ANDREW CRUMEY

SPUTNIK CALEDONIA

PICADOR

First published 2008 by Picador
an imprint of Pan Macmillan Ltd
Pan Macmillan, 20 New Wharf Road, London N1 9RR
Basingstoke and Oxford
Associated companies throughout the world
www.panmacmillan.co.uk

ISBN 978-0-330-44702-7

1 3 5 7 9 8 6 4 2

A CIP catalogue record for this book is available from the British Library.

Typeset by SetSystems Ltd, SaffronWalden, Essex
Printed and bound in Great Britain by
Mackays of Chatham plc, Chatham, Kent

SPUTNIK CALEDONIA

Andrew Crumey has a PhD in theoretical physics and was from 2000 to 2006 Literary Editor of *Scotland on Sunday*. He is the author of five previous novels, which have variously won the Saltire First Book Award, been long-listed for both the Booker Prize and the *Guardian* Fiction Prize, and been finalists in the Commonwealth Writers Prize. *Sputnik Caledonia* received the £60,000 Northern Rock Foundation Writer's Award. Andrew lives in Newcastle with his wife and two children.

ALSO BY ANDREW CRUMEY

Mobius Dick

Mr Mee

D'Alembert's Principle

Pfitz

Music, in a Foreign Language

For my family

PART ONE

1

For a long time Robbie Coyle used to wet the bed. On school days he'd be summoned from sleep almost without noticing what he'd done, but at weekends he'd slowly wake to find himself wrapped in soothing clammy moistness. At last his exasperated mother decided they should see the doctor.

In the waiting room you had to take a wee wooden token whose number told you when it was your turn, and whose colour indicated which doctor to go to. Robbie was due to be seen by someone named Dr Muir, who he didn't like the sound of. He read the magazine his mum had given him until at last his name was called.

Dr Muir was old and bald, and listened patiently while Robbie's mother explained the problem. 'Very good, Mrs Coyle,' he said, as if pleased by her son's condition, then spoke to Robbie. 'Do you have bad dreams?'

'Sometimes,' Robbie admitted.

'Do you play sport?'

Robbie said he liked running around playing at spaceships. He wanted to be an astronaut when he grew up.

'What sort of things do you read? Stories, comics? You don't buy those awful American ones, do you?'

Robbie didn't know quite what the doctor had in mind, so he showed him his *Look and Learn* and this was declared healthy enough. The doctor addressed Mrs Coyle again.

'Young Robert here strikes me as a nervous lad, though not excessively so. But he's bright for a nine-year-old, and that's the real problem. He's got a vivid imagination, and frets too much. What he needs is fresh air, an interest, good reading. Have you ever heard of Walter Scott?' he said, turning to Robbie, who shook his head solemnly. 'Try *Ivanhoe*, that's a fine story. I read it when I was your age.'

They left the surgery and went straight to the public library, where Robbie was registered with the same silent formality that had marked his induction into the care of the local health authority. Mrs Coyle then hunted among shelves as crammed as a chemist's drug counter while Robbie wandered off and pulled down something called *Rocket to the Stars*.

Mrs Coyle couldn't find *Ivanhoe*. Robbie, sitting on the floor with musty books towering over him, peered round the end of the bookcase and saw her go to the desk.

'I can put it on order for you,' said the assistant.

'Actually,' said Mrs Coyle, 'I just want something that'll stop him wetting the bed.'

'Oh,' said the assistant. 'Well, you could try *Kidnapped*, I suppose.'

As soon as they got home Robbie started reading *Kidnapped* and found it the most boring thing in the universe. There weren't even any pictures. In *Rocket to the Stars* there'd been a V2 painted like a chequerboard, a monkey in a spacesuit and loads of other things. But his mother and the assistant had both agreed that if anything was going to make him wee the bed it was stuff like that, so instead he'd been allowed *The Boy's Book of Facts*. Next morning his bed was wet again.

2

On Sunday, while the Coyles took their customary walk, the sky exploded. 'What was that?' Robbie asked fearfully, looking upwards.

'They're testing a new aeroplane called Concorde,' his father said.

'Why are they testing it over Scotland?'

'In case it crashes.'

A boat moving swiftly through water, Mr Coyle began to explain, kicks up a wave that forms the vessel's wake; supersonic aircraft do likewise, and the resulting shockwave was what they'd heard as an impressively reverberating thunderclap. Robbie's father left school at fourteen, worked in a factory in Clydebank and was never to be seen reading anything except a newspaper or a magazine, but he knew how to talk like an expert.

Mrs Coyle and Robbie's sister Janet were several paces ahead. Mrs Coyle turned and said, 'I wish they'd do all their sonic booming over the sea instead of over us. Did you not hear about Mrs Farrell's window cracking?' Mr Coyle agreed the choice of test area was another example of England's contempt for the Scots, but felt sure that supersonic air travel was the thing of the future. None of the Coyles had ever been in an aeroplane, but the thought that one could fly so fast was comforting all the same.

Robbie had stopped shaking and was hoping they'd hear another bang since he'd be ready for it this time. He said, 'If Concorde goes faster than sound, does that mean when the pilot talks his voice gets left behind and nobody in the plane can hear him?'

'No,' Mr Coyle reassured him, 'it doesn't work like that.' Then Mr Coyle asked Robbie to imagine a plane that could fly at the speed of a bullet. On board, a hijacker sits patiently waiting in seat 13C, gazing out at white clouds rolling like cauliflower beneath him. At a carefully chosen moment he will stand up, bring out the pistol he carries concealed within his clothing, and point it at an air hostess called Barbara Perkins who happens to be travelling on her very first flight and will subsequently describe the tragic events which follow to the world's press and television reporters.

Mrs Coyle turned round again. 'And Elsie Lang says her daughter's cat died of fright after one o' they sonic booms.'

The hijacker sees the second hand of his watch reach twelve; he stands, brings out a sleek, black and wholly persuasive firearm and declares, 'Nobody move. Nobody panic.'

Everyone panics. There are screams, tears, and doubtless a prayer or two. An old lady in seat 10B faints, her neighbour thinks she's had a heart attack, and the recently trained Barbara Perkins instinctively responds to the pressing of the overhead button whose bleeping summons her assistance.

'I said nobody move!' The hijacker's gun is pointed at the crisp firm breast of Barbara Perkins, who is paralysed by fear yet still heroically motivated by the sense of duty she will subsequently explain as being just part of her job, as she goes to receive an award for exceptional bravery wearing a smart pink outfit bought specially for the occasion.

'This lady needs help,' Barbara Perkins calmly explains. 'I think she may have had a heart attack.'

'And there are cracks in our close too,' said Mrs Coyle. 'I'm sure they weren't there before all this booming started.'

Far below, the hijacker's three revolutionary accomplices enter the private office of the French Ambassador, who sits at his desk while his secretary, her tanned legs crossed beneath his ruminating gaze, carefully takes notes. Three guns are aimed at them; one at him, one at her, and a third that swings persuasively between the ambassador's broad chest and the slimmer frame of the secretary. There's a noise at the door, someone has followed them; an armed guard enters and shots are about to be fired.

In the plane, Barbara Perkins is moving in a parabolic arc towards the unconscious lady while a male passenger in seat 16D – married with two children, the director of a pet-food company – gets out of his seat some distance behind the hijacker, who hears what's coming, turns and faces his assailant with gun raised.

The French Ambassador is about to receive a shot to the head issuing accidentally from the weapon belonging to the guard, who is himself collinear with the barrel of another gun in the room, and whose arm has been grabbed as two men struggle to subdue him. The secretary will take a shot in the stomach from which she will die two days later; her funeral in the small village from which she comes will be a scene of national grief. One hostage-taker, stumbling backwards, has his gaze directed towards the ceiling of the ambassador's office, whose elaborate plaster mouldings now take the form of a cloud-flecked sky and a newly developed airliner on its maiden flight, in which the director of a pet-food company is about to be united in death with a twenty-six-year-old woman below.

'What the devil are you two on about back there?' asked Mrs Coyle.

'I was just going to explain something,' said her husband. 'Suppose an aeroplane could fly as fast as a bullet,' he told Robbie. 'If you fired a gun backwards from it, what would the path of the bullet look like from the ground?'

Slowly, a round is entering the perspiring head of the French Ambassador; the secretary is taking within herself a projectile of equal calibre; and high above, a third identical bullet is completely stationary. The hostage-taker, gazing skywards through the ceiling, sees the bullet wait, hovering, while the barrel of a gun slides past to leave it apparently suspended in mid-air; yet the hostage-taker, in the last sweet moment of his life, knows this to be an impossibility. The bullet must surely be falling towards him, though in his final mortal instant it will descend no further than all the other bullets within this very room, even the one now parting the flesh of the French Ambassador's forehead. In the aeroplane, the bullet must descend with an acceleration that is universal and incontrovertible, while the body of a married father of two is carried towards it like a sacred offering. This is the last thing the hostage-taker sees; all subsequent acts of heroism, in which two more armed guards reach the ambassador's office and Barbara Perkins immobilizes the hijacker with the assistance of most of the passengers between seat rows 12 and 17, belong to a world which none of the terrorists survive to contemplate.

'So you see, Robbie, it's all quite simple. If you stand in a flat place and fire one bullet from a gun while dropping another from your hand, both hit the ground at the same time.'

That was all very well, but Robbie still hoped they'd hear another boom. As they walked behind Mrs Coyle and Janet, Robbie asked, 'Dad, if you were on an aeroplane and there was a hijack, what would you do?'

Mr Coyle looked bewildered. 'What do you mean? What made you think about hijackings?'

Robbie had been remembering something he saw on TV. A man waving a gun around. A shot.

'If anyone threatened me with a gun I'd let them do whatever they wanted,' said Mr Coyle. 'What's the point being a hero if you're dead?'

'Even if it was to save me or Janet?'

'That's different,' said Mr Coyle. 'I'd gladly give my life for you or your sister. That's the duty of any parent.'

'Why?' Robbie asked, and Mr Coyle explained that the biological purpose of every creature is to reproduce; though this didn't answer the question.

Janet and Mrs Coyle had reached the old memorial beside the river, a granite obelisk against whose mute support they were having a rest. 'I'm fair jiggered,' she declared. This was one of Mrs Coyle's customary sayings; she had many, and Robbie assumed such habits to be a general maternal phenomenon. Every night, for instance, she would send Robbie off to bed with a formula inspired by whatever he happened to be doing at the time: 'You can just

Spirograph off to bed now, Robbie'; or 'Time to Action Man upstairs.' Once, after the end of a film, he was told he'd better Gregory Peck into his pyjamas, and for the rest of his life would associate the great actor with his tank- and soldier-embellished night attire at the time. On another occasion, following a gruesome documentary which Mr Coyle had insisted the whole family should watch as a solemn warning, Robbie was cheerfully instructed by his mother to 'Belsen up to bed', so that the word acquired a warm domestic glow which was not at all what Mr Coyle or the film-makers had intended.

Mrs Coyle and Janet were leaning against the memorial as Robbie and his father joined them. 'Have you ever read what it says on this thing?' Mr Coyle asked his wife, who stood away in order that the whole family could follow the inscription:

ON 31ST DECEMBER 1860, DURING SEVERE FLOODING,
JAMES DEUCHAR, 20, A DIVINITY STUDENT AT GLASGOW
UNIVERSITY, LEAPT INTO THE RIVER NEAR THIS SPOT
IN AN ATTEMPT TO RESCUE GEORGE LAIDLAW, 5, AND
MARY LAIDLAW, 7, WHO HAD FALLEN IN. HAVING SAVED THE
YOUNGER CHILD, MR. DEUCHAR RETURNED TO SEARCH
FOR THE GIRL, WHO WAS WASHED UP ALIVE FURTHER
DOWNSTREAM. MR. DEUCHAR, HOWEVER, PERISHED IN
HIS NOBLE ENDEAVOUR. THIS MONUMENT TO HIS HEROISM
WAS ERECTED BY PUBLIC SUBSCRIPTION, 3RD JANUARY 1863.

Mrs Coyle shook her head in sympathy. 'Poor lad.'

'They'd all be dead by now anyway,' said Mr Coyle. 'You see, Robbie? What difference does it make in the end whether or not he decided to be a hero?'

'That's a terrible thing to say,' Mrs Coyle declared, and Janet agreed.

Mr Coyle shrugged. 'It may be terrible, but who can deny it? Unless he's up there now on a cloud looking down at us, it makes no odds what he did.'

Mr Coyle had many times invited God to strike him down for his blasphemies, but had so far survived. His own experiences as a child, he'd told his offspring, had been enough to convince him that the Catholic Church in which he was raised was only another way of controlling people's minds, along with capitalism, television and golf, the latter being one of Mr Coyle's pet hates. 'If God doesn't like what I'm saying then why doesn't he send a thunderbolt right now?' Mr Coyle had told a pair of Jehovah's Witnesses standing at the front door one evening while Janet and Robbie lay on the floor watching *Mission: Impossible*. Robbie wanted to go to the door to get a look at the brave souls who dared challenge Mr Coyle's unarguable logic, but was sent back to the living room for his own protection. 'At least he was a good socialist, I'll say that much for Jesus,' was the comment Robbie overheard from his father. 'It's these people who want to bow down and worship him I can't abide.'

Standing at the memorial, Robbie now said to his father, 'Don't you think it was a good thing that man done, jumping in after they children?'

'No,' said his dad, 'I think it was daft. It meant a grown man died instead of a boy, that's all. And where were the children's parents? What were they playing at, letting them fall in like that?'

Janet and Robbie had been lying on their tummies on

the floor watching *Mission: Impossible*. A newly developed super-fast airliner was flying high above the clouds, and in seat 13C a man of dangerously foreign appearance was preparing to bring out a gun. Some rows ahead, an elderly actress recently seen in a hospital drama enjoyed by Mr and Mrs Coyle got ready to faint. 'How can you prove to me there's a God?' Mr Coyle was saying to the two neatly dressed Christians at the door. Then the elderly actress swooned theatrically, and the one playing Barbara Perkins went to give assistance but found the sleek barrel of an imitation gun pointed at her crisp firm breast.

Far below, a hostage-taker was falling backwards, his gaze directed through the plaster mouldings of the ceiling to the silver dot in the sky where a bullet, he felt sure, really was held completely stationary in mid-air, in complete contravention of the laws of physics, so that he immediately learned the appalling truth of his situation. Everything around him, he realized, must be an illusion. He had joined the People's Liberation Army after the gunning down of his brother during a demonstration intended to be peaceful; he had volunteered to participate in capturing the French Ambassador in the full knowledge that he might die, convinced his sacrifice would not be in vain, and this morning he had recited his prayers with a feeling of lightness and ecstasy. But now, in his final moment, he understood that every passenger in the aeroplane was an actor; so too were the French Ambassador and his secretary, who would later remove capsules of fake blood, and crack jokes with the guards whose blank rounds had been so convincing. The hostage-taker watched his life become an airborne speck and knew his death to be futile; so too, therefore, had been his very existence. He was no more than an incidental character in a story he'd been unaware of; and in the final credits – his epitaph – he would be known only as 'Terrorist # 2'.

'Galileo stood at the top of the Leaning Tower of Pisa,' Mr Coyle explained once the family left the monument to continue their Sunday walk. 'He dropped a cannonball and a wee marble; both hit the ground at exactly the same time. The cannonball was bigger and heavier, which meant gravity was pulling it more strongly; but it was also harder to budge. The two effects cancel out; everything falls at the same rate.'

'What about a feather?' Robbie asked.

'Air resistance slows it down.' Aristotle believed a feather floats slowly because its natural realm is the sky; a stone hurries to return to the ground where it belongs. Everything has its proper station in the world. 'But that's rubbish,' said Mr Coyle. 'Like the idea that people should know their place. We're all equal, Robbie; you and me, we're as good as anybody.'

'What are you telling the boy now?' Mrs Coyle intervened, turning to examine the pair walking behind her.

'Just teaching him what's what,' her husband replied.

Mr Coyle originally came from a part of Glasgow called the Gorbals. It sounded very much like Goebbels, a name that had figured significantly in the documentary after which Robbie had been told to 'Belsen up to bed'. The Gorbals was a ghetto for Glasgow's poor, though Mr Coyle always spoke warmly of it, insisting it was never as bad as people made out. There had been sensational books about razor gangs, films showing criminals and drunks, but that was only because the ruling class are afraid of poverty and live in constant fear of revolution.

When they got home Mr Coyle positioned himself behind the raised pages of a camera magazine while Mrs Coyle decided to Paxo off to the kitchen. Robbie and Janet watched a film in which harsh-voiced German soldiers were killed in a variety of ways.

Robbie was troubled. James Deuchar must surely have been a good man; yet what scale or balance might measure and prove it? How to demonstrate, just as Galileo had shown the equivalent descent of all falling bodies, that a man who gives his life for a just cause is worth more than a uniformed actor blown up in an imagined spectacle?

'Dad,' said Robbie, 'why would you save me and Janet if we fell in a river, but not somebody else's children?'

The glossy cover of *Photographer's Weekly* showed a heavily made-up woman on a couch who now descended to reveal the all-knowing face of Mr Coyle. 'It's every parent's natural duty to protect their own children.'

'Is that all?' Robbie asked. 'Just something you've got to do, like going to work?'

The magazine sank lower still, onto Mr Coyle's lap. 'No, I'd want to save you because I love you.'

The words had the ominous finality of a judicial sentence.

Robbie said, 'Can't you love somebody else's children too?'

'Not the same way,' said his father. 'It's instinct. It's how we've evolved. It's why you're here.'

Mr Coyle then spoke about giraffes, saying they all used to look like horses until one day a giraffe was born whose neck was half an inch longer than usual, so it could reach leaves half an inch higher up the trees. There was a bad year, not much to eat, and most of the regular giraffes starved to death, but not the one who could nibble that extra half-inch. It grew up and had lots of baby giraffes, similarly blessed. That was evolution.

Robbie liked this story; all you had to do was keep repeating it over the generations, and you could see why giraffes ended up with long necks. Except that he couldn't see why the same thing hadn't happened to horses.

'Dad,' he said, 'why didn't the giraffes just get big long noses like elephants, then they could still reach up into the trees?'

'Because the special giraffe that got born one day had a neck that was half an inch longer than usual, not a nose.'

'But surely another giraffe could have been born with a long nose?'

'No,' said Mr Coyle. 'Otherwise giraffes would look like elephants now, but they don't, so it never happened.'

It was fairly plain to Robbie that people could be born with long noses – Mr Connor two doors along being a prime example – so he couldn't see why the same wasn't true for giraffes. Come to that, why hadn't humans evolved giraffe necks, or elephant trunks? Was Mr Connor the advance guard of a new master race? But his father had explained evolution, and there was no more to be said about it.

'So do you only love me and Janet because that's the way you've evolved?'

'I suppose so,' said Mr Coyle, and the reclining woman on *Photographer's Weekly* began once more to ascend.

'If I was bad, would you still love me?'

'Of course, even if you killed someone. Even if you were Hitler. It's my parental duty.'

An infernal cycle presented itself to Robbie's imagination, in which successive generations follow a script laid down for them millions of years previously. On a wild and fierce night in 1860, a man departed from the script by doing something for which there could be no logical explanation, no justification other than pure goodness. James Deuchar defied the gravitational pull of death; therein lay the kernel of his immortality.

3

Next morning Robbie's bed was wet again. He sincerely hoped his condition would improve before he grew up because he was sure it would count against him when he applied to be an astronaut. *The Boy's Book of Facts* included a section on 'careers' in which necessary qualifications and personal attributes were itemized for every occupation a young man might care to undertake: plumber, soldier, engine driver. Astronauts, the book declared, would need excellent powers of concentration and a cool head. Peeing the bed wasn't specified as a cause of automatic disqualification, and Robbie would of course point out to the selection panel that a small bag within an astronaut's pressurized suit is there to collect every weightless drop of urine passed while waking or asleep; nevertheless he knew it made him look like someone whose head was far from cool, since in all his comics not a single hero ever woke to find his mattress soaked through every intervening layer of bed sheet and folded towel, all because he'd had a drink after seven o'clock the night before.

The problem was that he had a vivid imagination, and his mum said this meant he spent too long in his own thoughts instead of going out and playing. The word sounded like a cross between 'livid', meaning angry, and 'Vivian', a fat woman in the baker's who was always laughing. 'Vivid' was a confused and insoluble state somewhere in between.

A man on television gave advice to children wanting to go into space, saying they must first work as US Air Force test pilots. Robbie told his dad later that night; Mr Coyle folded his newspaper, looked disapprovingly at his son and said, 'You'd only end up getting sent to Vietnam.'

In that case, Robbie countered, he'd be a Soviet cosmonaut.

'You don't speak Russian.'

'I'll learn.'

The Americans and Russians were enemies, but the Russians were better at sending people into space, and Robbie's father had once said that some of his friends in the Trades Council went on a delegation to Leningrad and found it a very happy place where there was no crime or unemployment, women worked as lorry drivers or mechanics, and people could do whatever they liked, within reason. In America there was segregation and organized crime, and hidden capitalists controlled the lives of millions, helped by the CIA. Anyone wanting to be an American astronaut would wind up dropping napalm on children, according to Mr Coyle, while in Russia the only hard bit was learning the alphabet.

Robbie asked him, 'Why do some people not like the Russians?'

'Because the workers there had a revolution against the capitalists, and one day the Scots'll get the gether and do the same. We nearly succeeded in 1919, until Churchill sent the army into Glasgow to stop it.' Then Mr Coyle began to speak of a future socialist paradise in which everyone would be equal, dressed in a classless uniform which sounded to Robbie a bit like the costumes of higher life forms in *Star Trek*. Money would no longer exist. 'Why should one man get paid twice as much as another for doing exactly the same work?' Mr Coyle said. And it was true; when did anybody in *Star Trek* ever open a wage packet, or put his hand in his pocket in search of change? Come to that, did they even have pockets? In the age of socialism, Robbie realized, such things would no longer be needed. It would be a world without competition or strife, his father promised, with no more war, since there would be no capitalists left to encourage hostilities. Every factory and shop would be owned by the state. You wouldn't have to traipse from C&A to Marks and Spencer and back again to find the best deal, said Mr Coyle; you'd just go by free public transport to the nearest, most convenient shop, and what you'd get there would be exactly the same as you'd get anywhere else. And when you bought a cup of coffee you wouldn't have to wait and see whether you got it in a big mug or a wee teacup, because coffee would be served in a standard size, for a standard price (they do it with beer, so why not everything else?). Of course, not everyone might be happy in the new utopia. The people who used to run the shops and factories, for example. But they'd be made to realize they'd lived a life of selfishness, sponging off their fellow man, always grabbing and clawing and trying to be richer than anyone else. In a capitalist society, you could only better yourself at the expense of others: if you got richer, it meant someone else was getting poorer, and that's not fair. Most of the capitalists would accept that in their old ways they were no better than thieves, but if the retraining and education didn't work then they'd be asked to leave, so that everyone else could get on in peace.

Mrs Coyle, coming out of the kitchen into the living room, decided to chip in. 'It'll never work. Do you really want us to live like Russians?'

'If Russia's got problems it's only because there's half the world agin them,' her husband retorted. 'And look what they did for us in the war. We'd never have won without the Red Army. The Americans only joined in when they knew they could be on the winning side, same as they did in the First.'

'Well, it's time to Red Army upstairs, Robbie,' Mrs Coyle announced.

'I'm still talking to the boy,' Mr Coyle protested from his armchair.

'Filling his head with nonsense, that's what you're doing.'

Mr Coyle flushed. 'You call it nonsense to say we should all be equal?'

'I say you can't go against human nature. And this lad needs his sleep – you've got school in the morning, Robbie.'

Mr Coyle was having none of it. He turned to Robbie, who stood immobilized wondering which parent to obey, and said to him, 'You see what we have to put up with? The prattle of women.'

Mrs Coyle went out in silence and from the kitchen came the thud of cupboard doors, leaving Mr Coyle to resume his lecture while his face assumed a triumphantly beatific look. 'It's not human nature that makes people exploit each other,' he told Robbie. 'It's animal nature, a relic of the beasts we're descended from. But people progress, the species improves. Capitalism's the law of the jungle, and we're evolving beyond that.' While giraffes had for aeons been putting all their efforts into perfecting their necks, humans were on the way to becoming spacesuited socialists. 'Are you putting on the kettle?' Mr Coyle called to his wife, smiling at Robbie with a conspiratorial wink.

'No,' she shouted back. 'I'm having a revolution. If we're all going to be equal then you can do it yourself.'

4

The Coyles' next-door neighbours were the Dunbars, who had a telephone, a car, took package holidays in Spain, and would face summary execution come the uprising.

It was Sam Dunbar's fondness for golf that really seemed to irritate Mr Coyle more than anything. 'Look at him!' he said, standing inside the front door staring through the net curtain of the hall window at Sam, in tartan cap and white golfing shoes, depositing a bag of clubs in the back of his car in readiness for a session.

Sam's two daughters were a few years older than Robbie and seemed to him like grown-ups already, objects of fearful fascination. He'd see them come and go in their secondary-school uniforms, smiling beings from another world.

It was a pity they'd probably be shot, and all because their father thought himself a cut above the rest of the scheme. Sam Dunbar worked for the GPO, from which it was deduced he must get a good salary and cut-price phone calls. The Coyles could afford a phone, but Mr Coyle cited a number of reasons against getting one. He didn't want to be pestered about union subscriptions, or have to listen to the problems of his older sister who lived in England and existed for the Coyles only by way of Christmas cards inscribed in evenly sloping handwriting. Most of all, Mr Coyle feared installation of a telephone would prompt MI5 surveillance, for being treasurer of the local branch of the ATWU made him an inevitable target for the authorities.

Cars were unnecessary since the public-transportation system was perfectly adequate, and so Mr Coyle had never learned to drive one. As for holidays in Spain, why go there when there was so much to see in Scotland? The Isle of Bute was a lot more interesting than Majorca, and even had a fairly bustling nightlife if that was what you wanted. This left golf, to which the plain objection was that it was totally pointless.

'Just look at him!' Mr Coyle said as Sam Dunbar came back out to his car. 'What's he like in that bunnet? Chic Murray, eh? The Tall Droll with the Small Doll!' Pleased by the resemblance he discerned between his next-door neighbours and a famous Glasgow double act, Mr Coyle would for a while call Sam and his petite wife Maureen 'Chic and Maidie' when referring to them in private.

'I think he looks very smart,' Mrs Coyle ventured. 'Maybe you should get yourself a hat like that.'

'I'm not going to the plant in one of those.'

'I don't mean for work. And I could do with getting you a new pair of shoes an' all, for if we go out.'

'You're not using the housekeeping to get me shoes. Besides, we never go out.'

'That's why you need new shoes.'

Robbie and Janet were in the living room watching the final of *Top of the Form*, a competition played between teams of strange-voiced English schoolchildren and presented by a man with crinkly hair held rigid by Brylcreem. 'Forms' were mysterious things found only in English schools, where boys in smart uniforms played cricket and grew up to be prime ministers or television announcers. Anybody wanting to go to one of those schools had to pay lots of money and then their name was put on a form. If you were top of the form that meant you were the best, and you'd get first choice when it came to deciding between being a politician or a presenter. At least, that's what Robbie had understood of his father's explanation, from which he'd also learned that there were schools in England where children didn't go home at night but stayed in dormitories, and there were some in Scotland too, for the offspring of English lords who owned castles and were only interested in grouse and salmon and forests, decking themselves out in kilts to go to fancy balls, then heading straight back to London as soon as the party was finished.

Mr Coyle didn't go to parties. He wouldn't leave his children all alone to go jigging around somewhere like an idiot.

'But Moira says she'll come and keep an eye on Janet and Robbie,' Mrs Coyle implored. 'When was the last time we went anywhere, Joe?'

'That's not the point,' said her husband, watching the cloud of exhaust left by Sam's disappearing car. 'And he needs to fix his silencer.'

The Brylcreemed announcer's was the next voice Robbie heard. '*Which King of England signed the Magna Carta?*'

'John!' Robbie shouted.

'Show off,' Janet snorted, as the answer was confirmed. The useless fact was one Robbie had learned from another quiz programme, though whatever was going on in Scotland in King John's time was a complete mystery to him, since no one had ever asked about it on telly.

'So do I just tell them we're not going?' said Mrs Coyle. 'And all because you won't let me get you a decent pair of shoes?'

'There's no need to be irrational about it, pet. You may be a woman but we should still be able to discuss things logically.'

The overheard conversation continued while Robbie and Janet gazed at the mounting triumph of St George's School over Langham Priory.

'Why do you not want to go, then?' Mrs Coyle asked her husband. 'We haven't been to a dinner dance in years.'

'I don't like leaving the children. What if Moira puts her cigarette in the ashtray on the arm of the chair . . .'

'She hardly smokes!'

'. . . then goes into the kitchen and forgets about it?'

The struggle of Langham Priory was overtaken in Robbie's imagination by the terrible scene his father proposed. Distracted by thirst and welcoming the opportunity presented by the adverts in the middle of some boring play, Moira decides to go and make herself a cup of tea. She takes a last ladylike drag on her slim cigarette, held between narrow long-nailed fingers, then deposits the fag on the edge of the heavy glass ashtray. She stands, and in the sort of close-up featured regularly in fire-brigade films, the cigarette is seen still smouldering where it lies, its lipstick-smeared end dangling terrifyingly over the arm of the highly inflammable armchair.

Upstairs, we see two children lying together in bed, Robbie and Janet, a convenient wedge of pale light making their monochrome faces clearly visible. Janet clutches her favourite doll; Robbie has dozed beneath *Tom Sawyer*, unopened and unread but recently checked out of the library by his mother, her faith in Dr Muir's prescription still not dashed. The next scene shows the dinner dance, Mr and Mrs Coyle sitting at a table with unknown friends. Mrs Coyle raises a sherry glass to her smiling, painted lips; Mr Coyle silently eyes his pint on the table, his face showing sudden doubt.

The cigarette is toppling. The burning of its tip has caused an imbalance, wholly in accord with the law of leverage discovered by Archimedes and explained at great length by Mr Coyle one Sunday afternoon. The cigarette, the ashtray and the chair arm fill most of the screen, but beyond them, in the background, we see an illuminated kitchen doorway where Moira pauses, lost in fluffy-headed feminine thought. It's exactly as Mr Coyle feared, sitting gazing at his flattening pint. Moira's wondering about a nice dress she saw in Arnott's, or her next haircut. She's forgotten the kettle, never mind the cigarette, and it's just as well the former is electric or else the stupid woman would be blowing up the entire street. Our next view of the fatal fag has it starkly presented in silhouette, falling, nestling comfortably among the synthetic fibres of the seat-cover like a slain bird tumbling onto heather. The swirling smoke thickens and becomes a flame.

In the pub, Mr Coyle turns to his daft wife. 'I think we should go home.' And in a rain-slicked street, another hopeless female screams for help, pointing up at the smoky bedroom where two suffocating children lie trapped. '*Remember*,' the film concludes, '*fire kills*.'

'So can I tell Moira we'll be going, then?' said Mrs Coyle.

'Aye, all right,' her husband conceded.

Robbie and Janet watched St George's romp to victory. '*And thank you to Langham Priory for being such good sports, just bowled out in the final innings*,' the Brylcreemed announcer cryptically concluded.

Robbie later contemplated, over his tea, the forthcoming destruction by fire of himself and his sister while his mum and dad went off jigging like idiots somewhere.

'You're very quiet, Robbie,' said Mr Coyle.

'I was wondering if you really could move the world with a lever.' This was what Archimedes had claimed he could do.

'You just need the right place to stand, that's all,' Mr Coyle explained. 'And a very big lever.'

On a golf course somewhere, Archimedes was swinging

a club. Archimedes became Chic Murray, the golf ball became the earth, and the Coyle family were launched along with everyone else into outer space.

'Robbie,' said his mother after tea, 'can you nip next door with these things for Mrs Dunbar?' She handed him the dress-making paraphernalia she'd borrowed from her neighbour.

'Is the Small Doll in?' Mr Coyle asked his wife from behind the dog-eared cover of *Modern Photographer*.

'She's a doll now is she?' The nickname would not survive for long. 'I've no reason to think she's out. Off you go, Robbie.'

A moment later he was standing outside his house clutching the sewing box, feeling like astronaut Ed White when he made the first space walk. Four paces separated him from the Dunbars' front door, where he managed to free a hand and reach for the doorbell. Within the house a mellow two-note chime was heard, and the figure who opened the door was young Sheena Dunbar, fair-haired, rosy-cheeked, inhabitant of another planet. She looked disappointed but amused. Without saying anything or acknowledging his existence, she looked over her shoulder and with raucous confidence called, 'Maw!'

Sheena was made of plastic from a faraway galaxy. Robbie wondered if she had a button you could press that made her hair grow. Her mother appeared.

'There you are, Mrs Murray,' Robbie announced, immediately realizing his mistake. 'I mean, Mrs Dunbar.' He tried to be casual about it, but errors of speech aren't the sort of thing you can rub out so nobody will ever notice them. The two dolls, mother and daughter, were gazing at him as he held out the stuff Mrs Coyle had borrowed. Sheena was smirking.

'Thanks ever so much, young man,' said Mrs Dunbar, stooping to pat Robbie on the head while on a golf course her husband stood frozen in post-swing, shielding his eyes and watching the earth retreat into space. 'My, what a big lad you're getting. Here, come on in and I'll gie ye a wee treat.'

Robbie followed them into the doll's house. He'd been here once or twice before, but never without his parents, and it was like the question on telly once about how to change a left-handed glove into a right-handed one. Answer: turn it inside out. Built to the same pattern as the rest of the scheme, the Dunbars' was nevertheless a mirror image of the Coyles', so that instead of going left into the kitchen you went right, which was where Robbie was led while Sheena returned to join her sister in the living room, the two of them erupting into big girls' laughter.

The kitchen was like the flight deck of a spaceship, very white with lots of cupboards, and with the smell of a hostile life form issuing from something simmering on the stove. 'Here y'are, son,' said Mrs Dunbar, selecting from a jar brought down off a shelf a bright red sweetie wrapped in cellophane. 'Still doing well at school, are you? Aye, you're growing. Won't be long before you're taking lassies out to the dancing, I'm sure.' The thought made Robbie feel instantly sick – or perhaps it was just the alien smell of the Dunbars' evening meal. 'You run along now and tell your mother if she wants the sewing machine she can have it any time.'

Then Robbie found himself in space again, with the

airtight hatch of Number 24 closing behind him. He drifted back to the safety of his own craft, quite forgetting about the sewing machine but thinking instead of Sheena and Louise laughing in the living room. Would there still be smiles on their faces when the Revolutionary Committee sentenced the whole family to death? At the last minute, Robbie would intercede to save them, and they'd realize he wasn't such a wee squirt after all.

'There he's there,' Mr Coyle announced to his wife later when Sam Dunbar returned in his timber-trimmed Morris Traveller, a puttering Tudor cottage on wheels. Robbie briefly stood up to look out of the window. 'No need to stare,' Mr Coyle told him, but Robbie had time to see Archimedes in his bunnet, coming home after moving the world with a golf club.

5

The combined efforts of Stevenson and Twain having done nothing to stop Robbie from wetting the bed, when he next visited the library with his mother she allowed him to exchange *Tom Sawyer* and *The Boy's Book of Facts* for *Russian In One Month* and *Rocket to the Stars*. The woman at the desk eyed him with some incredulity as he checked them out. 'He's going to be an astronaut,' Mrs Coyle explained.

In Russian some letters are written back to front and others are completely made up. Robbie mastered the equivalent of 'good morning', but felt the phrase would be of limited value during a solo mission into the endless night of space. The only place in the phrase book where the Moon was mentioned was in a section called Making Friends, whose chattiness sent shivers of revulsion down his spine. *Do you like opera? Are you married?* Surely astronauts didn't have to say stuff like that. But the numbers from zero to twenty were useful, and Robbie recited them in reverse order while training in his flight simulator. Really it was a cupboard under the sink that smelled of Pledge and dead beetles, and he could only just fit inside if he took the boxes out first; but by overcoming his fear of getting stuck in it he felt sure he could attain an astronaut's obligatory coolness of head, and when he pulled the door closed the darkness was no simulation; it was the true blackness of space, the loneliness of the grave, as he counted down to blast-off from a windswept cosmodrome in Central Asia.

In space there's no air and no gravity. You wear a helmet like a goldfish bowl (or in Robbie's case a balaclava and his dad's welding goggles), and things float around if you let go of them.

'Why's there no gravity in space?' he asked his father, who was mending a watch.

'Because gravity can't go on forever, it runs out after a while, and space is a long way off.'

But Robbie knew that tides are caused by the gravity of the Moon. 'Dad,' he said, 'if the Moon's gravity can get to Earth then why can't the Earth's gravity get into space?' His father, peering by the light of a table lamp at a gleaming, lifeless mainspring, said it was all a wee bit complicated. And for the first time, Robbie glimpsed the shoreline of paternal fallibility.

Apart from his cupboard simulator, Robbie's other main

piece of training equipment was the radiogram in the living room. A great four-legged box of veneered chipboard whose teak finish matched the G-plan dining table, the radiogram was receiver and gramophone combined, a melding of parts and ideas into a single word that was new and modern, like 'electromagnetism' or 'Politburo', the former being the means by which all the world's radio stations could be brought into a Scottish living room, the latter the source of a viewpoint more balanced, in Mr Coyle's considered view, than the sly propaganda of Radio Free Europe or the BBC World Service.

Electricity is like water, Robbie learned. Current is the amount that's flowing, capacitance is the volume of a flask, and voltage the height of a waterfall. We all of us exist at the bottom of a deep sea filled with invisible particles and fields, rebounding signals made murky during daytime by the heat of the sun, but becoming clearer in the cool of the night, just before bed, when, at the turn of a knob, the endless hidden flux could be summoned into life, of waltzes and jazz combos, whistles and pops, emanating from gold-lettered cities strung out across the dial – Frankfurt, Paris, Madrid – filling the room with monotonous foreign chatter or the distant echoing of an ancient dance band whose music would rise then slowly fade into crackling surf, like an ocean liner battling against a long rolling swell. Such nocturnal voyages were a treat both children enjoyed if there was nothing on television, and in this way Budapest had become more familiar to Robbie than the bus ride into Glasgow; Warsaw for him was a polar island built out of four notes played on a vibraphone each hour and the voice of a woman for whom the world news was a random floe of harsh syllables, out of whose icy depths an intelligible name would occasionally crest like the sudden fin of a whale. By day, when the cosmic signals were kept dormant by the sun's harsh glare, the radiogram still served its purpose in Robbie's conquest of space, for then it was his mission-control centre, its every city a planet, and simply by pressing one of the waveband buttons he could transport himself across the galaxy at the speed of light.

His best friend Scott failed to see the excitement of fiddling with the silent radio dial when the two of them played together in Robbie's house after school one day. Robbie described the alien planets they both could fly to in an instant, but Scott was more keen on going outside to play football.

'That's a very good idea,' said Mrs Coyle. 'And you could do with the exercise, Robbie.'

'Can't we go to the burn instead?' Robbie pleaded, his opinion of ball games being much like his father's.

'We could look for tadpoles,' Scott suggested.

'All right, but be careful,' said Mrs Coyle, fetching two empty jam jars for them from the kitchen. 'And don't be too long.'

She saw them out the door, and as the two boys headed along the street towards the waste ground a few hundred yards away where the little burn flowed past slag heaps from a former colliery, Scott said, 'You're maw's dead nice. I'm always getting a leathering off mine for something. Then when my da gets in he leathers me for getting leathert.' Robbie didn't know what to say; he was just glad not to be Scott, who began describing how his mother would beat his knuckles with a wooden spoon whenever she got annoyed with him.

The burn was little more than an ankle-deep trickle offering purpose to a crack in the ground, but frogs and newts could be found among its fronds of weed, and soon Scott was on his bare knees, clawing spawn by the handful and dropping gobs of curranty snot into his jam jar, while Robbie, kneeling beside him, took a more cautious approach, scooping his chunky glass container through the turbid water, releasing fat bubbles from his submerged jar but catching nothing.

'Don't you ever wonder why they're so nice?' asked Scott.

'Who? My parents?'

'Aye,' said Scott. 'Maybe they're hiding something.'

'What do you mean?'

Scott had seen it in a film; a mum and dad who were absolutely perfect, always good to their weans and everyone else. All because they had a secret.

'What sort of secret?' Robbie asked him, rising to his feet with a full jar of murky water in his hand.

The perfect parents in the film were spies who told the Russians how to make bombs, and they got caught and put in jail. 'Maybe your parents are spies,' Scott suggested.

'They are not!'

'Or maybe they stole a load of money and they're on the run frae the polis.' The sheer glamour of this scenario was enough to make Robbie dismiss it instantly, but Scott then offered another. 'Maybe the people you call your mum and dad kidnapped the real ones when you were a baby. Maybe they're aliens in disguise. How would you know?'

This was an altogether more powerful hypothesis. The thought that aliens might abduct and impersonate one's parents was eminently reasonable to Robbie, since that was just the sort of thing aliens did. By nature cruel, intelligent and devious, they delighted in subjugating their inferiors in whatever way they could. Somewhere, on a distant planet, the real Mr and Mrs Coyle might now be heaving sacks of glistening toxic dust, in a mine populated by slaves taken from every corner of the universe. Mrs Coyle would be saying, 'I wish we could toxic-dust back where we came from,' and Mr Coyle would be telling her, 'It's your fault we got here in the first place, woman.'

'Maybe your pretend parents wear rubber costumes,' Scott continued, 'and when you go to bed at night they take them off, and they've got horrible ugly faces with big long fangs, and they get their orders off the telly.'

It all sounded so plausible.

'And maybe they're just waiting to finish mending their spaceship, then they'll go away and take you as well.' From where he knelt, Scott stared up at Robbie, seeing the fear and doubt he'd caused. Then with a loud laugh and a flick of his arm he hurled the frogspawn into the air, launching it on an arc that Robbie barely managed to avoid. 'Can you no tell I'm only kidding? You should see the look on your face!'

Robbie silently emptied his jar into the burn. 'I'm going home.'

Scott scowled. 'Don't be such an eejit.'

'You're the eejit.'

'Aye, well, mind they aliens in your hoose.'

Angry and upset, Robbie turned and walked pensively home, leaving Scott to continue the spawn hunt alone. 'Enjoy yourself?' his mum asked when she opened the door, and Robbie nodded silently. He'd got the whole thing worked out by now.

'Just going upstairs,' he said, then went to his room, where he lay down on his bed. His sister Janet wasn't an alien, he'd decided, but he couldn't say anything to her in case she gave the game away. His pretend dad was probably behind it all. Robbie would just have to keep quiet and act casual until he could grow up and call in the army to demolish the entire house. His mum came in, and he sat up.

'Everything all right?' she asked.

'Fine,' said Robbie, feeling tense as he spoke.

'Did you fall out with Scott?'

Robbie told her about the frogspawn Scott had thrown, but not the rest. His mother sat beside him on the bed, put her arm round him, and immediately he wondered how he could ever have doubted she was human. Then as soon as she left, his fear returned.

She was meant to be just like his real mother; that was the whole point. He could never know for sure that her warmth and kindness were genuine. He couldn't be certain that he would never wake one night, in darkness except for an orange gleam across the ceiling from the streetlight outside, then leave his bed, go downstairs and enter the living room, there to see two hideous creatures with fangs and tentacles sitting on the settee calmly watching a secret alien channel on the telly. How could anyone ever prove otherwise? It was like God; either you believe or you don't.

He didn't know if he truly believed it himself, but just thinking it amounted to a form of belief. And the alien theory explained so much: why he was sent up to bed at fixed hours; why his father couldn't ride a bike (clearly an extraterrestrial foible); and why, when Robbie had got bored with the telly and wandered into his parents' bedroom one Saturday afternoon some years ago and found them lying together partly clothed on their bed, there had been a swift awkward fumbling between the two of them as their human disguises were hastily restored.

Surely there must be some way to verify his unique predicament. In every account of alien life forms, he recalled, some trait distinguishes the creatures from humanity, and becomes the weakness which ultimately proves their undoing. But Robbie's parents weren't unnaturally sensitive to light, or to diseases such as the common cold (once the downfall of an entire race of invaders). They didn't retreat at night to a cupboard in their bedroom containing a sleek metallic pod (or did they?), nor devote mysterious evenings to the care and maintenance of an inscrutable electrical device. As far as he could tell, his parents were pretty much like anybody else's; though it was this false normality that was most damning of all.

Treading softly downstairs, Robbie wanted to go and think about it in his cupboard space simulator, but his mum was in the kitchen, standing at the sink and blocking the entrance to the musty capsule beneath. So Robbie went instead to the living room, where his flight-control panel was situated. Janet was at Guides and Dad wouldn't be back from work for ages; Robbie had the precious equipment all to himself. Lifting the heavy lid of the radiogram, he saw the tuning knob and dial which were his link to the truth that lay beyond the stars. Twisting the control, watching the moving pointer on its journey past the planets, Robbie thought how powerful it was, the electrical illusion that could place a voice inside a living room, or an artificial mother inside a house. She must have heard him, because Mrs Coyle came through from the kitchen and saw him playing. 'Are you going to tell me what's wrong?' she said, kneeling beside him, enfolding him in her arms. 'What've you and Scott been up to?'

He came straight out and asked her. 'Are you an alien?'

She laughed and kissed him as Robbie explained what had happened, then said, 'I'll have words with that wee devil, so I will, for putting daft ideas in your head.' When she left him to carry on playing with the radiogram, Robbie knew his fears about his parents were groundless. Of course they weren't from another planet: they were sensible grown-ups who knew the right way to do everything. But what about Robbie himself? He was a bewildered traveller in a strange world who couldn't even stop peeing his bed. He was the alien: a space foundling dropped one night into the back garden by a smouldering comet, unable to relocate his cosmic home except by a process of random tuning which one day, if he was very lucky, might bring him to the comforting frequency he sought.

6

The time came for Mr and Mrs Coyle to go off jigging like idiots somewhere. It was a particularly unfortunate night on which to die by fire, Robbie thought, as he had a loose tooth and would miss out on the fairy-borne sixpence that was his due. His parents were already decked out for the evening when Moira arrived at the door and was shown into the living room, tall and blonde and with a fur-collared light-blue coat whose big buttons were more fascinating than her face.

'I'm sure we'll have a lovely time together,' she was saying to Robbie's parents. 'You just go out and enjoy yourselves.' Janet was hovering, awestruck, beside the newcomer, and Mr Coyle was hovering too, but Robbie remained silent. Moira took off her coat, handed it to Robbie's father who went out to the hall to hang it up, and sat herself down beside her quiet young charge. 'You don't look very pleased to see me. Maybe this'll cheer you up.' A Milky Way emerged from Moira's small handbag.

'He might not be able to eat it,' said Mrs Coyle, barely recognizable to Robbie in her make-up and jewellery. 'He's got a wobbly tooth.'

'Have you got a Milky Way for me too?' Janet asked.

'Don't be rude,' her mother intervened, glancing at herself once more in the mirror and pouting in a mysterious way that must have had something to do with all that lipstick, Robbie reckoned.

'Of course I've got some chocolate for you,' said Moira, opening her handbag again. As she reached for the second bar, Robbie glimpsed other items that lay beside it – keys, a purse, a cigarette packet – all of which made him even more certain of imminent death at the hands of a woman who didn't belong in the Coyle family home. 'Is it all right for them to have these now, Anne?'

'They've had their tea,' Mrs Coyle nodded, then addressed the children. 'I want you both to be very good. No fighting, and don't be too late going to bed.'

Mr Coyle had come back from the hall. 'We'll expect to hear a good report from Moira.'

'Oh, I'm sure it'll be glowing,' Moira insisted. 'And I'll bet these two children have got lots of things they want to tell me about.'

Mrs Coyle had got to know Moira through a keep-fit class they both went to. Moira was younger, probably fitter too, and the fags in her handbag were a very bad omen. Robbie watched carefully for signs of female incompetence when Moira closed the front door on the departing parents then looked at the fashion designs Janet was keen to show her. 'You drew all these yourself?' Moira said with exaggerated incredulity. 'I think you'll be an artist when you grow up.'

'What's your favourite colour?' Janet asked her, as Moira positioned herself between the two children on the settee.

'Sky blue,' said Moira. 'It's a healing colour.'

Janet was nestling beside her like a pussy cat, but Robbie kept his distance. Things so far were certainly looking bleak.

'What do you mean, healing?' Janet asked.

Moira went into an explanation of how every colour,

fragrance or mineral was part of a cosmic scheme. 'Opal is my birth stone – look at my ring.'

'It's so beautiful,' said Janet, Moira's hand resting in hers.

Robbie was having no more of this. He got up and announced he was getting something from his room. The two females barely acknowledged his departure, so wrapped up were they in their conversation about clothes and other nonsense, and when Robbie arrived at his room he wondered if he might be able to improvise some kind of fire extinguisher, perhaps using the shower hose. Robbie liked making things; he often created space capsules from bits of card, then with a carrier bag or handkerchief tied on as parachute he would throw them from the landing window, watching their descent onto the back garden. Americans always came down on the sea, but the Russians did it on land, because their spaceships were stronger. Robbie had found that toilet rolls were a superior material in spacecraft design, and Russian scientists had evidently made a similar breakthrough.

There was a fire in a spaceship once. All the astronauts were locked inside, waiting on the launch pad, when a tiny spark erupted into a ball of flame. It was an American spaceship, filled with pure oxygen instead of ordinary air like the Russian ones, so the wee spark instantly exploded and the astronauts were fried. One of them was Ed White, who had made the first space walk – Robbie read all about it in a space magazine his mum bought him, and when he told her about it she took the magazine straight back off him. Weeing the bed was nothing, though, compared with getting burned alive. It made Robbie all the more certain that the only kind of spaceship he'd ever go up in would be a Soviet one, preferably with a fire extinguisher on board just in case.

That still left the problem of daft Moira downstairs, who was probably already dropping matches on the carpet while getting all excited about Janet's stupid drawings. What was so great about clothes – couldn't Janet design a spacesuit? At least that'd be useful. Fancy outfits were only good for jigging about in like an idiot, the way Moira probably did every week. But how was he meant to make a fire extinguisher? He'd just have to be sure there was a full bucket of water handy for when the emergency arrived. Better sleep with one beside him. Or even drink it, then his bed would end up too wet to burn.

His dad was brilliant at making things – it was part of his job. Mr Coyle often explained to Robbie the workings of machines, frequently with the aid of sketch drawings, and in this way Robbie had seen pumps, motors and circuits, all of which made about as much sense to him as the Russian alphabet. From time to time, though, his father would show him some piece of machinery – 'junk' as his mother called it – which would come home in Mr Coyle's canvas tool bag and end up at the bottom of a cupboard, saved for a possible future use that never seemed to come.

Those oily gear assemblies and grubby switch units had the smell of work about them, the odour of the real world of factories, men in overalls, sweat, progress. Every item looked to Robbie like part of a spacecraft, and his favourite was one he had been allowed to keep on a shelf in his room – a technological treasure. Made of iron, it had come off an old steam engine; a single component only six inches long, called a governor. Two metal balls were fixed on moveable struts, able to spin freely around the central shaft like horses in a merry-go-round. Twirl them, and the balls would rise outwards and upwards. If the steam engine ran too fast, these rising balls would close a valve, reducing the steam. If too slow, the balls would sink, opening the valve to let more steam through. The result was a happy medium: the little governor could keep an entire locomotive in check.

Robbie took it from the shelf and lay on his bed, twirling it in his hand and watching the metal balls rise and fall. He could hear laughter downstairs, then quiet. Laughter again, and the baffled murmur of Janet's excited voice, her actual words unintelligible. They were probably talking about Robbie. More laughter, followed by further silence. There was a mechanism spinning the females into hysterics, shutting off the pressure, then letting it build again; though when the quiet continued for a longer time, Robbie wondered if the two of them had run out of steam altogether. He put the precious governor back where it belonged and went downstairs. Opening the living-room door, he saw Moira and Janet squatting cross-legged on the floor, eyes closed, in some kind of trance.

Moira's eyes blinked open. 'Come in and I'll teach you the lotus position.'

This sounded like the most absolute invitation to death by idiocy that he'd ever heard. 'What's the locust position?'

'Lotus,' said Janet, staring at him with the superiority of a hostile extraterrestrial intelligence. 'It's a kind of flower that grows in Egypt.'

'It's what we're doing now,' said Moira, whose platform-soled shoes had been removed and placed neatly beside the settee. Moira was wearing a black miniskirt, and through the thick but taut material of her matching tights, the lotus position offered an unequivocal view of sky-blue knickers whose healing properties Robbie preferred to do without. He sat himself at right angles to both Moira and Janet so that he wouldn't have to stare either of them in the face or anywhere else.

'That's right, just sit cross-legged in the normal way,' Moira instructed. 'We'll start with the half lotus. Here, like this.' She was bending her leg like it was made of Plasticine; Robbie tried and fell over. Now he knew what had been causing all the laughter, a renewed portion of which Janet directed at him with evident satisfaction.

'It's not hard,' said Moira, 'but it takes a wee bit getting used to. Look, I can do a full lotus.' The children watched in silence as Moira adopted the posture, placing her upturned hands on her knees and curling her fingers in a gesture of transcendental peace.

'Fab!' Janet exclaimed with an admiring sigh. Moira's closed eyes allowed Robbie to examine the babysitter's face in detail, making him even more convinced he and Janet were in the incapable hands of a maniac.

'I can do other positions,' Moira said brightly, her eyes popping open again.

'Does my mum know them?' Janet asked.

'I don't know,' said Moira. 'I could teach her. I'm sure I could show your dad a few as well.'

Janet shook her head. 'I don't think he'd like it. Please don't tell him about any of this.'

'All right,' Moira said with a laugh. 'If you want, it can be our secret.'

Robbie felt his stomach tighten. What had seemed merely pointless now became sinister – why should any of this be kept hidden? And was he going to be part of the conspiracy? 'I don't want to learn any more positions,' he said, standing up. 'The load-us'll do me.'

'Teach me more!' Janet implored, and so the yoga lesson continued while Robbie turned up the volume on the television and went through the three channels to see if anything was on. The choice was between Cilla Black, cowboys, and an announcer. The first two were hardly better than Moira's meditating, so he picked the BBC2 announcer, hoping something good would come of it. '*And now* Horizon, *investigating a strange new type of star.*'

'Great!' said Robbie, turning up the volume knob until the opening music set the television rattling.

'Not so loud!' Janet shouted.

'Quiet!' Robbie snapped back at her.

'Right, you two,' Moira interrupted firmly. 'Robbie, turn it down to where it was. And Janet, come over here away from the telly so we can do this quietly.'

Robbie stared at the screen while the other two took up new locations. Moira was still visible in the corner of his eye, but Janet was thankfully out of sight. The television showed the white dome of a mountaintop observatory.

'*For decades, astronomers thought they knew all about how stars work. But new discoveries have cast this into doubt. The universe could be much stranger than we think.*'

The shot changed to show a man with thick-rimmed glasses and enormous sideburns. '*Stars go through life, just like people do, and what we're really interested in is what happens when stars die. Some fade away slowly, but others go with a bang. And they blow inwards as well as outwards. That huge implosion could give rise to something called a black hole, and we think we know exactly where we can find one in the sky.'*

Janet and Moira were doing a new position now. Reluctantly but unavoidably, Robbie felt his gaze swing away from the television towards Moira, who was on all fours and had bent herself into an unnatural angle with her miniskirted rump held high. He watched her for a few moments, wondering what satisfaction or benefit there could possibly be in such absurd contortions, the like of which he'd only previously seen done by a Chinese girl in a sparkly leotard in Billy Smart's circus on telly at Christmas. Moira's backside was trembling with concentration, and Robbie looked at the screen again so as not to miss what the sideburned scientist was saying.

'A black hole is a state of matter that is infinitely dense and infinitely small – a singularity – lying hidden from view inside a spherical region termed the event horizon. You could fly right through the event horizon without noticing anything at all, but once you're inside there's no turning back – you get sucked straight into the central singularity.'

Another position now, just as daft as the last. Janet was taking it all in, following Moira's every move as though the stupid woman were a teacher in school. Robbie listened to the voice-over commentary on the television while his puzzled gaze lingered again on Moira's shifting form.

'To unsuspecting astronauts, a black hole could prove a deadly trap. According to the predictions of Einstein's theory of relativity, space travellers would be unable to detect what they were approaching, but colleagues back on Earth would

get some inkling. Messages from the spacecraft would appear to be in slow motion – an effect called gravitational red-shift. The closer the spaceship gets to the event horizon, the slower everything inside will appear to observers on Earth. But before mission control can send any warning to the crew, the slow motion comes to a total halt. On their screens, the controllers see the crew frozen in time, completely immobile. This marks the moment when they've crossed the event horizon. Already, by the time the signals reach Earth, the spaceship and crew have been destroyed, every last drop of space and time squeezed out of them.'

Now Moira was lying on her back, her conical breasts jutting into the air like a pair of command modules orbiting in tandem above a mysterious world. Her legs were bending and stretching in an alternating rhythm; she was a machine performing a pointless ritual. Maybe she'd left something switched on in the kitchen, or perhaps the cigarettes in her handbag were on fire and the whole house was about to explode; she didn't care. She was in slow motion, and there was nothing Robbie would be able to do to save them all from tumbling into the lethal singularity, other than make sure he kept plenty of water handy when he went to bed. Maybe a wet towel too, to douse the flames.

Moira lifted her head and noticed Robbie staring at her. 'Enjoying it?' she asked calmly.

The remark gave him an unworldly sensation; he was startled to receive her communication so quickly across so many light years. 'It's about black holes.'

'I know,' she said, lowering her head again and steering her limbs into a new but no less improbable arrangement.

'Your mum tells me you want to be an astronaut when you grow up.'

'That's right,' said Robbie, feeling slightly embarrassed and wondering what else his mum might have told Moira, not to mention half the town.

'Better watch out for black holes, then. They sound mind-blowing.' The television showed a dazzling photograph, taken through a huge telescope, of a million stars swirling like foam round a plughole, and as he looked at it, Robbie thought of his mind being blown clean out of his space helmet by an unexpected event horizon inadvertently smuggled into the mission by way of Moira's handbag. She, meanwhile, was relaying further instructions about the mission to Janet. 'Breathe slowly and steadily. Let your chest rise and fall. Don't force it. Relax.'

'*Could black holes truly exist? Einstein thought no, and for a long time all other physicists agreed with him. But matter whirling around a black hole would emit intense flares of light, radio waves or X-rays that would allow the hole to be detected, and astronomers think they can see this happening right now in the constellation of Cygnus, the swan. If humans had X-ray eyes, the brightest place in the entire sky would be a tiny point orbiting one of the swan's faint stars. More than six thousand light years away but perhaps only a few hundred miles in diameter, Cygnus X-1 is almost certainly a black hole, the first to be positively identified.*'

Then it was the astronomer's turn once more, describing what it might be like beyond the event horizon. '*You'd find yourself in a rapidly collapsing universe – everything would be blue-shifted and you'd very quickly reach the singularity marking the end of everything. That's the complete opposite of what we see on the outside – an expanding universe evolving away from an initial singularity, the big bang. So a black hole is a bit like a universe turned inside out. Or maybe it's the black hole that's the right way round, and the rest of the universe that's inverted.*'

Robbie watched a succession of experts carry the subject far beyond anything he could hope to comprehend, so that soon his brain felt as sore and twisted as his legs had been while trying to adopt the locust position. But the pictures were good – one sequence showed what would happen if a probe encountered a black hole whose horizon was small.

'*The spacecraft orbits the hole perfectly safely. Then one of the astronauts needs to go outside to do some repairs.*'

Robbie was carefully steering the capsule through the X-ray flashes of matter whizzing round the invisible hole when a voice calls out from behind. 'Captain, I think we have a problem here.' Robbie turns to see the ship's engineer trying to make the governor work. 'It's stuck, Captain, maybe a bit of meteorite's got lodged in the flue. I'll go out and check . . .'

'No!' Robbie insists. 'This is my job.' He tunes the control panel to Athlone, switches to medium wave, then goes and puts on his spacesuit.

'Let's try something easier,' Moira suggested, but Robbie was already going through the airlock and floating out into space.

'*Our astronaut could orbit the black hole safely too, but any change of course might send him tumbling inwards, and that would mean trouble. All objects falling into a black hole are directed towards the centre, so if the astro-*

naut falls feet first, his left and right sides will get squeezed together, both trying to reach the same place. But in addition, the astronaut's head – being further away from the hole – feels less gravitational pull than his toes, so he is stretched like spaghetti.'

Over the intercom in his space helmet, Moira's voice was beckoning him. 'Stretch – relax – push – relax.' Robbie tries to keep his attention on the small chimney projecting from the side of the spaceship which appears to have been fouled by dust, leaves, crisp packets and other space debris whipped up by the cosmic tornado. Faces are at the window, looking out at him. Be careful, Captain! Mind and don't tear your suit! Get back in here before you're blown away!

Robbie tugs at the space rubbish but loses his grip – his flailing arm connects with the jet pack on his chest, the ignition button is inadvertently pressed and in a single terrible moment a powerful blast of compressed gas is released, accelerating Robbie away from the safety of the mother ship, away from the agonized faces of his colleagues at the window, and directly towards the black hole. 'Relax!' the voice inside his helmet still insists, 'Let go!', and he feels himself being stretched and squeezed, squeezed and stretched, sucked and blue-shifted into oblivion.

'I think we've had enough now,' said Moira, standing up. 'Is your programme nearly finished?'

'I don't want to see it any more,' said Robbie. 'It's just people talking.' The screen displayed an equation containing lots of Greek letters, and a man in old-fashioned clothes.

'It's time for you two to get ready for bed. If you go first, Robbie, I can read you a story. Have you got a favourite book?' A few minutes later he was tucked up warmly with Moira sitting beside him holding *Rocket to the Stars*. 'It's not the sort I had in mind,' she said. 'Which bit shall I read?'

'The start.'

Moira recited, 'In 1957 the world was amazed when Russia launched the first artificial satellite, Sputnik 1. Its name means "fellow traveller", and the small unmanned probe marked the beginning of the space race. But man's dreams of conquering space go farther back in time.' She stopped and looked at him. 'You're really serious about wanting to be an astronaut, aren't you?'

'I'd prefer being a cosmonaut.'

'Because of your dad? He's got strong views, but there are other ways of seeing things.'

'I'd feel safer in a Russian mission, that's all. They build things better.'

Moira rolled her eyes. 'So it is because of your dad. Well, I'm sure you'll grow up to be whatever you want to be, because you're a clever boy. Do I need to keep reading this book or can I leave you to sleep?'

'Read,' he said. So she carried on, kept away from her cigarettes by the history of rocketry, and in this way Robbie's life was saved.

7

When the new school term started, Robbie found himself in Miss McPhail's class and the first thing she made them do was write about their summer holiday. The Coyles had been to Rothesay where it rained for two weeks solid, so he decided to write instead about his space programme and how it was progressing. Eventually Miss McPhail started asking pupils to stand up and read their work, and after choosing Ian Brodie and Margaret Pollock she alighted on Robbie. He got to his feet and began: 'I spent the summer training to be an astronaut.'

The entire class erupted. Miss McPhail was laughing too, but called the class to order so that he could continue.

'The job of astronaut requires excellent physical fitness and much technical expertise. Each day I lifted shoes, baked-bean tins and other heavy weights so as to build up my strength. I have also been studying the Russian alphabet so that I will be able to communicate with the ground crew, and I am learning the constellations because they help in navigation.'

Frank Coulter was staring at him, open-mouthed. 'You're mental.'

'Quiet, Frank,' the teacher said. 'Have you written anything else, Robert?'

'No, Miss McPhail.'

'Did you go away anywhere on holiday?'

'Only Rothesay.'

'That's a very interesting place. What did you do there?'

'Nothing.'

'Well, try writing about it. Now, Suzanne, let's hear what you've got for us.'

Suzanne had written about the kind of nothing that consists of a caravan in Ayr, a black-and-white dog, a new friend called Elaine. Miss McPhail called it excellent. Later she stood at Robbie's desk looking over his shoulder to read the rest of his piece. 'It's very well done,' she said, 'though not what I had in mind. Wouldn't you rather write about real life and ordinary people?'

'Why should I? It's boring.'

Miss McPhail frowned. 'Do you really find life boring, Robert?'

He nodded. 'The doctor says I've got a vivid imagination.'

'He's right about that,' said Miss McPhail. 'But we'll find something to keep it occupied.' Her solution was the same as the doctor's: she prescribed a book which Robbie dutifully took home with him that afternoon. The author's name reminded him of brontosaurus, his favourite dinosaur, so that was a good sign; but the title – *Jane Eyre* – was too much like the place where Suzanne had gone on holiday, and the book turned out to be a girls' story much like hers, with not so much as a pterodactyl in sight. He quickly gave up.

It would be good to have wings like a pterodactyl's, Robbie thought; great webs of skin connecting arms and legs, enabling flight. If there was nothing on television you could fly out the window instead. There'd be shops in treetops, play parks on cliff edges. If only there'd been a child born, some time in history, with the tiniest bit of wing, able to jump a little bit further whenever sabre-toothed tigers ran after it. Then evolution would have taken care of the rest – just like brontosaurus with its long neck. But humans can't fly, so the winged baby never happened. It was all so unfair.

There was another way of looking at things, and they sang about it at school. All things bright and beautiful – the

Lord God made them all. Robbie imagined it being like the Airfix kits he'd started making, ever since he was given a Lancaster bomber for his tenth birthday, all in pieces in a box with a tube of glue and an instruction book that was nearly as long as *Jane Eyre* but made a lot more sense once you got the hang of it. There was God one day, feeling bored in heaven with nothing to do, when suddenly he decides to take up a hobby. So he gets this enormous box called The Universe, with a picture on it showing trees and fields and birds, and people too. All he's got to do is put it together in the right order.

'Aye, but who made the pieces?' asked Scott, when Robbie explained the idea to his friend one Saturday while they threw stones at cans lined up beside the burn.

'The pieces were always there,' said Robbie. 'Nobody made them.'

'That's pointless,' said Scott.

Certainly it was one of the weaker aspects of the theory; nevertheless, Robbie liked to think of God sitting with all the parts of the plant and animal kingdom laid out before him on an enormous table, a tube of glue held in his hand, the liquid at the tip of its silver nozzle congealing into a gummy bead as the Lord inspects page after page of instruction. We would all be like Lancaster bombers, Messerschmitts, Panzers or any other machine in the Airfix range; different combinations of the same pre-moulded components.

A minister visited the school. He introduced himself as the Reverend Donaldson and spoke to the assembled children about his work in Africa. He said that an old woman took a pot of boiling water from the fire and spilled a drop on her foot but didn't feel anything, and this meant she had leprosy. The Reverend Donaldson was a bit like Dr Muir, old and bald. He came round the classrooms after they had all gone back to their lessons and when he got to Robbie's class he was shown the pictures and stories on the wall. Everyone carried on with their work but tried to see what the Reverend Donaldson was looking at.

'This is an interesting piece,' he was saying to Miss McPhail. Robbie had written it, about the Apollo Moon landings. Miss McPhail brought the minister over to meet the proud author. The reverend beamed down at him and placed a broad, brown-spotted hand on his shoulder. 'How old are you, young man?'

'Ten.'

The reverend raised his bushy eyebrows. 'Ten . . . what?'

'Ten years.'

The reverend chuckled and smiled encouragingly. 'Ten years . . . what?'

Miss McPhail seemed to be mouthing something at Robbie, who was trying to do a mental calculation. 'Ten years, three months and . . . eight days.'

'Don't you know you ought to say "sir"?' said the minister, turning away and about to move on to look at someone else's work. Robbie put his hand up, and Miss McPhail asked what he wanted.

'I've got a question for the minister.'

'Go ahead and ask me, lad.'

'Please – sir – how do you know God's real?'

Miss McPhail frowned, but the reverend kept beaming

and spread his hands in a grand gesture of benevolence. 'You only need look around and you'll see his works everywhere.'

'Did God give that woman in Africa leprosy?'

Miss McPhail intervened. 'Quiet now, Robbie, the minister has better things to do than answer impertinent questions.'

'On the contrary,' the minister said genially. 'This young fellow has asked a very important question, and I think the whole class might like to know the answer.' The raising of his voice had caused every head to turn in Robbie's direction; Frank Coulter looked ready for more fun at Robbie's expense.

'Now, children,' said the minister, 'we all know that sad things happen in this world. Can anyone tell me something sad – yes, you, young lady.'

'My goldfish died. She was called Polly.'

'Well, that really is very sad,' the reverend told her, 'and I'm sure you must have felt awful about it. But fish do die, don't they? A fish can't last forever, no more than anything else can, so when the time comes we have to be strong and remember all the happy times we've had looking after it.'

'I used to feed her every day,' said the girl, Fiona McBride, who was already on the verge of tears just thinking about it. Miss McPhail didn't look too happy either, and the raised hand of Margaret Cooper at the other end of the room offered a diversion.

'You shouldn't feed them every day,' said Margaret, 'so maybe that's why she died. I've got a hamster.'

'Oh, hamsters are lovely creatures,' the Reverend Donaldson agreed, and this prompted yet more hands.

'Please, sir, I've got a dog. A collie.' Stephen Fraser looked suitably gratified by the reverend's endorsement of collies as wonderful companions.

'Children, children,' said Miss McPhail, 'we really don't have time to hear about everyone's pet. The minister knows you all love your animals and look after them.'

'That's right,' he agreed. 'But . . . oh dear.'

Fiona McBride was sobbing uncontrollably. 'It's not true – I didn't feed Polly too much. I didn't kill her!'

'Of course you didn't,' Miss McPhail insisted, going to comfort her.

'You see, boys and girls,' the reverend concluded. 'Sadness is part of life, and there are times when we need to be strong.'

Robbie put up his hand again. 'Sir, did God make Fiona's fish die?'

Miss McPhail shot an impatient glance from the shaking, tearful former fish owner she had almost calmed before Robbie's intervention.

'Of course not,' said the reverend. 'God didn't kill wee Polly.'

'It was because she was fed too much,' Margaret Cooper helpfully reiterated.

'It wasn't that either,' said the reverend. 'It just happened, that's all. These things happen.'

'But God can do anything,' said Robbie. 'So why couldn't he cure the woman with leprosy, or make the fish stay alive? Or the two children who fell in the river and got saved by the man who drowned – the one on the memorial.'

The reverend nodded. 'That's a famous story, young man, and a very great example of what faith can do. James

Deuchar gave up his own life so that others could have theirs.'

'Then why can't God do that too?' said Robbie.

'What, kill himself so a wee fish could stay alive?'

Everyone laughed, even Fiona, so caught up was she in the edgy hysteria which now relieved the classroom's tension. Frank Coulter pretended to be a goldfish, gulping and flapping his arms most convincingly.

While Miss McPhail subdued the class, the reverend patted Robbie on the head. 'You asked a serious question and I can see that you're a thoughtful fellow. What do you want to be when you grow up?'

From the corner of his eye, Robbie could see that Frank Coulter's fish impression had turned into a rotating finger at the side of his skull. 'I want to be a scientist. Maybe an astronomer.'

'Oh, that's a fine ambition,' said the minister. 'And do you go to church?'

Robbie felt his mouth go completely dry. 'No, sir.' Nor did most of the rest of the class, but there was a palpable sense among them all that a great naughtiness had been publicly exposed.

'Sunday school?'

'No, sir.'

'You should. You'd have lots of fun and all your questions would be answered.'

Robbie said, 'Don't you think maybe all the animals and plants are made of pieces, like a machine, and one day the machine stops working?'

'I think that's a very sensible and scientific way of looking at it,' said the minister. 'And when you see a complicated machine like a clock, you know that somebody must have made it. And a goldfish or a hamster is a lot more complicated than a clock, which is how we know there must be a God who created all these wonderful things. But if God made them last forever then there wouldn't be room for all the fishes and hamsters and everything else that would soon fill up the world, so each of them has to go when the time comes. No matter how we feel about it, everything is for the best, because that's how God made it. He wants us all to be happy, and the only way we can know what happiness feels like is by being sad now and again, so we've got some kind of comparison. Well, children, are we all happy now?'

'Yes, sir,' the class chanted, prompted by Miss McPhail.

'That's lovely. And I hope you'll all say your prayers tonight and be at Sunday School at the weekend.'

When Robbie got home his mother challenged him straight away. 'Jessie told Janet you were cheeky to the minister.'

'I wasn't, honest.'

'Now go up to your room and wait for your dad to come back.'

Robbie passed the time in an African prison. There were huts with roofs made of big leaves, and guards in Nazi uniforms, and he was tied to the floor with the Reverend Donaldson sitting next to him slurping from a bowl of soup. The reverend offers the soup to Robbie, accidentally spills some of it on him, yet Robbie feels nothing. 'I think I've got leprosy, sir,' Robbie tells him calmly. 'You can make it out of here, but leave me behind.' Trapped by wicked Germans, the famous Professor Robbie knows the only hope for mankind is for him to die without revealing the secret he has discovered – the formula explaining how all the bits of atoms fit together like parts in an Airfix kit, and if you smash them in just the right way then you get an incredible explosion, able to blow the Reverend Donaldson and everybody else to smithereens.

When Mr Coyle returned he called Robbie downstairs and demanded an explanation. Janet had been sent to the kitchen to do her homework and Robbie found the living room eerily calm, the television having been switched off. His parents occupied two thirds of the recently acquired three-piece suite whose hire-purchase terms implied a strict code of use so as to prevent spills, and Robbie stood to attention beside the coffee table awaiting his fate. His father's face was impassive, but his mother, he noticed, had a sorrowful look, as if she'd been crying. 'We don't want you getting in trouble at school when you're doing so well,' she said.

'But I only asked the minister how he knows God's real. What's wrong with asking a question?'

'It was the way you asked,' said his mother. 'Just don't go getting too big for your boots, Robbie.'

His father had meanwhile been collecting his thoughts. 'What do you mean by God?' he asked.

Robbie pondered. 'I don't know.'

'Then how could you expect anyone to tell you if God's real?'

This puzzled Robbie since his father regularly debated with unwitting Christians who came to the door and invariably went back down the path defeated. Maybe his dad was a believer after all, and those doorstep arguments were only a way of passing the time. Robbie asked him, 'Did God make everything?'

'No,' said Mr Coyle. 'Your mother and me made you, and we were made by your grandparents. That table was made by men in a factory, and so was this cup. The light coming through the window was made by the sun, and the sun was made by dust and gravity.'

'But who started it all? Why?'

'Nobody did,' said his father. 'The universe has always been here, it never had a beginning and it doesn't have an end. It's infinite. Go for a million billion miles and you'll still have just as far to go if you want to reach the end of things. Live for a million billion years and you've had no life at all, compared to infinity.'

Mrs Coyle said, 'I don't think this helps, Joe . . .'

'Let me finish, pet,' he said firmly. 'Now, son, next time you see the Reverend Donaldson, just ask him this. In the Bible it says that first of all there was nothing, and then God said let there be light, and there was light, which was the first thing. Well, where did the light come from? You've got to have something that's shining and making all the light, so it doesn't really make sense, does it? And another thing: if God spoke before he switched the light on, that means he must have made sound first. But it doesn't say that in the Bible . . .'

'Joe,' said Mrs Coyle softly, 'that really isn't the point.'

'Will you mind not interrupting me or I'll lose my thread. Now, son, all I'm saying is that if you want to get into discussions about things then you need to know your facts, you need to be polite, and you need to be completely logical. But you weren't, were you? You asked an old man, who's spent years and years believing in God, how he knows that God's real. That was a damn stupid question to ask him, don't you think?'

'Joe, please . . .'

Mr Coyle was reddening with irritation. 'Can you not go and see to the tea, Anne?' Then he addressed Robbie again. 'Let me tell you how it all started. When people lived in caves and wore animal skins they didn't know how anything worked. If it rained, they said it was because of the rain god, and when they wanted to grow crops they prayed to the rain god because they were afraid that otherwise they might starve. All these people started out free and equal, but then there were one or two of them put on fancy gear, feathers on their heads and the like, and said they knew all about the rain god. These were the priests, and they started telling everyone what to do. And because the people were frightened and ignorant, they obeyed.'

It reminded Robbie of the African village. The German soldiers had run away and the Reverend Donaldson goes round the huts, telling the people with leprosy what to do. 'We all get a wee bit ill now and again,' he says soothingly to a lady with no arms. 'That way we know what it's like to feel healthy.'

'Eventually things started to change,' said Mr Coyle. 'People worked out that water evaporates from the sea and condenses as rain. So there was no rain god any more, but there was still a god of war or love. Then they thought of evolution, so there was no need for those gods either. In the end there's no reason for any of them, except as a way of making people feel less frightened about dying, though it doesn't seem to work too well at that either.' Robbie's mother was coming back from the kitchen. 'So you see, son,' Mr Coyle concluded, 'you just have to be logical about these things.'

Mrs Coyle sat down again, and Robbie stared at his parents' faces. For a moment, the only thing to be heard was the traffic outside and the transistor radio in the kitchen, accompanying Janet's art homework with a song that went *Oo-ee, chirpy chirpy cheep cheep*. Eventually Robbie said, 'Is that it?'

'Aye,' said his dad. 'You can switch on the telly now.'

8

Sometimes Mr and Mrs Coyle would have a 'wee night'. Grown-up friends would be invited; peanuts would be served from wooden bowls left strategically placed around the living room; tins of beer would be opened, their discarded ring-pull tops serving as toys or jewellery for the excited children in the half-hour of socializing they were allowed before being sent upstairs. These wee nights mostly weren't wee at all; they necessitated a major rearrangement of the living-room furniture, with chairs being carefully positioned so as to allow ease of access, and the gate-leg dining table being opened to its full splendour to bear the weight of all the sausage rolls, Scotch eggs and tinned Russian salad it was called upon to support. There might even be dancing, with Mrs Coyle's favourite Carpenters record doing a few turns on the radiogram.

The children learned there was to be a wee night with Moira, whom they'd not seen since she had babysat almost a year previously. In fact the night was to be one of the more truly wee, since the only guests would be Moira and her new boyfriend David, who taught science at a Glasgow secondary school. While Janet eagerly looked forward to being with Moira again, Robbie was more excited about meeting a real scientist for the first time in his life, and as the date of the wee night drew nearer, his mental image of David crystallized in increasing detail, until Robbie knew with complete certainty and confidence that he was shortly to become the trusted companion and assistant to a man with the wisdom of Dr Who, the courage of Captain Kirk, and the physical appearance of Tony Curtis in *The Persuaders*.

The fellow who showed up at the door alongside Moira was so totally unrecognizable that for at least the first ten minutes Robbie was struck completely dumb. David was short and skinny with receding hair and a thick moustache that hung over his mouth and served as a trap for the peanuts and crisps Robbie was told to offer him, reminding Robbie of the filter-feeding mechanism of blue whales which he'd seen on a wildlife documentary. He wore a caramel-coloured corduroy jacket and brought from his inside pocket a pipe which he lit, filling the room (and, as it turned out, the entire house) with a pungent odour that matched his marine appearance.

'Robbie starts secondary school next year,' Mrs Coyle told the visitor. She was wearing an orange dress that Robbie had never seen before and sat forward on the edge of her chair in a way that made her look both nervous and uncomfortable. 'Janet's there already, doing well at art. Robbie's more interested in science.'

'That's good,' David said between noxious puffs. 'What sort of things do you like, Robbie?'

'Space. Stories about other planets.'

'Secondary science isn't really like that,' David informed him, a remark as disappointing as his appearance. 'It's physics, chemistry, biology.' He took the glass of whisky Mr Coyle had poured. 'Chemistry's the most interesting, because that's the one with all the experiments and bangs and clouds of gas.'

'You're biased, darling,' Moira laughed, nuzzling against him, an ornate sherry glass delicately held in her hand while Janet sat silently beside her in the third space on the settee. Chemistry, with its clouds and smells, sounded to Robbie no different from what his mum did in the kitchen every Sunday when roasting the dinner.

'I want to learn about gravity,' he told the teacher.

'You will,' David said bluntly, and Robbie retreated with the peanut bowl, leaving the adults to talk now that Mr and Mrs Coyle were both seated with their guests.

'I hear you're a union man,' said Mr Coyle, going straight for his favourite subject.

'EIS rep for the school,' David replied. 'We've got pretty much all the teaching staff signed up.'

After listening to the men exchange union initials for a few minutes, the women broke off into a conversation of their own while Robbie, sitting silently and ready to be called on for nut duty at any moment, idly flipped his attention from one grown-up speaker to another, as though scanning radio frequencies.

'You ought to try yoga classes, Anne. You might even find there's one where you could take Janet, too.'

'That's right, Joe, we're having to consider a work-to-rule.'

'And are your mother's legs any better?'

'The only way we can get anywhere is through collective action.'

Robbie stared down at the peanut bowl on his lap and began counting the contents. He'd never noticed before how interesting peanuts could be – each one was different from the rest, if you looked closely.

'Of course there's a socialist way of teaching, and that's what we try to do now. It isn't the old rote learning, top of the class or dunce's cap nonsense any more. Comprehensive education is about equality.'

Mr Coyle had already explained to Robbie that the secondary school he was to attend was the new and modern kind in which children weren't segregated by ability. Being clever didn't make you more special than anybody else; it was no different from being a bit taller or a bit faster, or having blue eyes instead of brown. Since everyone's different it means that everybody's really the same. Like peanuts.

'And I hope you like chicken, Moira, because I've made coq au vin. It's a Fanny Cradock recipe.'

Moira's sudden intake of breath was enough to tear Robbie's attention away from his laboured fascination with the bowl; Moira had a hand to her mouth in a gesture that made him wonder what was so terrible about Fanny Cradock's cock o' van. 'Did I not tell you, Anne?' she said with a heavily apologetic air. 'I've gone vegetarian.'

The sense of domestic calamity was enough to interrupt

the men in mid-flow. 'Vegetarian?' Mr Coyle sceptically echoed. 'Since when?'

'Nearly a year,' said Moira. 'I became a Buddhist.'

The raising of eyebrows this caused sent tremors of interest through the two children.

'A Buddhist?' Mr Coyle again repeated, incredulously now. 'You mean you meditate 'n' that?' Moira nodded with an air of sublime contentment. 'But do you not need to get your head shaved and go to a monastery?'

'There's lots of ways of being a Buddhist,' Moira told him. 'I do it my way.' Janet was gazing at her with strengthened admiration, and if Mr Coyle noticed then it could only have added to the threat he felt at having a mystic loony inside the four walls he rented.

'Since you've only been doing it for less than a year, do you not think you could have a night off for the sake of a piece of chicken?' he suggested.

'Joe, don't,' said his wife. 'It's no problem at all.'

'I'm so sorry, Anne, I was sure I told you.'

'I expect you did and I forgot.' Mrs Coyle said there was plenty of other food she could eat. 'And I could make you an omelette if you like . . . or does that count as an animal?' She and Moira laughed, Janet joined in.

'That's a very good question,' said Mr Coyle, smiling too, but with sarcasm rather than humour. 'The chicken or the egg, eh? If you're going to be reincarnated as a chicken then you've got to be an egg first, so I suppose you don't eat eggs, do you, Moira?'

'No, Joe, I don't eat eggs.'

'Bread?'

'Yes, I eat bread.'

'Ah, but it's got yeast in it, and that's alive, isn't it, David?'

'Joe,' said his wife, 'let's drop it.'

'Yeast is a fungus,' David declared, 'so it's no problem.'

'What about a sea urchin?' Mr Coyle suggested.

'Come on in the kitchen, Moira,' said Mrs Coyle, standing up. 'Let's see what we've got. No sea urchins, that's for sure!' The three females exited the room, creating their own half-heard island of laughter behind the closed kitchen door while Mr Coyle continued to contemplate the infinite paradox the wee night had unexpectedly raised.

'Well, David,' he said, raising his whisky glass with a clink of ice, 'as a scientist and a socialist, I'm sure you regard all religions as the opium of the masses.'

'Certainly,' David agreed, taking a puff on the pipe which might have been part of the reason why the women were so eager to escape, and which was now making Robbie consider joining them. 'But Buddhism isn't a religion, Joe.'

'How do you mean?'

'It has no god.'

'What about Buddha, then?'

David briefly exchanged his pipe for his glass as a way of keeping his whiskery lips occupied, then said, 'Millions of uneducated people worship Buddhist idols, and for them it might as well be a religion, which is why Mao has done the right thing in China. But Buddhism's really a philosophy, not a religion. In fact, when you read Engels, you can see that Buddhism and Marxism have quite a lot in common. You know how Engels defined dialectics? The science of interconnections. That's what Marxism's all about – it says that everything in the universe is connected to everything else.'

Mr Coyle looked doubtful. 'I can't say I've ever thought of socialism in those sorts of terms.'

'It's true, though,' said the teacher. 'You take any person, Napoleon, say. Did Napoleon change history? No – history made Napoleon. He was a product of particular socio-economic conditions, that's what Marxism tells us, and it was only at a particular stage in the historical evolution of the class struggle that Napoleon could have emerged. If he'd been born in the Middle Ages then he'd never have become an emperor. And if Napoleon had died when he was a baby, somebody else would have grown up and done pretty much the same things he did. We're all connected to each other through the dialectics of history.'

Mr Coyle gave a dismissive laugh. 'That's very clever, David, but I don't think it's got much to do with anything the lads at our branch meetings would understand.'

'Maybe not,' David conceded, 'but revolutions aren't started by people at branch meetings; they come from the intelligentsia, the petit bourgeoisie.'

Robbie took in this lesson while staring at the peanut bowl. He liked the sound of the petty boor-joys, whom he imagined wearing pretty, frilly nineteenth-century clothes, jigging about like idiots in ballrooms. He wondered if the student who leapt in a river to save two children was one of them. If James Deuchar hadn't jumped, would the Daleks of history have made somebody else take the plunge instead?

From the kitchen, more liquid female laughter rippled into Robbie's consciousness. Here, though, everything was in deadly earnest, as the revolution was plotted that would send Sam Dunbar straight from the putting green to a firing squad and make it possible to buy yourself a new spacesuit without having to traipse from Marks and Spencer to C&A in search of the best deal.

'If you ask me, David,' said Mr Coyle, 'it's the intellectuals who cause all the worst problems for the labour movement. When you've got a truly popular force uniting workers then you don't need all these Fabians and the like.' It sounded to Robbie like a rude grown-up word.

David was shaking his head, spreading grey smoke before taking the pipe from his mouth, waving its spittle-moistened end in the air. 'If you want to get the means of production into the hands of the workers then it's no use waiting for an uneducated mob of coal miners and shipbuilders to storm Buckingham Palace, because it won't happen. Look at the sort of direct militant action that's happening now. Look at the revolution in Northern Ireland. If that was only about some Paddies with religious differences I don't suppose the special forces would be quite so keen on shooting dead every Marxist they can lay hands on.'

Mr Coyle had had enough, and Robbie could sense the tension as his father rose to his feet. 'I'd better see how Anne's getting on. Fancy another drink?' He went through to the kitchen, leaving his peanut-attendant son alone with the revolutionary in a smoky silence whose seconds lasted longer than either found comfortable.

'So, Robbie,' David said at last. 'You want to learn about gravity?'

Robbie nodded, and it occurred to him that this boor-

joy intellectual might be able to answer a question his dad had struggled with. 'How can the Moon's gravity get to the Earth, but the Earth's gravity can't get to the Moon?'

'What do you mean?' asked David, as the others began trickling quietly back into the room.

'Well, if you're in a spaceship then you're weightless, right? But the Moon's gravity makes tides on Earth.'

David nodded in understanding, moving along the settee to bring himself closer to Robbie while Moira and Janet sat down again beside him. 'That's a very common misconception,' he said. 'But let's imagine you're inside a lift compartment and the cable snaps. While you fall downwards, everything in the lift falls at the same rate, so you feel weightless. Now suppose you're in a capsule that's fired through the air. Again, as the capsule falls towards the ground, you'll be weightless. But suppose the capsule is fired so powerfully that it flies clear over the horizon, and the Earth itself curves away underneath the capsule faster than it can descend. Then you'll fall right round the Earth, and you'll be weightless – that's what's happening in an orbiting spacecraft.'

All the others remained silent while David continued his lecture, making Robbie feel as though it were he, the intended audience, who was the focus of attention. 'When a spacecraft flies to the Moon it's much the same kind of situation – the capsule falls in the combined gravitational field of the Earth and Moon. Every space journey is really a kind of falling. The Moon's revolution round the Earth is actually the fall of both around their common centre of gravity. But the field isn't the same everywhere, and the difference is what causes tides.'

Now Robbie understood. A revolution is a tide in history, and it was how you could get into space.

'There,' said Mrs Coyle, 'we've all learned something. And we won't have to be Mooning off to the chippie for Moira because I've cooked enough vegetables to feed an army.'

'We do have such a laugh, don't we, Anne!' said Moira, touching the corner of her eye where the mascara was still smudged from the fun that had gone on in the kitchen.

'Now, Robbie, it's time for you to spaceship up to bed. And Janet, you need to go upstairs too. Say nighty-night to Moira and David, both of you.'

Janet gave Moira a kiss; Robbie wondered if he was supposed to do the same, but hovered far enough away for the moment to pass without incident. 'Thank you for telling me about gravity,' he said to David.

'You're welcome. Good night, now.'

Robbie lay in bed with the unintelligible burble of adult voices rumbling beneath him. Even in his sleep he could still smell the pipe smoke.

9

That weekend it was Halloween, but Robbie's excitement about the prospect of dressing up was marred by news of a bomb in London. The children watched in silence as the lunchtime bulletin showed a gaping hole in the side of the Post Office Tower from which the tiny faces of police investigators peered down. Robbie hoped the crisis wouldn't stop him being allowed out later.

'They're saying it's the IRA,' Mrs Coyle commented to her husband, who came and sat down with them.

'That's propaganda,' he replied, while the camera panned across the twisted metal of the observation deck where the explosion had happened before dawn when no one was about. Robbie was sorry to see the tower in such a state; with its rocket-like shape and futuristic looks it had always been a building he longed to visit, perhaps to dine in the revolving restaurant as a grown-up astronaut in a Captain Scarlet uniform, casually gazing at the slowly swerving metropolis five hundred feet below.

Mr Coyle said, 'It's more likely the Angry Brigade.'

Robbie had heard of those people already – there'd been a series of bombs and fires – but he didn't know what they were so angry about. The Post Office Tower was meant to be the communications hub of the entire country, beaming telephone signals and making sure every call went to the right place. The Coyles didn't even have a phone but Robbie still felt grateful for the tower's existence. Perhaps the Angry Brigade had kept getting wrong numbers.

'Somebody from the IRA claimed responsibility,' Mrs Coyle pointed out.

'They could have been anybody,' Joe protested. 'And how do we even know they said it? What we hear on the news is whatever the government want us to think.'

Losing interest in the screen when the news moved to other items, Robbie considered the problem logically. The IRA lived in Ireland and probably couldn't even pick up British telephone signals so why would they want to bomb a tower in London? And why set it to go off at four o'clock in the morning? He imagined a big black time bomb with digits sliding through the minutes and hours like they always did in *Thunderbirds* or *Joe 90*, and maybe you had to select a.m. or p.m., so the bombers really meant it to go off at four o'clock in the afternoon but got it wrong. The science teacher who visited, David Luss, had said there was a revolution in Northern Ireland, which sounded as exciting as the rotating restaurant Robbie would never get to visit now that the Post Office Tower was to remain closed to the public indefinitely and security was being tightened at other potential targets. But Robbie's father didn't like David. After the wee night, Robbie had overheard him say that he never wanted that man in the house again. Robbie supposed it was because of the pipe smoke but couldn't be sure.

He said, 'Dad, are we having a war with Ireland?'

Mr Coyle must have been no more interested in the next news item than Robbie was, because he began a long story about Catholics and Protestants, and how it was the Catholics that got all the worst jobs and the poorest housing and had to put up with Orange walks every year, same as came round the scheme here in Kenzie; though Robbie always enjoyed the banners and the bowler hats, the rattling drums and gleaming flutes and the swaggering fellow at the front twirling a stick in the air. It maybe wasn't everybody's cup of tea but it was hardly reason for blowing up a building.

'If the British government don't like a Catholic in Northern Ireland they can lock them up,' Mr Coyle explained. 'It's called internment. There's no trial, no charges, no evidence.'

'That's not fair,' Robbie said indignantly.

'If we were living in Northern Ireland we'd all be classed as Catholics and could be locked up.'

'But we're not Catholics!'

'I was born and brought up one,' said his father, 'and as far as the Vatican or the government's concerned, I still am. That makes you Catholic too.'

'That's daft,' Janet said sourly, getting up to go to her room and carry on reading her *Jackie* in peace, but Robbie liked the thought that he was by birth part of the revolutionary underclass, like the Thals against the Daleks.

'So is that why they think the IRA blew up the Post Office Tower?'

Mr Coyle shook his head. 'The government want to blame the IRA so they can keep locking people up. It was the Angry Brigade done it. They're some crowd of dropout malcontents, probably a load of druggie squatters who all went to public school and now they're playing at being anarchists.' Robbie imagined them competing on *Top of the Form*, bowled out in the final innings by an opposing but identical-looking team of future cabinet ministers. One way or another, those posh-voiced people on telly had the whole world carved up between them, so what chance did Robbie seriously have of ever being an astronaut? He definitely needed to go to Russia where they didn't have Catholics and Protestants and no one had ever heard of *Top of the Form*.

'I know why the IRA couldn't possibly have done it,' he declared triumphantly.

'Why's that?'

'Because they claimed responsibility. Nobody's ever

going to do something bad and then straight away own up to it.'

Mr Coyle chuckled and rose from his chair to switch off the television. His wife had finished peeling the potatoes for dinner so it was time for their walk. 'Come and get your shoes and coat on,' he called up to Janet.

'Oh no,' she moaned from the landing. 'Do we have to?'

'We can't leave you here on your own.'

Half an hour later the four of them were taking the familiar riverbank path, Janet walking silently and despondently beside her mother with her hands buried in the pockets of her duffel coat while Robbie and Mr Coyle marched ahead in the cold autumnal air. Behind them, the path led past the memorial and then through the centre of Kenzie, but it was the other way Joe Coyle had opted for on this occasion, into the open countryside beyond the town's edge, and it was by means of this abundance of choice that he had easily countered his daughter's objections; for as well as being free to go east or west along the river there was the additional variable factor to consider of how far they should go, and whether indeed they should simply turn round after an hour's healthy strolling and retrace their steps or else – Mr Coyle's favoured option – pursue a circular route that could take all manner of forms. Having such a wealth of opportunities within a five-mile radius, it was a wonder that anyone ever left Kenzie at all; and if Janet wasn't happy with it then she'd just have to wait until she could grow up and find a husband and move away, then maybe she'd appreciate what she'd left behind. This waiting process was what she now appeared to be earnestly engaged in as she hid behind a hanging fringe of hair her father reckoned needed cutting or else tying back like his mother used to do.

Mr Coyle was telling Robbie how the Scots were so much better than the Irish at dealing with English persecution. 'Take the Queen, for example. She's called Elizabeth the Second but she's the first we've ever had by that name. She's Elizabeth the Second of England and First of Scotland, same way James the Sixth of Scotland was the First of England. And you know all about him, don't you?'

Robbie was gazing at black crows perched on bare trees at the opposite side of the river.

'Gunpowder plot?' his father prompted. 'Thing we're celebrating in a few days' time? Are you not doing it at school?' Robbie had learned so many times about Guy Fawkes that there seemed little else to be said about him, but Mr Coyle's version of history invariably differed from the authorized account. 'King Jamie was the cause of all our troubles, going down south and forgetting where he came from. But you know, when the Queen got crowned, some Scottish protestors rubbed down coins stamped Elizabeth II to make them Elizabeth I. That's our way: no bombs or riots, just peaceful resistance with a bit of Scots humour. Show the southerners what idiots they are.'

Evidently the Angry Brigade weren't Scottish, then, unless you could call it a humorous touch to have left the bomb inside the ladies' toilet, as the television had reported. Or was the joke that it was meant to be timed to explode on Bonfire Night, not Halloween? Anyway, neither had been cancelled, and that was the important thing to Robbie, who was still watching the crows which were wheeling now in the overcast sky ahead of them as they walked along the empty path. He could hear Janet's footsteps scraping reluctantly a few paces behind.

'Thing you've got to wonder,' said Mr Coyle, 'is what that Post Office Tower is really about. When they opened it a few year back they said it was to improve telecommunications but you only need an aerial for that, not an office building. All they parabolic dishes on the side aren't for ordinary radio signals, they're for microwaves.' These, he explained, were an electromagnetic frequency far beyond the end of any radio dial, a form of energy that could even be used to warm a bowl of soup – he'd seen it on *Tomorrow's World*. 'And they're sending these signals all over London. They must be cooking people's heads!'

Robbie imagined the slowly poaching brains of a million daft southerners sitting at their breakfast tables; TV dad in suit and tie, mother wearing a string of pearls while serving him Kellogg's Corn Flakes enriched with iron, and two smiling children sure to be top of the form even when all the contents of their posh skulls were hardened and congealed like overheated egg yolks.

'They people who bombed the Tower,' said Mr Coyle, 'they must know what the place is really about. Inside job. So now MI5's got the task of covering it all up, and they'll arrest some poor Irish people for it.' He halted and turned to check that the ladies were keeping pace. 'No dawdling back there,' he called to Anne and Janet, who had paused to watch something in the twitching reeds.

'I think it's a frog,' Anne shouted.

'Rat, more like,' Joe suggested, which was enough to encourage them to keep moving. 'Put a foot in that water and you'll go catching Wheel's disease.' They all re-gathered pace, and Mr Coyle explained to his son that Wheel's disease was something you got from rat's urine. 'Never used to be so many illnesses – makes you wonder where they come from.' Then, after wondering a bit, he said, 'There was a story in the *Post* or some other Tory rag about this great big radio transmitter in Russia, meant to be beaming deadly waves at us. I think they called them scalar waves – some made-up name I'd never heard of. And this was supposed to be why we were getting so many flu outbreaks and wet summers and the like. But you've got to ask your self, what's a more likely cause – an aerial thousands of miles away in Siberia, or one closer to home? That's why we need to know about the Post Office Tower.'

Mr Coyle fell silent and Robbie thought about his Halloween costume. There'd been no question about it: he was to go out this evening dressed as an astronaut. Janet said she was too old for guising and would stay indoors, not even tempted out by the prospect of sweets and coins from the neighbours, but for Robbie it was a chance to show himself to the world as he really was, and nobody would laugh at him for it. He imagined himself strapped into a padded chair in the nose-cone of a fireproof Soyuz rocket, while in London his Brylcreemed adversary was counting down to lift-off at the top of the repaired Post Office Tower, a cunningly disguised missile whose launch into space would leave the city blasted.

Mr Coyle paused again, this time to take in the scenery, because the bushes lining most of the riverside path were absent here, and they could look out across green fields to the distant hills. 'We should try going up one of them some time.'

'No way!' cried Janet.

'It'd be a bit of a hike,' Anne warned.

'Or we could see if there's a path takes us round the Vernon Estate. I hear it's a nice walk.'

'I thought the estate was private,' said Anne.

Joe laughed. 'Private? There's been nobody living there for years, the house is in ruins.' Then to Robbie he explained, 'Place belonged to some English aristocrat family – great big fancy Victorian house you could fit half the scheme in, and it was only their holiday home, their hunting lodge. Derelict now, so there's no reason why we shouldn't go round some time and see how the other half used to live.'

'You can other half it on your own,' said Anne. 'I'm not getting myself shot in the bahookie by some gamekeeper so you can have your right to roam or whatever you call it.'

'I keep telling you, there's no law of trespass in Scotland,' Joe reminded her, and from the look on her face it was clear she needed no more reminding. 'Why don't we go there now?'

Anne held firm. 'We'd all be tearing our clothes on barbed wire trying to get in. And we're needing to be getting home before too long so I can cook the chicken. Let's turn round and head back.'

Joe looked dejected. 'Already?' Robbed of the circular route he'd mentally prepared, he was like a child ordered indoors just when he was starting to enjoy himself. 'Let's go, then,' he said resignedly.

That evening, as soon as it was dark, Robbie put on his spacesuit. His mother's swimming cap had been modified with a layer of tinfoil and the addition of a microphone on a stalk, cleverly fashioned from part of a metal coat hanger. Together with rubber gloves, wellington boots and a padded winter coat and matching trousers that were the most extraterrestrial-looking items of clothing in the house, it made a most convincing costume, to Robbie's eye at least, when he proudly posed in front of the long mirror in his parents' bedroom. Mrs Coyle had carefully drawn a NASA emblem to pin on her son's arm but he refused, saying he should wear a hammer and sickle and the letters CCCP. Robbie's father was all for it but his mum was sceptical about the proposed insignia's door-to-door earning potential, so they settled instead for their own national flag, the Saltire. Robbie was then ready to go into the world: a Caledonian cosmonaut.

Mr Coyle held the front door open for him, giving Robbie a view of the interstellar darkness outside. 'Are you going to sing a song or say a poem?' his father asked. So concerned had he been with his appearance, Robbie had forgotten about the need to perform for the neighbours who were meant to reward him; and seeing his son's hesitation, Mr Coyle re-sealed the exit hatch.

'I don't know what to do,' Robbie confessed.

'Sing something,' Mr Coyle suggested. 'A good Scots song for Halloween. Do you know "The Wife of Usher's Well"?' Robbie had never heard of it, prompting complaints from his father about the state of schools, as well as an offer to teach it. He began chanting, 'There lived a wife at Usher's Well—'

'He's got no time for that now,' Mrs Coyle interrupted, while Janet hovered at the top of the stairs, suppressing laughter. 'Just tell a wee joke, Robbie.'

'I don't know any.'

'He's the joke,' Janet called down.

'If you've nothing useful to contribute then go back to your room,' Mr Coyle instructed her.

'What about "Roses are red, grass is green, so please help Halloween"?' she suggested.

'That's rubbish,' Robbie called back.

'It's the best any of us can think of,' said Mrs Coyle. 'So off you go exploring.'

Then the hatch opened once more and Robbie began his mission. It was cold outside, and breezy, hence his first concern was that the tinfoil might blow off his head and away down the street so he'd have to go chasing after it, but the glue and Sellotape held firm. Robbie couldn't see any other guisers, only an elderly life form on the opposite side of the street who glanced bemusedly at him while he decided which neighbour to visit first. Going right would mean the Dunbars but he wasn't yet mentally prepared for Sheena and Louise, so he went left instead to the Shaws. They weren't in. It was the same at the Connors, and he moved on dejectedly, thinking of an item he'd seen on television about an American custom called trick or treat. Mr Coyle considered it hideous blackmail and quite typical of that country: if you don't get what you want then vandalize your neighbour's house out of revenge, same way they treated places like Cambodia. Right now, though, Robbie thought it not such a bad idea. He was sure he saw a curtain twitch in the Connors' darkened house, and felt angry that grown people could be too mean to spare a gobstopper for a passing space explorer.

In London right now, an evil genius was preparing to

unleash his secret weapon: the wave-emitting missile that was the Post Office Tower. The only way to save the country and the planet was by hiding an explosive device in the ladies' lavatory – but could Robbie get there in time? Not at this rate, that was certain – it took him twenty minutes to reach the end of the street, though he was rewarded by four householders who liked his inane poem. All the while, the digital counter flipped steadily towards the moment when the missile would fire. Robbie had to try and save everyone – even the daft southerners who'd wonder why he was blowing up a building. Couldn't they see it was for their own good?

Imagine something the size of the Post Office Tower falling down on London. Robbie thought about it while pocketing a Mars Bar from the old lady at the last house on the street. The Angry Brigade made it go off when nobody was around because even wee bits of glass can do a lot of harm if they fall on you from five hundred feet up; like the shrapnel Robbie's father used to collect during the war and swapped for sweets with his schoolmates. But if the tower was really a missile and you had to destroy it, like the V2s with their chequerboard pattern – what then? There was Robbie, smuggling the bomb into the tower, knowing it would have to go off when the street below was full of men in bowler hats, women pushing prams. It was like all they people in Hiroshima. Shame they had to die, said Mr Coyle, but they brought it on themselves.

In his spacesuit, Robbie secretly enters the Post Office Tower by climbing through air-conditioning ducts. Every large building on Earth or anywhere else in the universe, he knows from countless television shows, is laced with such silver-lined tunnels, always man-sized and conveniently horizontal. Robbie pushes aside a metal grille and drops into the main computer room, where a man sits bound and gagged. It's the Reverend Donaldson.

'What are you doing here?' Robbie asks him, pulling the gag loose and beginning to untie the ropes around his body.

'They caught me trying to sabotage their plans,' the reverend explains. 'Now only you can save the world.'

'But have I the right?' says Robbie. 'If I destroy the missile I'll kill thousands of innocent Londoners.'

'Oh, don't worry about them,' says the reverend, and Robbie finds himself back outside his own house. He can stop now, or else continue and add the Dunbars to his list. He decides to take the risk, and goes to ring their bell, whose posh chime fades slowly while he waits.

Sometimes it's right to kill somebody if it's for the greater good. Like if you went back in time and found Hitler as a baby – you'd smother him and six million people would be saved from getting bulldozed into a pit like he saw once on telly. Only maybe it wouldn't work like that. Maybe someone else would step into Hitler's place, like that man Gorbals.

The door opened and there stood Sam Dunbar. 'Well, what do we have here!' Standing before a firing squad one day, Sam would have reason to recall this moment.

'Oh my, you're a fine sight,' said Maureen Dunbar, coming to join him.

Robbie had decided to abandon his poem: the situation called for something more imaginative. 'I'm collecting money for Scotland's first space mission. I also take sweets or nuts.'

The Dunbars looked at him with perfectly straight faces, and for a glorious moment it felt to Robbie as if he was being taken seriously.

'I'll see what I can find for you,' said Mrs Dunbar, retreating from view while Sam eyed his outfit, noticing the St Andrew's Cross on his arm. 'A Scottish astronaut, eh? That'd be a fine thing. No reason why you shouldn't do it some day.'

It was one of the most extended conversations Robbie had ever had with Mr Dunbar, and it prompted him to raise what had been on his mind. 'You work for the GPO, don't you?' Sam nodded. 'And did you hear what happened to the Post Office Tower?'

'Aye, terrible,' said Sam. 'These Irish fanatics. At least they didn't hurt anyone.'

'But what's the tower really for?'

Maureen was coming back to the door with a handful of sweets and a 10p coin which she held out to Robbie, his question to her husband making her wonder what the two of them were talking about.

'It's the main telephone exchange,' said Sam.

'It looks like a rocket.'

'I suppose it does,' said Sam, laughing.

'And doesn't it send some kind of special wave?'

'Only microwaves,' said Sam, evidently heartened by a chance to discuss technicalities with an interested listener.

'Not scalar waves?'

Sam shrugged. 'I've never heard of those.'

'Maybe they're trying to brainwash people.'

'Oh, you and your vivid imagination,' Maureen interrupted, and Robbie wondered how much she knew about it. He'd stopped wetting the bed a long time ago but felt depressingly certain that the whole saga of his condition and the various measures adopted against it would have been discussed at length over the garden fence every day while he was at school.

Robbie countered, 'My dad says . . .' then fell silent, sensing that in his young throat the argument might be as weak as his bladder had been.

'Don't believe everything your dad says,' Sam Dunbar suggested gently, and his wife gave him a subtle but unmistakeably disapproving look, as if he'd said something to Robbie that he shouldn't have. It was like a small chink in a vast alien conspiracy.

'Off you go now,' said Maureen. 'You've got some money there for your astronaut training and a snack to keep you going. One day we'll see you launching into orbit and the whole of Kenzie'll be proud of you.'

She began to close the door and two other figures appeared behind her, Sheena and Louise, their terrifyingly beautiful faces being rapidly swallowed from view, but not before they could see Robbie in his outfit. Simultaneously, like a pair of witches, they burst helplessly into laughter, and although the door quickly put them out of sight it could not contain the sound of their mirth, which Robbie held in his mind as firmly as the sweets in his hand.

He was flying towards a black hole in space, and a great building was crashing down on top of them.

10

Robbie's Christmas present was a telescope. It stood on a tall tripod and was the most precious thing he had ever possessed; Mr Coyle had been careful to choose the best he could afford, and on cloudless nights the two of them would stand together in the back garden, finding constellations with the aid of a map. Mrs Coyle was tempted outside on one or two occasions but expressed disappointment that magnification showed the stars to lack the projecting points she had always taken to be their most essential feature, so she Ursa Majored back into the warm, leaving the males to share that particular form of love that consists of silent, mutual fascination with inanimate objects, especially ones with screw fittings.

Robbie had grown out of his simulator. It wasn't only a question of no longer being able to fit inside; he was eleven now, and whenever he thought back to his training programme he felt a knot of embarrassment in his stomach. Frank Coulter was right; he'd been mental, but now he'd changed. Space had grown too, becoming far bigger and emptier than Robbie had ever dreamed. Patrick Moore explained it all on television: if the Sun were an orange then the nearest star would be another orange three hundred miles away. And that was only the nearest; try to imagine the furthest and you'd end up with distances that were themselves astronomical, implying that the only thing space could adequately be compared with was its own immense and inscrutable self. The Apollo programme had quickly faded from public interest and even Robbie now realized that it had taken humans no nearer to the stars. The only way to get there was in the mind.

Robbie and Janet settled to watch *Star Trek* one evening while Mr Coyle flicked the glossy pages of *Hi-Fi Monthly*. On a cloud-wrapped world, a peace-loving and rationally ordered civilization had been erased by nuclear attack, but the thoughts of its leaders were preserved in a small dark object the size and shape of a cigarette packet.

'That's impossible,' muttered Mr Coyle, looking up from his magazine.

'Ssh, Dad!'

Mrs Coyle, who'd come back from the kitchen to bring him his cup of tea, politely told him to shut up and read.

'I'm only trying to explain something,' he replied, his voice a mixture of sheepishness and indignation. 'Can a man not even talk in his own house these days?'

Mr Coyle was surveying the popular high-fidelity literature with a view to finding a more modern replacement for the radiogram, which had by now become as dated as the Apollo Moon missions, though Robbie still loved to play with its tuning dial and could never tire of the unintelligible voices that emerged from it at night. Mr Coyle said these all-in-one units were a thing of the past and the way ahead was a modular approach of turntable, amplifier, tuner and speakers, a cumbersome arrangement dictated by cost and expediency which sounded to Robbie more like the proposed Skylab space station than the sleekly romantic Starship *Enterprise*.

'Dad,' he said while the end credits rolled, 'what will you do with the radiogram when we get the new hi-fi?'

'We'll have to put it somewhere, I suppose,' Mr Coyle

ruminated, it being out of the question to let go of any piece of furniture so venerable and precious.

'Can I have it in my room? Oh, please,' Robbie begged, and Mr Coyle agreed. A few weeks later, the old wooden coffin on legs was carried upstairs by Robbie and his father and put in position near Robbie's bed; then Mr Coyle went back down to begin trying to make sense of all the hefty cartons that had been delivered, searching each for some kind of instruction book that would explain how to connect the components properly. Robbie lifted the familiar lid of his new possession. The simulator in the kitchen was retired from service, but the flight-control panel was his to play with as much as he wished. He switched it on and heard the low hum; the fifty cycles per second of alternating mains current which was like the throb of an antimatter engine about to go into warp drive.

The hi-fi, by contrast, was unattractively mundane. When Mr Coyle got it working and invited the whole family into the living room to hear it, he proudly turned up the volume control and said: 'Listen!'

They all listened, but there was no record on the turntable or radio station selected on the row of silver buttons. 'I can't hear anything,' said Janet.

'Exactly!' Mr Coyle cried delightedly. 'No hum at all, perfect silence. That way you hear the music better.'

'Why not put on a record, dear?' his wife suggested, fetching the Carpenters from the rack, and a moment later they leapt at the almighty thud of the needle hitting the spinning vinyl disc, Mr Coyle having forgotten to turn the sound back to a normal level.

'Dad!' Janet complained.

'All right, don't get in a flap.' After a few crackles the machine came to life with 'Rainy Days and Mondays'.

'It sounds very nice,' Mrs Coyle conceded, though to be honest she was a bit dismayed to find the music no different from what she was used to, having somehow supposed the expensive new equipment would transform their entire record collection. Hi-fi units, it seemed, were like telescopes: they worked by subtracting something from the usual experience, not adding to it.

'You can hear the treble far more clearly,' Mr Coyle explained. 'And the stereo effect'll be better once I get the speakers mounted on the walls.'

Mrs Coyle frowned. 'Mounted? You mean you're hanging those big things up?'

'Of course, Anne, that's what we agreed. There's no point spending all that money on a hi-fi if you're not going to make the most of it. And when I get the other two speakers on the far wall so we can have quad . . .'

'Oh no,' said his wife, raising her voice to beat the enhanced bass which Mr Coyle had proudly provided with the deft twirl of a knob. 'There'll be no quads here unless you want to turn the whole house into a discotheque.'

'Don't be unreasonable, Anne.'

The Carpenters continued to supply an inappropriately mellow if somewhat over-amplified accompaniment to what increasingly became an all-out row, and Robbie retreated back to his room, where he found a science documentary to listen to. A sombre man with the unimpeachable voice of a newsreader spoke about secret telepathy experiments allegedly being conducted in both Russia and America; a psychic arms race. It might be possible to see inside enemy bases from a thousand miles away, flick switches using only the power of thought. Or why not visit the stars, thought Robbie; they'd be far more interesting than a missile silo in Kamchatka. Another voice countered that any theory of instantaneous thought transference would have to be consistent with special relativity. It sounded as big a problem as hooking up a hi-fi correctly, and not the sort of thing you'd attempt without an instruction manual.

Next day after school, Robbie went with his mother to the library. They hadn't been for a while, but the librarian recognized them both at once. 'What's it to be today?' she asked Mrs Coyle.

It was Robbie who spoke. 'Do you have anything about the theory of relativity?'

The librarian cocked a pencilled eyebrow and looked quizzically at Robbie's mother. 'Is he still . . . ?'

'Oh no,' Mrs Coyle reassured her. 'We've sorted that out now.'

'All right,' she said, putting on the black-framed spectacles that hung on a cord round her neck. 'Let's see what we can find, though I'm sure it won't be for children.' Soon afterwards she was reluctantly rubber-stamping *The Meaning of Relativity* by Albert Einstein. Robbie had two whole weeks to understand it.

Relativity, he quickly found, is a bit like Russian: very hard. But Einstein's book, propped on his chest as he lay in bed with a Polish orchestra playing waltzes on the radiogram, started well enough. '*The theory of relativity is intimately connected with the theory of space and time.*' As first lines went, this was one of the best Robbie had come across: certainly a lot better than *Kidnapped*. Straight to the point, no pussyfooting descriptions. Relativity is the theory of space and time – terrific. If the rest of it's like this, thought Robbie, I'll be passing exams on it by the twenty-fifth when the book goes back.

'*The object of all science*,' it went on, '*whether natural science or psychology, is to co-ordinate our experiences and to bring them into a logical system.*' Robbie needed longer to take this in, but understood that psychology's not natural: it's about telepathy and remote viewing and putting minds in a cigarette packet then sending them to other planets. '*We are accustomed to regard as real those sense perceptions which are common to different individuals, and which therefore are, in a measure, impersonal. The natural sciences, and in particular, the most fundamental of them, physics, deal with such sense perceptions.*' So there it was: physics is what matters – all the rest is in people's heads. He'd been at it only twenty minutes and already Robbie reckoned he'd just about got the hang of this relativity business. But that was only the first page: there were 169 to go, most of them filled with equations, and he soon realized he might need more than two weeks.

This was Robbie's new project, a training regime that was mental, not physical. As the days and weeks passed he felt there to be even less development occurring in his brain than had manifested itself in the mild thickening of his arms in response to much secret heaving of baked-bean tins the previous summer. *The Meaning of Relativity* was dutifully returned and renewed with each successive expiration of its growing list of date stamps, punched by the librarian who looked pityingly at him. 'Still not ready to give up?' she would sometimes ask, and then Robbie and his mother would go home once more with the book that was his Bible; sacred, encyclopaedically authoritative, open to infinite interpretation, and almost entirely unreadable.

11

There was a council election, and as always on such occasions, Mr Coyle was canvassing for the Labour Party. Politics isn't about people in Westminster, he told his son, enlisted as poster carrier and afraid his supply might blow away at any moment; no, it's about talking to ordinary people on the doorstep. A bit like Halloween or evangelism, in other words, though the reward wasn't sweeties or heaven – it was keeping the Tories out.

'Hello, Bob, can we rely on your vote next Thursday?'

Bob was wearing a string vest to hold in his paunch; silver bristles carpeted his double chin like iron filings round a magnet. 'S'pose so,' he grunted without losing grip of the cigarette disintegrating on his lip, then closed the door.

Bob's neighbour was a neat but anxious-looking old lady who said the problem was the unions and the immigrants and children who didn't know the meaning of respect, and she'd be voting for Heath.

'But it's a council election,' Mr Coyle reminded her. 'Ted Heath isn't standing.'

'That won't stop me voting for him,' she said, sealing her door on the windswept figures.

Robbie looked at his wad of window posters. 'Do we have to keep going until we get rid of all these?'

Mr Coyle patted him on the shoulder. 'It's good training.'

Robbie couldn't imagine what his father was training him for; his ambition was to be teleported into space, not become a door-to-door salesman. The people they visited divided evenly into those who could see the light of Mr Coyle's reason and needed no further persuading, and bigoted Tory nincompoops who were beyond salvation and deserved locking up. Electioneering was a complete waste of time.

'This is real politics,' Mr Coyle redundantly reminded his son while they walked. 'Not books and theories and having secret meetings like that idiot David Luss.'

'You mean Moira's boyfriend?'

'I think they've split up now, which is just as well, not that Moira's got much more sense, though don't tell your mother I said that. But Luss, he's your typical Trotskyite agitator.'

'I thought he was a science teacher.'

'Aye, that makes it even worse. These people are wreckers, they're not interested in making people's lives better. They only want to stir things.'

They walked up the path of an overgrown garden and Mr Coyle rang the doorbell; it was answered by an elderly man whose grey hair was combed in a way that looked almost femininely flamboyant.

'Thanks for calling, but I'll be voting Liberal.'

'You mean you're going to waste your vote!' Mr Coyle's voice had a forced chumminess, heavy with ironic sympathy. 'I thought an intelligent man like you would support Labour.'

Surely they must know each other already, Robbie decided. This was merely some kind of banter.

'Yours is the only party that's bothered to come to my door, Mr Coyle, I'll say that much for Labour. But I've little time for Wilson.'

'I'm inclined to agree with you, Mr Tulloch, but we have to think about local issues.'

'Oh, I do,' said Mr Tulloch. 'Like this new military installation they're talking about building.'

The Vernon Estate had been sold to the Ministry of Defence, and now as well as being unable to exercise their right to roam, the people of Kenzie would have to put up with an army base. It sounded an issue of great importance but this was the first time Robbie had heard it raised, and the debate that ensued between his father and Mr Tulloch seemed no more than a good-humoured sparring match. Robbie was startled when the old man looked down at him with a smile.

'This is child number two, then?'

'That's right,' Mr Coyle replied, 'you'll be seeing him after summer.' Robbie cringed. So this was to be one of his teachers at secondary school.

The pair moved on to complete their tour of duty. 'What will the army do in their new installation?' Robbie asked his father.

'I don't know, these things are always kept secret from the likes of us who have to live with the consequences.'

'Will there be nuclear missiles?'

'Who knows?' said Mr Coyle. 'It wouldn't surprise me.'

There was something almost glamorous about it, the thought of deadly weaponry existing a short walk away from Kenzie town centre. Robbie would be able to practise remote viewing on it, trying to see inside the secret complex. Perhaps such experiments were what it was being built for. The rest of the houses they visited made no impression on Robbie; he was too busy dreaming of the installation whose promised existence made the little town of Kenzie seem significant at last.

Labour won the council election and Mr Coyle was soon taken up with a new campaign to try and block the army base. In the following months there were meetings and petitions, but Robbie managed to avoid them. Instead, when the summer holiday came, he and his friend Scott began regularly visiting the old estate, which still lay lonely and neglected, the unguarded holes and gaps in its surrounding fence big enough for them to get their bikes through. The crumbling mansion was boarded up; the grounds were wild and overgrown. Near the house, a flat expanse of grass could be imagined as a former bowling green or future landing pad. What had once been well-tended rhododendrons were now the dense tangle of a tropical jungle.

'Let's go that way,' Scott suggested one afternoon, pointing into some woods on the estate. They left their bikes on the path then crackled over twigs into the cool undergrowth. 'I'll be the British and you're the German.' He ran off and quickly disappeared, leaving Robbie to creep in search.

Robbie liked being the German. As well as *Achtung* and *Schweinhund* he'd learned other words; *vector*, *tensor*. They weren't exactly German but they might as well have been since they came from *The Meaning of Relativity* and he hadn't a clue what they meant, he just liked rolling them in his head. Robbie heard another sound; it must be Scott. He turned, alert, but in the empty sun-dappled woods he could hear only the twittering of finches, crows cawing in the air above, an aircraft miles away. 'Scott!' he called, waited, but there was no reply. 'Scott!'

His friend was gone. Robbie was alone in the enemy base, on an impossible mission requiring all the psychic powers he could muster. It was suicide to continue, but he had to. He tensored carefully through the trees, hoping the *Schweinhund* wouldn't jump out suddenly and scare the Riemann curvature out of him, but found it harder going as the birch wood gave way to denser pine, the ground a soft carpet of pale needles more hospitable to mushrooms than human feet. There was no track here, no route to follow, only a labyrinth of crowded trunks and perilous branches, a place where you could be stuck for thirty years, unaware the war was over. Robbie was lost.

'Scott! Where are you?'

His voice was weak, made weaker by the hostile forest. One day they'd find his skeleton with toadstools growing out the eye sockets. He stumbled, scraped his arm, saw a thin bloody line mark his papery torn flesh, thought of panicking but was already onto the next stage, the acceptance of certain death, when up ahead he glimpsed the promise of a sunlit clearing and ran joyfully for it. Scott wasn't there. What he saw instead was something from another world.

There was a circular pit some fifteen or twenty feet across, the kind of hole a flying saucer would leave behind. An access road leading to it that a tractor could manage, one the investigators could have used. And in the pit, filling it completely, an extraterrestrial gift, was a head-high mountain of green glass, glittering so brightly in the sunshine that it took a moment for Robbie's eyes to adjust and resolve the miracle into what it was: an enormous heap of marbles. He went to the edge of the pit and grabbed a couple in his hand, setting off a small clinking avalanche. Bigger than the ordinary marbles he played with, and without the coloured centre; these were heavy spheres you could look straight through, crude and flawed with rough surfaces, indentations like the marks of strings or fibres in the mould they came from on another planet. Here was the true secret of the Vernon Estate: the site of an alien visitation, now to become a military installation dedicated to re-establishing contact with a superior intelligence from the other side of the galaxy. Or maybe they were just marbles. Robbie put two of them in his pocket as souvenirs and headed down the access track.

He should tell Scott about the alien treasure. But Scott might blab, the pair of them would get arrested, interrogated, brainwashed so they wouldn't remember any of it. Thing was, Robbie knew these wee glass balls couldn't really be from a flying saucer, more likely industrial waste. Except that they might be. He stopped on the rutted track and drew one marble from his pocket, held it to his eye, looked through it and strained with all his telepathic energy, trying to view the world where the mystic sphere belonged. All he could see was upside-down trees.

These psychics, though, they could look into crystal balls and find all sorts. Russian bases, other planets, the future – a doddle. Robbie cupped the marble in his palm, willing it to show him the astral life he dreamed of, but it stayed stubborn and inert, not even a wee bit glow to encourage him. Why can't life be like a story?

It was more than glass, he knew it. You don't drag a ton of glass up a special track through a forest because you can't be bothered phoning the council to get them to take it away. Robbie thought about it logically, like his dad would. This stuff was hidden for a reason. Nobody was meant to know about it, like the Post Office Tower with its secret transmitters or that damned Concorde, military spy jet they put a few people in to make it look legitimate.

Could be radioactive.

Robbie dropped the marble, looked at his palm. No scar or burn but it can take days before your hair and fingernails fall out. Best not get involved. He carried on walking, took the other from his pocket and threw it. He'd only had a few minutes' contamination, wouldn't do him any harm. Then he thought what an eejit he was. He went back and picked up the one he'd dropped. It was only a marble.

Eventually he was able to regain the path where his bike lay; Scott was still looking for him, exasperated by his disappearance, and they went home together in sulky silence. Robbie found his father already home from work, counting out a pile of leaflets on the living-room coffee table.

'Are you going to come and help me distribute these?' Mr Coyle was about to go and post them through every letterbox in the scheme: *Block the base!*

Robbie said he was too tired, but what he feared was that if he went round people's doors he might not be able to keep quiet about his discovery. Instead he went to his room, hid the marble beneath his pillow, and hoped his dad would never find it.

12

When Robbie started secondary school the first thing they had was a talk from Mr Sneddon, the head, who everybody called Archie and Mrs Coyle said looked like Fulton Mackay off the telly. He said how important it was to work as a team and uphold community values but all Robbie could think was how he'd look in an officer's uniform. Then they got English with Mr Bryan, a fat man with a beard who went on about Shakespeare, and by ten o'clock Robbie was already beginning to think he'd be better off running away so he could get abducted by aliens. Science was next, and the man who came into the room was Mr Tulloch.

Slim and agile despite his age, he stood before the class with arms akimbo, surveying them with a teasing smile. 'A fine batch of recruits!' His eyes rested momentarily on Robbie,in recognition of their earlier encounter, then he started telling them all what science was. Yes, it was test tubes and atoms and frogs' legs and electric wires, but really it was simpler than that. Science, said Mr Tulloch, is the study of everything that is real.

Robbie listened with a warm sense of optimism, determined that he wasn't going to make a fool of himself like he did last year in Miss McPhail's class. He wasn't going to put up his hand and say he'd spent the summer learning Einstein's theory of relativity, even though he had, sort of.

He wasn't going to tell everyone how he still imagined that the radiogram in his bedroom could tune into extraterrestrial signals, or that the metal governor on his shelf was part of a ray gun, or that the marble beneath his pillow came from a time machine. Instead he was going to listen to this famous scientist telling them all about the top-secret project they were embarking on. The rocket was on the launch pad and already the countdown was in progress: *33, 32, 31 . . .*

Mr Tulloch said to one girl, 'Do you have a brother in this school?' She nodded.

28, 27, 26 . . .

He asked a boy, 'What unit can we use to measure time?'

24, 23, 22 . . .

He said to Robbie, 'How old are you?'

'*19*.'

The entire class erupted. Frank Coulter looked like he might need medical assistance, breathless and bright red with laughter.

'Nineteen?' Tulloch said with theatrical incredulity.

'I mean eleven.'

'An interesting mistake,' the teacher mused, quietening the class. 'But we all make mistakes, otherwise we'd never learn.' He glared at Frank. 'And we don't make fun of people.'

At the end of the lesson Mr Tulloch drew Robbie aside while the rest filed out, convinced he was to be punished for daydreaming, but the teacher spoke benevolently when they were alone. 'You're the one who reads Einstein, aren't you?'

Robbie was too embarrassed to speak.

'I know Mrs Lightfoot in the library, she told me she's been signing that book out to you every fortnight for months.'

Robbie nodded. 'I think I nearly understand some of it.'

'That's good, keep trying. And don't forget to read other books too. Have you ever heard of a writer called Goethe?'

It was like being with Dr Muir all over again. 'No.'

'He was a scientist as well as an author. Or you could try Immanuel Kant, he made a very important discovery in astronomy. If you like hard books about the universe, Robbie, there are plenty of them around.'

When Robbie emerged from the classroom it was with a glow of pride. Even Frank Coulter could see it. That night he lay in bed listening to the radiogram while the lucky marble formed a barely perceptible lump beneath his head; Mr Tulloch was telling them about the next space mission, and Robbie was to be its pilot. Distant foreign music had been playing on the radio, found through random tuning, but had sunk beneath the interference so that it was only an interstellar hiss that accompanied Robbie's thoughts. His first day had been a success: he'd learned that science is the study of all that's real. Made him wonder why the teachers bothered to teach anything else. Then from across the cosmos he heard a faint message: '*Voice of the Red Star.*' At least that's what he thought he heard; the name of a radio station on the other side of the Iron Curtain, its signal almost completely shielded by it, the announcer trained through spying or telephone interception to speak with what was nearly an American twang, but not quite; surfacing for an instant then quickly retreating to safety. It was a voice from beyond the event horizon; the place Robbie was meant to fly to.

Mr Tulloch's science lessons were unusual, like the man himself. He would make the class perform as molecules, planets, blood cells or blades of grass. They wrote poems about photosynthesis, made words out of the names of atomic elements, created pictures with chemicals. He was enthusiastic but aloof, regarding the human tableaux he orchestrated with a ballet master's cautious eye, one finger propped against his cheek.

'Tulloch's what you'd call a confirmed bachelor,' explained Mr Coyle, who had a label for everything. 'Lives with his mother, she must be in her eighties.' Never having married had given the teacher a distorted view of life: that was why he voted Liberal. Nor had Tulloch joined the public demonstrations against the military base, saying it was good for the local economy and would keep a few uniformed idiots safely out of harm's way instead of shooting people in Northern Ireland. Already the estate was being cleared; the fence was fixed and guarded, and Robbie had never again been able to reach the spacecraft crater.

'Maybe Mr Tulloch never met the right woman,' Anne Coyle suggested, bringing tea to her spouse, who sat behind a newspaper.

'Or he's gay,' said Janet.

'There's no need for that,' her father snapped over a crumpling *Glasgow Herald*.

'But there's nothing wrong with being gay.'

'You shouldn't voice opinions about matters you don't understand – I've been through life and I know a slate when I see one. If not being married makes a man queer then what about the Prime Minister? Do you think he's one?' The paper rose with a snap, Mrs Coyle Ted Heathed back to the kitchen with a disapproving sniff, and the children carried on watching *Top of the Pops*.

The spring term brought a new surprise: the appointment of David Luss as head of science. He walked into Mr Tulloch's class to introduce himself to the pupils, the Trotskyite wrecker pacing companionably before them and betraying no recollection of the quaking boy who'd formerly served him peanuts and hoped the favour would save him from a bullet in the neck come the revolution. Mr Luss's moustache was gone now, while the pipe – a sinister affectation, Joe Coyle thought, in any man below forty – was reserved for the staff room, where everyone soon grew sick of it. Science for Luss wasn't stories or pictures about everything that's real: it was physics, chemistry and biology, with a separate jotter for each.

Mr Tulloch had held Robbie back again at the end of a lesson one Friday afternoon to talk about books, when Luss came in and found the two of them sharing a private joke. 'Sorry to disturb you,' he said with an irony intended to be subtle.

Tulloch was unperturbed. 'We were talking about Goethe, Mr Luss; do you know his theory of morphology?'

Luss evidently didn't. 'I wonder if we could swap dining-hall duties this week . . .'

'I'm sure it can be arranged,' Tulloch replied with casual magnanimity. 'Now, what are we to do with this young fellow?' he said, indicating his pupil. 'Robert has been spending his time reading Einstein, you know.'

'That's a bit advanced.' Luss's visit to the Coyles, like

the woman he'd gone there with, were erased from his personal history, airbrushed from his past. He stared blankly at Robbie, then at Tulloch, who took the hint and dismissed his favourite pupil with a friendly pat on the back; but Robbie, thinking the teacher wasn't yet finished with him, waited unseen outside the open door.

'We need to talk about the strike action,' said Luss. 'All the union members are backing it.'

'I'm not in the union, David.'

'Most of the non-union staff are coming out in sympathy.'

'If the strike goes ahead then I'll be coming in to teach as normal.'

'You don't mind being a strike-breaker? You know the feelings it can arouse.'

Robbie saw Mr Bryan waddling along the corridor. He moved away from the door, not wanting to be caught eavesdropping, and was surprised when the plump English teacher turned, ignoring Robbie completely, and entered the science room.

'Ah, Willie,' Luss greeted him. 'Reckon you can make Gordon see some sense?'

Robbie could hear Willie Bryan panting as he caught his breath and looked round the room. 'Is that Voltaire on the wall?'

'He was a scientist,' said Tulloch.

Mr Bryan sputtered with laughter. 'What the devil are you teaching these kids?'

Mr Luss intervened. 'It's the attention he showers on one or two of them that bothers me. You know, Gordon, good intentions can be misinterpreted. That's why we all need to be in the union, so we've got legal protection if ever there's a problem.' Footsteps came towards the door, which closed firmly, and Robbie left, bewildered by what he'd heard.

Mr Tulloch didn't know about the alien signals on the radiogram; Robbie would have liked to have told him. In space they didn't have unions or free collective bargaining or beer and sandwiches in smoke-filled rooms. They didn't even have pockets. The gentle whistle and crackle Robbie fell asleep to each night was a shortwave promise of prosperity without strife.

Television programmes were interrupted to show Mr Heath announce that negotiations with the miners and power workers had fallen through, and that industry would consequently be limited to a three-day week to conserve coal, while electricity supplies were to be periodically cut off. It prompted Mrs Coyle to candle off to the shops first thing next morning, and by the end of the week she had filled an entire cupboard with sugar, butter and other essentials in readiness for what seemed more like a coming war than a few prearranged blackouts.

It was the biggest fun Robbie had ever had, counting down to the moment when the lights went out and the television died. The family sat round the dining table watching flickering flames and each other's spectral faces. 'This is the sort of thing we went through when we were weans,' Mr Coyle said, adjusting a candle that looked in danger of toppling.

'It's like being in Russia,' his wife said gloomily.

'They don't have power cuts in Russia.'

'They do in Albania,' Robbie said. 'Mr Tulloch told me.'

'And what does he know about Albania?'

'He knows about everything,' said Robbie.

'Oh, he does, does he?' Mr Coyle laughed. 'And how about Mr Luss? I expect he'll be wanting the school to go on a three-day week along with the rest of industry. He'll be having sit-ins in the assembly hall before we know it. The man calls himself a socialist but he's only a trouble-maker.'

'Joe, you shouldn't talk like that about school teachers in front of the children.'

'He's learned his socialism off a lot of fancy books and student debates, but these teachers don't really know what they are because they're not like us, Robbie. All workers are socialist by birth. Talk to any of the men in the plant, even the lads that have only just come in straight from school, and they know what's what though they don't yet have a name for it. They join the union because it's the only thing that stops them getting thrown out for nothing or having their pay packet cut. Luss, Tulloch, these so-called intellectuals – look where they end up, the hippie left or the bloody Liberals. Never trust anyone who's only learned about life from reading books.'

Robbie went up to bed in darkness. The radiogram was as inactive as every other electrical appliance in the house, but he had a secret nuclear fuel cell beneath his pillow, and this was what he placed beside his ear. Through it he could hear the voice of the Red Star, where everything was so much better.

13

One evening after school, Janet said sheepishly, 'Mum, can I go to the dance next week?'

'What dance is that?' asked Mrs Coyle, who was darning socks. Robbie was sitting nearby, watching *Young Scientist of the Year*.

'It's at St Mary's,' said Janet. 'Rhona's going.'

Mrs Coyle studied very carefully the needle she was re-threading. 'I don't know. You'd better ask your dad when he gets in.'

On the television screen, a trio of neatly shorn English schoolboys were showing the presenter a new gadget they had invented for cleaning windows. '*At first we found the motor kept getting wet*,' one said with a plummy chortle. '*Then we tried the polyester casing*.'

'*And I understand you all have interesting career ambitions*,' the presenter prompted, leading the boys to explain how business, law and politics beckoned. They went to the kind of posh school Mr Tulloch said Robbie ought to be in – he should try and get a scholarship. But Mr Coyle said that in the future these elitist places would be abolished completely and in the meantime he wasn't going to have his son brainwashed by upper-class twits.

'Does it have to be up to Dad?' Janet pleaded. 'Can't you decide about the dance, Mum?'

'We decide things together,' Mrs Coyle said loyally. 'Would you be wanting to go with a boy?'

Robbie snickered; Janet scowled. 'I don't have to,' she told her mother. 'I could go with Rhona. It's only a dance.'

'But we'd need to take you there and back, otherwise it's a long walk for you on your own.'

The haggling continued while Robbie watched the second team in the competition, three girls from Dame Margaret's College in Devon who had made a sugar-powered car. There it was, a real vehicle with four bicycle wheels and an engine, bits of Meccano and wires all over the place, must have taken them months. It was like something off *Tomorrow's World*, and it had been done by three girls who were only a few years older than Robbie. Why was there no one like that in his school? The blonde one, for example, team captain with sparkling eyes and a way of tossing her head like it was all nothing, really, this brilliant contraption they'd made. Could probably manage a milk-powered spaceship if they put their minds to it. She was called Rosalind.

He was on *Young Scientist of the Year*, showing off the device he'd made with no help from anyone. 'It's a telepathy machine,' he tells the presenter.

'Show me how it works.'

'You put your head close to the loudspeaker, like this.'

'I see.'

'That way the electromagnetic fields can enter your brain.'

'So you're actually tuning your mind into the ether, so to speak?'

'No,' says Robbie firmly, 'the ether theory was disproved by Albert Einstein in 1905.'

The team captain from Dame Margaret's College is watching with a mixture of envy and desire. 'All right, we give up,' she says at last. 'Our sugar-powered car is no match for the Coyle Mind Transducer.'

Robbie was in his room later, making some adjustments to the machine, when Mr Coyle came home and was greeted at once by his wife and daughter; Robbie heard what was said in the hall below.

'She wants to go to the dance.'

'Is it a discotheque?'

'It's at St Mary's, Joe, so I don't think they'll be letting them get up to anything.'

'Aye, but who's taking her?'

'I'll go on my own, Dad.'

'That's even worse – but can I not get in and take off my coat before you bombard me with all your problems?'

Mr and Mrs Coyle went to the kitchen; Janet rushed upstairs in tears, anticipating a bad result, and shut herself in her bedroom. Robbie crept down to the hallway and overheard his parents' conversation.

'There's going to be layoffs at the plant, Anne, it's looking definite.'

'Will you get made redundant?'

'No one knows how they'll do it but we're holding a strike meeting tomorrow.'

The doorbell rang, startling Robbie, who either had to answer it or else run away, but he still hadn't reached a decision when his mother came out of the kitchen. 'Let's see who it is,' she said, apparently unaware he had been listening.

Sam Dunbar was at the door. 'Hello, Anne,' he said with a smile.

Joe came up behind his wife. 'Come on in, Sam.' There was no more trace of worry or despondency, nor of the contempt that underlay his grudging friendship with Sam; instead there was a perfect mask of cheerfulness.

'I've a wee proposal to make,' said Sam, stepping in.

Mr and Mrs Coyle exchanged a puzzled glance. 'What sort of proposal?' asked Anne, closing the front door and beckoning Sam towards the kitchen.

'You're a big fellow, Robbie.' Sam patted him on the shoulder. 'Do you like dancing?'

It was all, to use a word Robbie had learned recently from Mr Tulloch, surreal. The telepathic waves of his machine had begun to scramble up the space–time continuum.

'Dancing?' said Mrs Coyle. 'No, he's not much of a dancer.'

'That's too bad. Maybe he needs a bit of practice.'

Robbie hung back as the three adults went to the kitchen, each of them looking just as awkward as Robbie felt. Janet appeared on the stairs, wondering what was going on.

Sam explained, 'There's a dance next week at St Mary's.'

'We know,' said Mrs Coyle.

'Sheena really wants to go but she's got nobody to take her.'

'I see,' Mr Coyle said with a knowing smile. 'Is she looking for a suitable boy?'

'That's it exactly.'

Janet rushed into the kitchen. 'Then Robbie and me can both go.'

'Eh, wait a wee minute,' her father said touchily. 'It's not up to you to say what everybody does.'

'I'd take them in the car and pick them up afterwards,' Sam explained. 'I could have them home by nine.' He smiled at Janet. 'So you're wanting to go too are you, poppet? Have you got someone taking you? I suppose I could squeeze the four of you in the car.'

'Hang on,' said Mr Coyle. 'Janet, you were talking about going with Rhona. If you don't mind going with a girl then why don't you go with Sheena? You see, Sam, it doesn't have to be boy–girl couples – they don't need a lumber like in these American films with all their proms and winching and that, not kids this age.'

'Is that so?' Sam replied, rubbing his cheek ruefully. 'To tell you the truth, Joe, I was already winching when I was their age and that's why I want Sheena going with someone I know won't try and get up to anything.'

Another word Robbie had learned recently was 'ignominious', and it was how he felt now.

Mrs Coyle tittered. 'You were an early starter, Sam.'

'Just an ordinary lad, Anne. The most dangerous animal in the world is a teenage boy – if you've got two daughters, that is.'

'Doesn't your Louise want to go?' asked Mrs Coyle. 'She could look after her wee sister.'

'She says the church-hall dances are for weans. Look, why don't I take the three of them: Sheena, Robbie and Janet?'

'I'm sure Robbie doesn't even want to go,' said Mr Coyle.

Robbie's fate was completely out of his hands; he was like the shiny projectile in a pinball table, buffeted from one post to another. First Mr Dunbar would light up, then his father, but the mounting score meant nothing to Robbie. All he saw was the pleasant possibility of spending time with Sheena.

'I want to go,' he said.

'Eh?' His father looked at him as if he'd just volunteered for a one-way trip to Pluto.

'You're only doing it to spite me!' Janet told him angrily. 'I was the first who said anything about the dance and if you go then you'll ruin it.'

'Then it's decided,' Mr Coyle said flatly. 'Robbie goes with Sheena. Janet, you're staying at home.'

'What!'

'Sam came here to invite Robbie; he's the one with the car and the plan and it's not for us to upset everything.'

'But, Dad, that's so totally . . . I hate you all!' She left the room in more tears.

Mr Coyle told Sam, 'Sometimes you've got to be hard with them for their own good.'

'Maybe not that hard,' his wife said quietly.

Sam looked equally pained. 'It's no bother taking the three of them . . .'

'No,' Mr Coyle insisted. 'Even if I'm wrong I never go back on my word. You only confuse your children that way. To be honest, Sam, I've got other things on my mind more important than dancing. Take Robbie with you next week – he'll keep an eye on Sheena.'

Sam shuffled uneasily towards the front door. 'We can talk about it another time, Joe.'

After Sam left, Robbie felt even more awkward. The ominous momentum of his father's mood had overbalanced the entire house, so Robbie climbed back to the safe equilibrium of his mind transducer. The sun was setting now and the tuning dial could begin picking up the interstellar signals.

'*Don't worry, kid.*' It was the voice of the Red Star. '*Things'll work out, wait and see.*'

'But will I ever meet someone like her?'

'*Who?*'

'The captain of Dame Margaret's . . . Hang on, I shouldn't need to tell you this, we're meant to be in telepathic contact, aren't we?'

'*It's not that simple. Just go to the dance next week and await further instructions.*'

14

The dances at St Mary's church hall were intermittent affairs organized with the stated aim of 'keeping youngsters out of trouble'; and since trouble, as Mr Coyle often warned, was something you could encounter almost everywhere, these dances had to be kept scrupulously clean and free of any contamination from the unpleasantness of the real world. 'There's a lot of funny characters around,' Mr Coyle had often told his children, and these characters who pushed drugs, knifed strangers or abducted the innocent into a life of crime and prostitution could be found in every town, in every inadequately lit street, in every shop or park, waiting to pounce on any unwitting and unescorted youngster who crossed their malevolent shadow. The only way to survive in a world invaded by aliens was to trust no one, and to carry a laser at all times.

Robbie and Sheena stepped together into the church hall's decontaminated zone. No aliens here; only a hundred or so children aged eleven to fourteen sipping lemonade served from a table in the corner of the brightly lit room. During the whole car journey Sheena hadn't said a single word to Robbie, and now that Mr Dunbar had released the two of them for their evening together she showed little sign of becoming any more talkative. It was her father's idea that she go with Robbie, not hers, and she was determined to make this clear. Janet was at the cinema with her mother, and Robbie wished he was there too. The evening stretched before him like a noose.

'I'm going to talk to my friends,' Sheena said, abruptly departing to the opposite side of the room where some girls excitedly greeted her. They all stared in his direction and broke into giggles. He wanted to shoot them dead.

A man in a cardigan was fiddling with a record player which didn't seem to be working, while a fat woman with a sweaty forehead called to her lanky son about checking the loudspeaker leads. Robbie went to the refreshment table and saw it was 5p a cup. He had no money; Mr Dunbar had bought the entry tickets and Robbie hadn't thought to bring any.

'Do you want something?' He looked up from the paper cups and saw an older girl in a white dress, or maybe it was some kind of apron that you wore when it was your job to sell lemonade at church-hall dances, Robbie wasn't sure. She didn't look anything like Sheena or the captain of Dame Margaret's science team. She looked kind.

'I haven't any money,' he said meekly.

'Then you won't be buying anything.'

He felt totally foolish. Ignominious and surreal. It was only in the *Star Trek* future that money would be abolished and pockets made unnecessary; here in St Mary's church hall they were still essential.

'It's OK,' she said quietly, glancing around. 'What do you want?'

'Really?'

'Come on, don't let me get caught. Lemonade, cola or Irn Bru?'

'Irn Bru.'

She poured so hurriedly she created an orange bubbling fizz that volcanoed over the edge of the cup onto the paper tablecloth. 'Oh no!'

'Sorry,' he said, taking the dripping cup and sucking the sweet froth into his mouth.

'You're trouble,' she told him. 'So much for me and my good deeds.'

It was the longest conversation he'd ever had in his entire life with a female who wasn't a member of his family or somebody's pet hamster. It all felt so easy, he thought, while walking away from the table, wondering if he'd ever speak to her again. Too bad he couldn't go back and cadge a free bag of cheese and onion. Safely positioned at the far wall he turned and looked towards the table but now somebody else had taken over; a greasy-haired boy. She was gone like a radio signal.

There was a loud popping from one of the loudspeakers, then the cardiganed man began speaking into a microphone. All fell silent.

'Hello, boys and girls, and hello, too, ladies, because I can see that a few parents have managed to come as well. It's always nice when people of all ages can mix together, because we oldies still know how to have a good time, don't we? And I'm glad to see so many familiar faces from St Mary's and the youth club, as well as a few newcomers who I hope we'll meet again. Obviously a splendid occasion like this involves a great many people behind the scenes so to speak making sure everything goes all right on the night, and I can't list everyone now, but I'd just like to say a special thank you to Agnes Ritchie and to Mr and Mrs Morrison, and also to young Alan. Do be sure to partake of refreshments and please try to avoid spillages on the floor. Now without further ado let's on with the show.'

There was another loud pop and then a tune no one recognized, which clearly went back a generation or two. Nobody was quite sure what to do with it until the fat woman pulled a short bald man, her husband or someone who was simply unlucky, out into the middle of the floor, where one or two other brave individuals of comparable vintage went to join them. The children carried on sipping and talking in the clusters they had formed, none of which had room for Robbie.

He didn't recognize a single person here, and in an effort to appear less conspicuous began walking slowly round the room, carefully studying the pictures on the walls and sipping his Irn Bru. When his drink ran out he was left awkwardly holding an empty cup; locating a bin for it offered a welcome diversion, but afterwards as he carried on examining the decor with the attentive gaze of a connoisseur he found himself troubled by his empty hands, weighty and superfluous at the ends of his unoccupied arms. He linked them behind his back like Prince Philip being shown round a new building, while all the other children stared at him (or rather ignored him, which amounted to the same thing), and a few grown-ups jigged around like idiots. It was so ignominiously surreal.

'Hello.'

Robbie turned and saw the girl in the white dress. He wondered if he was about to be thrown out for being totally useless and didn't know what to say in his defence, so he settled for the first thing that came out of his mouth. 'I was looking at the pictures.'

'My name's Dorothy.'

It was as if she were holding it up for him in bright painted letters, expecting his opinion. He kept his hands clasped politely behind his back.

'I got named after the girl in *The Wizard of Oz* – have you seen it?'

'I don't think so.' It was a very old film and as far as Robbie could remember it had never been on television.

'Have you not?' Dorothy sounded surprised. 'There's this girl goes to a magic place and all these people she's known in her real life get turned into different ones like a witch and a lion and that. It's dead good.'

It had all been so easy when he was spilling Irn Bru on her table but now there was nothing to occupy his hands, and he'd never before realized how important it is not to think about your hands when you're trying to think about how to make your tongue move, because maybe there's a nerve goes between all of them and your brain pulls them like strings on a puppet, so it can't cope with working too many bits at once.

'What's your name?' she said.

'Robert.'

'Why did they call you that?'

He'd never really thought about it. 'I don't think it was from a film,' he said, feeling envious of the Hollywood pedigree that would give Dorothy a sure-fire conversation starter for the rest of her life.

'Do you want to dance?'

'Not really.'

'Me neither, I only come because I've got to. That's my dad over there.' She pointed to the cardiganed man, who was sliding an LP from a paper sleeve browned with age, and was too distant and preoccupied to notice his daughter. 'Do you go to church?'

'No.'

'Don't you believe in God?'

It was even worse than having no money – he'd been stupid enough to come to St Mary's church hall an atheist. He'd definitely get thrown out now. 'I don't know,' he said evasively.

'You've got to love Jesus and repent your sins otherwise you'll go to eternal damnation. Do you know what that is? It's these flames that burn you up only you don't go black and charred, you just keep burning forever. You don't want that, do you?'

'I suppose not.'

She was sizing him up like a new recruit. 'They've got a ping-pong table – do you want to see it?'

'All right.' It sounded better than eternal damnation and was sure to be an improvement on the music here.

'Come on,' she said, leading him to a swing door at the other end of the room where a large handwritten notice directed over-eager lemonade drinkers to the toilets immediately beyond. Opposite the toilets was another door with a sign saying *Staff Only*.

She looked back to make sure no one could see them. 'In here,' she said, opening the door.

'Are we allowed?'

'It's OK.'

She switched on the light and closed the door. They were in a small, cluttered storeroom with wooden shelves along one wall, piled with art materials and discarded decorations. Robbie and Dorothy had to share the limited floor space with the folded ping-pong table standing forlornly upright beside them, as well as somebody's bike.

'We can't play table tennis here,' Robbie observed with logical precision.

'It goes outside in the hall. The youth club use it.'

The light above them was a bare bulb hanging from a wire, and the air their entry had displaced had set it swinging gently but perceptibly. She was standing close to him, and for the first time he noticed the thin silver necklace she wore. 'When I was wee my dad sometimes used to let me play in this room,' she said. 'I pretended it was a house.'

'I used to play games like that.'

'Houses?'

'No, spaceships.'

'This room'd make a good spaceship.'

She rested her hand on the upper edge of the folded table and gazed at her fingers. Robbie, following her lowered eyes, looked too and saw that they were very thin, delicate fingers, gentle and artistic, and they were nearly touching his arm.

'Sometimes people get caught kissing here,' she said without looking at him.

'What happens to them?'

'Nothing.'

'Don't they get told off?'

'Maybe a bit. But telling off isn't the worst that can happen to you.'

'Not like eternal damnation?'

'No,' she said, still looking intently at her fingers. 'You only get that for doing really bad things like not believing. Have you ever kissed anyone?'

It was an interrogation even more perilous than her questions about religion. 'Yes,' he lied.

'Did you like it?'

'I suppose so.'

Then she said, 'Do you want to kiss me?'

He couldn't quite believe that he was actually here, right now, with this girl who genuinely wanted to be with him and was treating him like a film star or something, taking him totally seriously, it had all happened so fast and so unexpectedly when only a wee while back he was looking at pictures on the wall and now here he was, with a girl asking if he wanted to kiss her. That was amazing. But at the same time it felt more real than any moment in his whole life. All the rest was imitation.

'Would you mind if I kissed you?' he asked solemnly, and she turned her face up towards his. Her eyes were closed, she said nothing. He took this as a yes.

He was a space rocket and she was the launch tower. There was a tiny bridge between them, and a man in a control room counting down. As his face slowly moved closer to Dorothy's he felt some kind of force field electrifying him and making him tingle. When their lips touched he was blasted into space.

Everything was dark and the mission was very brief, but Robbie would describe his feelings afterwards to the flashing lights of a press conference. 'You see the whole world from up there, small, precious and beautiful, and you realize how lucky we all are to live on this planet. It's both glorious and humbling, reassuring yet somehow scary. It's something I'll never forget.'

They disconnected with a last faint click as their access chambers repressurized. Dorothy opened her eyes and looked at him gravely. 'I can't go out with you,' she said.

'Why not?'

'My dad won't let me. If he knew we were here he'd kill me. We'd better go back.'

The threat of cardigan man coming after him was enough to break the spell; Robbie made straight for the door.

'Wait,' she said, but it was too late. Robbie had abruptly opened without listening to make sure no one was there. Coming out of the toilet at the same time was Sheena Dunbar, who stopped in her tracks and at first looked unhappy to have encountered him, then strangely pleased when she saw Dorothy emerge behind, switching off the light and closing the door.

Sheena stared at the two of them. 'You're not allowed in there.'

Dorothy went silently back through the swing door into the hall, leaving Robbie to try and explain himself. 'We were just looking . . .'

'Who's your girlfriend? Do your mum and dad know?'

'Don't tell them.'

'Why not?' She drew closer to him and lowered her voice. 'Were you winching?'

For the first time he could see in her face a hint of admiration. 'Aye, so what?'

'So . . . she's a slag.' Sheena turned and strutted aloofly back to the hall; Robbie followed afterwards. Dorothy was behind the lemonade table again and refused to look at him, but the intangible bond still hovered in the air between them. The rest of the time went quickly; Robbie no longer cared about anyone else here or what they did. It was all the other kids who were ignominious: he was a hero at a press conference.

Sheena said nothing about it when her dad arrived to pick them up, and as soon as Robbie got home he went to share his news with the only person in the whole universe he could confide in.

'Did you see it?'

'*I don't really have eyes as such. I'm more what you'd call a disembodied transcendental higher intelligence.*'

'But did you see it?'

'*Sure.*'

'Even when we kissed?'

'*You bet.*'

'And will I see her again?'

The answer came after a while. '*Yes.*' It was like reading tea leaves of sound; anyone else would have heard only the quiet hiss of a radiogram tuned between stations, but the magic marble focused the random noise into the authentic voice of the Red Star. '*You wish you'd gone and said goodbye, don't you? Then you could have arranged a date. Sam Dunbar wouldn't have minded, your father would never find out. Sam and your mother are very good at keeping secrets, you know . . .*'

'Where will I see her again?'

'*I can't tell you that.*'

'But you know everything, don't you? The whole of the past and the future?'

'*There are lots of pasts and futures. Which you get is up to you.*'

'Take us both to your planet.'

'*Whoa! You want to cross the inter-dimensional void?*'

'Can't you give us a date there?'

'*You're a twelve-year-old kid!*'

'But you could make me older, couldn't you? And braver? Then I could meet her in your world and we'd both be grown-ups.'

'*What you're requesting is a gross violation of the special theory of relativity.*'

'Please take me.'

'*We'd have to wipe your memory, create a different life for you.*'

'I'd give you my pocket money.'

'I mean erase and rewrite, start from scratch. Whole new story. Could be very disorientating.'

'I know what I'm doing.'

'*Oh no you don't. Here we go . . .*'

'I feel weird . . .'

'*Faster.*'

'My head's hurting.'

'*Faster.*'

'It's sore. I'm spinning.'

'*Faster.*'

'Stop this! Mum!'

'*I guess we're not in Kenzie anymore.*'

PART TWO

1

'Are you listening to me, soldier? Can you hear me?'

Robert Coyle opened his eyes and saw a circle of men's faces staring down at him where he lay on the hard, cold ground. It was the oldest of the men, the most superior in uniform and demeanour, who was speaking to him.

'Come on, get up, otherwise I'll have to call for the medics and you can be sure you'll be deselected forthwith. You only slipped on the ice, man. If nothing's broken can we please continue?'

Where was he? For a moment his mind was a slate as smooth and blank as the ground he lay on; then he remembered that he'd been getting off the bus with the other volunteers and had foolishly slid on a glassy patch of frozen tarmac. Perhaps he was concussed. One thing was certain: he'd given himself an icy arse and made a complete tit of himself.

'Here, let me help you.' One of the other volunteers reached down and aided Robert to his feet. There had been no introductions on the bus journey through the forests and minefields of the security cordon, no conversation as they passed each checkpoint on the deserted road into the most secure research facility in Scotland. Instead the six of them had sat separately and silently, watched by two armed guards and the pipe-smoking Party minder at the back; but now that they were safely within the Installation, it seemed permissible to extend some basic human courtesy. Robert smiled in gratitude and shook a white snowy dusting from his greatcoat.

'This way,' the adjutant barked. 'And mind the ice. We don't want any more accidents.' He led the volunteers across the empty expanse of the vehicle area towards a long, low wooden hut at whose door a helmeted sentry, his breath billowing in the frigid air, snapped crisply to attention. Inside it felt immediately warmer, and soon the volunteers were seated in a brown-walled briefing room heated by an iron radiator whose pipework, snaking along the walls like a road map, provided the nearest thing to decor. There were a dozen or so desks for the volunteers to choose from and they instinctively distributed themselves as they had been on the bus, in isolation from each other, while the Party man took his place at the rear. The silence in which they waited was like the prelude to an exam; Robert hoped he'd do better here than at Cromwell.

He sat in the middle of the room, staring forwards at the simple oak lectern which stood beside a white screen with a slide projector aimed at it, not yet switched on. A blackboard was fixed to the wall, well wiped, but Robert was still able to discern, in a lower corner, an imperfectly erased string of symbols which appeared to be part of a scientific equation, together with the legible but cryptic inscription: *scalar field*. He wondered where it might be, this grassy pasture inhabited by tile-skinned lizards that must have been the subject of a seminar.

Such dreaminess was what had got him kicked out of the best university in the Republic – in the general paper he'd been meant to write about the social impact of quality versus quantity but instead had ended up describing how as a small child he'd always wanted to be a spaceman. His tutor said it was an interesting approach to urban regeneration and one he would have ample time to ponder in the regiment he was now being assigned to under Article 17 of the Military Service Act.

From the open door at the back of the room, out of Robert's view, a guard called the men to attention, and they all stood rigidly while a senior officer strode smartly past them towards the front. Around fifty years old, with neatly shorn grey hair visible beneath his perfectly positioned cap, and with his baton held smartly under his arm, he walked purposefully to the lectern, then stopped and turned to survey the new recruits.

'Sit down, lads,' he said, his carefully measured tone of familiarity only adding to his dignified air. Once they were all seated he introduced himself. 'My name is Brigadier Archibald and I am commander-in-chief of military operations at the Installation.' His clipped accent was redolent of a frugal Scottish upbringing and a belief in the virtue of hard work and cold showers; he would have made a good headmaster. 'Officially, the Installation does not exist. It is on no map and is referred to in no document. Right now you are in a non-existent place.' The comment brought the hint of a smile to the edge of the brigadier's thin lips, as though he had cracked a joke. 'But everything that we do here is real enough, oh yes.' Gathering his thoughts, he took a few paces, pensively turning the baton beneath his arm. 'It is entirely possible that you have heard rumours about this non-existent place of ours.' He halted and stared at the volunteers with cold blue eyes that had seen decades of patriotic service and tolerated no nonsense. 'You might even have indulged in speculation about the nature of the special duties for which you have all freely volunteered.' He looked from one recruit to another. 'Let me dispel straight away any half-baked, nonsensical and irrelevant ideas that might have formed in your heads, and let me instead tell you exactly what you need to know about the Installation, and what you are allowed to know.' The brigadier's mobile neck was like that of a crow, enabling him to fix his gaze on whoever he wished without the need for any movement below the level of his collar. He was looking straight at Robert now. 'This is where we made the Bomb,' he said simply, allowing a moment of silence so that the information could sink in. 'Yes,' he resumed, 'that's right – you're in the most secret, the most important, the most valuable military asset in the whole of the Republic. If the imperialists ever decide to commence hostilities, you can be sure that this non-existent place – which they're sure to have found already from satellite photographs – will be top of their target list.' The brigadier straightened. 'I consider it an honour, as well as my duty, to be first in line.'

Robert watched the brigadier once more begin pacing, speaking to the windowless walls as much as to the young men. 'The Installation was created over thirty years ago, right at the end of the Patriotic War, when the invading

Nazi scum who terrorized this land of ours for five dark years were defeated by the People's Army. The Central Committee knew that if such horrors were to be prevented from ever happening again, then Britain needed to have its own nuclear deterrent alongside that of our Soviet allies.' He stopped. 'You all know the proud achievements which resulted from this. Our nuclear tests were the fear and envy of the world. Granted, our bombs might not be the largest, but they're the best designed.'

Beside the blackboard was a door that now sprung open. The brigadier turned to look at what all the recruits had seen already: a sleek, fair-haired woman in civilian clothes.

'Ah, Rosalind,' he said. 'Is Professor Kaupff ready?'

'He's on his way.' She looked to be in her late twenties – quite a lot older than Robert or any of the other volunteers – and had the ease to match. Her hair was pinned neatly in a bun behind her head; her drab blouse and long utilitarian skirt were the typical outfit of any office worker or shop assistant; yet the signal they sent, just as powerfully as the epaulettes on the brigadier's shoulders, was one of superiority. Rosalind stood by the open doorway staring at the volunteers with a curiosity whose casualness appeared almost insolent; and it was only when her dark eyes met Robert's that she folded her arms with a flicker of defensiveness.

'Yes, the Bomb,' the brigadier resumed with a tone of nostalgia. 'The technological miracle that has maintained world peace for nearly four decades and epitomizes the special relationship between the British Democratic Republic and the USSR. It was a huge undertaking, involving hundreds of scientists and technical workers, secretarial and administrative staff, support personnel – and you will shortly meet the man who did more than anyone else to make it a reality. But that was only the start. Nuclear power, chemical weaponry, navigation systems, artificial satellites; all have been developed here. The Installation nowadays is a complete town, totally closed to the outside world, containing families, schools, bars, a cinema – everything you'd expect to find in any normal community. You'll be lodged with resident families who'll look after your domestic needs, and all the people you meet will be involved in the hidden life and work of the Installation in one way or another. The golden rule is that you don't ask unnecessary questions, and you don't answer them. Whatever your superiors tell you may, in the interests of security, be a lie – but you can rest assured that it will be a significant lie, told for good reason, because here in the Installation, everything has a purpose. Nothing is accidental.'

Robert had already had enough accidents for one day – his head was still sore from his fall – but before the brigadier could say any more there was an abrupt interruption. 'He's here,' said Rosalind, standing away from the door to let her colleague enter.

'Professor Kaupff, at last,' the brigadier, turning, said to the brisk figure who came in: an older man, in his sixties or even seventies, tall but stooped, slimly built and wearing a jacket and tie, and surprisingly youthful in his swiftness.

'Sorry to keep you waiting,' Kaupff said to no one in particular, his voice having only a hint of the foreign accent his name might lead one to expect, masked by a convincing Scottish burr. 'Can we begin?'

'We've begun already, Professor,' the brigadier said

indulgently, clearly used to situations of this kind, and tolerant of his civilian colleague's lack of military precision. 'I've been explaining in general terms the work of the Installation; now I shall let you take over.'

'Of course,' said Kaupff, though when the brigadier retreated to the rear of the room it was not the vacated lectern to which Kaupff moved, but rather the blackboard, as if he might be about to pull a stick of chalk from his pocket. For a moment he stood thoughtfully with one finger on his lips while Rosalind, still at the open doorway, watched him with the admiring air of an acolyte, his attendance here evidently being an intrusion upon the profound intellectual labour that was his vocation. This man, Robert realized, was the father of the Bomb – though few outside the Installation had ever seen or heard of him.

Kaupff faced his small audience, moved slowly towards them with his hands in his pockets, and smiled. 'So these are our young recruits,' he said with satisfaction. 'What fine specimens you are.'

There was an impish warmth in Kaupff's voice that Robert found appealing; there was also something vaguely familiar about the old man's appearance, though Robert knew he couldn't possibly have seen him before; most probably there wasn't a single photograph of him in the whole of the Republic. Kaupff approached Robert's desk and looked down at him. 'You, young man, how old are you?'

'12.'

The whole class erupted. What the hell had he just said, where had it come from? Mortified, Robert looked round and saw the smirking faces of his fellow volunteers – even the Party man was grinning – and although the laughter quickly ceased, their mockery was deafening. With his single inexplicable error, Robert had uncorked their anxiety and transformed it into mirth. 'I'm sorry . . . I mean . . .'

'Don't worry,' Kaupff said calmly. 'How old are you?'

'Nineteen, sir.'

'You're the one who slipped outside, aren't you? And you were in hospital recently – I hear they nearly killed you.' Robert looked in startled amazement at the old man standing over him, but Kaupff immediately clarified his remark, as if it were a gaffe like Robert's. 'Those doctors didn't quite manage, eh?' he said with heavy irony. 'You bounced back.' Then Kaupff looked at the other recruits spread around the room and said to them, 'Only a short time ago this soldier was dangerously ill, he went to the very brink. His heart stopped – I've seen the report. We owe him our respect.' He addressed Robert again. 'Do you remember any of it?'

'Not really, sir.' His illness had started only days after he submitted his application for special duties, and at the time he thought it would mean being struck off the list so that he would have to find some other way of escaping the tedium of the regiment; but when his condition quickly deteriorated he found such mundane worries flowing out of him along with the sweat of his mysterious fever. Now, restored to health and ferried at once to the Installation, it was almost as if his illness was the reason he was here, for Robert could think of no other explanation why Kaupff should have singled him out. Nor could anything except residual weakness explain his foolish slip of the tongue – as foolish as his other slip outside.

'Let us proceed,' the professor announced. 'Rosalind, would you please prepare the projector?'

A moment later the lights were put out and the screen was illuminated by the lantern's white beam. Rosalind, dimly moving in the pale reflected glow, was like a cinema usherette tending ice creams at a romantic matinee. Then with a snap the screen went dark again. It took a moment for Robert to realize that this was the first slide: a picture of blackness, pierced with small, randomly scattered points of light.

'This photograph,' Kaupff explained, 'was taken twelve weeks ago by astronomers using one of the most powerful telescopes in the Republic. It shows a star field in the constellation of Cygnus, roughly one arc minute across, and if you can be bothered to count, you'll find that there are one hundred and fifty-three stars. Next please, Rosalind.' Again a snap, revealing a second picture that looked identical to the first. 'Same telescope, same part of the sky, but taken one night later. I don't suppose you'll notice anything different, but the trained eye of an astronomer – together with sensitive photometric equipment – reveals a number of changes. Some of the stars are fractionally brighter, others fainter – this variability is perfectly normal, and is what the astronomers were monitoring as part of an ongoing survey. There is, however, one other modification here which is highly unusual. I told you that the first picture contained a hundred and fifty-three stars. This second has a hundred and fifty-four. I'm sure you can appreciate that the sudden appearance of a new star is not the sort of thing that happens all the time.'

Professor Kaupff approached the screen and pointed

with his arm towards the top right of the image. Briefly bathed in projected sky, his face and body bore pricks of light while he indicated the area of interest. 'Let's see an enlargement of this very small region. Rosalind . . .' Obeying his prompt, she inserted a new slide in which the stars were far fewer in number and looked large and fuzzy. Kaupff retreated to allow his audience a complete view. 'This is the original shot,' he explained. 'Notice the group of three stars close to the centre. But if we now look at what has happened on the following night – thank you, Rosalind . . .'

It was there for all to see: the triangle had been joined by a fourth star. In fact it looked to Robert as though one of the stars had split like a fertilized embryo, creating two identical copies side by side, close enough together that they appeared to be touching.

'There's the evidence,' Professor Kaupff said grandly. 'One becomes two. Quite extraordinary. But our wise astronomers knew what they must be witnessing, and their suspicions were confirmed when they took a further image on the following night, which my assistant will now show us in the same enlarged form.' This time the stellar group was again a triangle, the interloper having completely disappeared. 'The star which appeared to split lies some six hundred light years from Earth. The star itself did not divide; what happened was that some other object passed in front of it, something small and dense, whose gravitational field bent the star's light in a way predicted by Einstein's theory of general relativity. By a happy stroke of luck, the invisible object briefly covered the more distant star so exactly that its light was split in two, half of it bending one way around the object, and half the other. Seen from Earth, the effect is to create a double image – a phenomenon known as gravitational lensing. Lights please, Rosalind.' She switched off the projector, and soon the small audience were blinking in the restored illumination of the fluorescent strips overhead. 'I expect the brigadier has told you that the work of the Installation encompasses far more than weapons research. Science, gentlemen, is the study of all that is real, and space lies within our remit. You have been brought here to assist in the most remarkable project ever sanctioned by the Central Committee. You are here to make history.'

Whatever relaxation of tension might have been achieved by Robert's foolishness was instantly undone; the recruits attended Kaupff's words in rapt anticipation.

'Scientific discovery has many aspects,' he continued. 'Some of it is purely intellectual, much of it mechanical and routine. Our astronomers engaged a team of workers to study photographs of large areas of the sky in painstaking detail, in the hope of uncovering more instances of star-splitting, and their laborious efforts were rewarded by two more lensing events. Yet on each occasion it was a different star that was distorted.'

Robert, like the other volunteers, was trying to work out what relevance any of this might have to a group of young soldiers. It sounded as if their special duties would consist of counting stars through a magnifying glass: history-making of an esoteric kind.

'Let's try and think about this scientifically,' Kaupff proposed. 'Or should I say – for it amounts to the same thing – dialectically. We have the splitting of one star, then of another that is nowhere near it in space, but which lies close to it in the sky as seen from Earth. Then, a little later, a third briefly alters. Moreover, the successive abnormalities form a line. What might be going on?'

In the ensuing silence, it gradually became clear to the recruits that they were being asked to do something that was not part of their normal military service. They were being invited to think. Robert, having twice made himself ridiculous already, risked little in raising his hand. 'Well?' said Kaupff.

'Perhaps they're all connected,' Robert suggested.

'Indeed,' Kaupff agreed warmly. 'The fundamental law of nature which Marx and Engels discovered is that everything is connected to everything else. But can we be more precise?'

Robert pondered briefly, then asked, 'Could the same invisible object have caused all three stars to split?'

Kaupff smiled and nodded. 'That is exactly what our finest astronomers concluded – you have the wisdom of Meno's slave.' Neither Robert nor anybody else had any idea what was meant by this, but it sounded like a compliment. 'An unseen object is moving across our sky, and from its pace we deduce that it is far closer to Earth than the background stars it occasionally occludes. It is within our own solar system, following a trajectory resembling that of a comet, falling very rapidly towards the Sun, which in a few weeks' time it will sweep closely past. Then like a slingshot it will fly onwards, surpassing the orbit of Pluto in a matter of months. But this mysterious visitor is clearly no comet. What, then, is it?'

Kaupff made another rhetorical pause, offering his audience a chance to muster their thoughts, but Robert felt as bewildered as the others. Rosalind calmly and deliberately studied their puzzled faces, her narrow eyes assessing each young man in turn with the self-satisfied expression of one who already has the required answer.

'We know the object possesses considerable mass,' Kaupff hinted, 'since it is able to bend starlight.'

One volunteer raised his hand. 'Is there any risk of it hitting Earth?'

'None,' said Kaupff. 'The object is in a highly elongated orbit, its plane of motion being at an oblique angle to Earth's path. At its closest approach, in about five weeks' time, it will be roughly one hundred million miles away – further than the Sun. It poses no danger; nor will its gravitational field perturb the solar system to any significant extent, though its mass is comparable to Mercury's. For the short duration of its visit, the object is an unobtrusive tenth member of our solar system.'

Now the historic nature of the discovery was apparent. One of the recruits exclaimed, 'Our astronomers have discovered a new planet!'

'What should it be called?' another asked.

'Can we send a rocket?'

This last comment brought an icy silence as Kaupff glared at the stocky recruit, seated at the front, who had allowed himself to be too bold. Then he addressed the whole company again, his voice firm and clear. 'The object is of planetary mass, but it is not what you or I or anyone else would consider a planet in the ordinary sense. We know how far it lies from Earth, and our astronomers know that at such a distance their telescopes should be able to resolve it, even if it were only a few miles across. Yet they see nothing. The strange new visitor to our solar system, whatever its origin, contains a world's-worth of matter squeezed into the size of a small town.'

It sounded almost like the Installation itself, and Robert imagined it tumbling through space, shrouded in pine needles, patrolled by dogs, lit only by the flicker of search-lights. Inside that world there might be another Robert, another Kaupff, another Rosalind.

'For some time now,' Kaupff continued, 'astronomers have taken quite seriously the idea that under certain conditions, matter can become compressed to such an extremely high density that light itself is unable to escape. In the capitalist world, such hypothetical objects are referred to as black holes.'

The phrase, thrilling and disturbing, made Robert shudder; and like the dials of some inscrutable machine, Rosalind's coal-dark eyes appeared to register the effect. The refolding of her arms this time had a less defensive, more triumphant quality.

'Of course we reject the term, with its colonialist implications, its unsavoury air of medieval clericalism, its sheer inaccuracy. The object is not a hole or void, not a gap in the universe – it's not even completely black, but a very dull red. We follow the Soviet nomenclature and call it a frozen star. What to capitalists symbolizes a fate worse than death represents for us the highest form of astrophysical evolution. Our visitor is not a monster – it is a unique opportunity for socialist exploration.'

Now in the mind of every volunteer the same revelation flashed. They were on a space mission. They had been brought to this closed Scottish town to become the Republic's first cosmonauts.

Rosalind began stalking around the room like a tiger, moving between the desks where the volunteers sat, while Kaupff continued. 'Why should the object have arrived now, at this precise point in human history, when we are in a position to understand it?' She came to a halt behind Robert, and as Kaupff spoke he directed his eyes at his female assistant, whom Robert could sense and even smell, for a whiff of unknown perfume had reached his nostrils. 'All knowledge is historical knowledge,' said Kaupff, lowering his eyes from Rosalind to Robert. 'To understand the visitor we must know its past, the method of its formation; yet here we encounter a great mystery, since physics offers no natural mechanism for the production of a frozen star of planetary mass. What sent it on its rapid flight through space – why has it been captured by the Sun? We almost sense the guiding hand of some higher intelligence . . .'

Robert could taste the air of another world. A creaking of floorboard behind him signalled Rosalind's departure, and when he saw her walk towards the door at the front of the room, as if preparing to return to her scented alien domain, she again looked to him like a figure from cinema; not the humble usherette he'd previously pictured, but a star.

'Science frowns upon mere speculation,' said Kaupff, 'yet our mission demands mental strength, intellectual courage and above all imagination, for no possibility can be excluded from our deliberations, nothing can be dismissed as too outlandish. Together we must lift the veil of Isis and penetrate the infinite unknown.'

She was like the girl in a public-service film he used to see every Saturday morning, Robert remembered. A beautiful woman sits smoking in an armchair; she gets up to go to the kitchen, leaves her cigarette dangling over an ashtray, forgets about it . . .

'Permission to speak, sir,' said a volunteer.

'Go on,' Kaupff told him impatiently.

'What would happen if a spaceship tried to land on the frozen star?'

Kaupff touched his lips and assumed his earlier ruminative expression, then shook his head in answer to some unspoken internal remark. 'A frozen star has no surface in the ordinary sense. It has an event horizon, and no one knows what might lie beyond.'

Remember, the film always concluded, *fire kills*; the same message reiterated every week to an audience of short-trousered Pioneer Cadets peeling oranges and picking their noses between *Workers Newsround* and *The Crazy Club*; though to Robert it felt like a million years ago, a billion light years away in another galaxy, because the vertigo that had made him slip outside and rendered his life momentarily weightless was reinforced by the strangeness of what he had learned, the awareness that a world is nothing but a marble slung through space by unseen forces, our existence a glimmer through flawed glass. As a child he had been terrorized by the safety film, but now, seeing Rosalind standing at the doorway, he was gripped by an irrational excitement at the retreating thought of it. The forested security cordon was a horizon he had crossed and the closed universe he had entered was one where everything could be reversed with the ease of a light switch.

'Sir,' the volunteer pursued, 'can you tell us if there are any plans to send a space probe to the object?'

Kaupff smiled. 'Of course not.' It took a moment for everyone to appreciate the delicate ambiguity of this statement, but already Kaupff was turning on his heels to walk out of the room, followed by Rosalind, who closed the door behind them. Even the brigadier appeared stunned by the sudden termination of the briefing; he returned to the lectern, a figure diminished by the ignorance he now knew himself to share with the recruits. 'I expect you've all got lots of questions, but rest assured, you'll be told everything at the appropriate time. At this point I formally hand you over to the jurisdiction of the Installation's civilian authorities – you won't be seeing me again unless one of you comes up on a charge, so mind and behave yourselves. Let's get you to your quarters . . .'

'Wait please, Brigadier.' The voice came from the back of the room. All the volunteers turned to see the balding Party observer, his black fur-collared coat still tightly buttoned despite the room's warmth, and his expired pipe propped in his hand, awaiting relighting. 'I have a few words to say.' A small man, he rose from between the armed guards flanking him and walked to the front, displacing the brigadier, who moved deferentially to one side.

'My name is Commissioner Davis,' he announced. 'I am your Party representative. I'm here to help.' He took a box of matches from an inside pocket and slowly lit his pipe. Robert searched with his nostrils for a last hint of Rosalind's perfume before Davis shook the match to extinguish it, and woody smoke began to rise around his bare head. 'I'm hardly more of a scientist than any of you,' he said.

'Physics, chemistry, biology – those are the divisions and that's about the limit of my knowledge. In other words I'm on your side, one of the rank and file.'

As with Kaupff, Robert almost felt as if he might have seen Davis in another life, but knew he couldn't have. There could have been no forgetting that pipe smoke.

'We are, as you all appreciate, at war. It's not being fought with tanks on battlefields, but the capitalist-imperialist aggressors are constantly seeking to disrupt our way of life – they want to turn back history, destroy the prosperity we enjoy, undermine the freedoms we cherish. Penetrating the Installation is one of their highest priorities, and don't think all our security measures can render everything safe. There are spies here. We shot one only last month. It is entirely possible that you will encounter an infiltrator – you could even be sitting next to one right now. Keep that in mind as you do your patriotic duty.' He took another puff of his pipe. 'There's something else I have to tell you, and this comes straight from the top. I know all about the duties you will be undertaking here and I can assure you that they are of the utmost strategic, political and ideological importance. Success will be appropriately rewarded. So will failure. You understand what I mean.'

The creaking radiator on the wall could do nothing to avert the chill that ran round the room. Davis marched out, followed by the guards, signalling that the meeting was adjourned.

'Well then,' said the brigadier, toying nervously with his baton. 'Now we've all heard it. This one's as big as the Bomb, maybe bigger. Just as well we've got Kaupff.' He looked at the men with the pleading eyes of a spaniel.

'Don't let me down, lads.' He expressed what all felt: chance and fate had fallen together across their lives like searchlight beams, selecting them out of obscurity into a position of the most perilous responsibility. Robert ought to have been terrified, yet instead he was buoyed by the carefree elation this new world, by means of some unknown secret ingredient, had somehow instilled within him, while it was the wrong-footed brigadier who blinked with apprehension. 'Your quarters,' he reminded himself hesitantly. 'You need to be taken to the places where you're staying . . . I wonder who has the list?'

'I do,' said the woman who came in from the rear door where Davis and the guards had just gone. It was Rosalind again, materializing like an all-pervading spirit, holding a clipboard. It struck Robert that she must be the source of his new valour: for her he would walk through fire. 'Gentlemen,' she said, 'if you will all now follow me, I shall escort you to the bus.' They sat waiting for the brigadier to dismiss them but quickly realized that his renouncing of authority was complete, for he gave only a slight rolling of his sorrowful eyes and a wistful craning of his neck as indication that they should do Rosalind's bidding; so they all rose and filed out past her, and when Robert reached the doorway she gently pulled on his arm. 'You are invited to dine with Professor Kaupff at eight o'clock tonight.'

He was taken aback. 'Thank you, ma'am. But where, ma'am?'

'You will be collected at seven thirty. And stop calling me ma'am.' She released him so that he could walk on with the others, and he wondered what he should call her instead.

2

The six volunteers became more relaxed as they crossed the icy tarmac, Davis having left them in the more pleasant care of Rosalind, who walked behind them to the waiting vehicle, its motor idling.

'Make sure you don't slip this time,' said one of Robert's companions – the fellow who had helped him up earlier. He extended a hand to shake and introduced himself while they walked side by side. 'John Harvey, Third Armoured.'

'Robert Coyle, Ninth Infantry.'

Others were chatting too, and when they all climbed onto the bus they arranged themselves in pairs near the front, leaving the seat closest to the driver for Rosalind, who looked round at her charges with the air of a schoolmistress. 'Gentlemen,' she said, adding sardonically, 'or if you prefer, lads. We're going to drop you one by one at your billets, and it will give you an opportunity to see the general layout of the Installation. There are of course no maps here, no street names, no signs. We navigate this place by memory, so it's quite likely you'll get lost a few times initially. But believe me, you'll soon get to know every inch.' There was a hint of weariness in her voice. She turned and nodded to the driver, who clunked into gear and steered the vehicle around, then headed into the heart of the Installation. Robert wondered how long it was since Rosalind had been outside, beyond the pine-forested perimeter. And what about the bus driver? Would he be going home to his wife in the real world tonight?

'Here's the main street,' Rosalind announced, and from

the trundling bus the men saw a dull and chilly vista little different from the centre of any small town in the Republic. The buildings were all of equal and recent age, in the plain and functional reconstructivist style that had been the blueprint for countless communities devastated in the final stages of the Patriotic War then subsequently rebuilt. It was all about quality and quantity, Robert reminded himself, and about how each is really a version of the other; though when he thought of his essay at Cromwell, and his lamentable failure in it, he could only laugh with the same distant fondness he already felt for his silly comment in the briefing room. Condensing in his mind like a crystal was the conviction that no matter what happened to him, all would ultimately be well, because wise architects controlled his destiny.

There were shops along the main street, Robert noticed, though they didn't bear the signs you would find in the world outside. Instead of 'Fashion' – the ubiquitous red-on-yellow design above clothes-shop windows – there was only a blank wooden board surmounting a display of outfits much like Rosalind's. No doubt this exaggerated anonymity was a security measure; though any spy would easily be able to deduce the nature of each shop, even from frontages so sparse and austere as these. A few pedestrians, women mostly, several pushing prams, were pausing before the shops, and one of the doorways had attracted a substantial queue. The moving bus was the only vehicle on the road, yet no one turned to examine it.

'The cinema,' Rosalind drawled, nodding towards a squat, flat-roofed brick building whose peeling whitewash made it look older than it probably was. 'A different programme every night.' Then, as the bus crawled onwards, she indicated other highlights: the swimming baths, two pubs, a fish-and-chip shop. 'Oh, and there's the lending library – though you probably won't be needing it. Professor Kaupff will give you whatever is necessary.'

As she turned in her seat towards the window, shielding her eyes with one hand against the glass, Rosalind's flat-shoed foot and stockinged ankle jutted into the passageway and into the view of Robert and the other volunteers, all of whom studied it with the same immediate and instinctive interest. For a blissful moment Robert imagined the unpeeling of that foot, ankle and leg.

She turned again, pointing towards the opposite window. 'The bowling alley,' she said. 'You see, lads, the Installation has everything.' That sly smile again, and now a better view of her legs. 'Everything you could want.'

Her commentary finished, she faced primly towards the front and studied the typed list on her clipboard. She murmured something to the driver, who took a left turn past a terrace of identical pebble-dashed dwellings just like any scheme you'd find elsewhere. The bus pulled up in front of one of the houses, whose lace curtain twitched in response. 'Volunteer Forsyth,' she said, looking round and scanning the group until she saw the one she wanted: a gangly, horse-faced man grinning in response to the familiar syllables of his name. 'You may alight.'

Forsyth got out, followed by the driver, who left the vehicle running while he went round the side of the bus and wheezily opened the hold so that the recruit could retrieve the kitbag which had been stowed there for him. A plump grey-haired woman had emerged from the house, evidently destined to be Forsyth's landlady. The others watched silently as he shook hands with her and followed her inside. The driver having already taken his seat again, they moved on to the next destination in Rosalind's list.

'Volunteer Harvey,' she instructed.

'See you later,' Robert's companion said, getting up and offering another handshake before dismounting to be met by an elderly couple. Those two must have spent most of their working lives here, Robert thought, and now their retirement too. The next drop-off points were not far away, and once three more human deliveries had been made it transpired that Robert was the sole remaining recruit.

'Last but not least,' Rosalind said to him from her seat at the front when the bus embarked on the final stage of its tour. Already the streets were beginning to assume an air of repetition as trivial landmarks that had somehow fixed themselves in Robert's mind began popping once more into view. 'We're going to the Franks,' Rosalind instructed the driver, speaking loudly enough for Robert to hear now that there were no other passengers. She looked round at him again. 'I'm sure you'll have a lot in common with the Franks' daughter, Miriam. She's about your age.' Her eyes narrowed mischievously. 'Nineteen, I mean, not twelve.'

'It was a foolish mistake, ma'am.'

'Yes, but an interesting one. And I told you already to stop calling me ma'am, or have you forgotten that too?'

'I'm sorry,' he said, 'but I don't know your second name.'

'You don't need to.'

'I mean as a matter of respect.'

'In this place women are usually called by their first

names,' she told him. 'Surnames, Coyle, are not how we show respect.' He felt humbled and chastised, and saw on her face the satisfied mark of some minor victory in a larger campaign beyond his ken. 'You could take her out to the pictures.'

'Who?'

'Miriam.' The bus halted, having reached its destination. 'But don't forget you've got a date tonight with Professor Kaupff – you'll be collected from here.'

He got out and saw a house just like all the others they had visited. The front door was opened by a jovial middle-aged woman.

'Goodbye now, Volunteer Coyle,' Rosalind called to him from the bus. 'See you later.' The driver, returning to his seat after handing Robert his bag, closed the automatic door and drove off as Robert's new landlady came down the path to greet him.

'Well, look at you, Mr Volunteer,' she said with blunt cordiality. 'I'm Dorothy Frank.' She extended a welcoming hand, but Robert was using both of his to clutch his green canvas kit bag, which he was holding upright in his arms like a heavy roll of carpet, obscuring most of his face from the kindly lady to whom he could only stretch the fingers of his occupied right while introducing himself. 'I expect we'd better volunteer ourselves inside,' she said cheerfully, leading the way into the house, where Robert dropped his bag on the hallway floor and hung up his coat. The decor made him feel at home – the garish flowered wallpaper, the small framed pictures hanging on the walls.

'I hope you'll be comfortable here.'

'I will, Mrs Frank.'

'Cuppa?'

'Please, I'm parched.' He followed her to the kitchen where she switched on the electric kettle and spooned tea leaves from an enamel caddy into a glossy brown earthenware pot.

'Hungry too, I expect. They're in the tin there.' It was marked 'biscuits', and she gave him a small plate on which to put some. 'You go and sit yourself in the lounge and I'll bring this in. Then once we're sorted I'll show you your room.'

He did as he was told, settling himself in an easy chair which sagged receptively beneath his weight. A heavy glass ashtray rested on the arm, clean and empty in anticipation of visitors such as himself.

'Here, get some of this down you,' said Mrs Frank, coming through with a tray and placing it on the coffee table. 'Did you have any lunch?'

'Sandwiches,' said Robert.

'Nice, were they?'

'Standard service issue. I really need this tea, though. We sat through a whole long briefing and they never offered us anything . . .' He realized he was saying too much. Mrs Frank noticed too.

'My husband Arthur comes home at half-past five and we usually dine at six.'

'I'll be eating out tonight. I'm being collected at seven thirty.'

'Oh well,' she said, holding out the plate so that he could help himself to another biscuit. 'You could always have a nibble with us first if your stomach can't hold out. I've made a coq au vin, you know.' She announced it with evident pride, going on to explain exactly what coq au vin was, since she was sure her guest wouldn't know. 'We don't get chicken here all that often,' she added. 'Or wine. So it'd be a shame to miss out.'

'I'll see what I can manage,' Robert said diplomatically. Dorothy had gone to great lengths to make sure his first evening here would be pleasant.

'And I expect you'll be late,' she said with an involuntary hint of self-pity. 'If you're eating out, I mean. I'll give you the key and you can let yourself in.' He drained his teacup with a tip of his head, gritting his teeth against the final wash of unstrained leaves. 'Now let's get you organized,' she said. 'Your room's ready if you want to come upstairs.'

They went back to the hallway and then up the carpeted steps to the landing, where a photograph on the wall showed a recognizable but much younger-looking Mrs Frank holding a baby.

'Is that your daughter?' Robert asked.

'That was my son James,' she said. 'He's with the angels now.' Immediately changing the subject, she pointed to the open door at the end of the landing and said, 'There you are – go on in and set your things down.'

Doing as she said, Robert found himself in a room that was small and neat, decorated with a feminine touch. The narrow bed was plumped high and topped with a quilted eiderdown. 'It does get chilly at nights,' Dorothy explained, watching him prod the bedding's ample convexity. 'My husband reckons they didn't insulate the walls properly when the place got built, but this lot should keep you warm. I can give you a hot-water bottle if need be.'

'It all looks perfect,' said Robert. The few simple furnishings were luxurious compared to what he had been accustomed to in the regiment. A shelf bore some books and a pretty vase; there was a small table which he could use as a desk. A large old Bakelite radio stood in one corner, the kind whose tuning panel would light up when switched on. The panel was dark, but the pointer could be seen indicating London. 'Does it still work?' Robert asked.

'Of course,' said Mrs Frank. 'But it's pre-war, mind. We're allowed them here, you know, but . . .'

'I understand,' said Robert. Radios made since the Liberation were restricted in the frequencies they could receive – this antique would be forbidden outside the Installation, its use punishable by a prison sentence. Different rules evidently applied within the closed town's forested perimeter, though Dorothy's unspoken instruction told Robert that if he were to use the radio he should restrict his tuning to the authorized wavebands.

'And if you should want to use it,' she added, 'best not do it after ten o'clock at night when we go to bed. You can hear it all over the house, even when it's turned quiet.' This sounded like another subtle message, reminding Robert that nothing in the Installation, lawful or otherwise, was ever completely private.

'Thanks, Mrs Frank. If you don't mind I'll have a wee bit rest, then freshen up.'

'That's a good idea – you saw where the bathroom was, didn't you? I'll leave you to yourself, then.'

Robert closed the door and heard her pad away along the landing and downstairs. He pulled off his boots, tunic and trousers, and lay down on the bed in his underwear, soon feeling the draughty accuracy of Mrs Frank's comment about the chill, though remaining reluctant to climb beneath any of the immaculately arranged and densely packed layers of bedding.

Nevertheless he dozed, until a noise downstairs startled him. Someone was coming in the front door – he heard Mrs Frank greet the newcomer, and after briefly supposing it to be her husband, realized it must instead be her daughter, Miriam, returning home from wherever she worked in the Installation. Robert got up and pulled on his trousers, then went quickly to the bathroom, carrying his tunic and the towel that had been left for him. From behind the locked door he heard Miriam ascend the stairs. 'He might be asleep,' Mrs Frank called up to her in a solicitous stage whisper.

'He isn't,' Miriam answered in a firm, no-nonsense way. 'Looks like he's in the bathroom. I'll come down when I'm changed.'

She went to her room; and after hurriedly washing, Robert went back towards his, carrying his damp towel and passing Miriam's door. It sprang open.

'Hello,' she said abruptly. She was short, small featured, with dark shoulder-length hair and a matronly plumpness.

'You must be Miriam.'

'That's right, I must.' The way she stood looking impassively up at him made Robert feel he was blocking her way.

'Nice to meet you,' he said, walking onwards to his room.

'We'd better get used to it,' she said to the back of his head, and when Robert closed his door and hung his towel over the wooden chair, he concluded that Rosalind's comment about the pair of them going to the cinema had been ironic.

A renewed disturbance in the hallway soon afterwards encouraged Robert to emerge again, and this time it was Mr Frank who had entered. Robert saw him from the top of the stairs – a thin man, greying but not without a lingering trace of youthfulness, divesting himself of the red scarf in which he had braved the cold weather outside. 'Hello, sir,' Robert called, descending with his arm outstretched.

'Lovely to see you,' said Mr Frank with unforced sincerity. 'Settled in all right?'

'Yes, thank you. I'm really grateful.'

A rueful smile graced Arthur Frank's features. 'It's not as if we had much choice in the matter . . . Please don't take that unkindly. All I'm saying is that it's our duty to look after you, and we welcome it and shall do our patriotic best.'

'That's very nicely put, Arthur,' said his wife. 'Now if you two gentlemen would like to settle your patriotic bahookies in the lounge I'll get on with preparing dinner. Coq au vin, Mr F?'

'You're an angel and a goddess, my love.' Then, as if sharing a manly secret, he said to her with a tilt of his head towards Robert who was his intended audience, 'In a happy marriage every day should be like every other, and every night should be like the first. Or to put it more succinctly: every night a bit of the other – eh, Robert?'

Mrs Frank rolled her eyes at the indelicacy and went to the kitchen while the two men did as she had requested, taking themselves to the living room.

'How long have you lived . . .' Robert, seeking small-talk, began, before correcting himself. 'I'm sorry, Mr Frank, I shouldn't pry.'

'Arthur. And don't worry yourself,' he said, settling into his favourite armchair while Robert returned to the one he had occupied earlier. 'I'm Category A, general workforce. I can say what I want in this place because I don't know anything worth spreading.'

'Hear, hear!' Dorothy called from the kitchen.

'Listen to that sauce,' Arthur chuckled. 'Can't live with them, couldn't live without them. We've a closed existence here at the Installation but it's good – twenty-three years, I've had. Or is it more?' He began trying to count but quickly gave up. 'In a town of nearly five thousand people there's never a dull moment. I wouldn't want to leave even if I had to. Worst thing I could imagine would be relocation, though it never happens. Once you're in, you're in; unless you're Category C and can be trusted to leave without saying anything. I could be trusted, mind – it's just that I prefer not to go. Different for Dot and Miriam, of course, but you know what they say about the tongues of women and children.'

Miriam came in. 'And what do they say, exactly?'

'Never mind,' said her father. 'Have you two been introduced?'

'We've met,' Miriam told him, then asked Robert, 'Do you like my room?'

'Pardon?'

'My room. The one you'll be sleeping in.'

Mr Frank smiled nervously and rubbed his hands in a futile gesture of reconciliation. 'I should explain, Robert, that when we got the billeting instructions we saw we had to provide adequate space, so we felt we'd better give Miriam the back room and let you . . .'

'I really don't want to inconvenience anybody,' Robert immediately insisted. 'I'll take any room you want – I'll even sleep on the floor. Really, I'm used to all sorts of conditions and as long as there's a roof over my head . . .'

'Don't you worry,' said Mr Frank. 'It's done, it's what we've decided, and it's the right way to do it. Miriam, I think we should show a little more hospitality to our very important guest.'

'I'm about to lay the table,' she replied coldly. 'Then I'll help Mother serve the food. Excuse me, both of you.' She went to the kitchen.

'I'm sorry about that, Robert,' said Arthur. 'That girl always has to be making some kind of point. Been like it since she was wee – I can't think why. But as I was saying, the Category A workforce . . .'

'Please,' said Robert, 'I don't want you to compromise yourself through generosity. The less we know about each other, the better for everyone.'

Mr Frank looked crestfallen. 'Aye, all right. You realize we don't get to see many outsiders. Not that we mind, of course, but that's how it is here. Even the new lad who just started last week at the cold-casting works – I've known him since he was in nappies; his father got killed in the reactor leak fifteen year ago. Terrible, it was, seeing poor wee Stephen grow up without a father. He was at school with Miriam.' Robert waited silently for Mr Frank to run out of steam, but the convivial host clearly had a lot to get rid of. 'And that leak – we all thought we were done for. Cloud came off that fire looking black as hell. Reckon the whole town was irradiated but what can you do? And the lassie Stephen's courting, wee Joyce, lovely girl, works in the baker's so you'll likely see her soon enough, she's got something wrong with her, a funny kind of boil on her neck. I only noticed it the other week when I was in getting some potato scones, big livid lump, like a walnut, almost. Beautiful lassie, so she is, and I'll say that for the Installation, there's some bonny girls here. I reckon it's the sort of breeding stock they bring in – know what I mean? There's all the best scientists and top military people, the Category B's and C's, and they marry here and settle and have children – or they don't marry or settle but have children, eh? Because don't think it doesn't all go on here, oh no. But then you've got these sons and daughters of the elite growing up and marrying, and more and more of the elite keep coming in. Quite a gene pool, as they say. And my Miriam should find a good match – she's got her mother's firm figure, nice chest on her and strong thighs. She'll be someone's catch if only she knew it.'

Miriam had already re-entered the room before Mr Frank's unsubtle attempt at matchmaking had finished, and she deposited the knives and forks on the dining table with a clatter, quickly turning on her heels and going back to join her mother.

'Have you got a girlfriend, Robert?'

The question took him by surprise, as he'd been letting Mr Frank's monologue wash over him, trying not to let any unwanted details stick and register in his consciousness. 'Girlfriend? No.'

'And you an army boy too? Lad like you could have any girl you wanted, I expect. All the lassies love a uniform, don't know why but that's women for you. And while you're here with us you'll have your pick, you know. Every

Friday night they're all at the dancing. You'll be needing your key to get in because the missus and myself like to retire early, specially on a weekend, eh? "Something for the weekend, sir?", you take my drift? But I'll sort you with the spare key if Dorothy hasn't already, and the only thing is, if you do bring a lassie back, you know, be discreet about it, because I wouldn't want Miriam hearing any, you know, goings-on, because she's only a girl, same sort of age as you, and if she heard, you know, moaning and such like, well, it might put her off the whole idea altogether and you know how it is. They don't always realize it feels nicer than it sounds. Dot and I used to have to . . .'

'Ah, there you are, Mrs Frank.' Robert stood to greet the incoming coq au vin with a relief he never thought any cooked dish could possibly inspire.

'I hope I won't be spending all my time reminding you my name's Dorothy,' she told him as she deposited the hot casserole on the table, then gave the oven glove on her hands a triumphant clap. 'Nobody touch that yet, mind. Arthur, will you see to the wine?'

'Wine?' said Arthur, evidently puzzled by this unprecedented novelty in dining chez Frank.

'Aye, well, half of it's in the meal already,' his wife explained, going back out for the vegetables and nearly colliding with the incoming Miriam, who'd beaten her to them.

'I don't know if you're having water or anything else to drink with the food so you'd all better sort yourselves out,' Miriam declared, seating herself at the table.

'I'll get that wine,' Arthur decided. 'Where is it?'

'And the glasses too,' Dorothy ordered, telling him where

in the kitchen to look. 'Sit yourself down, Robert. Even if you're eating out I'm sure you can still squeeze in a bit to tide you over.'

'Eating out?' Arthur chimed in, returning with the half-empty bottle and four stemmed glasses on a tray. 'You're not forsaking us for the officers' mess, are you?'

'I'm being picked up shortly,' Robert said apologetically.

'We won't let Mum's efforts go to waste,' Miriam commented, helping herself.

Mrs Frank hunted for some chunks of meat amid the sauce and deposited them on a plate. 'Just a taste, Robert. Veg?'

'No, thanks,' he said, reaching over the table for the worryingly ample portion she offered. 'It's more than I need.'

'And less than you deserve,' said Mrs Frank. 'Young lad like you, far away from home. I wouldn't want your mother thinking I was starving you. Bread and butter?' Robert shook his head, but as soon as he tasted the food he appreciated just how hungry he was.

'That's it, go right ahead,' Mr Frank told him, offering Robert a paternal pat on the shoulder while pouring out the wine. 'No need to wait for everyone to be seated – we don't hold with formality. You're one of us, now, Robert – part of the gang. It feels good not to be the only man about the house.'

'Here you are, Arthur,' his wife said, passing him a filled plate in what appeared partly a gesture aimed at shutting him up as swiftly as possible.

'I think we should have a toast,' said Arthur, raising his

glass. He had given himself the smallest share of the half bottle of red wine, his guest the largest. 'To Robert. May your stay here be a happy one.'

'To Robert,' his wife repeated, and Miriam raised her beaker of water.

'Thank you so much, all of you—'

'We haven't known each other very long,' Mr Frank interrupted, 'but I can tell that you're a young man after my own heart. I like you, Robert.'

'You're too kind . . .'

'We have our own ways and customs at the Installation – our own unique way of life, which we're very proud of. You've joined a community with strong traditions and a big heart. We know how to look after outsiders – we see so few of them! But one thing you should know about us, Robert, we aren't afraid to show our feelings. I know you've come here with your outsider ideas – "silence is golden", "never talk to strangers" and the like – but I'm Frank by name . . .'

'*Frank by nature*,' his daughter mouthed in weary unison.

'And true to form, I want to tell you that while our life here may have been good, it hasn't always been easy, and I know Dot might not want me to say this just yet, but I've always longed for a son of my own . . .'

'Arthur, please not now.'

'And I want you to know that as long as you're here you'll be like a son to me. If there's anything you need, any bother, I'm here for you. That's the sort of people we are. We're Installation folk, and your ain's oor ain.'

His wife gave a sniff. Robert saw her get up and go to the kitchen, wiping a tear from her eye with a corner of her apron.

'She gets a bit sentimental sometimes,' Arthur said by way of explanation, tapping with gentle camaraderie on Robert's forearm.

'It's no time to remind her of Jamie,' Miriam said, adding for the lodger's benefit, 'I had an older brother that died—'

'I know,' Robert replied, cutting her off.

'Right. So you know not to mention it.'

Robert could understand her displeasure at losing her room, but Miriam's habitual hostility was beginning to irritate him. And while her father was at the exactly opposite end of the hospitality spectrum, Robert felt that Mrs Frank's happy medium was the best way of ensuring everyone got along together in the new regime. She came back from the kitchen, lacking any sign of her momentary distress except a slight smearing of mascara. 'More food, Robert?'

'Really I mustn't.'

'Oh, go on. We won't be eating coq au vin every day.'

He consented to another portion, and by quarter past seven the whole lot was gone and he was as full as every other member of the household. The doorbell rang.

'They're early,' Dot said calmly. Arthur and Robert hurried to the door, Mr Frank struggling to detach a spare key from the bundle drawn from his pocket while Robert answered the bell's second ring.

'Coyle?' said the waiting driver. A white Morris Commonwealth, its headlights shining in the darkness, stood idling on the road behind him, conspicuous for being the only vehicle in the street.

'I'm coming.' Robert grabbed his coat from the hook; Arthur held him back.

'Here's that key. Now, if you look at the lock . . .'

'I'll manage,' called Robert, dashing after the driver, who was already at the car, holding the rear door open for his passenger. 'See you later.'

3

They drove swiftly through the streets, darkened now, that Robert had seen earlier from the bus. There again were the terraces of white-walled houses with their curtained windows gleaming cosily, and then the deserted main thoroughfare of unlit, unmarked shops, and in the pallid glow of the streetlights, standing like benevolent watchmen, the obligatory statues of Marx and Shaw which made the Installation look like any ordinary town. The taciturn driver was wrapped in a thick coat, necessary since the car was as cold as the air outside, and he wore a battered old leather cap, leaving as Robert's only view of him in the dim light a fat neck with a ragged tangle of unclipped grey hairs shedding dandruff on a dark blue collar. The driver whistled occasionally, as if oblivious to his passenger's presence, and Robert gazed out at the nocturnal vista, seeing the buildings give way to dense trees which after a while were in turn replaced by what looked like an industrial zone, harshly illuminated by white floodlights. Steam belched from aluminium flues jutting out of concrete towers too tall to be seen in their entirety from where Robert sat. He was passing a complex of factories, refineries or power plants; and there was a further change of architecture as a series of low structures, fabricated from corrugated steel, passed his sight. These, Robert suspected, housed facilities used by the night workers who kept the Installation's mechanized hub in operation.

A brightly lit window gave Robert a brief view of a group of overalled men laughing together; another showed a stout woman in military uniform, writing at a desk. Then, as if whole regions or countries were being traversed in this drive across the Installation, the surroundings restored themselves to native moorland, and they came to a check-point where the driver halted to show his pass to a shivering guard. Satisfied with their credentials, the guard waved them on, and soon the vehicle began rising up a gentle hill towards twinkling lights which slowly resolved themselves like the stars in Professor Kaupff's presentation, enlarging however not into circles but instead into the windows and lamps of an imposing mansion, patrolled by pacing guards. The car came to its final stop, the driver got out and held the door for Robert, who emerged into the winter night to see a warm, open entrance.

'This is the Lodge, sir,' the driver explained, getting back into his car. Robert began walking towards the doorway, hearing the vehicle start up behind him in preparation for its return journey, and when he crossed the threshold he found himself in a wood-panelled lobby. Deer antlers, swords and shields were mounted on the wall, and on the right there was a solid desk where a uniformed butler stood waiting.

'Good evening, Volunteer Coyle,' he said, approaching to close the glass-paned inner door and then take Robert's coat. 'Professor Kaupff will receive you in the Maxwell Room, to which I shall now escort you.' The butler placed Robert's coat over his red-cuffed sleeve in a well-practised manner. Lithe and smooth-skinned, probably not much older than Robert himself, he had an air of confidence and experience which added to Robert's unease at this wholly unfamiliar place with its deep-piled burgundy coloured carpet, its gilt-framed pictures and ornate carvings. Robert was led along a corridor to a heavy panelled door, which the butler opened, revealing a room dominated by the glow of a log fire.

Kaupff sat alone in a leather armchair. 'Welcome, Coyle.' He rose and shook his visitor by the hand while the butler silently retreated to leave them in private. 'Quite a nice place, don't you think? Are your quarters satisfactory?'

The gulf between the Franks' house and the room Robert now stood in was too great for him to express, even if he had time to consider how best to put it, so he settled instead for polite agreement. 'Fine, thank you, sir.'

'Well, Robert, let us sit down so that we can get acquainted.' There was another armchair beside Kaupff's, the two positioned at right angles with a small wooden table between them on which stood an empty whisky glass. 'Like a drink?'

'I'm not thirsty.'

'Come now,' Kaupff laughed. 'A small aperitif? What you Scotsmen call a "wee dram"?' Fixed into the table was a brass push-button like that of a doorbell. Kaupff pressed it, and a moment later the butler reappeared.

'I shall have another Glenlivet,' Kaupff instructed. 'And you, Robert?'

He had no idea what he should ask for – he had been a half-hearted social drinker at university and in the regiment, accustomed to little except beer and sherry, but guessed Glenlivet must be a kind of whisky sold in the foreign-currency shops that only Party people could use. 'I'll have the same,' he said.

'Ice and water, sir?' the butler asked, casting a smile at Robert that showed an effortless sense of superiority.

'Yes, please.'

'I drink mine straight,' Kaupff said as the butler left them once more. 'I know the true Scot adds a dash of water to enhance the aroma, but I was born with schnapps in my blood, and though it was a long time ago – nearly seventy years – nevertheless I retain my German barbarism even here, so I'm afraid you shall just have to indulge me, dear boy.' He reached across and gave Robert's knee a friendly pat. 'Now, tell me why you volunteered for special duties.'

The question was so blunt it caught Robert completely off guard. 'Why . . . ? Well . . .'

Kaupff smiled. 'You're a patriot, of course; that's one reason. And the pay's better, that's another. You want to help your country and enjoy a few perks – it's perfectly understandable.' Robert nodded silently, gratified by Kaupff's pragmatism; then the professor grew more serious. 'There are dangers, you understand.'

'I know, sir.'

'You signed a form consenting to all risks, your life is in our hands – and you willingly put it there.' The door opened and Kaupff fell silent. The butler was carrying a tray on which stood an almost-full whisky bottle, a jug of water, a small ice bucket and glass. He placed the items on the table, stooping near Robert and exuding a soapy scent. His clothes seemed to crackle as he straightened; then he nodded and left. Kaupff uncorked the whisky bottle with an appetizing pop and generously filled the bottom of his crystal tumbler, then turned the bottle's tilted neck to Robert's glass, sending an equal quantity gurgling into it. 'Help yourself to water and ice.'

'I think I shall try it your way, sir.' Robert raised the whisky to his lips, finding its oily smell almost nauseous, then let the alcohol burn on his lips and tongue, filling his head with warmth.

'Do you remember exactly when you volunteered?' Kaupff asked.

A man came and talked to the regiment, there were interviews and meetings. Robert described the events to the professor but was aware how remote and vague they felt in his mind.

'Do you remember a session at District HQ?'

'Yes, but not very clearly. I've been ill . . .'

'I know,' said Kaupff. 'Do you recall having tea with some people from the Ministry?'

'I think so . . .'

'And do you have any memory of what they looked like? What they said? How the tea tasted?' Kaupff was staring fixedly at Robert who sensed the significance of the half-forgotten meeting but couldn't guess what it might be until Kaupff said, 'They put something in the tea. That's what made you ill.'

Robert froze with the whisky glass beneath his lips and looked down at it.

'Don't worry, Coyle, it's pure Glenlivet and won't do any more harm to you than it does to me. But the experimental drug you took had unexpected side effects; you developed an adverse reaction that nearly killed you.'

'The doctors told me it was meningitis.'

'Quite possibly that's what they thought it was,' Kaupff said with a shrug. 'But you see, you consented to all risks, and luckily you've survived to hear the tale – though never tell it, of course.'

Kaupff seemed to take it all so lightly, the days and nights when Robert had been close to death, feverish and delirious. 'I don't remember ever being told I might be given a drug . . .'

'You weren't,' said Kaupff. 'It's designed to be administered secretly, and if you'd been warned then the conditions of the experiment would have been ruined.' Seeing the shock on Robert's face, Kaupff mellowed. 'Don't blame me; I had nothing to do with it. But you realize now, don't you, that what you signed up for isn't just perks and an easy time. What we do here is a matter of life and death – and it's the preservation of our society that counts, not the fate of individuals. People here are privy to the most sensitive classified information – a few of them go back outside, and that poses a security problem. Wouldn't it be good if there were some harmless way of regulating their memories? A departee could go home having forgotten everything about the Installation – it would be like a dream. And if a spy were to be sent inadvertently into our midst, he could be purged on arrival, given a potion like the waters of Lethe, so that all his mischievous plans would be erased and he would instead become a willing patriot.'

'Did they think I was a spy?'

Kaupff shook his head. 'It was only a test of an evidently imperfect strategic tool.'

It had worked well enough, though, and Robert appreciated now why the life he had left behind felt so alien and insignificant to him. 'Were the others given the same drug?'

'I can't tell you that,' said Kaupff. 'But you were the only one who fell ill – which suggests your brain functioning may be of an unusual kind. When you were feverish, did you hallucinate?'

Robert struggled to remember, but all that came to mind was the radio beside his bed, left quietly murmuring day and night, which he was powerless to silence. 'I heard voices.'

Kaupff raised an eyebrow. 'Intelligible voices?'

'It was as if the radio was speaking to me.' Robert was embarrassed to admit such lunacy but Kaupff, intrigued, leaned closer.

'What did the radio say to you?'

'I don't recall – I expect it was nonsense.'

'I've no doubt it was,' Kaupff agreed, almost too readily, 'but I'm sure Rosalind will want to follow this up in her own way.' Then, without saying any more about his assistant or her ways, he changed the subject. 'You're not here to do drugs trials, you realize.'

'I gathered that from the briefing, sir.'

Kaupff took a sip of whisky, thought silently for a moment, and said, 'Gravity.'

'I beg your pardon, sir?'

'That's what our mission is about. Just as the proletariat had to surmount the barrier of class, we have to defeat the tyranny of gravity – a revolutionary endeavour. You always wanted to be a cosmonaut, didn't you?'

Now Robert understood – he was here because of that damned essay. Having got him thrown out of university and nearly poisoned, his foolish reminiscence had been interpreted as a job application. Yet the chemical lingering in his system made him willing to fulfil his childish dream. 'I still want to go into space,' he said.

Kaupff looked sceptical. 'Even if it might mean death?'

'Yes,' said Robert, embracing as an asset the spiritual lethargy he had been given in a cup of tea, surprised by his own boldness. 'If there were any chance of flying to the frozen star – I'd do it.'

'Then let's consider the technicalities,' said Kaupff. 'The frozen star is moving very quickly at the edge of our solar system, which means it has a great deal of angular momentum. Do you know what angular momentum is?'

'No, sir.' Robert's mental image involved an angler throwing bait into a sluggish river but that certainly wasn't right.

'It's what keeps a bicycle from falling down,' said Kaupff, so the fisherman now had wheels to ride home on. 'Rockets launched from Earth need a tremendous boost, which is why they are launched from sites as close to the equator as is politically and technically possible, thus lending them some of Earth's own angular momentum as an initial gift.'

'Scotland is a long way from the equator,' Robert observed sagely, feeling himself to be on somewhat safer territory with geography since it was one of the few subjects he hadn't failed at Cromwell. But in the silence which Kaupff allowed to ensue, Robert realized that his comment had instantly stripped the Installation of the hidden launch pad and floodlit rocket he had imagined seeping clouds of icy vapour into the night. He was back to a bloke with a fishing rod.

'The most conveniently equatorial part of the free world is the Indian Federation of Socialist Republics,' Kaupff continued. 'But you know the delicate nature of relations between the Asiatic and Euro-Soviet powers. For Britain, the Pacific island territories have always been the best available option, which is why our unmanned satellites have all been launched from there. But we aren't sunning ourselves on Mayday Island, are we? We're here, warming ourselves against the Caledonian winter outside.' It was a riddle Kaupff left unexplained; instead he glanced at the clock on the mantelpiece. 'Are you hungry?'

It had been Robert's vain hope that the whisky he had been sipping might displace or dissolve Mrs Frank's coq au vin; instead it had enriched it. 'To be honest, Professor, I don't have much appetite.'

Kaupff looked puzzled. 'You mean you don't want to visit our dining hall? We lucky residents have the best cuisine in the whole of the Installation – the pheasant and venison are superb, and either goes very well with the excellent Saint-Émilion they cellar here. Well, to be honest, I'm not starving either – how about biscuits and cheese in my rooms?' The professor rose, indicating it was an instruction rather than a suggestion, and Robert followed him to a door at the far end of the room which led onto a corridor simpler in appearance than the panelled one by which he had entered. This was more like an access passage, the plastered walls painted green and white and starkly lit by overhead electric bulbs; and as they followed its twists and corners it soon became apparent that this labyrinth constituted the true core of the building, rather than the ostentatious periphery Robert had first been shown. Along the corridor there were grubby numbered doors, most of them bearing the occupant's name, with a sliding indicator to show whether each was in or out.

'It's all a little bit like how I imagine the old public schools might have been,' Kaupff commented over his shoulder, walking ahead of his guest. 'And guess who's top of the form?'

They reached a narrow spiral staircase, which Kaupff began to ascend. At the top there was a landing with a lace-curtained window looking out onto a dark courtyard, and two doors. 'This is where I live,' said Kaupff, taking a key from his pocket and opening one of the doors. He switched on the light to reveal a shabbily furnished room whose walls were almost entirely lined, from floor to ceiling, with books. 'Sit yourself down, Robert, make yourself comfortable.' The wooden-framed sofa had a light foam upholstery covered in checked fabric, frayed in places – the kind of basic and not particularly comfortable furniture Robert had seen in countless homes and shop windows. He sat down and surveyed the rest of the room: two armchairs matched the sofa, and beyond them there was a Government-plan deal table on which a small chipped vase bore a plastic flower. A framed picture on the wall appeared to be a print of an old-master painting; there was no television, only a portable radio on one of the many bookshelves. Robert watched Kaupff go through to the adjoining kitchenette, from which came a clattering of cupboard doors and a rustling of packets. 'Like a sherry to go with your cheese and biscuits? Or a cup of tea?'

Robert gave no answer; and Kaupff, understanding why, looked round the doorway at him. 'It won't be spiked, I promise.'

'How can I be sure?'

'Trust me,' said Kaupff. 'Those games are over. Tea, then?'

At Robert's nod he turned away to prepare it, leaving the recruit to gaze at the crowded library that was the professor's home. Many of the titles on the spines were in German or Russian – Robert remembered only a smattering of the latter from his schooldays, and the polyglot shelves made him almost forget which country he was in. Nowhere near the equator, though. Kaupff returned and saw his companion staring with tilted head at the volumes. 'Let me find you something useful to read,' he said, depositing on the table a board bearing a wedge of orange cheese and then going with perfect and immediate accuracy to the place he wanted, taking a book and handing it to Robert. It was called *Rocket to the Stars*. 'You'll find the basics of interplanetary travel very clearly explained here,' he said, going back to the kitchenette to get the remaining items for their snack.

Robert leafed through the book. There was a photograph of a German missile painted black and white like a chequerboard, a monkey in a spacesuit. He felt sorry for the monkey.

'Here we are,' said Kaupff, returning. 'Biscuits, pot of tea, the works.' Kaupff unloaded the tray onto the table and invited Robert to come and join him. 'Shall I be mother?' he asked with a smile, pouring the tea into two china cups. 'You see, I've picked up all your British expressions over the years. People guess I'm a foreigner but they never identify my accent as German. I'm rather proud of that. I can read the language of Shakespeare and Coleridge as well as any native.' He passed a cup to Robert, who helped himself to milk from the open bottle, and sugar from the blue-and-white bowl Kaupff had assembled alongside the block of cheese, the half-eaten packet of crackers and a couple of small plates and knives. 'Don't go thinking I'm trying to turn you into some kind of teacher's pet, Robert. All six of you have an equal part to play in the mission – but your case is particularly remarkable. When you were close to death, did you have any kind of mystical experience? Light at the end of a tunnel, perhaps? The neural basis of religious superstition is something that interests me . . .'

'All I remember is the sound of the radio,' Robert reminded him. 'It was always tuned to Red Star, for the news bulletins I suppose.'

'Naturally,' Kaupff said, then paused. 'You know, it's a very apt description of the object that has entered our solar system: Red Star. Its event horizon is a zone of infinite redshift.'

Robert was grateful for this arcane piece of information, though less appreciative of the single dry cracker he accepted out of politeness and started laboriously chewing, hoping it wouldn't undergo an explosive chemical combination with chicken à la Frank.

Kaupff said wistfully, 'Perhaps what you heard was the voice of the Red Star – yet you remember none of it! We shall have to probe that young mind of yours – and we shall have to nurture it carefully. You are here to be trained and educated – you are here to grow.'

Robert looked over towards the settee he had been sitting on, and the book he had left lying there. 'I shall read my homework very carefully,' he promised.

'Good,' said Kaupff. 'Then you will understand the sheer impossibility of reaching our Red Star by conventional means. The object is too distant, too swift. If we had ten years to get there then it might just be possible – but in a matter of weeks, forget it. We must think hard, Robert. We must find another way.' He sipped his tea with rhetorical deliberation. 'What do you suppose is the most important attribute for a space explorer?'

Robert thought about it. 'Courage . . . determination . . . a cool head.'

'And do you have those?'

'I don't know, sir.'

'There's another equally important quality we require, and you do have it. I mean a vivid imagination. You sit in an exam hall at Cromwell University and instead of writing about social policy you describe how you used to do exercises with baked-bean tins so you could become a cosmonaut. I like that.'

'My tutor didn't,' Robert said glumly.

'Your tutor knows nothing about the frozen star, nothing

about the Installation or how we do things here. The finest military minds in the Republic – we need them. The finest engineers and scientists – we need them too. But when we hit a barrier and are unable to move forwards we must be prepared to take a sideways step around the obstacle. That takes a kind of imagination one could almost call poetic.'

The only verses Robert could remember were a few lines of doggerel he used to recite when guising door-to-door on Fallen Comrades night. 'I'm no poet, sir.'

'I use the term loosely,' Kaupff assured him. 'Sonnets and villanelles will never make anyone airborne. But our programme requires a mind that is open to association, able to make unexpected connections; a mind that can perceive what others miss. And it's not only your little essay or your unusual reaction to a drug that have made us bring you here. Other factors are right too.'

It was all so flattering: already a thin crust of pride was beginning to envelop the young man whose talents had been too subtle and refined for the doltish eyes of Cromwell's geriatric professors.

'Intelligence has nothing to do with it,' Kaupff added. 'In fact your score was rather low, but that doesn't matter to us, so don't feel put off by all the brainy people you'll meet here, such as Rosalind.'

'Does she live here in the Lodge too?'

'No, her home is in the town. She's Category D – has anyone explained the system to you?'

Robert recalled Mr Frank's overly detailed but apparently incomplete induction. 'I was only aware of three categories,' he said. 'A for the general workforce, like the people I'm staying with, then B and C for the higher levels.'

Kaupff explained, 'Something the A's aren't allowed to know, at least not officially, is that there are more than three categories. You will of course say nothing to them about this.'

It was another secret to add to Robert's burgeoning stock. 'And what category am I?' he asked.

'I can't tell you that,' said Kaupff. 'But one thing you'll know already is that some people are allowed to leave the Installation and others aren't. I can never leave, because my brain holds too much strategic information. Then there are those whose minds are less nimble than their tongues – they might reveal the most trivial details about the Installation which would nevertheless assist our enemies. We see people come and go – but we can never be sure exactly where it is they go to.'

Robert caught his drift. 'You mean . . . ?'

The professor shrugged. 'I don't know. People disappear from the Installation and no one ever sees them again – to us they might as well have gone to another world. We get news from the outside, we get mail . . . but evidence has to be placed in context. What I'm saying, Robert, is that anyone who enters the Installation must be prepared for the possibility that they will never see the outside again. This was what you freely consented to – it is the cost of all the rewards you will be given.'

It was an enormous cost, yet Robert wasn't afraid of having to pay it. The men from the Ministry who spiked his tea had performed a delicate act of kindness.

'We all have our patriotic part to play,' Kaupff continued. 'What matters is freedom of the people as a whole, not our own personal interests: that's the cause I've believed in and fought for all my life, it was why the fascists threw me in prison. My father was a Nazi, you know. He wasn't a bad man, he never beat me or my mother – but he was in there at the very start, strutting along the street in his brown shirt like an idiot. And I became a communist, determined to make sure that the speculators and bankers and arms dealers and factory owners who made fascism possible would never again be able to enrich themselves by perverting the minds of honest workers like my father. He wasn't an evil man, Robert. When I was small he dandled me on his knee, sang lullabies to help me sleep, played games with me, taught me how to send a kite whirring into the air on a beautiful summer's day I shall never forget. If I fell and hurt myself he would comfort me; if I did well at school he expressed pride and joy. You see, he was no brute. Nor did he lack culture, though he was rough-hewn and self-educated. It was from my father that I first learned lines of Goethe, before I was ever taught them at school. Was he an angry man, a disappointed man, spiteful or petulant? I wouldn't say so. No, he lacked only one thing, Robert. He lacked imagination. And that is what all of them lacked, that single quality that could have made them stop the disaster. Have you ever read Goethe?'

No doubt brainy Rosalind was an expert but Robert felt no embarrassment in admitting an ignorance he shared with nearly every one of his countrymen.

'In the Installation, all this must change,' said Kaupff. 'I consider a certain amount of Goethe to be compulsory for every human being who aspires to have an imagination.'

So she was an expert, then. Perhaps a few choice lines would be the way to impress her – but did he have to impress Kaupff too? 'How is Goethe relevant to the mission?' Robert asked. He could see the point of *Rocket to the Stars*, but not some dead German poet.

Kaupff smiled. 'When I was seven I learned to recite "*Wandrers Nachtlied*" – a pretty little poem about being in the countryside at twilight. Then when I was your age it became a different kind of poem for me, about being at one with nature and beauty. And when I was rotting in a labour camp it was about the indestructible value of German culture, which even the fascists couldn't destroy. And now that I'm old, it's a poem about the final rest that comes to us all. The same lines, Robert, the same words I learned when I was seven – the same primal material recurring in renewed form, because this is what life is. If we taught seven-year-olds only what is relevant to seven-year-olds then they could never grow. So if I should ask you to read some Goethe, then I hope you will understand it as a kind of mental insurance, like making you pack sandwiches and an umbrella before a long journey. You never know if you'll need them, but you'll appreciate them when you do.'

Robert looked toward the window beyond Kaupff's shoulder, and between the faded flower-patterned curtains that remained opened, he thought he could see the feeble twinkling of a star.

'I lead a double life,' said Kaupff.

'What do you mean?'

'My research has been along two paths: the development of weapons, and the theory of fundamental forces. The great problem we would all love to solve is the unification of general relativity with quantum field theory. Do you know anything about relativity?'

If Kaupff thought Robert's vivid imagination could be of any help in that department then he'd picked the wrong man.

'You'll be taught whatever you need to know,' Kaupff assured him. 'But you see, this problem of quantum gravity is every bit as hard as trying to reach a frozen star – people have been banging their heads at it for decades. Maybe we need to go around the problem instead of trying to blast through it. So I've followed a different approach from other physicists – and many of my ideas have come from reading works that have no obvious connection with the subject. Yes, even Goethe, who did a great deal of scientific research. Here, let me show you something.' He got up and went past Robert towards a door at the other end of the room. Robert, turning to watch, saw through the opening what he took to be the old man's bedroom, revealed – when Kaupff switched on the light and moved to a region beyond Robert's view – to be a place filled just as completely with books as the rest of the flat. Kaupff came back a moment later, switching off the light and closing the door before bringing to the table a small contraption of rusted iron. 'Now, Robert, take a look at this.' Kaupff handed it to him; a device consisting of two metal balls on struts. By twirling it in his hand, Robert found he could make the balls rise outwards and upwards. 'Have you ever seen one before?'

'I think I might have. I can't remember where.'

'It's called a governor. I first saw one when I was a child – it was spinning around on a steam engine, and I thought it a lovely thing, like a miniature carousel. Then when I was older and knew a little physics, it meant something deeper. Just like a poem, in fact.'

Robert spun it to and fro in his hand, and the only association it suggested to him was a pair of testicles and a very thin penis.

'Nineteenth-century mathematicians tried to work out an equation for the way it moves but found they couldn't, because it exhibits a kind of behaviour they'd never encountered before: a feedback loop. The rotation of the spindle affects the steam flow, which in turn affects the rotation. Goethe would have called that sort of mutual dependency organic; Engels would have said it's dialectic. The other word we have nowadays is cybernetic. And that's the approach I've been taking to quantum gravity: a cybernetic one. You see, Robert? Everything in the universe both determines and is determined by everything else. Everything is connected. To understand the part we must perceive the whole.'

It still looked like a rusty cock and a pair of balls, but Robert was having fun playing with it.

'I hope you realize now that our mission is both an intellectual and a moral one; both scientific and visionary. Only by approaching it from every possible angle can we hope to find a solution – which is why a simple young fellow like yourself can potentially have as much to offer as an army of professors. So don't be surprised if you find yourself having to read poetry or take part in experiments or exercises that might seem strange, irrelevant, bizarre. Everything here has a purpose, Robert. I've even arranged for a prominent writer to join our research team in the hope of generating new ideas – he'll be giving a lecture tomorrow.'

Robert glanced at his watch – it was after ten o'clock and he had heard enough lecturing for tonight. Kaupff noticed his tiredness. 'We should go and call for your car.' Robert collected his book from the sofa while Kaupff put on a thick coat and scarf, apparently intending to wait with him in the night air. On the landing, Robert pointed to the second door beside Kaupff's.

'Who lives there?'

'No one, it's a spare apartment. Sometimes it's used by visiting scientists who come to the Installation. Rosalind occasionally sleeps over if she's been working late here.' He led the way down the narrow flight of stairs to the brightly lit corridor below.

'Will I sometimes be working here with you?'

'We shall see,' Kaupff said curtly, making Robert wonder if he was still the teacher's pet Kaupff's hospitality had made him feel, despite the professor's denial. They walked swiftly past doors whose occupants were now nearly all marked 'in'.

'Shall I meet any of these people?' asked Robert.

'Too many questions, Coyle.' They reached a more opulent corridor that led to the front lobby, where both walked more slowly in deference to the burgundy carpet and panelled walls. The butler was still at his desk. 'A car, please, Jason.'

'Certainly, Professor.' Almost lizard-like with his unerringly precise movements, he lifted the receiver of the large black telephone at his side, said 'Car – main entrance,' hung up, then announced with silky assurance to Robert, 'About ten or fifteen minutes. Do please relax in the bar.'

'If you'd like to give our guest his coat, he and I can both go outside to take the air,' Kaupff told him.

'Of course, Professor.' The butler fetched Robert's military greatcoat and handed it to him; *Rocket to the Stars* slid neatly into one pocket. Then he opened the glass-paned door for the two men, wishing Robert goodnight as the pupil followed his master through the outer doorway and into the dark gravel-covered courtyard.

'Just look at the sky,' said Kaupff. Above them, stars glowed in the clear, moonless night.

'It's beautiful,' Robert murmured obediently. Cold too.

'It's why you're here,' Kaupff reminded him. 'Do you know your constellations?' Robert guessed this was something else the brainy ones were expected to be familiar with. 'What do you think that star there must be?'

Robert saw a brilliant light which would have been an aeroplane if it moved. 'The Red Star, sir?'

Kaupff sighed. 'It's Jupiter, dear boy. What we seem to have officially decided to call the Red Star is invisible – and in any case its present position is below the horizon, in roughly that direction.' He pointed at a far-off piece of ground towards the main part of the Installation, whose lights glowed in the distance; almost as if he were indicating the Installation itself. The two of them kept pacing, and Robert began to notice they were walking away from the building and its bright windows, so that very soon they left the courtyard for a smooth path that took them through a copse of trees. The increased darkness, and Robert's growing acclimatization to it, made the stars above them swell in number and brilliance.

'Doesn't it make you feel both small and magnificent?' said Kaupff. 'Here beneath the stars we are reminded that all nature is one. *In tausend Formen magst du dich verstecken . . .*'

Robert ought to try that one on Rosalind, if only he could figure out how to say it, and what it meant. He could manage a little Russian, but didn't suppose 'Do you like opera?' would have much use in a closed town with two pubs and a cinema.

They walked through the trees and emerged onto the smooth expanse of a bowling green. 'I often come here,' Kaupff said, standing closely at Robert's side. 'I sometimes bring a telescope – as you can see, we're far enough removed here from electric lights to get a superb view. Of course, telescopes aren't the sort of thing you normally find in the Installation – they're banned for security reasons. But an exception was made for me. And there's something else I like about this place – can you guess what it is?' Robert felt an arm across his back, a hand rising and coming to rest on his shoulder. Kaupff whispered in his ear. 'No bugging devices. This is where we can share our deepest secrets.'

Robert moved away. 'My car will be here soon . . .'

'We'll see its headlights coming up the hill,' said Kaupff. 'It won't go back down without you. Enjoy the stars and the fresh air. Can you see the Milky Way?' Robert looked upwards and Kaupff embraced him once more. 'There it is,' he said, tracing with his free arm a faintly glowing band, brightest where it dipped towards the northern horizon. 'A hundred million suns at a single glance – can anything be more wondrous?'

Robert was unnerved. Kaupff's comment about bugging devices was a hint of danger: their electronic presence beneath the soil, or in the neighbouring trees, would have been reassuring. It was as if Kaupff were deliberately showing him the one place in the Installation where they could not be overheard – the sort of place in which a spy might choose to linger.

He heard a crackle among the trees – it sounded like twigs breaking beneath a shoe. More probably a fox, but Robert could feel the short hairs on the back of his neck rise and tingle. Even a fox was threatening now; a nocturnal beast in search of prey, in its dark element while Robert strained to see anything but distant lights.

'I learned these constellations as a child,' Kaupff said dreamily. 'The poetry of the sky – the beacons we steer by. What's wrong?'

'I heard something. An animal, I think.'

'Only a child fears darkness, Robert. You're not a child.'

'I'm sure I can see my car.'

'Is it the night that scares you?' Kaupff drew closer to him, breathing warm vapour across his face, speaking with sudden and surprising passion. 'Or is it me? Do you think I'm a mad old fool with my talk of poetry and stars?'

'No, sir.'

'Don't you see that we must have courage and daring – even if it means daring to be mad? And you worry about an animal! We're confronted by the infinite, Robert, and all you notice is a scurrying rat.' Excited clouds of the old man's breath were urging themselves against Robert's cheek, almost like the prelude to a kiss. Robert was confused and embarrassed, and when the crackling of twigs became a heavy breaking of wood beneath a dark figure emerging from the trees, he leapt away with a start.

'Good evening, comrades. I hope I didn't frighten you, though it's very late for you both to be wandering around the grounds like this.' It was Commissioner Davis, who, while hiding himself among the trees so as to eavesdrop on the conversation, had kept his pipe strategically unlit.

'I've been telling Volunteer Coyle about astronomy,' said Kaupff, hardly less unnerved than Robert had been.

'I know,' said Davis. 'It was an interesting disquisition, which I hope you shall share with all of us in a seminar. It seems a pity to waste such entertaining ideas in a place where no one can hear.'

'Unless he tries,' Kaupff added, regaining his composure. For a moment, all three men were swept by pale light: the swinging beams of the car that had rounded the bend at the foot of the hill and was beginning its ascent towards the Lodge. 'We need to get you home, Robert,' said Kaupff. 'Let's go to your car.'

'Why the hurry?' Davis interrupted. 'As you said yourself, Professor, it won't leave without him.' Then he turned to Robert and asked him, 'Has anything improper happened during your visit here tonight?'

Kaupff was outraged. 'I beg your pardon!'

'Quiet, please. I have asked Volunteer Coyle a formal question in accordance with my duties and responsibilities under the Judicial Code, and I shall make an official note of his response, which will be kept on record. Well, Volunteer?'

Robert spoke softly. 'I am not aware of any impropriety.'

'Not aware?'

Robert coughed nervously. 'Nothing improper has happened. And if I may say so, sir, I see no reason why any such allegation should be made.'

'I make no allegation,' said Davis. 'I observe, I take note, I record. You could say I'm a scientist of the human condition. And I'm sorry if I have caused any misunderstanding, any offence or embarrassment, but I'm sure you can both see why two men lurking on a bowling green at night, in a place of the very highest security which has been breached in the recent past by enemy agents, might attract official attention.'

'We understand,' said Kaupff. 'Now please let us send Coyle home to bed. And the next time I bring my telescope here I shall be sure to invite you along as chaperone, Commissioner.'

'It would be most educational,' Davis replied, leading the way back to the courtyard. The car was waiting at the Lodge's doorway, engine chugging, its headlamps dazzling as they approached, so that Kaupff and Robert had to shield their eyes in order to see the commissioner's silhouetted figure when he came to a halt. 'I have an idea,' he said, turning to face his blinking companions. 'Let's convene here tomorrow night – you can give us a tour of the heavens, Professor Kaupff. I should very much like to find out what you're able to see with that instrument of yours.'

'I shall be delighted to show you,' Kaupff said calmly. 'Let us hope for another clear sky like tonight's.'

Davis went to the car and pulled open the front passenger door; Robert followed, going towards the rear, then realized that the open door was meant for him. 'Goodnight, Volunteer,' Davis said when Robert climbed in. 'You will be collected from your quarters at eight a.m. Sleep well.' The driver was the same man who had brought him earlier; and during the whole journey back, neither he nor Robert said a word.

4

The Franks' house was dark. Robert left the car as quietly as he could and walked up the path, hearing the vehicle drive away along the empty street. Even as he stood at the door and reached inside his pocket for the key Mr Frank had given him, he could still hear the car in the distance – perhaps the only moving vehicle in the whole of the Installation.

He pushed the brass key into the lock, gave it a twist, and found it wouldn't budge. He should have waited for that lesson from Mr Frank after all. He tried again, turning the key this way and that, unsure which direction was correct, but finding either impossible. The key was defective, or the lock had been set in some unshiftable way, or else – most likely of all – it would only respond to the deft and expert fiddling of Mr Frank, or of someone schooled by him in the household's manifold idiosyncrasies. There was frost on the ground at Robert's feet; his ungloved hands were numb with cold. If he were to stay outdoors on a night like this he would quite possibly be dead by morning.

He did what most people will do in moments of utter hopelessness. He kept trying, silently twisting and forcing the immovable key, as if the weight of need and desperation would be enough to undo the mechanical laws of nature and of locks; as if willpower alone would persuade the key to change its shape, change its mind, and let him into the house. The thought of calling out and waking the Franks – and the whole street – or of lobbing pebbles at upstairs windows was more outrageous to him than the idea that he might soon be on the verge of hypothermia. At least he would die politely, expiring in a frost-crusted heap on the pavement while the Franks' precious sleep went uninterrupted. So he fiddled and fussed, he pushed and pulled, making no sound and achieving nothing except a worsening of the pain in his fingers. Then the door opened.

It happened so suddenly that he fell forwards, still holding the key, and collided with the figure emerging from inside whose intention had been to open the door only partially; a young man, just as startled as Robert, the two of them simultaneously stifling a joint cry of surprise.

'Who are you?' the stranger whispered, his voice a mixture of fear and anger. Inside the house, at the top of the stairs, Robert saw the pale figure of Miriam, in a nightdress, holding her hands to her mouth in a frantic mime of shock. She began tripping down the stairs as swiftly and silently as she could while Robert came inside.

Miriam told her companion in an agitated hiss, 'He's the volunteer they've billeted here – I did warn you.' Then to Robert: 'You've seen nothing, OK? If Dad finds out he'll kill me.' The man, his composure regained, looked at Robert and raised his palms in a gesture of truce. Robert stood aside to let him out. 'Goodnight, Tim,' Miriam whispered after him. 'Love you.' Then as soon as she sealed the door with a soft click, she turned to Robert, her glowering expression easily visible in the dim light. 'Well, Mr Volunteer, now you know.'

'I won't say a thing. I honestly couldn't care what you do.'

'I don't need your charity or your consideration,' she immediately interrupted. 'If you breathe a word to anyone then I'll personally cut off your balls and feed them to the cat. I want you to be clear about that as long as you're underneath this roof of ours.'

'No problem,' said Robert, whose interest in Miriam's private affairs – or even her public ones – was by now about as great as his concern for German poetry. 'I never knew you had a cat.'

'Figure of speech.'

'And the bit about my bollocks?'

'Literal.'

'Got you,' said Robert. 'But if you don't mind, I'm going to sleep. Long day. See you tomorrow.'

'Enjoy your bed,' she whispered sarcastically after him as he began to ascend. 'Maybe it's still warm.'

He reached his room and took off his coat, hearing Miriam quietly close the door of the spare room to which she'd been exiled. When he turned on the table lamp he saw that the bed appeared undisturbed – either Miriam had been teasing or else she had remade it very carefully.

He slept heavily until a knock signalled the start of his

first full day at the Installation. Mrs Frank was calling to him through the door. 'Will you be wanting a cooked breakfast?' It was seven o'clock, still dark outside, and sleep weighed more heavily than sausages on the scale of his desires, but Mrs Frank was quite insistent about getting an answer. 'We thought we'd better wake you,' she called in generous plural, 'because we forgot to give you the alarm. Miriam took her clock with her to the other room because she always starts early at the library and likes to get herself sorted first – will you be wanting hot water? Should be enough but we might need to set the boiler to come on a bit earlier if there's both of you using it every morning and I'll go and see to those eggs now but if you're wanting porridge too then I can always sort it out because Mr Frank sometimes has it . . .'

He heard her retreat downstairs, still talking, and got himself ready to face the world. Miriam was already out of the bathroom, and when Robert eventually came down he found her in the kitchen, seated with her father at the carefully laid table while Mrs Frank scraped bacon from an iron frying pan she rattled unnecessarily on the gas hob.

'Sleep well?' Mr Frank asked jovially. He had cut himself shaving, and a small corner of white tissue paper was stuck to the wound on his scrawny neck with a bloody spot.

'Like a log,' said Robert, seating himself and surveying the small regiment of toast slices lined up in a steel rack in readiness. The place mat in front of him showed a picture of the Marx Memorial in London – Mrs Frank soon buried it beneath a heavily burdened plate.

'A young lad like you needs a good feed in the morning,' she asserted, as though stating an axiom of logic.

'Nothing like home cooking, eh?' Mr Frank chimed in. 'Bet you don't get this sort of thing every day. Where did you say your base is?'

Robert hadn't said, and had no intention of doing so. He deposited a buttered slice of toast onto his feast and began eating. 'This is great,' he said, reverting the subject.

'Did you manage all right with the key last night?' Mr Frank asked. Robert shot a glance at Miriam, who ignored him and looked very steadily at her teacup.

'Yes, fine,' said Robert, called upon by Mr Frank's rapt silence to elaborate. 'I had to give it a few tries, but it opened.'

'A few tries?' Mrs Frank echoed with concern as she sat down.

'Only a couple,' Robert insisted.

Mr Frank looked sceptical. 'Maybe I ought to see that key. You weren't out there long in the cold, were you?'

'Not long – it's nothing, really. Don't trouble yourself.' Even as Robert offered these reassurances, he realized that not only was there no reason why he should cover for Miriam, but he also had a key in his pocket that he had found himself unable to use.

It was as if Mr Frank could read his mind. 'Let me have a look at it,' he said. 'We haven't tried it for a while so I'd better check.' Robert reached into his pocket, gave Mr Frank what he wanted, and watched his host rise from the table with a scrape of his wooden chair on the linoleumed floor. Through the kitchen doorway, Robert could see Mr Frank go to the front door and open it, admitting an icy chill from the early morning blackness outside that soon reached the diners.

'Do you have to be doing that now, Arthur?' his wife called.

Mr Frank was rattling the key in the exterior lock with the same difficulty Robert had experienced. 'That's odd,' he muttered. 'It's not usually this tricky.' He retracted the key, closed the door and stood in the hallway examining the gleaming paradox beneath the electric ceiling light. Still the truth had not materialized; and it was only when Mr Frank brought out his own key and looked at both side by side, one in each of his upheld hands, that his face transformed. 'I gave him the wrong one!' he exclaimed.

'Oh, you stupid man,' Dorothy scolded.

Arthur's smile froze as the full implication of his eureka moment bedded into his brain. He looked through the kitchen doorway at Robert. 'How did you get in?'

Robert didn't know what to say. Lying had proved the easiest way to deal with the Franks so far, but why lie for Miriam's sake? 'Actually . . .'

'I let him in,' said Miriam.

'You?' Mr Frank had evidently never before experienced so much puzzlement over breakfast.

'I heard him at the door,' Miriam said simply. 'All his struggling woke me up. So I came down and let him in.'

'Well then,' Mrs Frank chuckled, 'why didn't you say?' She seemed to sense there was more to it than either Miriam or Robert had admitted, but was still trying to pin down the natural conclusion that evaded her.

'I didn't want to make a fuss,' Miriam replied, taking a sip of tea, lifting a slice of toast from the rack, then changing her mind and putting it back again. 'I know how you and Dad want everything to be perfect for our new guest, so I thought I'd save your embarrassment and swap his key myself, without bothering to tell you.'

'Is that so?' said Mr Frank who came and sat down again, his words directed nowhere in particular, though his gaze was on the newcomer.

'Yes,' said Robert.

Dorothy Frank's ruminations were meanwhile leading her to an ominous deduction. 'I just hope you two don't catch a chill, wandering around the house at night together. And you'd only have had your nightdress on, Miriam. It's good to know you're looking after Robert and making him feel welcome, but you don't have to keep any secrets from us. It makes it all sound as if the pair of you were up to no good!' She chuckled again, even less convincingly than before, and remained quiet until breakfast was finished and it was time for everyone to leave. 'Arthur, get Robert sorted; and Miriam, will you stop off at the butcher's when you finish at the library this afternoon and get a kilo of diced mutton if they've got any? They'll be closed when my shift ends and I want to make a casserole tonight. Will you be eating with us, Robert?'

'I don't know—' He was interrupted by the sound of a horn tooting outside. 'I wonder if that's for me?' He went to the hall, looked through the lace-curtained window and saw a waiting bus like the one that had brought him the previous day. 'I've got to go,' he called back, dashing upstairs to get his greatcoat, which was in his bedroom, tossed over the old, bulky radio set where he had left it last night. The book Kaupff gave him was still wedged in one pocket, Robert pulled it out and threw it onto the bedside table; but when he glanced at the radio again he noticed something else. The radio had been tuned to London when he first saw it yesterday; now the pointer was aimed at neighbouring Athlone.

Mr Frank was waiting for him at the front door. 'You need the right key!' he exclaimed, handing over his own.

'And don't forget to leave out any clothes that need washing,' Mrs Frank interjected. 'Or put them in the laundry basket . . .'

'Yes – see you later,' Robert called, running out to the impatiently rumbling bus in which, when he climbed aboard, he found Rosalind and the recruits sitting amid the numerous empty seats.

'Good morning, Volunteer Coyle,' Rosalind said smoothly. 'Now that we're all here, we can proceed.' She gave a nod to the driver, who immediately set off, making Robert lurch as he went to sit down. There were four other volunteers, he noticed, sitting in pairs. Yesterday there had been five.

'We're going to the College,' Rosalind announced. 'This is the area of the Installation where all the highest-level scientific and technical personnel live, and where theoretical work is carried out.' She shot a glance at Robert, who realized he must have visited part of it last night. 'Any questions?'

One man asked, 'Why aren't we staying there too? My landlady's a sweet old dear but she can't boil an egg.' The others laughed.

'There is a reason for the present arrangements, Volunteer Macleod,' Rosalind told him. 'There is a reason for everything that happens here. But I am not able to discuss such matters.'

From behind Robert another man spoke. 'Where do you live, Rosalind? Can't they give me quarters nearer yours?' Again there was laughter, in which Rosalind allowed herself to participate, as if in a calculated gesture of informality like some prearranged elevation of the group to a new status in the Installation's social hierarchy. 'I find it best to keep some distance,' she said, her smile unwavering. 'I shall be watching you, Volunteer Forsyth.'

'And we're watching you!' he called back, to yet more laughter.

Robert felt unable to share the mood; he gazed through the bus window at a route he had already viewed in darkness, seeing it differently in the winter dawn. The industrial zone looked less dramatic now, almost shabby. When the bus began to crawl up the gently sloping hill leading to the Lodge it took a side road, bypassing the grand Victorian mansion and arriving instead at a group of modern buildings ringed by a security fence.

'All of this is what we call the College,' Rosalind explained to the volunteers. 'It was the original Installation – the first part to be built, with the old hunting lodge serving as an accommodation wing, and the newer research buildings alongside. This was where Professor Kaupff and his colleagues created Britain's nuclear deterrent.'

The bus paused at a checkpoint; two helmeted soldiers approached, one of whom came on board and silently scrutinized the occupants, then nodded towards Rosalind. 'All right, pet?'

'I'm fine.'

'Be seeing you, then.' He turned to alight, his sub-machine gun tucked under his arm with its barrel lowered.

'At the Blue Cat tonight?' he called back to her. She shrugged mysteriously, the bus doors concertinaed closed, and he offered a comradely wave as the vehicle proceeded slowly onwards through the raised barrier. Rosalind recommenced her commentary while the bus reached a car park beside a large ugly concrete-and-glass structure that in any other place might have been a theatre or civic centre. 'Fabrication was carried out in the industrial area we passed earlier – an interconnected suite of manufacturing and technical facilities we collectively call the Plant. As the Installation's activities expanded, the two zones became enclosed sectors of the single high-security community we see today, along with the military base where you arrived yesterday, and the Town where you are staying. Town and Base are the Installation's backbone; the Plant is its muscle, the College is its brain.'

'Where's its heart?' Robert called out.

She fell silent, and the bus doors clunked open.

5

Rosalind led them into a place that reminded Robert of the university he'd been slung out of: they were in the foyer of what appeared to be a lecture building. Several dozen people, mostly male and in their early twenties, stood in clusters, chatting and smoking, sipping coffee whose source was a wheeled trolley bearing a large copper urn. A tall woman stood beside it wearing the uniform of a caterer – a stiff blue blouse and coarse black skirt extending just below her knees, with a white apron in front. Her sleek black hair was tied up behind her head to reveal a long and delicate neck whose gracefulness was somehow incongruous. One of the waiting men brought his empty cup to her for a refill, and Robert saw that as she handed the replenished cup to him, she seemed to give his wrist a friendly pat. It was the same inscrutable familiarity he had witnessed on the bus, between Rosalind and the soldier. Everyone here knew everyone else; they were all interconnected, like Kaupff's vision of the universe. No, Robert didn't think Kaupff was mad, as the old man had petulantly suggested. Instead, in the waitress's handing over of a cup of coffee, Robert perceived something of the cosmic mission which had brought him here. He was also reminded that unlike everyone else, he knew nobody.

A tannoy crackled. 'The professor's lecture is about to resume in Auditorium A. Please have your passes ready for inspection at the door.' There was a swift stubbing of cigarettes and draining of cups as the crowd converged towards the open entrance of what Robert could see to be a spacious theatre.

'This building,' Rosalind explained to her charges, sweeping the emptying foyer with her outstretched arm, 'is the focus of the College's educational activities. New researchers need to be trained in advanced nuclear or plasma physics, aeronautics, nonlinear optics – much of it classified information of a highly sensitive kind.' Robert was in no doubt that his guide knew about every one of those topics – while he hadn't even been able to manage an essay on quality versus quantity. The imbalance was one that Rosalind seemed to relish. 'The discoveries we make here can't be published in normal journals. There are brilliant workers whose entire careers have been secret, known only to their fellow initiates – and now you have the privilege of being among them.'

She began walking towards the far end of the foyer, gesturing the others to follow her to the lift whose dark shaft was sealed by a steel door with a frosted-glass panel. Rosalind pushed the button and a few seconds later a wedge of light slid down inside; when she went to open the heavy door, Volunteer Forsyth moved in front of her.

'Allow me, dear,' he said gallantly, his gesture revealing the wood-lined compartment with its caged inner door, and a picture of Karl Marx on the rear wall.

'Your strength has its uses,' Rosalind said acidly, then observed the notice inside the compartment. 'I wonder if all six of us will fit in – the limit's meant to be five.'

'Let's make two trips,' someone suggested.

'Never mind,' said Rosalind, whose lips trembled with the rapid ticking of a mental calculation. 'Our combined mass is below the recommended maximum.' Being able to weigh a man by sight was evidently one of her many secret skills. She slid aside the cage and waved everyone in, entering after them and demonstrating when she pulled the cage back in place that they could indeed all fit, though not without touching. Robert had been the last of the volunteers to step inside and had immediately turned to face the door in order not to find himself staring at the other men; and when Rosalind came in, also turning so as to close the door, she backed into him until her shoulders met his chest, her hair stroked his chin, her rump touched his crotch.

'Press three,' she instructed, and somebody's finger found the appropriate button on the compartment wall she was unable to reach.

It was a comically crowded scene. When the lift began to move, Volunteer Forsyth said, 'I hope no one had beans for breakfast.'

'No, only that egg,' said Macleod, the compartment bearing its laughing occupants upwards.

For a few delicious moments, Robert savoured the numerous points of contact between Rosalind and himself. As well as the perfume he had noticed yesterday there was another scent now – the earthy, natural fragrance of her hair. No more than four slow breaths separated the ground floor from their destination, yet each was more delightful than the last, bringing a steadily intensifying image of Rosalind into his nostrils while his skin conceived its own detailed landscape of pressures and frictions. Most of all it was on the push of his crotch that his thoughts were concentrated; the dull prod of his folded member against a portion of her buttock which, in the short duration of the bumpy lift ride, was sufficient to elicit a rebellious swelling against the constrictions of the compartment. She, as if aware between the first and second floors of some impropriety, shifted slightly, but a moment later returned, contributing her own equal force to the unacknowledged encounter, having chosen for herself, it seemed, a more agreeable position during the final seconds of the ascent.

'Here we are,' she said when the lift stopped with a ping, and she extracted her right arm from the squeeze so as to pull back the cage and free them all from an experience Robert would have wished to last for hours. Her shoulder dug into Robert's chest and her unused arm found secret employment of its own as it brushed Robert's front, swiftly, but with an apparent precision he would mentally revisit many times afterwards, for it brought the ends of her fingers into glancing contact with his penis. It lasted no longer than the flash of a photograph but she'd done it on purpose, he was immediately sure of it. She pulled the cage aside, opened with her own weight the steel door beyond, and as the passengers disembarked into the fluorescent illumination of a windowless lobby, Robert reflected on the discreet but, to him, unmistakable message she had given.

Two middle-aged men came through a swing door, deep in conversation. One of them – short, balding and with a drinker's glowing face – looked pensively at the new arrivals and informed Rosalind, 'Kaupff is ready to start in the seminar room.'

'Thank you, Professor Vine,' she said, waving her charges to follow until they arrived at a small lecture room with enough moveable seats and desks for thirty or so people, though only a handful were present – all mature-looking men, whom Professor Vine and his companion went to sit among. Davis was there too, Robert noticed, but the commissioner did not look round at them, instead keeping his attention fixed on Professor Kaupff, who was slowly pacing before the blackboard, chalk in hand.

Kaupff turned and noticed the new arrivals. 'Ah, here are our brave volunteers. Come, Rosalind, bring them to the front, then we can be properly introduced.'

She led them in single file past the desks so that they could assemble in line for inspection by their elders. Like a choirmaster, Kaupff prompted them to recite their names one by one: John Harvey, Colin Forsyth, Lachlan Macleod, Gordon Beatty, Robert Coyle.

'These,' Kaupff said to his colleagues, 'are the cream of our youth. All of them, whatever happens, are heroes. Now, if you would like to be seated, we can begin.'

Davis rose from his chair just as Rosalind and the recruits were finding theirs. He paced slowly to the open door of the seminar room, stuck his head out into the corridor, looking both ways with great deliberation, and then, watched silently by everyone in the room, he closed the door and came to the front, where Kaupff stood aside so that he could speak.

'I have an important announcement to make,' he said. 'Last night an unauthorized radio signal was detected, coming from somewhere inside the Installation. It was too faint and too short to be decoded, but we know that it was on an illegal frequency reserved for military use. You are all scientists, and you all understand what this means. There is a spy in the Installation, and he – or she – is presumably transmitting information to the Yankee imperialists or their allies. If the capitalists discover the frozen star – and more importantly, if they discover the means by which Professor Kaupff hopes to reach it – then the consequences could be catastrophic. We all know the cost of failure. We all know that a great many lives – not only our own – are at stake. You can rest assured that my men from Department 5 are undertaking the most intensive search for the spy – the records of every single person in the Installation are being studied, and we are systematically interviewing personnel. You will all be invited to take part in this process soon. Security measures here, as you know, are always of the strictest kind, but we also value the freedoms that make it possible for people to live and work happily in the Installation. I assure you we will do everything in our power to preserve those freedoms. The spy will be caught. Justice will be done. The imperialists will not be allowed to win their war on our way of life.' Davis went to sit down again, the only sound in the room being the click of his heels and the nervous coughing of one or two elderly scientists who were no strangers, Robert guessed, to episodes like these.

Kaupff took the floor once more. 'The illegal radio signal was intercepted by Dr Simpson and his team.' Simpson, singled out by the point of Kaupff's chalk, smiled modestly from where he sat at one side of the room. 'When the frozen star was first discovered we hoped to detect X-ray or gamma radiation produced by dust falling and accelerating into the object's intense gravitational field. No such emissions were found, so we extended our search to radio frequencies, still without success, apart from the unexpected signal from within the Installation itself. I should further add that Commissioner Davis is wrong to assume the source was a transmitter. As all the physicists in this room will attest, any radio receiver re-emits a small amount of energy, somewhat like the reflection on a window. What Simpson's team may have detected was the illegal use of a receiver tuned to a forbidden waveband—'

'That still counts as spying under the Penal Code,' Davis interrupted. 'As every patriotic citizen in this room, with or without a PhD in physics, will attest.'

Kaupff was discomfited by the intervention. 'Quite,' he said. 'I merely reiterate what I said to you earlier, as soon as you informed me about the problem, which is that if your men from D5 spend all their time looking for a transmitter they might miss their target. If only we remember to approach the problem dialectically, we see that reception and transmission are two sides of the same phenomenon, as the Penal Code fully recognizes. And we can also apply this methodology in our efforts to reach the object – for which, incidentally, we have an appropriate name proposed by one of our recruits: the Red Star.'

A combination of muttering and mirth greeted what everyone conceded to be an ideologically acceptable nickname, and Robert was soon identified as the proposer of what he knew to have been Kaupff's own idea, donated out of paternalistic generosity.

'Some of you here know just as much as I do about the mission, its rationale and the physical principles it seeks to invoke; others do not. Those who remain in greatest ignorance are you, my young recruits, and so we must begin to educate you. No doubt you will already have noticed certain curious commonalities among yourselves – you are all exactly the same height, the same weight, the same age, and you all scored equally on the intelligence and personality tests that formed part of the initial selection process.'

None of this commonality had been apparent to Robert – nor, it seemed, had it occurred to any of the others, since all now shot comradely glances among themselves in acknowledgement of the new bond they had discovered, which explained among other things how Rosalind had known the lift would bear them.

'The allowed physical dimensions of our volunteers are constrained by the geometry of the capsule; but this mission is more than purely physical. It is also mental – indeed, one could say it is predominantly so, which is why our volunteers have to be of exactly equal intellectual capacity and development.' Thus at a stroke Kaupff confirmed what Robert had suspected then doubted. Regardless of Scotland's distance from the equator, they were somehow to be its first cosmonauts. 'Let's think about basics,' the professor went on. 'Something lies between us and the Red Star. What is it?'

He paused, waiting for an answer, but no one spoke. Robert was aware of the silent experts seated behind him – surely they were not the people from whom Kaupff hoped to elicit a response to so elementary a question. It was the volunteers he aimed to test, and Robert raised his hand.

'Yes, Coyle?' Kaupff spoke as if he had never met him before.

'Space, sir.'

'Very good, Coyle. But what is space? Harvey?'

The volunteer whom Robert had yesterday found so friendly had been noticeably quieter this morning, and took a moment to answer. 'Space is emptiness . . . it's nothing.'

The professor addressed his peers who sat further back. 'There we have it, gentlemen, the essential problem. Space lies between us and the Red Star – and if space is nothing then the problem is solved. So space must be something, and the question is what kind of thing. Any ideas, Macleod?'

'Eh . . . what about distance? Is that a thing?'

'I suppose we have to ask what exactly we mean by "thing",' said Kaupff. 'Do we mean that which is not a predicable attribute, or do we mean moveable substance? Distance is neither.'

Now Davis interrupted again. 'I can't quite believe what I'm hearing, Professor Kaupff. We have several of the finest physicists in the Republic gathered in this room, and you're taking us through some pedantic game that makes no sense whatsoever. Are you making the volunteers – and myself – the butt of an academic joke? What's all this nonsense about something and nothing? Get to the point, man!'

Professor Vine, claret-nosed and genial, spoke up for his colleague. 'Commissioner, I first worked with Heinz twenty-five years ago on the Pluto missile system, and I quickly learned that nothing this man says is without meaning. He's human and he makes mistakes – we've had our disagreements about all sorts of scientific questions, and sometimes I can't believe the damned foolish things he says. But even when he's wrong, he's meaningfully wrong, because he's a scientist, and that's how we do things. Now I admit that these volunteers we've brought here are still in the dark about matters you and I already know concerning the mission, and I also admit that giving them a quick lesson in Aristotelian categories might seem a strange way to start their education at the College. But I recall that when I studied the scientific writings of Engels as an undergraduate, as we all did, I learned from him that Aristotle was the founder of the dialectical method in Western thought, so although Heinz's approach is doubtless unorthodox, it's also ideologically impeccable, and I think we should let him continue. So, Heinz, you're telling us first of all that there's an opposition between being and nothingness?'

'Exactly, Roger,' said Kaupff. Robert understood that it

was a conversation they must have had many times, perhaps over a diminishing bottle of whisky in the wood-panelled Maxwell Room with its crackling log fire.

'And next,' said Professor Vine, 'you'll be pointing out that such oppositions can only be understood in relative terms, by virtue of the negation of the negation.'

'Precisely,' Kaupff agreed with a smile. 'You really deserve a house point.' There was laughter.

'But we're not in Pioneer Camp any more,' said Vine, 'so let's get to the nub of the question. We know from the deepest philosophical reasoning – from the materialist viewpoint that is basic to everything we do as physicists, as well as to everything we do as socialists – that space is not just some empty container, but is itself a thing, an entity with physical properties. Space can have pressure – Einstein found this nearly seventy years ago – and the pressure can be positive or negative . . .'

'We mustn't rush ahead of ourselves,' Kaupff said, silencing Vine as though wishing to still the inappropriate words of an adult before children. 'Let's stick, though, with your picture of an empty container. A jam jar, say, like the kind in which I collected pond life when I was a child.'

Robert had a similar memory: a gob of frogspawn crowded in turbid water.

'Let's pour out all the water and creatures and screw the lid firmly back on the jar,' said Kaupff. 'There's still air inside, of course. So let's get a vacuum pump and remove all the air. In fact let's imagine that our pump is fantastically powerful – more so than any on Earth – and that our jar is inordinately strong, so that we are able to remove every single gas molecule floating around in the jar. Not one of them is left – the jar surrounds a perfect vacuum. So what's inside – nothing or something?'

Robert glanced behind himself at the experts, one or two of whom were nodding in approval at Kaupff's lesson. Davis was still stony faced, unconvinced that there was any point to this charade.

'Well, Coyle?' Kaupff, wanting an answer, made him turn. 'You're holding the empty jar, looking through it. What can you see?'

Robert pictured the fictional scene. 'Someone else who's with me.' A face distorted by glass.

'Then there's our answer,' said Kaupff. 'Even when we thought the jar to be completely empty, light is still passing through. This transiting light shows that the jar is not empty at all – far from it. Photons of light, like tiny tadpoles, fill every part of the jar – and they fill our universe. The Red Star is not falling through a void – it is falling through the light and heat of the Sun, and before it entered our solar system it fell through the light, heat and other radiation of the stars in our galaxy. More than that, it fell through the photons of the microwave radiation which remain from the universe's birth, and which vastly outnumber all the particles of matter in the cosmos. So, if we really want to make a jam jar empty, we have to deal with these photons – we need a way of removing electromagnetic radiation. Any suggestions?'

Robert was still seeing the face through the glass. 'Cover it up,' he said. 'Wrap the jar in thick paper, or paint it black, then light can't get in or out.'

'Exactly,' said Kaupff. 'We can easily exclude visible light.

But it wouldn't block microwaves or radio signals, as Simpson and his colleagues could tell us. If you were sitting inside a blacked-out jam jar with a radio receiver you'd still be able to pick up the news bulletin.'

It was playing beside his bed in the military hospital, he remembered, and in all that time, when he was so close to dying, his mother and father never visited, Robert was sure of it. No one came, except the kind people from the Ministry. Now he wanted to cover the glass completely and never see through it again – never see the outside that had forgotten him. And another radio: the old device in his bedroom. Yesterday it had been tuned to London, this morning Athlone, and while Kaupff spoke of waves and frequencies, a possible explanation became apparent to him. Miriam and her boyfriend had been fooling with the radio late last night in the darkened bedroom – innocently turning the control they should not have touched, the volume so low that Mr and Mrs Frank heard nothing. Probably all they wanted was the soft illumination of its antique dial during their lovemaking, but the radio leaked some of the electromagnetic tadpoles it received from the sex-drenched ether, and a few of them had fallen into the prophylactic grasp of Simpson and his sleepless henchmen, who had monitored the treacherous droplets as they spilled onto the scientists' sensitive dish. It was a theory of unimpeachable logical rigour; and if it were empirically proven, Miriam and her boyfriend could end up being shot as spies. Robert couldn't stand her but there was no need for a firing squad.

'So there's a simple way to shut out radio signals,' Kaupff continued. 'All we need do is enclose our jam jar in a metal box, then any receiver put inside would remain silent. In fact, if we make the metal thick enough, and cold enough, then all electromagnetic fields will be excluded, and we shall have the nearest thing in the whole universe to a portion of perfectly empty space, devoid of matter, radiation or heat. Think of that perfect emptiness, comrades. Think how pure and sublime it would be.'

Robert saw the darkened bedroom where Miriam and her boyfriend had done what he wished to do with Rosalind. He imagined the room encased in thick metal, the radio falling silent, and only the glow of its silent dial caressing Rosalind's naked rump, whose curve he had felt in the ascending lift. She was sitting to his right, out of clear view unless he dared shoot his gaze at her, but he was sure she was watching him, monitoring his performance.

'Have we really attained perfect emptiness?' asked Kaupff. 'Our container holds no matter, no radiation – if we were to place a camera inside it would show nothing; a radio would pick up no signal. Yet we have forgotten something. The camera or the radio would have weight. Though we have made our container emptier than the most remote depths of space, still we find that gravity can act there. How can we shut out gravitational fields? H. G. Wells offered a fanciful solution – a magical substance which resists gravity in the same way that a curtain obstructs light – but that was only a novelist's dream. There is no such substance, and there is no evidence that anything like it could ever exist. But we do know a way to remove the effects of gravity. Think of the lift you all came up in.'

Robert had never forgotten it.

'Disaster strikes, a cable breaks – the lift compartment plummets.' A euphoric nausea gripped Robert as he imagined the shared moment of imminent death. 'The lift and its occupants are in free fall,' Kaupff explained. 'And we know what this implies. All objects accelerate through empty space at the same rate: a hammer or a feather, a human or a speck of dust. Everyone in the lift must therefore feel weightless, since the floor falls beneath them at the same rate as their own bodies.' In Robert's mind there dwelt no more the weight of inhibition which had burdened him during his brief ascent. Now he was freely moving his hands across Rosalind's light body, encircling her, reaching up towards her floating breasts. 'Gravity draws us like a roaring river, and rather than resist we can yield to it, going effortlessly with its flow. So to remove the effects of gravity from an empty container we simply let it fall freely through space.' There was only Robert and Rosalind now; the metal lift compartment was their orbiting bedroom. 'This is the freedom nature cherishes most,' Kaupff added; 'the freedom experienced by bodies which don't resist, don't remain stubbornly at rest – and it would seem that we have at last found an answer to our riddle. What can be left inside an empty falling container? Well, Coyle?'

He had been caught daydreaming. 'Pardon, sir?' Somebody laughed behind him.

'If we are to find a correct solution to the problem of being and nothingness we must think more carefully about the freely falling elevator – a thought-experiment which all these wise people behind you learned when they were no older than you are now, though they were perhaps a little more attentive.' Then Kaupff smiled. 'Don't worry, Robert,' he said softly. 'The path to enlightenment is never easy.'

The professor raised his voice again to address the whole audience, though all the volunteers knew by now that for the experts, the performance was purely rhetorical. This show was for the recruits, and perhaps for Davis at the rear. 'I feel the need of a diagram,' Kaupff said, going to the blackboard and drawing a small rectangular pillar above a large circle. 'This is the lift,' he said, pointing to the chalk rectangle; and then, indicating the circle beneath, 'Here is the Earth it falls towards.'

A symbolism as crude as that of last night's iron governor displaced Robert's effortful attentiveness: the pillar was a rigid phallus, the circle its desired destination; and while Kaupff explained the inevitable effects of downwards acceleration, he extended from the pillar two thick white lines converging on the central point. 'All matter is stretched and squeezed by tidal forces,' he explained.

Robert raised his hand. 'Is that how the Moon can move the sea, even though astronauts orbiting the Earth are weightless?'

Kaupff nodded.

'And if we were to fall onto the Red Star, would we be turned into spaghetti Bolognese?'

A burst of laughter from one or two recruits, then silence as the thought struck home.

'You're right,' said Kaupff. 'The Red Star could reduce any man to a limp string of blood and tissue. But those tidal forces, in far weaker form, are present everywhere in the universe, even here in this room – this is Einstein's answer to the riddle of empty space. The stretching and squeezing of freely falling matter is an effect we can never exclude. But can we be sure that gravity is always attractive?'

For every attraction there is a corresponding repulsion: it was a political formula Robert had learned at Cromwell. It was also a way of picturing his desire for Rosalind and the anxiety it instilled in him.

'Let's return to electromagnetism,' said Kaupff. 'Imagine two charged particles, an electron and a proton, held completely immobile in space. Think of them as being like two flies on the surface of a smooth pond.'

One of them was Rosalind, the other was Robert. The laws of evolution dictated that he had to get to the other side of the pond and put his thing in her, or on her, or whatever it is that flies do. Then she'd lay eggs which would turn into maggots.

'One of the flies begins to buzz – the water ripples. This trembling surface is the electromagnetic field. Motion in one particle has caused excitations of the field, and these propagate towards the other fly or particle, so that it too begins to move. Soon the two of them are dancing together, linked by the field. The speed at which these waves move through space is the speed of light, and when we look at a star twinkling in the night sky, the electrons in our eyes are set dancing by ripples first produced tens or hundreds of years earlier by charged particles vibrating at the star's surface.'

Robert was still stuck to the pond – his fly-legs were adhering to its viscous surface and his fly-brain was beginning to feel as if it were made of glue. Kaupff's lecture was evidently aimed at a higher form of life – Robert might as well resign now from the mission and concentrate his efforts on getting a date with Rosalind. Except that once he resigned he would never see her again.

'Notice that in order to produce electromagnetic waves it's enough simply to make charged particles dance up and down. Take a long piece of wire and entice electrons to waltz from one end of it to the other – this will create radio waves which pass through space until they meet another piece of wire, a receiving aerial, whose electrons obediently perform the same dance, creating a varying electric current which we can amplify strongly enough to push a loudspeaker back and forth, making sounds in our ears.'

Miriam and her boyfriend might have turned on the radio to hide their own sexual grunting. But Mrs Frank said not to use it after ten, Robert recalled, and if she and her husband had heard the radio they would have known Miriam was in there.

'Let's apply this to gravity,' said Kaupff. 'The Red Star and our own planet are two bugs on a bigger pond whose smooth surface is the gravitational field. Give the Red Star a shake, and gravitational waves could propagate – again at the speed of light – towards Earth. The difference now is that gravity's dance is more complicated; it's the stretching and squeezing of tidal forces. Electromagnetic waves are a dance of one dimension, gravity's happen in two. Coyle, are you feeling all right?'

'Yes, sir.'

'You look pale – do you need to go outside for some air?'

'No, sir.'

'As I was saying – we've been searching for electromagnetic waves from the Red Star and have found none. We've also tried looking for gravitational waves, but these would be extremely weak, and our detectors are insufficiently sensitive. What, though, if there were a third option – a dance of no dimensions? I am talking about a scalar field.'

It was what Robert had seen erased from the blackboard in the briefing room yesterday: this name suggestive of a snake in long grass. Kaupff had probably given his lecture already to Brigadier Archibald, to Rosalind, even to the bus driver or the tea lady. Volunteers like himself were the last to know everything.

'A scalar field would be something else we could never remove from inside a jam jar,' Kaupff explained. 'At every point in space it has a certain strength, measurable by its interaction with matter, and changes in strength could propagate through space as a wave. According to the theory of quantum gravity I have been developing, the Red Star ought to generate scalar waves, detectable here on Earth.'

Davis spoke. 'Is your theory verified?'

'The Red Star will be its verification: our mission is to detect and interpret the waves.'

Macleod raised his hand. 'Sir, you spoke of a capsule. Do you mean we're to fly close to the Red Star and pick up its signals?'

'All in good time,' Kaupff said soothingly. 'At this stage let me say only that we have made enormous advances in detector technology, but one crucial element remains to be added. You, my fine young men, are that final, indispensable component.' He glanced at his watch. 'Now we must begin the technical part of the seminar. Rosalind, you will please take the volunteers downstairs for some refreshment before they commence the exercise.' Appearing to know exactly what Kaupff was talking about, she rose and bade the recruits follow her out of the room while the experts – and Davis – remained seated. Leading them back along the corridor to the lift, she waved the men inside the waiting compartment where Robert found himself squashed against one wall, while Rosalind, when she followed them in, became pressed against Forsyth. Thus their descent was a further disappointment to Robert in addition to the renewed suspicion he now harboured that the mission Kaupff proposed was not really a journey into space at all, but only an Earth-bound twiddling of knobs on a scalar-wave receiver. Perhaps, in the end, the only signals to be detected would be the fugitive emissions of the Installation's own frustrated inhabitants.

6

They came out of the lift into the foyer where a new set of students were waiting. Rosalind led her charges to the trolley and greeted the woman at it.

'Hello, Dora.'

Dora nodded in response, a silent gesture curtly indicative of acquaintance, subordination and dislike.

'Serve the boys well,' Rosalind instructed her. 'They need something strong inside them for what's coming up.'

'And what would that be, miss?' Dora said, beginning to fill cups for the recruits and speaking as if to her elder and superior, though she and Rosalind looked to be of similar age.

'You know I can't tell you,' Rosalind replied, her smile inhabiting only her mouth, while her eyes sent a different message. As soon as the volunteers were all supplied with refreshment, Rosalind beckoned them to come with her to the open doorway of Auditorium B.

'Do you see that man there?' she said quietly, indicating a portly, bearded and somewhat self-important-looking figure who was leafing through his notes at the front of the empty lecture theatre in readiness for a forthcoming talk. 'That's Brian Willoughby.'

'Who?' said Lachlan Macleod, giving voice to what all the recruits were thinking as they looked at the short, fat man, rendered even smaller by distance, who was scratching at his greying beard in response to some difficulty apparently thrown up by his own lecture notes.

'Brian Willoughby, the famous writer,' said Rosalind. 'You surely must have heard of his novel *Shipbuilders*?'

'It rings a bell,' Volunteer Harvey admitted.

'I'm not much of a reader,' said Beatty.

'Me neither,' Forsyth added.

'I've heard of him,' said Robert, trying to equate the diminutive middle-aged figure with the correspondingly fat but for that very reason far more impressive novel he was sure he had seen in the Cromwell University library, and had never read.

'He won the Dickens Prize twice,' Rosalind whispered, with an inexplicably possessive pride that sounded almost maternal. 'I must have read *Song of Freedom* at least five times. Take a good look at him – there's a man who understands a woman's heart.'

Robert felt a twinge of jealousy. This corpulent, pug-nosed and frankly ugly little man meant more to Rosalind than he ever would. He reassured himself with the thought that it was only Willoughby's status that made him impressive. Take away his books and prizes and what was there left of him except a fellow with an unpleasant habit of scratching at his bearded chin?

'Professor Kaupff invited him here,' Rosalind explained to the recruits. 'He thinks scientists should spend as much time thinking about art, politics and philosophy as they do on science. The more rounded the person, the better the results.'

'He looks rounded, all right,' said Robert, causing laughter loud enough to make the overweight writer look up from his notes. Rosalind drew her charges away from the novelist's view.

'That's an impertinent and unpatriotic way to speak about one of our greatest living treasures,' she admonished, leaving Robert feeling instantly humbled. 'In the war of ideas, one novel by Brian Willoughby is worth an aircraft carrier. So I never want to hear another disrespectful word about a man who has served the motherland so well.'

The tannoy announced the imminent start of Willoughby's lecture; the waiting students extinguished and stored their cigarettes for later reuse, returned their coffee cups and began converging towards the open door. The volunteers found themselves at the focus of this activity; Rosalind said, 'Let's go inside – I'm sure Professor Kaupff would wish you to hear at least part of the talk, and the simulator exercises can't start without us.'

The volunteers shrugged with deference rather than

eagerness. Only Robert resisted. 'If you don't mind, I prefer to wait here for you. I have a headache.'

'We shall attend to it later,' Rosalind said briskly. 'I hope you are in a better state when we come back out.' She led the others inside, the door swung closed, and Robert was left alone in the quiet foyer with only Dora for company. She was leaning gently on the trolley, one elbow delicately placed on its handlebar, watching him silently. He walked over to her.

'More?' she said with a glance at his empty cup.

'No, thanks.' He put it on the trolley, the clatter exaggerated by the lack of other sound. 'So you're Dora?' he said with a boldness born of a lack of any desire, and a curiosity inspired by nothing more than idleness and the thought of a long wait.

'Yes, I'm Dora,' she said coolly. 'I expect we'll be seeing a lot of each other.'

Robert shrugged. 'I suppose so.'

'In the Town, I mean.'

'It's a small place,' Robert conceded.

'I work nights at the Blue Cat,' she explained. 'I'm a waitress there.'

It was what the soldier on the bus had mentioned. 'Is it a restaurant?'

Dora's plain features became animated with a hint of mischief. 'Oh, you can get a meal at the Blue Cat,' she said non-committally, 'if that's what you really want. Not many people do, though.'

'You mean it's a bar?'

'You can drink, too. Listen to music.' She was still

leaning casually against the trolley and appeared to be enjoying this chance to play the role of expert. 'The Blue Cat's the sort of place where every need is catered for.' It sounded like an erotic hint but there was also a note of apathy in her voice, the tone of someone reciting a mundane fact.

'Needs?' said Robert.

From between her pursed lips a puff of breath escaped, somewhere between a sigh and whistle. 'You know what I mean, soldier. It's a whorehouse.'

'And you're a waitress there?'

'That's what I said. I expect I'll see you and your friends there sometime soon – and I won't mind if you don't say hello. It's that kind of place. In the Blue Cat, other rules apply – people you never speak to in the street are suddenly your best friends, and the people you know on the outside turn into strangers who look the other way when you meet them coming out of a love booth. It's like they always say – discretion is the better part of valour. And you're such brave men here, aren't you?'

Robert resolved never to visit the place – but why would Rosalind go? 'You know a lot about what goes on here,' he said.

'You bet I do. Five years is plenty of time to get to know everything worth knowing. Not about the work that's done – of course I don't know any of that, and I don't care. But I know about people and how they operate. I know that everyone has an inside and an outside, and what you see on the surface usually has very little to do with whatever's underneath.'

'Can't you leave?'

She tutted as if in pity and amusement at his ignorance. 'I'm Category O. The only way out for me is if my sentence gets commuted.'

'You're a prisoner?'

Dora shrugged. 'Not officially – I don't get locked up at night. I've got my own place and I earn a wage. But nobody does what I do out of choice. It was either a jail term on the outside or community service here. And now that you know, I suppose you're going to stop talking to me, because nice people like you aren't meant to fraternize with O's. You're allowed to ask me for milk and sugar but anything else is a bad idea.'

'And in the Blue Cat?'

'It's like I told you,' said Dora. 'Different rules apply.' She began to push the trolley away from him. 'Got to go upstairs now to serve the seniors. Expect I'll see you again, soldier. Don't suppose we'll have many more conversations, though.' She wheeled the urn towards the lift.

'Wait,' Robert called, hurrying after her and reaching the lift door which he pulled open, as well as the inner cage.

'How very kind of you, sir,' she said, backing into the compartment with the trolley.

He still held the door open. 'How long do you have to be a prisoner here?'

'Forever.'

'What did you do?'

'It doesn't matter what any of us did,' she said. 'We're all prisoners here, one way or another. Now let me get on with my work. It was nice knowing you.'

'I want to see you again,' he blurted, immediately surprised by what he had said.

'You'll see me here every day.'

'I don't mean that.'

'Then come to the Blue Cat,' she told him. 'Ten till two a.m., any night of the week, and you can see as much of me as you want. Bring your friends if you like.'

Robert let his grip loosen. 'Goodbye,' he said weakly. The lift sealed with a thud, and through the frosted-glass window he soon saw the cabin begin to ascend.

The lecture was well underway by now; Robert went across the foyer to the closed door of the auditorium and put his ear to it. Brian Willoughby was in full flight.

'We have to consider the significance of King Lear's actions within the historical class struggle. Shakespeare's character is in effect a bourgeois revolutionary, trying to modify the existing feudal system without overturning it: he thinks he can create a kind of family democracy over which he will still preside. We are left in no doubt as to the folly of this political experiment. Lear himself admits that "nothing will come of nothing", a remark suggesting not only Aristotelian physics but also the symbol 0, the female orifice. Lear is a nothing born of nothing – "the quality of nothing hath not such need to hide itself".'

Two women were in Robert's mind, Dora and Rosalind; two hidden nothings combined in the vacuous jar of Kaupff's earlier discourse, the plummeting container which had resurfaced in altered form as the bobbing subject of Willoughby's disquisition. Something will come in something, Robert thought, imagining the plump, self-satisfied celebrity strutting as he spoke, scratching at his bristly beard, watched by Rosalind with crossed legs and a warm glow of hero-worship rising through her body. Robert tried to follow the lecture, straining to hear the passage of *Henry V* that supposedly demonstrated an understanding of materialist necessity, and the remark about an elephant in *Troilus and Cressida* that prefigured Darwinism. None of it made any more sense than Kaupff's tadpoles and flies, though it lasted a lot longer.

Footsteps – light, rapid, feminine – disturbed Robert, coming from the other end of the foyer. It was Miriam, dressed in the grey suit he had seen her wearing this morning at the breakfast table, carrying a pile of books. Robert was dumbfounded and stood open-mouthed as she came near. 'I thought you worked in the library.'

'I do,' she said. 'There's one here in the College, another in the Town.' She raised her chin with a superior air. 'You're not the only one with a high security rating.'

'But your father . . .'

'Is Category A,' said Miriam, 'and so is Mum. But I'm B. And now I have to get on with my work.' She began to move away.

'Wait,' said Robert, taking hold of her arm, almost pinching it.

She scowled at his impudent hand, then at him. 'What do you think you're doing?'

He lowered his voice to a whisper. 'They know what you did last night.'

Miriam's face went white. 'What are you talking about?'

'You know what I mean. It was on. In your bedroom.'

She moved so close to him that her pile of books pressed equally into both their chests in what was almost a strange kind of embrace. 'Later,' she hissed. 'We can't talk here.' Then she stretched up on her toes, puckered her lips, and planted on his cheek a kiss that startled him so much he put his fingers to it, as if on a wound, when she stepped back from him, turned, and moved on without a further word.

'See you then,' he called after her, slowly realizing that her kiss was a way of confusing anyone who might have been watching, by way of some peephole or security camera, into thinking that their only secret was a romantic one. With the fading of Miriam's footsteps and the swing of a door in a distant corridor, Robert became aware again of Willoughby's voice.

'Shakespeare was no Marxist – history did not offer him that option. The Copernican revolution was still fresh, and its implications were slow to reach British shores. Yet we should no more criticize Shakespeare for his ignorance of it than we should condemn Oliver Cromwell for not having instigated communism. Each was a product of his epoch, each was instinctively aware of the rights of the proletariat, and each played his part in the ultimate triumph of socialism. For that we should all be thankful.'

Applause rang out, and Robert pulled the door of the lecture theatre ajar, then slipped inside to see the novelist's appreciative smiles while the crowd cheered him. A few people rose to their feet, and this was swiftly copied so that soon a full standing ovation was being delivered to the academician's humbly outstretched arms. Willoughby's talk had clearly made an enormous impact on this gathering of scientists and technicians, most of whom presumably understood Shakespeare no better than Robert did. The recruits were all standing, applauding, as was Rosalind, who emanated the unsullied radiance of a political campaign poster.

Her clapping hands were held high, almost at her lips, as if to offer Willoughby a kiss of infinite gratitude. What exactly had he said? Robert tried to remember one of the quotes from *Henry V* – we are all nothing except place, degree and form: a certain time, a certain position. And here was Willoughby, in the position of a famous writer, being treated as a famous writer. Here, too, was Rosalind, a nothing, being nothing – an open, receptive nothing, waiting for Willoughby to come and help himself. There were only three other women in the room, and Robert couldn't imagine Willoughby preferring any of them to Rosalind, whom he appeared to look at momentarily but significantly, rustling his notes like bed sheets. And Dora, thought Robert, a different kind of nothing – the kind that never disappears, no matter how hard you try to erase its trace.

Willoughby had drunk enough applause now; he gave a last wave and lowered his head, moving away from the lectern as the clapping faded, stuffing his notes into a leather briefcase. It marked the breaking of a spell; Willoughby was once more a shambling academic with a slight limp evident in his heavy gait, and people began moving towards the exit where Robert stood.

'You missed an inspiring talk,' Rosalind told him.

'I heard some of it through the door.'

'Then I hope it cured your headache, because now it's time for us to go to the simulator.'

7

When they got back onto the bus that stood waiting outside, Rosalind told Robert to sit beside her. 'Your state of health concerns me.'

'It was only a headache. It's gone now.'

'Is it an after-effect of your illness?'

'I don't think so.'

She lowered her voice. 'Kaupff suspects you may be the best man to pilot the capsule. We can't let the mission be jeopardized by a migraine.' The bus revved into motion but soon halted again at a checkpoint. The driver leaned out of his side window to speak with the guard.

Robert said, 'To be honest, I didn't feel like sitting through the lecture; there was nothing wrong with me. Though from what I heard of Willoughby's talk, nothingness is a subject he's very interested in.'

'Then I'm glad you learned something.' They moved on, entering some kind of industrial complex.

'I had an interesting conversation with Dora about the Blue Cat.'

'She's Category O – if you speak to her again at the College I may have to inform Commissioner Davis.'

'Do you ever go there?' Robert asked. Through the window he could see a towering maze of pipes and gantries in which the only humans were tiny yellow-helmeted workmen on aerial walkways.

'Everyone goes,' said Rosalind. 'It's the only night spot in the Installation. You'll find Professor Vine there nearly every night with his colleagues, talking physics and doing calculations on the tablecloths. They have to take them away afterwards for security reasons – it drives the staff nuts.'

'Does Kaupff go?'

'He prefers to spend his evenings in the Lodge. Why are you so interested in the Blue Cat?'

'Dora told me it's a brothel.'

Rosalind fell silent for a moment. She glanced round at the other volunteers as if to see whether any of them had overheard. 'Don't believe anything you hear from an O. She's dirt, nothing but trouble. For your own good, stay away from her.'

They arrived at what looked like a blast-proof door on an otherwise featureless concrete building, as big as an apartment block, painted in green and black camouflage. 'All change,' Rosalind announced, and once everyone was off, the huge door began grinding open with a mechanical whirr.

What they saw inside was a kind of hangar, windowless but brilliantly lit by powerful floodlights, teeming with technicians who scurried purposefully like ants beneath a stone. Rosalind could no doubt have brought the volunteers in by some smaller side entrance; her purpose was theatrical, and the effect succeeded, because what the sliding door revealed to the recruits drew a unanimous gasp of wonder. Kaupff had been teasing them, giving them cause to doubt whether it really was a space mission they were embarking on; but here was the evidence standing before them, in the centre of the hangar, tethered by electrical cables. Here was the capsule that Robert was to command.

It was a tapering white cylinder some ten or twelve

metres high; a smooth metal craft with a large red star painted on its side and the initials of the British Democratic Republic arranged vertically beneath. It had no portholes, no visible means of propulsion, as if the object were designed to convey its passive occupants magically into orbit.

'It's beautiful,' Robert whispered.

The capsule was supported on a massive platform beneath which thick steel pistons could be seen amid a tangle of wires and tubing, tended by numerous white-coated engineers who inspected the jumble intently.

'It's not the real thing,' said Rosalind.

'What?' Robert was still as spellbound by it as the others.

'This is the simulator,' she told them. 'It's where you'll be trained.' It looked real enough – but that was because at this stage there was still so little of it for them to see. Even the entry hatch was hidden from sight, on the far side. 'Come this way,' she said, leading them along one wall of the hangar to a railed viewing area from which they could see the vehicle's small circular door hinged open while a technician crawled inside.

'Not much room in there for five,' Forsyth muttered. 'Worse than the lift we all squeezed in this morning.'

Rosalind looked at them. 'Haven't you understood yet? You won't all be going.'

The hatch closed, there was a loud hissing, and a moment later the capsule gave a shudder as its supporting platform rumbled into motion. A klaxon sounded, a red light flashed, the volunteers watched a spectacle they took to be routine;

but engineers were shouting, running. This was not routine: it was an emergency.

'I think someone's trapped inside!' Rosalind exclaimed.

The capsule shook and juddered on its platform while a squad of men leapt up to try and open the hatch, some of them stumbling and being thrown clear by the machine's violent motion. Suddenly it halted and gave a loud dying groan, then a moment later the hatch sprung open and the dazed prisoner stuck his head out, beaming. A great cheer went up.

'He could have been killed,' Rosalind gasped, then saw how the volunteers were staring at her. 'Don't worry, boys, you'll be securely restrained when you use it.'

While operations swiftly returned to normality, she led them through a swing door that took them into a corridor lined with offices and workshops, where she began explaining what went on, as though the near-disaster had never occurred.

'That's the imaging team,' she said, pointing into a room where men and women were looking at computer screens with colour pictures on them: something none of the volunteers had ever before seen, or even thought possible. 'Telemetry is over there, and around the corner is ballistics.'

They followed Rosalind past an encyclopedia of scientific specialisms until at last they reached her own. Bringing a key from her pocket, she unlocked the plain white door of her office and ushered them inside. 'Do make yourselves comfortable,' she said, though there were no chairs except the one behind her desk, positioned in a corner of the large room. There was a bookcase too, a filing cabinet and a blackboard on the wall; but most of the floor was taken up by a square woven rug, Turkish in appearance, on which plump cushions were scattered in an approximate circle, as if in preparation for an informal discussion group.

'Some people need the cushions but I prefer to do without,' said Rosalind, casually removing her shoes after having taken off her coat, then going past the volunteers to the far end of the rug where she kneeled down, her coarse grey skirt being long enough to cover her legs. 'Come, join me.'

It was an unusual situation for the volunteers, and after some embarrassed hesitation they did as she invited, taking off their coats and boots and finding a space on the carpet – though each of the men required rather more room than Rosalind occupied, since most stretched out their legs, trying to use the large cushions as a support for their backs.

'My field is psychophysics,' she explained. 'The relationship between mind and matter. And before we go any further, I should like to teach you all a better way to sit.' She hitched up her dress, exposing her stockinged knees and pink thighs without a qualm, and began to bend her legs into shape. 'This is the lotus position,' she said, though every man was more concerned with the way that Rosalind's pale-blue knickers – strictly utilitarian in form yet no less arousing in appearance – were freely revealed in the course of her demonstration. It was only when she had completed her adoption of the difficult posture that she draped the loose cloth of her hitched dress onto the floor before her lap, allowing only her knees and thighs to remain visible. 'You might prefer the half lotus,' she said calmly, 'in which just one foot is brought up onto the calf. Or else simply cross your legs.' Macleod rolled over a few times as he made a game attempt at the full lotus, but the others expended less effort. Forsyth, sitting directly opposite Robert, had his legs splayed to reveal a very obvious erection.

Rosalind looked from one volunteer to the next, examining each man's posture. What she saw in Forsyth was mirrored in other volunteers too. 'I'm glad you find yoga so stimulating. It demonstrates an important fact of psychophysics: mind affects matter. For example,' she said, nonchalantly adjusting her dress and revealing once more, for a deliberate moment, her underwear, 'if we feel a certain emotion, this can have measurable physical consequences. Fear or joy correspond to specific secretions, changes in pulse or perspiration. Sexual arousal has evident manifestations, so strong and powerful they even led some foolish male philosophers to think that all matter is really a product of mind, in which case the world is little more than a wet dream. This idealism may have suited bourgeois nineteenth-century professors who imagined their great mental systems would be a terrific way of impressing women – but I am not impressed.' One or two men gave a nervous laugh, but each now felt as Robert did – somehow invaded and abused by this strange manipulation, like the lewd stunt of a stage hypnotist in a fairground tent. 'Nor were Marx and Engels impressed,' Rosalind continued. 'Mind is made of matter – this is the philosophy of materialism – and we have a clear demonstration of its truth in this room. You see part of a female body, you become erect, and you think of sex. This is the order in which it happens, as we know from animals, who see a potential mate, become sexually prepared, but don't think anything at all. They just stick it in, and nature

– matter – does the rest. If any of you are now thinking about sex it is only because you received a visual stimulus – a material phenomenon – which caused a physiological modification in your body that has now acted on your mind.'

Macleod burst into laughter and started shaking his head.

'Is something wrong, Volunteer Macleod?'

'I'm sorry, but I can't quite believe this is for real.'

'I beg your pardon?' she said sternly.

'Well, what's this got to do with going into space? Are we meant to wank ourselves into orbit?'

There was an outbreak of sniggering which offered the men some relief, but Rosalind soon silenced it. 'How do you know you aren't?' she said. 'You know nothing about the mission, except that the frozen star possibly emits scalar waves which we have to find a way of detecting. You sniff a woman, Macleod, and you go hard. Source and receiver, signal and antenna – that is psychophysics, and your feelings count only to the extent that they are phenomena that can be analysed and if necessary eliminated from the experiment. If you cannot overcome embarrassment, gentlemen, what hope is there that you will conquer fear?'

Once more she looked at each volunteer in turn, assessing his posture and physique. Forsyth's erection, so prominent before, had wilted. The mood in the room was one of oppression – Rosalind had made clear to them the power she held, and each volunteer knew that the final selection would be a process in which she played an important part. Perhaps involuntary arousal had already cost one or two of them a place in the capsule – who could say? Yet suddenly she appeared more relaxed. 'I want you to perform some yoga for at least fifteen minutes every day – do try the lotus, though here is another position which is also very beneficial.' She uncrossed her legs, got up from the floor and squatted on all fours like a dog. 'The curve of the back is most important. Start like this, then slowly look down, stretching the neck.' The men watched her demonstration, then reluctantly made their own half-hearted attempts to copy. 'And back up again . . . raise . . . stretch . . . don't jerk.'

After a while she called a halt and stood up, performing this last move rather more gracefully than the men who followed. She walked barefoot across the room to the filing cabinet, pulled open one of its heavy drawers, and took out a manila folder. 'Let's try an experiment,' she said, handing out sheets of blank paper and pencils to the men. 'I am going to look through an ordinary pack of playing cards and I want each of you to try and guess whether the card I'm seeing is red or black. Simply write R or B on your sheet. I want no conferring, no copying and most all,' she looked at Macleod, 'no giggling. This is a serious task and I want to see how you perform. Now go and settle yourselves anywhere you like.'

Most of the men sat back down on the rug while Rosalind went to her desk. Robert moved towards the far wall and stood leaning against it, the sheet of paper folded small enough in his hand so that he could easily scribble on it while also keeping his answers hidden.

'Here is the deck,' said Rosalind. Held together with a rubber band, it looked no different from the kind the men might play pontoon with. She snapped off the band, put the cards face down on the table, and lifted the first so that the men could see only its back. 'Each time I raise a card you must think carefully and try to decide its colour.' There was a scratching of pencils as one or two volunteers immediately wrote an answer, but Rosalind held the card aloft for some time, encouraging them to concentrate. Robert stared at it, and in his mind he saw an eight of spades. He wrote B.

Rosalind made her own note, drew the next card, and again waited while the recruits guessed. In this way they slowly went through most of the pack, until after ten long minutes the experiment was declared finished. She instructed the candidates to write their names on their sheets and bring them to her desk, then sent them back to wait on the rug like kindergarten pupils while she marked their answers.

This was another guessing game, played in tense silence as the five men watched the flicking of Rosalind's wrist. Eventually she looked up. 'Macleod?'

He stood and took a pace forward. 'Yes, ma'am?'

'You are free to go.'

'What?'

'You will be escorted out by a member of the technical staff.'

Macleod was stunned. 'You mean I'm off the mission?'

'You will be assigned other duties,' Rosalind calmly told him, almost as if reading from a script. 'You will continue to serve in a significant supportive role but you will not proceed to simulator training.'

Macleod was still trying to take in what he was hearing; his fellow recruits were on their feet too, equally appalled by the abruptness of Rosalind's decision. 'All this because of a pack of cards?' he said, anger rising in him. 'Because of a pack of fucking cards?'

She was unmoved. 'Selection is not a simple process, Volunteer Macleod.'

'And what gives you the right to throw me off? You bring us here and do a mind-reading game and then that's it, go home. Don't you know how much this means to me, and to all of us lads? Don't you understand, you heartless fucking bitch?'

Still she was unperturbed. 'Volunteer Macleod, I am not a member of the armed services but I am of superior technical rank within the Installation, and I have the right, if I wish, to put you on a charge for insubordination.'

'Fucking well do it, then, whore!' He looked as if he might make a lunge towards the desk she sat behind – Harvey and Forsyth immediately offered comradely restraint, but he shook them off, regaining his physical composure though speaking with the same undiminished force. 'I'll go,' he said. 'Obviously I've got no choice in the matter and no right of appeal. But I'll tell you this – I'll tell all of you. If we're meant to put our lives on the line and risk our fucking necks for the sake of some bird who gets a kick out of flashing her knickers at us, then I say this mission is a fucking disaster from square one. If that's insubordination then you'd better put me on a charge, but I'm telling you, miss, the British armed forces aren't the sort of men you can fuck around with. And that's what you've been doing with us for the last hour – no, since we first saw you yesterday.'

Rosalind quietly interrupted him. 'Everything you say

confirms the correctness of the decision made yesterday by the selection committee which I am now officially delivering to you after having allowed due time for reconsideration. No one questions your loyalty, your abilities or your patriotism, Volunteer Macleod. This mission requires a certain kind of human being, and it has been established that you are not of that kind. You will be assigned other duties.'

Macleod's proud figure was hunched and drooping as he gave in to the inevitability of his dismissal. 'So it was already sorted yesterday?'

'I can't discuss details,' she told him. 'Volunteer Beatty, you too will be redeployed.'

Beatty's jaw fell at the news. All the men were by now too demoralized to respond, and Beatty made no complaint. Forsyth offered him a consoling handshake; Robert wondered whose name would be next on Rosalind's lips. Macleod was still seething but Beatty looked close to tears. All he could say, after a painful silence, was, 'Will my mum be told?'

'Of course not,' said Rosalind. 'Whatever part you play in the mission, successful or otherwise, the world will never know. Now, Volunteers Macleod and Beatty, please step outside, where you will find your escort.'

The three remaining recruits watched them leave, and no other name was called. Robert was still in the mission, along with Forsyth and Harvey. Outrage turned to quiet jubilation, each man registering a sudden improvement of his odds.

Rosalind behaved as if nothing had happened. 'It's time for lunch,' she told the lucky trio, putting on her shoes again, then lifting her small shoulder bag from the floor beside the desk where she had left it. 'I'll take you to the canteen, then we shall begin using the simulator.'

8

The dining area was not far from Rosalind's office; at the serving counter, three women in white aprons delivered the single available meal option: vegetable soup followed by gammon, boiled potatoes and peas, with a small moulded jelly topped by a swirl of synthetic cream to finish. Only in the matter of drinks was there any choice: it could be water, apple juice or tea.

'Simple but nutritious,' Rosalind remarked to her companions, quoting a well-known and widely mocked Food Board slogan while the three men lined up with her in the short queue that soon began to lengthen behind them with the arrival of other customers.

'More like cheap and cheerful,' Forsyth commented, though the carefully measured rations which the women behind the counter gave him soon afterwards did not come with a smile. 'I'll find us a place,' he said, bearing his tray towards the ranks of still mostly empty stools, followed by Harvey and Robert. They settled themselves at the far end of one of the long tables, Robert sitting opposite the other two, and when Rosalind joined them after paying the bill she put her tray beside Robert's.

'There's something I have to give you,' she told them, reaching into her bag and bringing out three long booklets of vouchers, which she distributed to the recruits. 'These are what we use here instead of money. The denominations are small but you can't get change with them, so if you only want a loaf of bread make sure you buy something else as well.'

Harvey leafed through the thick booklet, whose perforated pages were pink, blue or white according to value. 'Can we convert them into cash when we leave?'

Rosalind shook her head. 'These are only for day-to-day expenses,' she explained. 'Your service wages will continue to be paid into a fund while you're here – and if the mission is successful there will be other rewards.'

Harvey smiled contentedly and fanned the flimsy vouchers beneath his face. He seemed oblivious to what Robert knew and increasingly accepted: that they might never leave.

'Let me tell you more about my research,' Rosalind said between sips of her hot soup. 'Before I came to the Installation I was part of a team investigating the effects of strong electromagnetic fields on particular regions of the human brain. It has therapeutic uses in curing depression.'

'You mean shock treatment?' Harvey asked.

'That's what lay people tend to call one version of it. I was more interested in finding how artificial stimulation can affect an individual's personality and opinions. If a sufficiently intense field is applied to the temporal lobe, for instance, the subject will start to believe in the existence of God.'

The recruits were surprised and sceptical.

'It's perfectly true,' she assured them. 'When the field is switched on, the person has a tremendously powerful sense of being at one with the infinite – subjects in our experiments described a profound peace, a kind of floating on air, a benign spiritual presence.'

'And when the field was switched off?' Robert asked.

'It stopped,' said Rosalind. 'All the belief, all the irrational certainty they briefly felt; it vanished as they reverted to their normal, healthy selves. So now we know the origin of religion: it's a disorder of the particular brain region on which we experimented. A few people have strong, spontaneous electrical activity there. The research I carried out offers hope of a cure.'

They pondered it while they ate, then Robert said, 'What about drugs? Could they have the same effect?'

'I don't know. I think it would be very difficult to target a specific brain area.'

Harvey said, 'Do you still do these electrical experiments?'

'Yes.'

'Who on?' Forsyth asked.

'Psychiatric patients, convicts, military personnel.'

All three men stared silently at her. 'Are you going to be sticking wires on our heads?' said Forsyth.

'Other parts too. It's what you consented to. If you want to back out now—'

'No,' Forsyth immediately interrupted. 'I'm in this all the way.'

'Me too,' said Harvey.

'And you, Coyle?' Rosalind looked at him challengingly. 'Is it all for one and one for all?' He nodded. 'Good. I'm glad I have your support. If Professor Kaupff is right, scalar waves might interact with human tissue in a way similar to electromagnetic fields. Your minds could be the detectors we need.'

Robert was struggling to make sense of it. 'Do you mean these waves might transfer thoughts? Are we meant to get to the Red Star by telepathy?'

'We have to consider every possibility,' Rosalind said brusquely. She picked at the rest of her food then stood up. 'I have to go and find out how things are proceeding in the hangar; the simulator may have been damaged by the incident we saw earlier. Stay here and have some coffee if you like – it's one pink voucher per cup.' She went quickly out, leaving the three men to mull over what they had learned. None had much appetite for imitation jellies that owed more to cow bones and tree bark than anything resembling a strawberry.

'So now we know,' Forsyth said with resignation. 'We're guinea pigs, lab rats.' His brow furrowed as he looked at his companions.

'I knew it already,' said Robert, telling them how he had fallen ill. 'Maybe they gave you both the same drug too, but you weren't allergic.'

Harvey was pensive. 'It couldn't have worked on me – I don't feel any different from usual.'

'It's what we've signed up to,' Forsyth said ruefully. 'And we've got to see it through – right, lads?' With his elbow on the table, he extended his fist for the other two to hold.

'To the end,' they vowed.

'Now I've got to take a leak,' Harvey declared. 'Where's the lav?'

Forsyth had seen it, and gave directions. 'I expect it won't only be pish coming out your old man after that performance we got from Rosalind.' All three laughed, but as soon as Harvey left, Forsyth grew more serious. 'I reckon it's either you or me,' he told Robert.

'What do you mean?'

'Rosalind and Kaupff have got it sorted between them, they're stringing us along so that we'll do all these experiments they want. Harvey'll be next for the heave-ho, I get that off Rosalind's face, the way she looks at him. Then they keep us two going with the promise of a place in the capsule – maybe draw straws when the big day comes. Assuming the capsule even exists.'

'You think they might be bluffing?'

'Who knows. And all this spy stuff – what do you make of that? This Installation's a weird fucking place, no mistake. Not surprising since there's all these people never get out to the real world to see what's going on. They've even got fucking toy money!' He leaned closer. 'What I'd like to know is where we're meant to find ourselves some fanny. We're not going to last a few weeks here without any relief except the kind Harvey's probably giving himself now in the bog. Where's all the talent?' he asked, shrugging as he looked round the dining hall, almost all of whose occupants were male. 'Where do these blokes get their satisfaction? Are they all homos or what?'

'There's the Town.'

'My landlady's as old as my mum,' Forsyth said dismissively. 'And from what little I've seen out of the bus, this place isn't exactly heaving with birds. Fine for Rosalind, of course, getting her jollies prick-teasing us poor sods, but I'm damned if I'll be spending all my nights here shaking hands with the bishop.'

Robert suggested they start spending some of their toy money on coffee. 'I'll get the first round,' he said, going to the counter with his booklet of vouchers and offering them to the fat girl at the till, who was not much older than he was but had a blowsy air of worldly experience.

'You're a rich one,' she told him, tearing out two pink slips for the drinks, leaning over the counter as she did so, making one of her large breasts rest on the booklet. Beneath her white hat her pinned black hair was greasy, and the flesh of her bare neck looked mottled. She was coarse and unattractive, yet with Forsyth's banter still ringing in his ears, Robert imagined squeezing that heavy breast. She looked up at him, caught his gaze, and there was a moment of understanding between them. 'Spend some of it on me if you like,' she suggested with a wink. He said nothing more, but went back to Forsyth with two milky coffees in glass cups and saucers.

'That Rosalind,' Forsyth resumed, 'she gave me such a stonner when we were all sat on the rug.'

'I could see it through your trousers.'

Forsyth laughed. 'You can get slung out the forces for spying on a fellow's todger.'

'I could hardly help seeing it.'

'I have to admit it's an outstanding natural feature. But where's it going to get some exercise? Where's the fucking whorehouse in this place?'

'It's called the Blue Cat,' Robert informed him.

Forsyth was taken aback. 'And how come you're the

fucking expert, Casanova? Let's go there tonight. You, me and Harvey – boys' night out. After all, we've got to get rid of these vouchers somehow – and I'm not spending them all on this fucking acorn juice they call coffee. Hang on, here comes trouble.' Rosalind and Harvey could be seen coming into the dining hall together, both looking grave.

'Bad news,' Harvey announced on reaching their table.

Robert and Forsyth immediately had the same thought: Harvey was off the mission. They were wrong.

'The platform's still not operational,' Rosalind explained. 'The simulator's out of action – we can't do anything with it this afternoon. So the three of you have some free time. I can arrange for the bus to drop you anywhere you like in the Town – the bowling alley, perhaps?'

Forsyth looked at Robert with a sly smile, then at Rosalind. 'How about the Blue Cat?'

'That's for tonight,' she said, completely unfazed. 'It is now half-past one, and Professor Kaupff expects all of us to be back at the College for five, so I shall ask the bus driver to take you to the centre of Town where you can do as you wish. You'll be collected from the same place at four thirty. If you should visit one of the pubs, do not consume more than two units of alcohol or else I shall put you on a charge and possibly terminate your involvement in the mission. You may fraternize with women but should not engage in any lewd or immoral conduct. Now let me take you to the bus. I have faith in all three of you.'

9

The men were deposited beside the Freedom Monument at one end of the Town's main street; a white cenotaph resembling those found throughout the Republic to commemorate victims of the patriotic fight against tyranny and oppression; though this one bore few names, since, as the recruits had already learned, there had been only a small village here prior to the founding of the Installation. Where the people of that village had gone, and what had become of their houses and livelihoods, one could only guess.

It was a bright, sunny winter's day, but Forsyth was in little mood for strolling. 'Let's try that pub,' he said, pointing to a place whose nature was evident from the lamp over the door and the frosted-glass windows. The others complied, and soon all three were crossing the threshold of a dreary establishment that could have been situated anywhere, its interior an assortment of nicotine browns. The floor was sticky with spilled beer, and the only other customers were four elderly men who sat playing dominoes at a wooden table. They barely turned their heads to see the new arrivals walking straight to the bar.

'All right, pet?' Forsyth said to the middle-aged woman behind the counter.

'What'll it be?'

He quickly glanced at his companions on either side and asked them, 'Large?' They shrugged assent, and Forsyth ordered a round of Victory Ale. 'Just what we're needing,' he said to them as the drinks were poured.

'That'll be three, please.'

He brought out his voucher book, tore off the correct amount and smiled to his companions. 'Good system, eh?' Then he led them to a table some distance away from the old men, who they now could see were playing for matchsticks. 'Wonder how much it costs for a leg-over with auntie behind the bar,' he whispered once they sat down.

'Save it for the Blue Cat,' said Harvey, taking a sip of flat beer. 'Cheers.'

'We'll probably see her again there anyway,' Forsyth added. 'I reckon every woman in the camp doubles as a whore – workers for peace and all that.' A long-running campaign had encouraged people to take up a second occupation, and he saw no reason why the same principle shouldn't apply inside the Installation.

The beer was weak but Robert still felt its effect with the first sip he took, spreading a rich hoppiness through his palate and a lightness to his head. 'I'd better go easy on this,' he said. 'One's the limit for me.'

Forsyth looked puzzled. 'Not much of a drinker, are you? What sort of regiment are you from?'

Robert confessed he had been conscripted after failing university, and Harvey smiled. 'Spud peeler, eh? And an intellectual. Well, one's my limit too.'

'Rosalind said two,' Forsyth insisted.

'She meant that as a maximum, not a requirement – don't make Einstein here get a headache.' Harvey looked at Robert again. 'Now I know why you went straight to the top of the class – reckon they want you as the brains and us as the brawn.'

Forsyth asked Harvey, 'Make any sense of those lectures this morning?'

'Nope.'

'Me neither. Too busy thinking about fanny. And too thick. How about you, Professor?'

Robert swallowed a mouthful of beer. 'All I've worked out so far is that everything's connected to everything else.'

Forsyth laughed. 'Thank you, Confucius. Why can't they just tell us about the space capsule?' He saw how his careless remark made the others look nervously towards the old men and the barwoman. 'Don't get fucking paranoid,' he said, more quietly. 'We're still on the inside here. Everybody's doing something secret and they all know to keep their eyes, ears and traps shut.'

'I wonder what sort of experiments they got used in,' Harvey said mournfully, nodding towards the oblivious domino players.

'I expect they spent years making bombs and now they're allowed a bit of rest,' said Forsyth. 'And good luck to them.' One of the old men appeared to have noticed he was being observed; he turned and looked towards the recruits, and Forsyth raised his glass. 'Cheers, comrade.'

'And yersel',' the old man replied, resuming his earnest contemplation of the dominoes standing upright on the table before him.

Harvey was still watching them. 'Reckon we'll end up like that? Still here when we're old men, our brains dried up? Or else dead?'

Forsyth gave him a comforting pat. 'Nobody wants his arse shot off but that didn't stop us joining up, did it? Take the risk, make yourself a hero, and don't waste the best years of your life being a fucking coward. Of course, it's different for college boy here – expect you must be shitting yourself by now, eh?'

It wasn't meant in a hostile way; Forsyth was used to dealing with all things in life – from mortal danger to human sensitivities – by not thinking about them; but in any case Robert was not offended, because whatever fear he felt was as abstract and remote as the life he had left: he wasn't afraid to die because in some sense he was already dead. Harvey was the only one of them who seemed unduly stressed.

'For all we know,' Harvey whispered, 'those old codgers might be making a report to send to Rosalind. They could be part of the selection panel.'

'That's fucking mental,' Forsyth opined. 'Look, if we're going to live in this place without turning into headcases there's two things we need sorted. Regular fanny, that's priority number one, and the other is treating this place like any normal town – they work hard enough to make it look like one so we'd best go along with the pretence.' He quaffed the rest of his beer in a few gulps, then scrutinized the foam-lined glass in his hand with the tenderness of a connoisseur. 'I'm for another. Whose round?'

Harvey's glass was still half full. 'I'll get you it next time. I need some air.'

Robert, too, had drunk enough. 'I'll join you.'

Forsyth was unconcerned. 'I'll have that second one on my tod, then,' he said, calling to the barmaid for another measure. 'And one for yourself, pet,' he added as she began to pour, to which she nodded in customary gratitude. Forsyth got up to collect his ale; Robert and Harvey rose too, and took their leave, walking out to the bright street with shouts and laughter behind them, from the old men whose game had ended.

'Let's do some sightseeing,' Robert suggested. 'Should take us at least ten minutes.'

They walked along the main street, looking through shop windows at the sparse displays. Harvey was still preoccupied. 'This place is so weird,' he said, gazing at a newsagent's magazine rack.

'It's like an ordinary town – that's what's so weird.'

Harvey shook his head. 'No, there's more to it.' His voice dropped to a whisper while they walked. 'It's like everyone's brainwashed, hypnotized. But we're different.'

'The medication must have changed over the years,' Robert guessed.

'Or they're trying something new on us. Sending signals into our heads, controlling us.'

At the butcher's there was a queue of women, wrapped in thick coats, stretching out onto the pavement, and through the open doorway the volunteers heard the shopkeeper's gruff patter. 'Right, ladies, no more than one kilo each and don't ask me for anything but mutton because mutton's what I've got.'

'Nothing strange about that,' Robert observed.

Further along they stopped to look at a naked mannequin in a clothes-shop window; a hairless woman made of plastic, her arm raised, upturned palm outstretched. Harvey gazed at the dummy, then said, 'Do you reckon Forsyth's all talk?'

'Possibly.'

'And what about you? Have you ever . . . ?'

'No.'

'Me neither.' He continued to stare at the sexless static figure whose smooth breasts lacked nipples and whose groin was completely featureless. 'I like looking at a woman as much as any man but it's never been too much of a problem for me, not having a bird. Expect it's the bromide.'

Robert smiled. 'That story was made up in the Patriotic War because soldiers couldn't understand why they'd lost their sex drive. It was stress that did it, not something in their tea.'

Harvey glared at him. 'And what makes you so sure it was something in your tea that made you ill?' He looked at the mannequin again, his face a mixture of fascination and loathing. 'In this place everything's the other way round. Since we got here yesterday it's like I've had sex on the brain – they're messing with our minds. When Rosalind was flashing her legs at us and we all got hard, that wasn't natural, was it?'

'I suppose not,' said Robert, remembering the delicious but illusory moment in the lift, and wondering what truth there is in anything we feel.

Harvey glanced both ways along the street to make sure there was no chance of being overheard, then said quietly, 'When I left you after lunch to go to the toilet, I sat down in one of the cubicles in the gents, had a smoke and a crap, then reckoned I needed some relief.'

'Sounds perfectly natural to me.'

'I was sat there with cig in one hand and knob in the other when I heard the outer door swing open, somebody coming in. Another bloke needing the loo, I thought, but no. A few quick footsteps – a woman's walk. Cleaner?

Maybe – best stop tossing, have a drag and start whistling. Then who should I hear but Rosalind. "Volunteer Harvey?" she says. "Yes," I say back, "what's up?" And she says to me, "Are you masturbating?" Just like that. And I say no, of course, but she says, "I think you are." What do you make of that?'

'That's her style. Clinical, no nonsense. Did she leave you then?'

'No, she stood outside the cubicle, waiting. I could hear her shoes on the floor when she shifted position now and again. I could hear the movement of her clothes. After a while I could even hear her breathing. I said to her, "Are you needing in?" and she said no. I said, "Are you wanting me to come out?" and she said, "Only when you finish what you have to do." Too bad, I thought, save it for later, but then something else sparked in my head, like a switch. Fuck her, I thought. And the next thing I knew I had my chopper in my hand, pumping it like nobody's business, making no effort to keep quiet. I don't know what happened to me – I was like a madman, all I could hear was the sound of her feet, her clothes, her breath, my own gasping, and her voice in my head telling me what to do. Yes, she was controlling it, I don't know how, but she was. I shot my load all over the door. Instantly felt a complete fool. And she says, "Are you finished, Volunteer Harvey?" She even waited while I wiped it off the door – she must have heard all of that. I came out and washed my hands, hardly able to look her in the eye, and we came back to find you in the dining hall. I'm embarrassed enough even talking to you about it. Don't tell Forsyth.'

'I won't,' Robert promised, moving away from the shop window, prompting Harvey to follow.

'I don't like any of this,' Harvey said earnestly. 'Forsyth's right, we're lab rats – and it's got fuck all to do with spaceships. The simulator's only a way of conning us.' They reached the end of the main street; there was a small park ahead with a dry fountain and some empty benches. Harvey gave a contemptuous laugh. 'Lab rats in Toy Town. My mum's in a wheelchair and lives on the fifth floor of a block of flats where the lift never works. They said if I volunteered they'd move her up the rehousing queue, so here I am. Wanking for welfare. Funny way to help your old lady, isn't it?' He pulled his sleeve to inspect his wristwatch. 'Ages till we get picked up. Mind if I take a bit of time on my own?'

'Sure,' said Robert. 'See you later.' He watched Harvey walk dejectedly away and felt glad that the alteration in his own mind had been more beneficial. Then, wondering how best to fill the next two hours, he decided to visit the library. Rosalind had indicated it from the bus yesterday; a red-brick building, unimpressive in appearance but easy to find after a few minutes' walk, its entrance open. Going inside, Robert half expected to see Miriam again, but the only staff member – in fact the only other person visible in the place – was a spectacled woman sitting at a desk, busying herself with a dog-eared card index. She remained ostentatiously unaware of his presence.

Robert made his way to the contemporary literature section, intending only to kill time, and among the books soon noticed Brian Willoughby's *Shipbuilders*. Smartly bound and frequently borrowed, judging from the date stamps crowded on the label inside, the book's cover offered a condensed version of the author's illustrious career; an Alpine range of dizzying achievements whose peaks were various prizes, honours, professorships and distinctions, including presidency of the Writers' Union. Robert turned to the first chapter and made a start on it, finding it to be about an old, dying woman looking out of her slum window at smoke from factory chimneys, then expiring just before her son could get home from his night shift, having been refused leave by the shipyard foreman. Robert could see it all in his head – the woman, the slum, the grimy yard – and this was the mark of great literature, he supposed, in which case he grudgingly understood Rosalind's admiration. But then he reread the first paragraph, in which the old woman beheld chimney smoke 'curdling like sour milk against the anaemic dawn', and the sheer impossibility of this fine-sounding phrase was like a welcome revelation. What he had been seeing while reading the story, Robert realized, was the work of his own imagination, not Willoughby's, whose only achievement had been to elicit stock responses, like those aroused by Rosalind's bare legs. To call Willoughby great because of the effect he could produce in a receptive mind was like calling Rosalind beautiful because she had made brainwashed men go hard.

Robert put the book back on the shelf and wondered if he ought to do some private cramming. He had left *Rocket to the Stars* at home but could surely find something equally relevant. So he went to the desk where the woman sat, still thumbing cards as if computing the futility of her employment, and waited for her to notice his existence. Eventually she looked up. 'Can I help you?'

'Have you got anything by Einstein?'

Her eyebrows rose behind her spectacles. 'If you're looking for technical literature you need signed authorization, you ought to know that.'

Robert shrugged. 'I thought you might have something about relativity. Something that isn't technical.'

She looked penetratingly at his uniform, his haircut, his eyes. 'Come back with a properly completed green form and I'll be happy to assist you.'

'But where do I get a green form?'

'You should know that already.' She returned to the more pleasant company of her faded cards, and Robert went back to the book stacks. He was damned if he was going to spend any more time reading Brian bloody Willoughby; instead he tracked down a volume of Goethe's poems. He wanted to find the one Kaupff had mentioned, about being in the woods at night. But although the book had German and English texts alongside one another, and lists of titles and first lines in both languages, it lacked the one thing that would have been really useful: an index of what the poems were about. Robert searched in vain, trying to make sense either of the German texts or of what in many cases were equally obscure translations. *So let me seem, until I become*: what the hell was that supposed to mean?

Eventually it was time to go. Trying to borrow the book would be another exercise in bureaucracy, so Robert returned it to its place and walked towards the exit, pausing however at the desk where the librarian looked up. 'Remember the green form next time.'

This wasn't what he had intended to raise. 'Miriam Frank works here, doesn't she?'

The librarian's face was like ice. 'I can't discuss that.' She was in the lowest-rated part of the Installation and treated every piece of information within reach of her polished fingernails as if it were the most precious state secret: it was how she maintained her self-respect when all she did was stamp books and fill in cards. 'Just remember that green form.'

He left without a further word. Outside, the sky had grown dark, a few stars were shining, and when he reached the main street he found it even less animated than before. Forsyth was already waiting at the Freedom Monument.

'Hey, college boy. Find any fanny?'

Robert shook his head. 'What about you?'

'No luck. And both the pubs here are shite.'

'How many more beers did you have?' Robert was surprised at how perfectly sober Forsyth appeared.

He put a finger to his nose. 'Classified info. Want a mint?' Forsyth brought a packet from his tunic pocket. 'Here's Harvey coming.'

Robert turned to see the third recruit arrive behind him, looking more cheerful now, greeting them with a laugh. 'All right, lads?'

'You get your end away?' Forsyth asked, offering him a mint too, though it was only Forsyth whose breath needed masking.

Harvey shot a glance at Robert, then said to both, 'Fresh air did me good. Chance to get things in perspective.'

A pair of headlights swung into view; not the bus that had brought them, but a car that halted beside the monument and stood waiting with its engine ticking, the driver looking towards them in silent instruction.

'Here's our ride,' said Harvey, going towards the rear door.

'Hope it won't be the only kind we get,' Forsyth quipped, taking the door on the other side and leaving Robert to sit in front. It was the same driver who had taken him last night, the same car, but the driver said nothing to the recruits, merely putting the vehicle in gear and trundling off along the familiar route out of the darkening Town.

10

They stopped in the courtyard of the Lodge, where Robert had been delivered previously. Forsyth whistled appreciatively. 'Nice place.' The three got out, the slamming of their doors momentarily breaking the dignified calm; but once the car had crunched away over the gravel they were all struck by the peace of the fine mansion.

A distant voice called to them from the darkness. 'Over here!' They turned, and Robert realized it must be Kaupff on the bowling green.

'This way,' he instructed, leading his companions through a gloom which slowly eased as their eyes adjusted. When they came out onto the lawn they saw Kaupff's face glowing in the red light of a filtered torch held in his hand. There were other people with him – Davis, Vine, Willoughby and Rosalind clustered around Professor Kaupff's impressively large telescope.

'Now that we're all here,' said Kaupff, 'we can begin this evening's training session.' Using his red flashlight he outlined the workings of the telescope; a Newtonian reflector whose parabolic mirror, fixed at the bottom end of the tube, served the magnifying purpose of a lens. A handle on the heavy mounting, Kaupff explained, had to be turned at regular intervals so that the telescope's aim could keep pace with the stars' slow procession, induced by Earth's rotation. 'Who's first?' he asked.

Forsyth stepped forward and put his face close to the eyepiece. 'Oh my . . . !'

'What can you see?' asked Robert.

'It's incredible, like a picture in a book. Go on, see for yourself.' He moved away and Robert took his place, stooping towards the eyepiece and trying to locate in the darkness the small lens whose view had so captivated his colleague. Then he found it, and as he positioned himself properly he saw a bright globe circled with a ring.

'It's Saturn!' he gasped.

'Beautiful, isn't it?' Kaupff laid a hand on Robert's shoulder. 'Can you see the planet's colours? Yellowish towards the upper part, greyer further down. And look carefully at the rings, Coyle – do you notice the thin dark gap between them?' Robert struggled to see any of these features, too dazzled by the little world that slowly drifted across his field of view. 'We'd better let Harvey take a turn now,' Kaupff suggested, though when Robert stood away it was Kaupff himself who moved to the eyepiece, giving the crank handle on the mount a few turns so as to re-centre the planet for the benefit of the remaining recruit.

'Have all of you seen it already?' Robert asked the others, and they nodded.

'A very pretty sight,' Willoughby conceded, offering a

description of the experience somewhat less elaborate than the curdled smoke of his novel.

Harvey, awestruck, stepped back from the lens. 'It's like flying in space.'

'I couldn't get the thing to focus,' said Davis. 'Maybe I need to have my eyes tested.'

'Well, gentlemen,' Kaupff continued, calling the recruits to order. 'Why exactly have I brought you here this evening? To entertain or to educate? Both, I hope. Seeing another world in vivid detail is an experience no civilized person should miss. Whether through a piece of glass, or enacted in a Shakespeare play, or summoned by a Beethoven string quartet, these other realms help us place ourselves more solidly on the one beneath our feet.'

'An attractive sentiment,' said Willoughby. 'You are one of those few scientists who recognize the equal if not superior value of art.'

'We live in an age of specialization,' Kaupff continued. 'But a factory worker whose only job is to pull a lever or turn a spanner can easily become estranged from the end-product of his labour. Specialization begets alienation: that is the secret of capitalism.'

'And that is why we have political-education programmes in every workplace,' Commissioner Davis reminded him.

'Quite so,' said Kaupff. 'Yet go to any of our universities and you will find physicists who think they have no need of Shelley, or novelists who suppose they can live without Newton. I have always worked hard to resist this attitude within the Installation, which is why I am so pleased that I have been able to arrange for Academician Willoughby to visit us.'

'The pleasure is mine,' said Willoughby, who was standing, Robert noticed, closely beside Rosalind.

'I, too, was delighted,' Davis added, 'to have been instrumental in obtaining approval for such an unusual request.'

'Academician Willoughby, I'm sure you recall what Schiller said about the unity of art and science,' Kaupff continued. 'And do you remember Goethe's scene, when Wilhelm Meister is invited to look through a telescope?'

'Hmm,' Willoughby said, then gave a cough expressive of the effort involved in summoning the appropriate passage from a vast memorized stock. 'It rings a bell – though eighteenth-century German literature isn't my field, of course. And having wide interests is certainly admirable, Professor Kaupff, but if we all tried to learn everything there is to know, we would have no time for anything. We must always be on our guard against the dangers of eclecticism.' With this last word, a standard form of condemnation issued by Writers' Union headquarters against anyone deemed to have wavered from approved ideology, Willoughby's voice momentarily took on a frostiness which touched everyone present, as palpably as the cooling air.

Kaupff seemed unabashed. 'I understand you spoke today about *King Lear*.'

'That's right,' said Willoughby.

'And I believe you spoke eloquently about the rigid feudalism of Shakespeare's world.'

'It's a pity you were unable to be there to hear it,' Willoughby told him.

'Indeed. But this rigidity reflected a more general view of the universe. Our solar system, Isaac Newton noted, is like a flattened disc, with all the planets wheeling neatly in a single plane. Newton could find no reason for this orderliness, other than intelligent design.'

'Which goes to show,' Willoughby said drily, 'that physicists are not to be trusted to speak sensibly about anything other than physics. And even there, we must be on our guard!'

'You are perfectly correct,' Kaupff said over the ensuing laughter. 'Of course Newton's argument was fallacious. Look there, all of you, at that patch of sky above the far end of the College. Do you notice the faint white glow of the Milky Way?'

Robert had no difficulty tracing the luminous band, which Kaupff had already pointed out to him the previous night.

'I can't see it,' said Davis.

'I can,' Harvey declared, and for some time there was debate among the group about its exact position and appearance, until eventually a division established itself between those who had no trouble viewing it, and those such as Davis whose eyes would never register it.

'The Milky Way is a flattened disc of stars,' said Kaupff. 'It's a very interesting coincidence – our galaxy is like a vastly enlarged version of the solar system sitting inside it: the part mirrors the whole. Why should this resemblance exist? The answer was found by Immanuel Kant, who realized that both the Milky Way and the solar system must have formed in the same way, from a spherical cloud of dust and gas which stretched and flattened as it rotated.

The universe, Kant realized, is an evolving structure, impelled towards perfection by its own natural forces. Life itself is an inevitable part of this cosmic evolution.'

'All very interesting,' said Willoughby. 'And will you be making the recruits read the *Critique of Judgment*?'

Willoughby's tone made Robert wonder if the remark was a kind of baited trap, but Kaupff leapt at it. 'I would prefer them to start with Kant's *Theory of Heaven*, where he says that the state of gravitational perfection will only be reached after an infinite time. Marx, of course, revised this notion completely, showing how human society must attain perfection in a finite period.'

Davis sniffed. 'Your unorthodox reading has thrown up some remarkable observations, Professor.'

'And were not Goethe and Schiller prominent spokespersons for Kant's fideistic pseudo-theories?' Willoughby asked rhetorically. The esoteric ideas were lost on Robert, but not the tone of rivalry or simple malice rising fin-like through the opaque waters of the debate. Robert wished he could return to the telescope standing unused beside them, through whose lens Saturn had looked so peaceful and aloof. By now the planet must have drifted out of the telescope's view.

'In their very first meeting, Schiller and Goethe discussed the development of plant species,' Kaupff agreed, too enthused by his prestigious companion's apparent interest to notice the dangerous current in which he swam. 'They wanted to understand how evolutionary growth – *Bildung* – can work in living things, or in art, to create organic microcosms of universal order. This is the message we see in the orbits of the planets or the glow of the Milky Way:

everything is connected, cause and effect are circular, not linear. That is why we are gathered here beneath the stars.'

'We are here,' Davis reminded him, 'because I instructed it. And I have been greatly interested in everything you have said to us, Professor Kaupff, but I am beginning to fear that Academician Willoughby perhaps has a point when he speaks of the dangers of eclecticism. You are a great physicist, Professor, and you have the admiration of everyone at the very highest level of the Central Committee under whose authority I act. But Lenin once remarked that the greatest physicists can also be the very poorest philosophers, and your own example of Newton bears this out. I think it might be best for us to stick to physics and astronomy from now on, otherwise I fear you may inadvertently say something – through no more than inadequate acquaintance with the facts – which you and all of us would come to regret.'

Everyone was silent in the cold night air. Robert had struggled to follow the blows and parries of the confrontation, but he knew that if sides were to be taken, his sympathy lay with the professor.

'I think we had better adjourn,' Kaupff said. 'I have asked for warm drinks to be served inside, so let's go and refresh ourselves. There will be plenty of opportunity to look through the telescope again later.'

He led the party in a slowly proceeding file, back along the darkened path towards the Lodge. Robert walked behind Rosalind and Willoughby, overhearing their conversation.

'Stargazing might appeal to me if you could do it without catching pneumonia,' the bulky writer told his companion.

'Communing with the infinite surely doesn't have to be such an uncomfortable experience.' Rosalind's fawn-coloured coat stood out in the feeble light, and Robert saw the movement of Willoughby's arm across her back. 'We'd better mind our step,' he was saying to her as she allowed his steadying embrace, though they disengaged on reaching the brighter region of the courtyard. Soon the group were entering the warmth of the Lodge, where Jason the butler stood waiting to hang their coats, then showed them to the opulent Maxwell Room in which Robert had sat with Kaupff before. A table in the corner bore a large, ornate silver bowl, and Jason proceeded to ladle mulled wine from it into small glass goblets.

'I propose a toast,' Kaupff announced. 'To our honoured guest, Academician Willoughby, and to our three heroic volunteers. Long live the Republic!'

The others echoed Kaupff's words, then sipped with him in a moment's silence that allowed Robert to savour the cloying aroma of cinnamon and sugar, and to ponder the equally heavy sentiments combined in the professor's salutation. Forsyth interrupted his thoughts.

'Still up for the Blue Cat tonight, lads?'

Professor Vine overheard and smiled. 'You're going to join the night school, are you?' Forsyth frowned uncertainly. 'That's what we call it,' Vine continued. 'A group of us from the College go there most evenings to talk and relax. It's better than staying here.' He leaned closer. 'And there are other pleasures.'

Forsyth grinned with understanding. 'That's what I had in mind.'

Vine offered him a matey nudge. 'So I thought!' Then he

gave a sceptical look to the mulled wine in his hand. 'We'd better save ourselves for the main event. No point getting pissed on this when there's decent stuff to be had at the Cat.' He tapped the shoulder of Kaupff, who had been standing silently nearby with Davis, to bring him into the conversation. 'Heinz, are you going to break the habit of a lifetime and join us all at the Blue Cat later?'

Kaupff shook his head. 'The night school is for younger hearts and stronger livers.'

'I'm sure Commissioner Davis will wish to join us,' said Vine. 'And Rosalind? Academician Willoughby?' He had now embraced everyone except the butler in the evening's entertainment, which no longer sounded to Robert like a visit to a brothel. Forsyth, too, looked disappointed at the prospect of what must after all be an acceptable and anodyne part of the Installation's social rituals.

'Perhaps I'll come,' said Willoughby. 'Though first I might need to lie down for a little. I had a long journey here today.'

'Is your accommodation comfortable?' Kaupff asked. 'I believe you've been given the flat adjoining my own.'

'I haven't really had any time to see it yet,' Willoughby told him, still with some of the prickliness that had surfaced outside. 'Except to drop my bag and freshen up when I arrived this morning, before giving the talk you were unfortunately unable to attend.'

'It sounds as if an early night will be in order,' Kaupff suggested. 'You have a few days ahead of you here, when we shall be plumbing your thoughts for all the knowledge and wisdom you can share with us and which we value so highly – for I consider you just as much a part of our patriotic mission, Academician Willoughby, as any of the scientific or technical workers, and I hope our discussions will be long and fruitful. So we must allow you to rest – though should you seek any entertainment tonight here at the College, you might like to join me in hearing Dr Carter, who will be giving a piano recital at eight o'clock. In the meantime, if you need to go to your room then I can escort you there – the building is somewhat of a maze . . .'

'That won't be necessary,' Willoughby said abruptly. 'Rosalind has already offered to direct me. And I won't be joining you for the music. Good evening, gentlemen.' He gave a stiff nod to the company, handed his and Rosalind's glasses to the butler who came for them, then turned and left the room with her. Their sudden departure left the others standing in embarrassed silence.

'Writers are an odd lot,' Vine said eventually, looking at his nearly empty glass and deciding to finish it off, then calling on Jason for a refill. 'I really wonder if this approach of yours is such a good idea, Heinz.'

Davis, standing beside him, raised an eyebrow. 'Am I to understand that the new initiative is solely Professor Kaupff's idea?'

Vine sniffed danger. 'Oh no, it was a collective decision, as always. We are engaged in an extraordinary project, Commissioner, and it requires extraordinary measures.'

Davis's impassive face was that of the most skilled card player, who knows how to conceal his superior hand. 'The Central Committee watches your progress with great interest,' he said. 'And it is to be hoped, as a matter of economy, that the eventual rewards – or penalties – will be distributed among as few people as possible.' Then he, too, left the room, telling the butler who followed the snapping of his fingers that he needed to make a phone call.

For Kaupff, Vine and the three volunteers who remained, the atmosphere was distinctly uncomfortable. Forsyth stared into his glass, Harvey rubbed his chin.

'We may have taken one risk too many,' Vine said to Kaupff. 'These people don't play games – they want results.'

Kaupff, despite all that had been said, remained blissfully unperturbed. 'What? You think we should be building a rocket, as the planning group told us? Why, young Robert here already knows the impossibility of such a scheme, simply from flicking through the popular book I gave him last night. The Red Star isn't the sort of thing we can fly to.'

Forsyth and Harvey looked at one another in puzzlement, and eventually it was Harvey who spoke. 'Sir,' he said, 'if we aren't flying there, then what exactly is it we'll be doing?'

'Let's all sit down,' Vine suggested. 'We seem to have reached the next stage of your training a little ahead of schedule, but at least these leather chairs are more comfortable than the seats in the seminar room.'

Kaupff took over once the five men were seated in as close a circle as the large armchairs allowed. 'The universe, we understand, is in a state of perpetual evolution, as Kant and Goethe realized—'

'Please, Heinz,' Vine interrupted. 'Do we need to deal with this in literary terms? Can't we just try and explain to them the second law of thermodynamics?'

'That's exactly what I am doing,' said Kaupff. 'But all knowledge is historical knowledge – that's what Kant's discovery implied.'

Of more concern to Robert right now was the thought of what Rosalind and Willoughby might be doing, for there was no sign of Kaupff's assistant.

'What we see,' said Kaupff, 'is that *Bildung* is a fundamental force of nature. Goethe recognized this in his scientific work; but he added another insight, which came from his own poetic imagination. In any experiment, he said, the experimenter must himself be considered part of the apparatus. We cannot detach ourselves from what we observe.'

Perhaps by now she was making Willoughby do what Harvey had been forced to perform for her. Robert imagined the flat beside Kaupff's to be exactly like the old professor's, though without the books and other humanizing touches.

'Our bodies are investigative instruments!' Kaupff declared. 'We are pieces of scientific equipment; living test tubes and retorts, sensors and recorders. We are all participating in the great natural experiment of life.' He was speaking of the same psychophysics that Rosalind had described, confirming what the three recruits already knew.

'We're your guinea pigs,' Robert said quietly.

Kaupff shook his head. 'My dear boy, no! We're not bourgeois reactionaries who murder to dissect; we're not proposing to vivisect you.'

Vine interrupted. 'Professor Kaupff is trying to tell you that the entropy of the universe is a monotonically increasing function of time, therefore local regions of maximal entropy should contain the most advanced form of structure . . .'

'Can we have his way again, please?' said Forsyth, nodding towards Kaupff, who instead looked at his watch.

'We must save the rest for tomorrow.'

'No!' Forsyth demanded. 'There's a simple thing we need to know right now. You keep telling us about theories and structures and stuff that honestly doesn't mean very much to me. What exactly is it we're here for?'

Kaupff smiled. 'You want the short answer? Here it is. The Red Star is a collapsed state of matter of possibly infinite density. It may be emitting radiation in the form of scalar waves. We need to find a detector for those waves. A human body – yours, for example – might serve as such a detector.'

Harvey asked, 'Will any of us ever be doing any flying, or are we just radio antennae in your wave experiment?'

'This is a space mission,' said Kaupff. 'You can't do a space mission without moving through space. So yes, one of you will fly the capsule. And of course it has to be the right man, you all understand that. But now we should arrange your transport back to the Town – unless, that is, any of you would like to stay a little longer so as to use the telescope again.'

'I'll stay,' Forsyth said at once, hoping to learn more.

'Me too,' said Harvey.

'And you, Coyle?' Kaupff asked.

'I would prefer not to,' he said.

Kaupff raised his eyebrows. 'Has astronomy lost its appeal? Wouldn't you like to see Jupiter now that he's risen?'

Robert was tired, hungry, irritated by Rosalind's continuing absence with Willoughby, and in no mood to revisit the telescope now that he would be unable to feel the same pleasure it gave him earlier. But he also knew that he should do his duty unquestioningly. 'If you order me to stay, then I shall stay. And if you order me to leave, I shall leave.'

Kaupff looked puzzled, almost hurt. 'What does this mean?'

Vine chuckled. 'Quite the Cordelia, eh, Heinz?'

'So let me seem, until I become,' said Robert.

Forsyth stared at him like he thought he was mental; Vine and Harvey were equally nonplussed, but Kaupff gazed with a bemused fascination that quickly turned to warmth. 'Well, well,' he said to himself. 'The slave knows Goethe as well as geometry.'

'A very clever response,' said Vine. 'Very clever. Forsyth, Harvey, let's go and look for Jupiter. We'll leave your obedient friend here while Professor Kaupff works out what to do with him.' Robert's remark had been made innocently, but to his companions it was like the correct answer in an exam, found through cheating. Forsyth gave Robert a hostile look before following Vine and Harvey out of the room.

Kaupff and Robert were alone now, seated side by side. 'You realize, don't you,' said the professor, 'that those two are merely experimental controls?' It sounded a harsh way to talk about Forsyth and Harvey, but there was no contempt in Kaupff's voice, only detachment. 'They have important parts to play in the mission, and so do you.' Then, as if suddenly changing the subject, he said, 'Do you remember much about that essay of yours at Cromwell?'

Like everything prior to his illness, the memory was covered in Robert's imagination by an obscuring glass that rendered it distant and artificial. 'It was meant to be about housing-stock renewal.'

'A most worthy and important subject for rational enquiry,' Kaupff exclaimed with just a little too much false sincerity. 'It went into your file along with everything else. Now let's suppose a fire breaks out in the Ministry headquarters.'

'Why?'

'Never mind, boy, just imagine it.'

Robert had no difficulty: he saw a woman like Rosalind sitting in an empty office after hours, smoking a cigarette while through an open doorway a man straightens his tie in an adjoining room. The man calls to Rosalind, she gets up from her chair, leaving her cigarette dangling on an ashtray placed over a pile of papers, Robert's own file, whose top sheet is a page from his essay, and while Rosalind and her lover kiss cinematically, the cigarette falls, and a brown charring hole swells inside a circle of speeding flames.

'I see it,' said Robert.

'Your essay is burned to ashes and all the little pieces blow away. In fact the whole of your police file goes up in smoke. Now tell me, has the information been destroyed?'

'I certainly hope so.' Robert didn't like the thought that his story about wanting to be a spaceman could remain an item of mirth for D5 agents until the end of time.

'Well, it hasn't,' said Kaupff. 'The information has become very inaccessible, very well hidden among the air and dust surrounding the Ministry; but if we were exceptionally clever we could work backwards, step by step, and return all those atoms to their original configuration. You see, Robert, information can never really be destroyed: this is a fundamental law of quantum physics called unitarity. But let's think of the Red Star. Matter – your police file – falls across its event horizon and disappears forever. There's no getting it back. The information is lost, violating the law of unitarity. That's a paradox.'

It sounded to Robert like a very good way of getting rid of all his past transgressions, but Kaupff disapproved of such illegality.

'If information can't disappear then it has to go somewhere,' said the professor. 'Perhaps the frozen star is really the gateway to some distant region of the galaxy – or to an entirely separate universe, a mirror world whose history is quite unlike ours. There could be another you, with a completely different life.'

'Bet I'd still get kicked out of university,' Robert said balefully.

'Most probably,' Kaupff agreed. 'But if my theory of quantum gravity is correct, the Red Star ought also to be emitting information in the form of scalar waves. We have to ask where that information came from. Your body is the detector.'

Robert thought it even more absurd than his essay, though he had already seen the army of scientists and technicians devoted to making it work. 'Why me?'

'Rosalind showed me your score from the card experiment,' Kaupff told him earnestly. 'You got eighty-five per cent. Have you any idea how extraordinary that is?' Robert remained silent, still holding the empty glass that had contained his mulled wine, whose warming effect had quite worn off. 'The probability of obtaining a result like that from random guessing is less than one in a million. You're not the first person with such a gift that Rosalind has encountered; she has made a study of similar cases, and some of the people she identified went on to do patriotic work of a strategic kind. But none of them was physically suited to an active mission. You are.'

Robert had the gift of telepathy. Somehow he'd gone through nearly twenty years of life and had never even noticed it; but if he thought hard enough – or simply relaxed his mind – he ought to be able to see what they were doing right now, Rosalind and Willoughby, just as he had discerned the colours of playing cards seen by her eyes only. And so, with eighty-five per cent accuracy, he saw plump Willoughby sitting naked on the end of his disordered bed, Rosalind kneeling on the floor before him with her face buried in what lay beneath his hairy paunch. 'Why was I never aware of this?' he asked Kaupff.

'It seems that just before you became ill, your ability was artificially stimulated.'

'By the drug?'

Kaupff shook his head slowly. 'There was no drug.'

Robert was confused; why had Kaupff lied, and how had the lie so convincingly explained what Robert felt?

Kaupff saw his discomfort. 'You understand that information about the mission has to be carefully controlled. If we had told you prior to the card experiment that we were convinced you possessed extrasensory perception, it would have destroyed the experimental conditions. My story about the drug was convenient at the time; now I can tell you the truth.'

'How do I know it's the truth?' asked Robert.

'You can't. So if you prefer, let's call it the next stage. Do you remember the facility where you stayed during the induction period?'

'Not very clearly.'

'No, I suppose not. Nor, I expect, do you recall very much about the aptitude tests, or the pictures you were asked to draw, or the bedroom you slept in for each of the three nights you stayed there, or the pillow you laid your head on.'

'I thought it was because of the drug that all those things are like a dream now.'

'We were testing prototype equipment. It was inside your pillow.'

Now Robert did remember something very clearly. Something small, round and hard had been inside that pillow. At least, he thought he could remember it.

'We believe it was these trials that made you ill,' said Kaupff. 'But whereas before the experiment you scored little better than average in telepathy tests, now you get eighty-five per cent. That tells us we're on the right track, though more work is needed before we can launch you in the capsule.'

'But I might fall ill again.'

Kaupff nodded. 'You consented to all risks.'

'I'm still willing to take them,' said Robert; and it was true. Whatever had altered his mind – drug, hidden machine or the invisible waves of another universe – it had given him a genuine sense of courage and purpose. The facts were open to doubt, but not his feelings. 'I shall do my duty.'

'Let's go to my rooms,' Kaupff instructed, and they went out to the bare-walled corridor with its doors marked 'in' or 'out'. One of them, Robert noticed, belonged to Professor Vine, another to Dr Carter, who Kaupff had said would play the piano later. Life at the Installation for these scientists must perpetually revolve around a handful of locations, at each of which the same people would appear in permutation, like moving figures in a mechanical clock.

'Is Professor Vine married?' Robert asked.

'Yes. He's got two children.'

'Do they all live here in the College?'

'His wife does; the children board in the Town. All the Installation children do – it keeps them out of mischief.' They reached the winding staircase which took them to the landing where Kaupff's door stood beside Willoughby's. Robert waited while Kaupff found his key, and through the jingling tried to catch any sound that might be leaking from the neighbouring flat. Then, once inside, Robert saw again the private library that was so much more welcoming than the one he had visited in the Town.

'Come, let me show you something,' Kaupff told him, leading Robert to the bedroom where the professor switched on a table lamp that cast a glowing tongue of light onto the striped wallpaper. 'Sit yourself down while I find it.' The only chair was covered with books, so Robert sat on the bed while Kaupff began looking along the spines on the shelves. 'That's strange,' Kaupff murmured. 'I suppose I must have moved it.'

From the wall behind him, Robert heard a bump. On the other side of that wall, he realized, were Willoughby and Rosalind. Kaupff was still looking for the book he wanted, but the twisting of his head to read the spines appeared to be giving him neck ache, because he straightened and sat down on the bed beside Robert, casually placing his hand on the young man's knee. 'Don't know what's happened to it,' he said with an absent-minded air. 'Might someone have . . . ?' Suddenly he seemed concerned; Kaupff withdrew his hand and stood up, went to a bookcase at the other side of the room, and took from the top shelf a cardboard box which he put on the bed and opened. It was full, Robert saw, of handwritten notes. 'All seems well here,' Kaupff said with relief. 'I don't mind too much if a thief has stolen a single book from me, as long as there is no disturbance to my thousand pages.'

'What are those pages?' Robert asked, and Kaupff, still stooped over his precious work, looked at him gravely.

'The distillation of years of thought.' Kaupff sealed the box, returned it to its place of safe-keeping, and once more sat down beside Robert. 'Now tell me, what made you come out with that line you quoted?' Again he placed his hand on Robert's leg.

'So let me seem, until I become?'

'That's the one.' Kaupff's fingers tapped on the soldier's thigh as if on a desk in a seminar room. 'Do you know the source?'

'I found it in a book of Goethe's poems.'

Kaupff smiled. 'It's from one of his novels. But why that particular line?'

Robert could feel his leg being subtly stroked by a hand working independently of its genially innocent master, as if two entirely separate conversations were being conducted, each unnerving in a different way. Robert stood up. 'It was a random choice . . .'

'Nothing in the universe is random.' Kaupff's words

yearned, as they always did, for the stars; Robert struggled to interpret the second urge that the old man's hand had implied. 'You can have no idea how perfectly appropriate your words were; the song of a strange, beautiful child, neither male nor female, transfigured by death. A pale, angelic child . . .' Kaupff trailed off and looked down at his lap, where he folded his hands and rubbed his thumbs pensively. 'How I admire and envy your courage.' When he looked up again, Robert was surprised to see films of moisture in the professor's eyes. 'You really aren't afraid to die, are you?'

The possibility, despite all Robert had been told, still seemed as remote as the planet he had seen through Kaupff's telescope. 'I don't know,' he said.

'I was brave once. The Nazis could have shot me for being a communist – sometimes I almost wish they had.' Kaupff gave a wistful laugh, and at the same time there was another sound on the wall from the neighbouring room, this time like something small and hard being tapped against it. Kaupff appeared not to notice but Robert wondered if Willoughby and Rosalind were eavesdropping.

'If you'd been shot then you would never have been able to do your heroic work on the Bomb.'

'Someone else would have done it instead,' said Kaupff. 'In science, no one is indispensable. I console myself with a flabbier kind of courage – some would call it foolhardiness. For years I've worked alone on my theory of quantum gravity, and my ideas have come from unusual sources. That's what my thousand pages are about – quotations from authors down the ages, wisdom assembled in the hope of synthesizing a new approach to space, time, consciousness. An unorthodox approach, but we can already see the success of it in the progress we've made. Though if my academic peers outside the Installation knew how I got the initial inspiration for scalar-wave theory they'd probably think me a mad old fool.'

Kaupff was interrupted by a loud knocking on the door to the flat. He got up and went to see who it was; Robert went too, and stood watching in the main room as Kaupff opened the door to reveal the waiting figure of Jason.

'You are told to expect a telephone call in ten minutes, sir.'

'I'll be right down.'

Jason nodded and Kaupff closed the door on his retreating figure, then turned to Robert, his eyes quite dry now and his mood less intimate. 'Let me have another quick look for that book I wanted to give you, before we have to leave.' He rapidly scanned the shelves and at last cried, 'Ah, here's another copy – an even better translation.' Kaupff handed Robert an old leather-bound book that looked as though it dated from the turn of the century or even earlier. On its spine Robert saw, in gold letters, the name Goethe. 'It's the novel where your poem came from.'

'Do I have to read it?' Robert asked. He still hadn't even started *Rocket to the Stars* and already he was being given more homework.

'You probably don't have to. Information permeates the universe, and some minds have the disposition to detect it. I wonder if the whole of this book isn't already somehow in your unconscious mind, which is why you chose the line you did. How much else lies inside that head of yours?' As if to emphasize the point, Kaupff stroked Robert's hair.

'Science frees us from superstition and makes us see the world as it really is, but Goethe knew that if life is to have any meaning there must be more. We must see the world with love. Do you have love in your heart, Robert?'

It was like being asked if he feared death, and again the answer lay far off, drifting against a starry background. 'I don't know.'

'Love makes us do the strangest but greatest of things,' Kaupff said, his voice momentarily darkening. 'But come now, I must hear what some bureaucrat in London wishes to instruct, and you must be driven to your lodgings – I'm sure you are ready for a meal.' Kaupff opened the door and followed Robert onto the landing. There was another sound in Willoughby's neighbouring flat: a heavy bump, though no voices. Kaupff glanced towards Willoughby's door, then began to go down the spiral staircase with Robert close behind. It was only once they were in the corridor and well beyond earshot that Kaupff told Robert in a low voice, 'I didn't get off to a very good start with the Academician, did I?'

'I think not,' said Robert, glancing at the 'out' on Professor Vine's door.

'I'm beginning to wonder if it was a mistake inviting him here.'

They emerged into the panelled lobby, where Jason stood at the desk and silently pointed Kaupff towards the private booth in which the telephone call was to be received. 'Goodnight, Robert,' Kaupff told him. 'I shall see you here tomorrow morning at nine o'clock, and then we shall begin tuning that mental receiver of yours – who knows what frequencies we might pick up!' Kaupff stretched out his hand which Robert took in order to shake; but the young volunteer was surprised to be wrapped in a fatherly hug before Kaupff swiftly turned on his heels and went across the lobby to the booth, whose soundproof door he closed with a heavy thud. A moment later, a red light came on above it.

Robert, still holding the book Kaupff had given him, stood wondering what he ought to do next. He turned to Jason, whose head was lowered over some paperwork. 'I'll need a car.'

Jason looked up, his short fair hair and smooth, pale skin glowing in the yellow light of the desk lamp beside his hand. 'Not yet,' he said flatly.

A voice came from behind Robert. 'There you are.' He turned to see Davis standing at the far end of the lobby. 'Come with me, please, Volunteer Coyle.' Robert obeyed, feeling like an errant pupil called to see the head as Davis escorted him through a door to a corridor he had not seen before, just as cold and bare as the one leading to Kaupff's flat, but without any intervening row of other dwellings. Instead this corridor was a featureless tunnel, harshly lit, whose bricks were painted gloss white, and which had the appearance of the entrance to a prison. Robert walked silently with Davis, the clacking of both men's feet ringing in his ears, until they reached a reinforced door which Davis unlocked, bringing them into a shabby office. There were three desks, a typewriter and telephone on each, and one was occupied by a man in civilian clothes whose eyes never strayed from the keyboard at his fingers while Davis led Robert into a room with a plain wooden table and a chair on either side, lit by a bare bulb hanging from the ceiling.

'Sit down,' Davis instructed, remaining standing while he lit his pipe and closed the door on the clattering typewriter whose sound, now muffled, was like a last precious link with the world beyond the interrogation room. 'Did he do anything to you?'

'What do you mean?'

'What did you and Kaupff get up to in his flat?'

Robert stared at the wooden table. 'He gave me a book.' Robert laid it on the table; Davis picked it up for inspection.

'It's from Imperialist times,' Davis muttered, flicking through the first few pages while puffing on his pipe. He opened the covers to their full width and held the book up by them, letting the pages dangle in case some hidden note should fall, then peered into the spine's aperture in search of anything secreted there. 'I'll need to get this checked out,' he said, tossing it back onto the table. 'What else has he given you?'

'Another book called *Rocket to the Stars*.'

'We know about that,' said Davis. 'It's harmless.' The commissioner sat down. 'Has he done any more than hug you or put his arm round you?'

'No,' said Robert, still staring at the table and feeling unable to meet Davis's gaze.

'Kissed you? It's not illegal.'

'No, he hasn't kissed me, and I certainly wouldn't want him to.'

Davis sat back with a creak of his wooden chair. 'I don't think you're a queer. But you need to know one or two things about Kaupff. Hero of the Resistance, Hero of Socialist Labour – without him there would have been no nuclear deterrent and the capitalists could have walked straight back in. He's worth a lot to us and our way of life.' Davis leaned forward with another creak, resting his elbows on the table. 'Doesn't make him a perfect human being, though. We all have our weaknesses. And do you know what his is?'

'I think I can guess.'

'Let me tell you what it was like here in the Installation during the early days,' Davis continued. 'I never saw it, of course – we're going back twenty or thirty years, when there were far fewer people here, and the Bomb was the only project. Life was pretty basic – the scientists could bring their wives and children, but there were no facilities for them, so some of the personnel got together to run a makeshift school. Kaupff taught in it for an hour or two every week even though he was working night and day on the Bomb – very noble of him, you might think. Except that he had an ulterior motive. That's his weakness.' Davis lifted the small book and drummed its corner on the table to match the rhythm of his thoughts; a gesture not unlike Kaupff's on Robert's leg. 'He likes little boys, does our professor. In fact he likes them so much that he took one lad into a toilet and raped him.'

Robert's stomach lurched.

'I'm sure you feel exactly the same way about it that I do,' said Davis. 'Scum like that deserve the death penalty they get for it. In fact I'm sure you'll agree that hanging is altogether too humane – they ought to be castrated first as an example to other perverts. The question is, why didn't

Kaupff get what was coming to him? And the answer, of course, is that he was too useful. Not all perverts are equal, and when your pederast is one of the leading scientists in Britain's nuclear programme, well, perhaps it's best to brush things under the carpet. The boy's evidence was contradictory; there was bruising but no spunk; perhaps he fell and hurt his arse on the toilet and he made up all that stuff about a man coming in behind him, or else it was another man, because the boy never got a good look. Who knows? We have to accept that matters of national security and state secrecy are more important than any individual. So Kaupff was never charged – he got clean away with it. Except that he never taught at the school again, and soon a proper one was built, as the Installation expanded. It was all a very long time ago and I suppose we should let bygones be bygones. Oh, but there's another incident I ought to mention, happened fifteen years ago. Lady who lives in the Town took her toddler to play in the swing park. She got talking to a friend, next thing she knows, the kid's gone – wandered off. Every parent's nightmare. She looks all over the place – eventually it's half the Town hunting for the lad, who some say was seen in the company of a man. And where do they find the boy? Drowned in the river. Now what did a nice woman like Dorothy Frank ever do to deserve that, eh?'

'Was Professor Kaupff involved? Was there any evidence?'

Davis shrugged. 'The inquest concluded it was an accidental drowning and no one else was involved – I've looked through all the files. But when you've got a known pervert in the Town, and a child dies like that – well, you only need to put two and two together. Nobody wanted to dig too deep – better to let him get away with it, as long as he's useful.' Still Davis drummed the book on the table, anger simmering in his voice. 'And that's the key to it all – how useful is he? Nobody questions what he did in the past, but he's an old man now, and this so-called space mission is his last chance. If he delivers results he'll get another medal and perhaps be allowed to retire. But if he fails then it's time for him to get what he's long been owed. All I need is a little more evidence, which is where you come in.'

Robert mentally replayed the scene in Kaupff's bedroom and saw the tears in the professor's eyes. 'Even if he makes a pass at me, it won't prove anything about what he might have done to the children.'

Davis nodded. 'For queers it's only prison – the Penal Code is pretty lenient in that regard. But proof that he's a nancy would bolster the case regarding the boys.'

'And is that why you're here at the Installation?' Robert asked. 'To investigate Professor Kaupff?'

Davis's face hardened instantly and his voice became a quietly sneering hiss. 'Don't take it upon yourself to ask about my operation, you fucking squaddie piece of shit.' He let his words sink in, then adopted a conciliatory tone. 'There are people in high places who think Kaupff's latest scheme might demonstrate he's finally lost it. Kaupff's a national asset gone rusty – he's an old battleship you either leave to rust or break up for scrap. And while my superiors try and work out which to do, I get on with gathering evidence. He's taken a fancy to you – anyone can see that. Might be nothing more than an old man's fondness for a young protégé – I'm quite prepared to see the innocent side of it. Or he might want to wave his cock in your face. Whatever he does, you tell me – got it?'

'Yes, sir.'

'Has he kissed you?'

'No, sir.'

'In his flat, did he touch you?'

'No, sir.'

Davis sat back, apparently satisfied. 'I billeted you with the Franks for a reason – you understand that, don't you?'

'Yes, sir.'

'The woman made a full statement at the time, but she might have come up with her own ideas since then about what really happened. She might even have withheld information – it's not easy for a parent to admit they've been negligent. If you learn anything new, you tell me.'

'I shall do my patriotic duty, sir.'

'I'm glad to hear it.' Davis rose from his chair and lifted the book from the table. 'Let's go.'

Robert stood up, and when Davis opened the door it was like being released into life again, though it was only the office with its clattering typewriter that they emerged into. Davis led Robert out along the corridor and back to the incongruously cosy surroundings of the lobby. The red light no longer shone above the telephone booth – Kaupff's call had ended and he was nowhere to be seen. Jason, however, was still at his desk. 'Your car is here,' he said.

Davis gave Robert a pat on the back which almost felt like an ejecting push. 'Do your duty, Coyle.' Then Robert took the coat that Jason handed him, and went out to the waiting vehicle.

11

When Robert arrived back at his lodgings the hall was dark, the living-room door was closed, and from behind it he could hear raised voices. Miriam and her father were arguing.

'What do you mean, Dad?'

'Don't fly off the handle, Miriam. I'm only saying that whenever your mother and I try to tell you something you act as though we're attacking you.'

'But you are! You seem to think that just because we get this soldier dumped on us we have to treat him like the district governor. You could make him sleep in the bath and he'd probably be grateful, but no, you have to throw me out of my own room.'

'There's no need to be so hostile, either to him or to me. Robert's a good lad and we're lucky to have him here. A fine-looking man.'

'Don't give me any more about the son you never had, please!'

'You be quiet and don't talk like that in front of your mother. You're a grown woman now, Miriam, and we need to be realistic.'

'Meaning what?'

'Meaning sooner or later you're going to have to think about settling down.'

Robert stood in darkness, hearing Miriam's intake of breath as she tried to find her words. 'Settle down? Pardon me, Dad, but exactly what are you talking about?'

'You need to have plans, Miriam, you're not a wee girl anymore.'

'The only plan I have is to get myself out of this shite hole at the earliest opportunity.'

'You mind your language! You're not too old to feel the palm of my hand. And how dare you call this house what you did.'

'Not the house, Dad, the whole place – the Installation. Do you really expect me to spend the rest of my life here?'

'There's only one way you'll ever get out, Miriam, and that's if you marry up a category, and I see no developments on that score.'

'Oh, and you've got me lined up with soldier boy, have you?'

'Don't be so daft, Miriam, I wish you could at least try to look at things logically. I'm not lining you up with anybody. But you know what happens with a lot of these young recruits that come here – they do their training, meet a lassie and end up settling down in the Installation. Young Shona and John, for example. Or Karen and Tommy.'

'Karen had a black eye last time I saw her that she got off Tommy after he came home drunk from the Levellers. Tried to hit the baby too.'

'Is that relevant, Miriam? Is that the best you can do?'

'I don't need to listen to this.'

Robert moved away from the door, ready at any moment to proceed up the stairs as though he had only just entered, but the conversation wasn't over yet because now it was Mrs Frank's quieter voice he heard.

'Robert hasn't done anything wrong, Miriam, so let's

not take it out on him. And there's no need to rush – whenever you meet the right man you'll know it. The one thing you shouldn't do is latch on to a technical just because he can take you out of the Installation – we'd never see you again, and what if he turned out bad like Tommy? Who would you go to? Your father's right: unless there's an Installation boy you've always had your heart set on, an incomer's your best bet; a recruit like Robert or one of the other boys with him in town today. There'll be girls snapping them up while they're here.'

'Whose side are you on, Mum?'

'I'm not on anybody's side. Life isn't a contest.'

Robert waited to hear Miriam's response, but he waited too long. Finally realizing she was about to leave the room, he barely had time to make it to the bottom of the stairs before she opened the living-room door, flooding the hall with light and her own accusing stare. 'Well, well, look who it is,' she said sourly, evidently aware of what he had been doing.

'I just got back,' he said guiltily. Mr and Mrs Frank were on their feet and coming to see.

'Hello there, Robert,' Arthur exclaimed with forced cheerfulness. 'Welcome home. Come in and put your feet up.'

'Will you be wanting your supper?' Mrs Frank asked him, while Miriam slipped away from the three of them and up to her room.

'Yes, if you don't mind,' Robert said sheepishly, following Dorothy into the kitchen where, having switched on the light, she began inspecting the contents of a large saucepan that sat idly on the cooker, its rim smeared with tomato-coloured sauce.

'Spaghetti all right?' she said, igniting the gas.

'Perfect.'

He sat down at the table where Arthur came and stood beside him, casting him an apologetic look. 'We didn't know if you'd be dining with us, so we ate earlier. We can make you something fresh if you like.'

'Please,' said Robert, 'I don't want to cause you any trouble. The last thing I'd want is to disrupt your household. I can even eat out every night if it makes things easier for you.'

Mr Frank smiled. 'You're a good lad, Robert – and no trouble at all. Fancy a beer?' He went to the pantry and fetched a litre bottle of Victory Ale, pouring its brown, foaming contents into two glasses. 'Cheers, Robert.'

'Cheers.'

'Is Robert what you prefer? Or are you Rab to your pals?'

'At home I was always Robbie.'

'Then you're Robbie to us too,' Arthur declared, sitting down at the table as a steaming plate of spaghetti was placed before Robert.

'This looks great. You're very kind.' The relief of escaping from Davis had only added to his hunger; Robert ate voraciously under Arthur's attentive gaze.

'There'll always be a meal here if you need it,' Mr Frank told him, swigging his beer, while Dorothy silently assented to the domestic generosity her husband offered, which it would be her task to provide. 'We know you can't tell us what your daily schedule's like, or even why you're here. But there's three of you, isn't there?'

Robert paused, fork in hand, and looked at his host.

'You were in the Levellers today,' Mr Frank explained.

'Is that what the pub's called?'

'Jessie's lovely, isn't she?' Robert guessed he meant the bar lady, whose loveliness had been elusive. 'Don't be shy about bringing your two pals here if you like. This is your home, after all, as long as you're here.'

Robert carried on eating, aware that the invitation was part of Mr Frank's ambitions regarding Miriam, whose life the paterfamilias could plan with the same casual ease he applied to Dorothy's catering duties.

'I'll leave you men in peace,' Dorothy said, going back to the living room.

In two thirsty gulps, Arthur drained most of what was in his glass. 'I can open another if you like.'

'No, thanks.'

Arthur leaned towards him. 'We get lads like you coming to the Installation fairly often,' he said, as if sharing a secret. 'There's always some new project needs recruits. Some men do their bit and go, others find a reason to stay.' Clearly he had never doubted that disappearance from the Installation meant a return to life outside. 'Have you got a girlfriend, Robbie?'

'No.'

Arthur smiled. 'Footloose and fancy free – I almost envy you.' Then he lowered his voice still further. 'You lads, you'll probably find out where the special workers can go for, you know, women.'

'I've heard about it.'

'It's not for Category A's and I wouldn't go near a place like that if you paid me,' Mr Frank said, in what was little more than a whisper. 'But take my advice, Robbie, and don't get involved. I've heard all sorts of unpleasant stories. Men robbed and beaten up. Disease. Blackmail. It's a bad business.'

'I'll bear it in mind.' Robert scraped the remaining strands of spaghetti from his plate.

'Like another beer? More food?' Robert shook his head and said he ought to go upstairs and rest. It was only nine o'clock, but already he felt ready for sleep. 'That's fine,' said Mr Frank, a little crestfallen. 'Me and Dorothy'll be turning in before too long. Sure you don't want to look at the telly with us for a bit?'

None of Mr Frank's suggestions could compete with the one thing Robert wanted now. 'Good night, Arthur.'

On the landing, Robert saw that Miriam's door was ajar. Perhaps she had wanted to overhear what her father had been saying. Robert could see part of the room, but not Miriam herself. He knocked gently.

'Go away, Mum,' she said through what sounded like a sob.

'I'm not your mother.'

There was a pause. 'Go anyway.'

He waited, wondering if he should leave her, but decided he had to say something. 'I'm sorry if I've caused problems for you.'

'Good.'

'I want you to remember that I never asked to stay here, it wasn't my idea which room I should sleep in, and I have absolutely no interest in you, or what you do with your life. The war you've got with your father is none of my business.'

Miriam came to the open doorway and stared at him with eyes that were swollen and hostile. 'I know why they put you here.'

'You do?'

'I expect you've told them about last night,' she hissed, 'and no doubt Tim will be questioned, if he hasn't been already. Just remember that fornication isn't a crime. Neither of us is married and we can do what we like.'

From the living room downstairs, the jaunty theme music of *Variety Tonight* struck up. 'I've told no one,' said Robert. 'You think I'm here to spy on you and your boyfriend? Why should I do that?'

She snorted. 'Don't play the little innocent. I had sex here with Tim last night – all perfectly legal. He bumped against the radio in the dark, accidentally switched it on, and must have shifted the tuning too. We've had that radio for years, the authorities know about it, and there's never been any trouble. Suddenly you appear and there's a problem.'

'I took a risk warning you,' Robert whispered. 'I only wanted to help you, but you seem determined to take out all your anger on me, when it's your father who's the problem.' He decided on a change of tack. 'It must be hard for all of you, after what happened to your little brother.'

She rolled her reddened eyes. 'So now the little innocent's become a psychologist. Do you think any of us would really be happier if Jamie hadn't run away from that stupid park and drowned?'

'I heard he was abducted. Is that true?'

She sneered derisively. 'What the hell are you talking about? You'd better not tell any of these lies to my mother – she's suffered enough.' Then she closed the door on him and Robert turned to go to his room, satisfied that he'd fulfilled his obligation towards Davis, and relieved that he had learned nothing worth reporting.

He switched on the light, kicked off his boots and lay down to read *Rocket to the Stars*, but his mind soon wandered from the page. Today he had learned he was telepathic; yet apart from mild recurring headaches and a persistent sense of unreality, he felt nothing. The playing cards had provoked a response over which he had no conscious control, and when he tried to think what Miriam and her boyfriend must have done in this room last night he saw only her alarmed expression on being challenged by him at the College. The bed had been so carefully re-made by them afterwards; why not do it in the other room? There was something about the whole incident that didn't make sense.

He got up, pulled back the top blankets and looked at the unsoiled sheet beneath. He went further, lifting the sheet to see the mattress, convinced that no one had ever made love on it. Then he began to tuck the sheet back in place with the military neatness that was the one useful skill he had learned in his regiment; but as he reached beneath the far side of the mattress against the wall, his hand encountered something. He drew out a thin gold chain and straightened himself to view what hung from it: a simple cross. A religious symbol; not the sort of thing Miriam would be allowed to wear at work, and a type of jewellery considered so old fashioned that only the most eccentric or ideologically suspect would ever wear it in public at all. Was Miriam secretly a Christian? Robert remembered what Mrs Frank had said about the dead brother being with the angels: the proverbial formula of a grieving woman. Now he asked himself if there was more to it. But if the Franks were crypto-Christians, what was the daughter doing, having sex with her boyfriend?

Robert trickled the thin chain onto his palm and decided the best place to put it would be back where he found it. He hid it under the mattress with the same furtive care he might have given to a pornographic magazine, wondered if he should mention it to Davis, and found himself bearing yet another secret on Miriam's behalf.

A vehicle braked outside, soon afterwards the doorbell rang and he felt a tremor of anxiety, thinking it must be Davis's men. 'Robbie!' Mr Frank was calling up to him. He pulled on his boots, smoothed his shirt and prepared himself for further interrogation. He owed the Franks no favours – he would tell Davis all about Miriam's visitor in the night, and the radio, and the necklace, and if the Franks were thrown into prison it was not his concern. Reaching the top of the stairs he saw who was standing at the open door. It was Colin Forsyth.

'All set?' Forsyth beamed as Robert came down.

'Enjoy yourselves,' Mr Frank said to both of them.

'I don't understand.'

'Have you forgotten?' said Forsyth. 'Lads' night out. Harvey's in the car – we're all set to spend some vouchers.'

'I'd rather not.'

Forsyth frowned. 'Don't give us any more of that poncey talk like you did at the Lodge.' He gave Mr Frank a knowing wink. 'These college boys, eh?'

Arthur raised his eyebrows. 'College? You've been hiding your light under a bushel, Robbie. Now on you go, and remember your key.'

'Really, it's been a long day . . .'

The driver had come out of the waiting vehicle and was walking up the path behind Forsyth; the same man whom Robert had seen several times already but who never showed any recognition of his passengers. Reaching the doorstep, he said, 'You are instructed to come with us, Volunteer Coyle.'

There was an embarrassed pause, broken by Mr Frank. 'Hurry up, Robert. Here's your coat.' Arthur lifted it from the hook, eager to send his guest away without further fuss or influx of cold air.

'Cheer up,' Forsyth said brightly as they followed the driver to the car. 'Now we'll see what sort of fanny they've got at the Blue Cat.'

12

It was a place without a sign, like everywhere else, but the Blue Cat lacked a front too. The car halted at what appeared to be a darkened industrial warehouse; a high brick building with unlit windows in a part of town so desolate and anonymous that Forsyth, voicing the unease of all three recruits, said, 'Is this it?'

'Just go and ring the bell,' the driver told them, pointing to a closed and featureless entrance.

Forsyth, sitting in front, opened his door. 'Will you be waiting here for us?'

'No,' said the driver.

'Then how do we get back?' asked Harvey.

'Everything's arranged.'

Robert said, 'I don't like this.' Harvey and Forsyth turned to him; the driver continued staring impassively forward into the empty road his beams illuminated, the car engine rattling. 'This place is deserted. I don't . . .'

He tailed off; the driver looked round. 'Happy fucking, boys, but I need to be off.'

'Come on, you poofters,' said Forsyth. 'Party time.'

The others had no choice; they got out and all three went to the black door. It was Robert who rang the bell, and soon it was answered by a bald, heavily built man in a dark suit and tie. 'Evening, gentlemen.' He gave a nod past them to the car, which rolled away.

The entrance led straight down a flight of stone steps that bent at the bottom, taking the visitors into a large basement bar lit by blue neon tubes; a noisy, convivial place where most of the tables were occupied by groups of men – laughing, drinking, talking – and a few women too. Music played from loudspeakers somewhere, and an empty stage at the far end was set up for a band. The atmosphere was that of any lively city pub, a lot more welcoming than the sleepy boozer they'd been in earlier.

'Place is heaving,' Forsyth said approvingly above the hubbub. All the tables in the sunken central area were occupied; around the indigo-coloured walls, a series of booths separated by tall wooden partitions offered more hope of free space. Scanning them, Robert saw the miniskirted rump of a stooping waitress serving drinks to elderly cigar-smoking men; and it was only when she turned with her empty tray that he recognized Dora, the woman he had met at the College. She saw him too; then in a moment she was lost among the crowd.

'There's an empty one near the stage,' Forsyth shouted. 'Let's get us a sit-down and work out whose round it is.' He led them in a snaking procession through standing drinkers until they reached their goal, each recruit taking one side of the continuous bench, upholstered in imitation black leather, which surrounded three sides of the large square table.

Harvey unbuttoned his greatcoat and glanced round the busy room. 'You don't think this one's reserved, do you?'

Forsyth jeered. 'No fucking sign on it, is there? Your shout, I reckon, college boy. Mine's a Victory.'

Robert could see customers standing at the brightly lit bar counter, and was about to go and order when a waitress came to their table.

'Can I help you, gentlemen?' She was blonde, pale-skinned and smiled broadly, though all three men found their gaze resting on her uplifted bosom rather than her yellow teeth.

'You can help me any day, pet,' said Forsyth, 'but how about bringing us three Victories first?'

Her glance fell on the coat he had deposited beside him. 'Weren't you asked to check that in?'

Forsyth couldn't see why it should matter. 'Never know, might feel like wrapping up later. So it's three large – our man here's paying. And, eh, where do we go for extras?'

The waitress was still perplexed by the unchecked coats. 'Did you reserve this table for dining?'

'It's oats we're thinking of, pet, if you get my drift.'

She was stony-faced. 'This table's reserved for Daddy, you know that, don't you?'

Forsyth gave a bemused laugh and looked to the other two for help. 'I'll be your daddy, love.'

'You didn't check in, did you?' she said accusingly.

'All we're after is a drink,' Forsyth told her with growing exasperation, 'and a wee bit adult entertainment, seeing as they all say this is a knocking shop.'

'Excuse me.'

The waitress retreated, and Harvey muttered, 'I knew we shouldn't have sat here.'

Robert could see her go to a small counter they had walked past on entering, which he now realized was a coat-check desk. The waitress conferred with the grey-haired woman seated there; both looked towards the volunteers' table. There was a shaking of heads, an exchange of words, and the ladies were soon joined by the burly doorman offering his own opinion about the anomaly.

'I think we're going to get flung out,' Robert said when the waitress began making her way back towards them.

'Don't talk pish, we only parked our fucking arses in the wrong place.'

She reached them and said, 'It's all right for you to keep your coats if you want. Or I'll take them for you.'

'So we can stay here?' Harvey asked doubtfully.

'Certainly. What drinks do you want?'

'Three Victories,' Forsyth reminded her cheerfully, his mood reverting with the swiftness of a child's.

'People here usually prefer the German beers, they're stronger.'

'You've got foreign beer?' Harvey asked incredulously.

'We've got pretty much everything.'

The waitress recited a Teutonic list like something out of the poetry book Robert had thumbed in the library, and Forsyth ended it by saying, 'Aye, three of those.' When she left, he grinned broadly. 'We're in, lads. Reckon she's a hoor?'

Harvey was unimpressed. 'Who's Daddy, that's what I want to know.'

Robert continued to look round the low-ceilinged cellar, searching for familiar faces. There was no sign of Rosalind, but at the far side of the room he saw some young men he thought he recognized from the College, seated round a table, talking earnestly. And coming down the steps he saw Professor Vine, who went to join the debaters.

'Your drinks, gentlemen.' The waitress positioned three tall glasses on circular beer mats.

'Didn't know Jerries drank out of flower vases,' Forsyth said sceptically.

Robert brought out his voucher book. 'How much?'

'We settle bills at the end.'

'And what if Daddy shows up?' asked Harvey.

The waitress stared at the three of them and smiled. 'You really don't know very much about this place, do you?'

'There's one thing we know, pet. Not only drinks for sale, eh?'

'You'll have to wait,' she told him. 'No access without authorization.' Then with a wink she left to serve another table.

Forsyth was stupefied with delight. 'Hear that?' he said, lifting his glass. 'I'm having her, no mistake. Soon as Daddy comes and signs our forms.'

Getting a woman here was like borrowing a library book. How many date stamps did Dora have, Robert wondered, seeing her with two bottles of wine, a large jug of water and several glasses held high on a tray she delivered through the crowd without incident; a heavy load for her to bear after a long day serving tea and coffee at the College. It was to Vine's table that she went; for there, in full progress now that he had joined his students, was the night school the professor had spoken of. One of the physicists was jotting something in a notebook while the others huddled round to see; all ignored the waitress distributing refreshments among them.

Harvey noticed the music striking up on the PA; a slow ballad meant to create an atmosphere of sophistication. 'This is an old one,' he said.

Forsyth quaffed his beer. 'I can't stand that shite.' Somehow goaded by the music's gentle pace, he quickly emptied his glass, then declared himself ready for a slash and got up to find the toilet.

Harvey moved round the table to sit next to Robert. 'My mum loves this song.'

Robert imagined her leaning over a small record player, drawing comfort from the vapid melody. 'I hope you manage to get her rehoused,' he said, though Robert knew it would never happen; his two fellow recruits were experimental controls whose bodies were simply the right size and weight.

'You know what I said to you today, about Rosalind? Forget all of that, will you?'

'Let's not even mention it again.'

'That idea I had, about her beaming signals into our heads . . .'

'Don't worry, it could never happen.' Robert looked towards the entrance and saw who was coming down the steps now. 'Here's Daddy.'

Davis and Willoughby were being greeted by a red-haired waitress who supervised the checking of their coats and then began to lead them through the crowd. So Willoughby had changed his mind about retiring early, Robert thought; or else had been brought here at Davis's behest, like the recruits. They arrived at the table just as Forsyth returned from the lavatory; the volunteers shuffled together so that the overweight academician could be comfortably accommodated.

'We were unexpectedly delayed,' Davis, standing beside the waitress, explained to the volunteers, addressing none of them in particular and not really explaining anything at all. 'What shall we have to drink?'

Robert and Harvey still had most of their beer left; Forsyth stared into his empty glass and said, 'Same again?'

'Or how about some wine?' Davis proposed, describing for Willoughby's benefit a range which, to the discerning customer, was the Blue Cat's principal attraction. 'Medoc, perhaps? They have a very good one.' Willoughby nodded assent, and Davis instructed the waitress accordingly, adding, 'Three more beers for our young friends,' before she departed.

Then he sat down, and although he had one of the square booth's three sides to himself – Robert and Harvey being opposite him, Forsyth and Willoughby between – and although Davis was a thin man whose sense of physical space and its attendant proprieties appeared keen, nevertheless his presence, his quiet air of authority and control, now made the table feel closed to any further visitors. 'How very agreeable to see you all again in such relaxed and informal surroundings,' he said, his cold eyes dwelling on Robert's face, and when no one spoke, he turned towards Willoughby, saying in a comradely way, 'Don't you think the Installation's scientists have an enviable existence?

'Certainly,' Willoughby agreed. 'I only wish the same opportunities existed for writers.'

Davis laughed. 'You should suggest it at the next Party Congress: a city of literature. Closed to outsiders, of course.'

Willoughby picked up the joke so eagerly that he almost appeared to take the proposal seriously. 'We'd have residencies, retreats, a research institute. We'd invite a physicist or mathematician now and again to try and give us some new ideas.'

'And of course you'd have a Blue Cat of your own,' Davis added. 'With all the delights such establishments offer.' He scanned the recruits' faces once more. 'Gentlemen, have you fully explored the facilities yet?'

Forsyth, tearing at his damp beer mat, snickered and said, 'We've been waiting for Daddy.'

Davis smiled knowingly; Willoughby was bemused and asked the commissioner what it meant.

'Blue Cat slang,' Davis explained. 'Daddies are people of Category D. It brings benefits.'

'So we're daddies?' Forsyth said with wonder at the new discovery. 'That bird only wanted some proof?'

'I'm all the proof you need,' Davis said flatly. 'Who do you want? The redhead, Beth? Here she comes now.'

She was bringing their drinks, and after giving the soldiers their beers and placing empty wine glasses before Davis and Willoughby, she poured a sample from the open bottle for the commissioner to try. He raised it to his thin lips, sipped delicately and rolled the fluid in his mouth, watched by the others who knew that what was really being sampled was the waitress herself.

Davis swallowed and said to Forsyth, 'Well?'

Forsyth shrugged. 'Aye, sure.'

'Or should we send for another?' The waitress still held the bottle in readiness, and seeing her uncertainty, Davis said to her, 'Pour.'

She filled both glasses. 'Anything else?'

'I don't think he's decided yet, Beth.'

Taking his meaning, she turned and stared at Forsyth; a gaze that was simultaneously inviting and contemptuous. 'Well?' she said, echoing the commissioner's challenge.

Forsyth was hesitant. 'No offence, but I was thinking maybe . . .'

'You want another girl?' she said abruptly.

'The blonde that was here before.'

She looked to Davis for further instruction, and a nod from him sent her in search. Then he addressed Willoughby again. 'Brian, perhaps you might like some time alone with one or two of the hostesses.' Willoughby beamed but shook his head. 'No need to be shy, Brian, we're all grown men here, and whatever happens in the Blue Cat goes no further

– not even into the rest of the Installation. Not a word. Anyone who comes down those steps becomes a different person, and anything he does here can be forgotten as soon as he leaves. When we come to the Blue Cat we hang up our moral qualms along with our coats. Your wife need never know a thing.'

Willoughby, his curved lips pursed in a suppressed, embarrassed laugh, shook his head again, and in response to Davis's insistence said by way of excuse, 'I have already had all the stimulation this evening that a man of my age requires.' Robert knew at once that he referred to Rosalind. 'The nimbus of pleasure is not to be evaporated through over-hasty repetition.'

'Spoken like a true poet!' Davis chuckled. 'But really, you ought to see what's available here.' He snapped his fingers at the nearest waitress he could find; a woman who was out of Robert's view but quickly came at Davis's bidding. It was Dora.

'Good evening, gentlemen,' she said. 'Can I be of service?' While she spoke, she never met Robert's eyes – nor, it seemed to him, those of any other man at the table. Her words were completely impersonal, her actions those of a convincing robot.

'Hello, Wanda,' Davis said with confident familiarity, using what was clearly her pseudonym here. 'My friend Mr Clark would like to see the show – will you take him?'

'Certainly, sir.'

Once more, Willoughby offered polite resistance, but Davis was not to be refused. 'Please, Mr Clark,' Davis said to him encouragingly, 'Wanda will escort you to the peep show next door. It's highly entertaining – stay as long as you wish. And if you feel like anything else while you're through there, it's all on me.'

'You're very kind, Commissioner,' said Willoughby, immediately covering his mouth at what he thought might be a gaffe, and squeezing his weight along the space which Davis, rising, made for him. 'Sorry if I said something I shouldn't have.'

'It's quite all right, Mr Clark,' said Davis. 'There's no need to be discreet on my behalf. Now go and enjoy the performance – it's not Shakespeare but it's totally sincere.'

Davis sat down again, and Dora and Willoughby made their way across the room to what Robert saw to be an inconspicuous yellow door distinguished only by the dark-suited man standing in attendance who opened it, then sealed the pair from view.

There was no music on the PA system now; the only sound was the clatter of glasses and the clash of a hundred voices, but beyond the yellow door, Robert thought, something altogether more single-minded must be happening. Just as he had wondered about Willoughby and Rosalind, he tried to imagine how the Writers' Union President might be entertained by Dora; but the task was impossible, the cards remained hidden from view.

Soon they were joined again by the first hostess they had seen that evening, her manner transformed. 'I see you've got your authorization sorted, boys,' she said teasingly. 'Want some fun?'

Forsyth needed no further asking; he got up straight away. 'Take me to heaven, baby.'

Davis nodded approval, then the girl took Forsyth to the same yellow door, not far from where Vine's night school was still progressing, and when it opened Forsyth turned, looked towards his comrades and gave them a thumbs-up gesture, as if about to climb into the space capsule and disappear forever.

'And then there were two,' said Davis, sipping his wine.

There was some activity on the stage; Robert turned to see three men with permed hair and spangled jackets lift the electric guitars resting on steel stands in readiness for their act. A paunchy drummer took his place at the rear and then a tired-looking woman in a long purple dress came to the microphone, unannounced and unnoticed by the crowd. A moment later the band struck up, offering a live version of the same kind of music that had been playing earlier, whose principal aim was to encourage people to talk over it.

'A fine place, don't you think?' Davis said to the recruits. 'You can see why everyone wants to come here.'

Harvey nodded. 'Beer's good.'

'And not only the beer, of course. There's also a certain matter of fucking. Most of the people here wouldn't be allowed so much as a grope of a waitress's arse – they'd get thrown out at once. But you're part of the elite, and that brings privileges. The best girls aren't even on view, they're all through there.' He pointed to the yellow door, from which a middle-aged man could be seen leaving, then going to collect his coat. 'Want me to get you an escort?'

Harvey took a gulp of beer. 'Still plenty left. Let's see how it goes.'

The red-haired waitress came to see if they wanted any more drinks. 'Not yet,' said Davis, 'though I really don't know why that oaf didn't take you when he had the chance.

Harvey, what do you think, beautiful, eh? Wouldn't you like to screw her?' Beth gave an oddly modest smile, as if Davis had made no more than a mildly inappropriate but vaguely complimentary comment. 'Good tits, nice arse. On you go, Harvey, let her make a man of you.'

Harvey stared into his glass. 'No thanks.'

'What? I offer you a lovely woman, free of charge, no strings, and you refuse? What are you talking about?'

Beth was about to leave the table; Davis swiftly reached out and held her arm. 'Wait,' he said, and she stayed. There was a new note of hardness in his voice. 'Go with her, Harvey.'

'I don't want to.'

A half-hearted flutter of applause greeted the ending of a song. 'I don't care if you fucking want to, man, it's an order. Screw her good and hard.'

Both Robert and Harvey had their eyes lowered in fear and shame. 'It's a strange order,' Harvey murmured.

'Strange? You think fucking a woman's strange? What are you, some kind of pervert?' As Davis's voice rose, Robert looked up to see the vein that had begun bulging on the commissioner's forehead; his grip on Beth had tightened and she was staring helplessly over her shoulder towards the doorman who watched everything from the foot of the stairs but appeared unwilling or unable to come and intervene. At last Davis released Beth, but his nod told her she must stay and wait for further orders. Another dismal ballad started up on stage. 'Well, Harvey?' he said. 'Are you a homo?'

'No, sir.'

'So what's up? Afraid your girlfriend will find out?'

'I don't have one, sir.'

Davis looked mystified. 'What earthly reason can there be for refusing this lovely, willing woman? She's trying to earn a living and you're wasting her time. You needn't be afraid of catching anything – the standards here are very high and all the girls get regular checks.'

'It's wrong.'

'What? Whoring is wrong? Beth, do you enjoy working here?'

'Yes, sir,' she said.

'There you are, Harvey, she loves it, so what's all the fake moralizing for?' He paused. 'Don't tell me you've got religious principles.'

'No, sir.'

'You'd be slung out of the forces if you did. Or maybe you don't fancy her, is that it? Then shut your eyes and think of someone else. You're supposed to be a professionally trained killer; if your commander ordered you to stick a bayonet in a baby, that's what you'd do. I order you to stick a hard cock in a whore and you go all limp on me.'

'With the greatest respect, sir,' said Harvey, 'you're not my commanding officer . . .' He tailed off as he saw Davis's face. It was the face of someone whose power was self-appointed, illegitimate and absolute; someone who could have Harvey beaten up in a soundproof interrogation room and then shot as a spy.

Davis spoke quietly. 'You're the luckiest fucker in the world, Harvey, do you know that? If you'd said that to me anywhere else but here you'd be a dead man, and I'd see to it that your whore mother got kicked out of her wheelchair and down the stairs. Do you know about her and the schoolteacher?'

'What?'

'Her and Mr Wilson, did she never tell you?' Robert was almost as stunned by this latest provocation as Harvey was. 'Now get up off that pink arse of yours and let this woman show you what life's about. Stick your dirty little thing wherever it'll fit. And Beth, tell me all about it afterwards.'

Harvey rose from his seat as if he were being taken away for torture. Beth forced a smile. 'Come on, soldier, I'll look after you.' There was something painfully maternal about the way she took charge of him, leading him across the bar and through the yellow door.

'I do like to spread a little happiness in the world,' Davis said to his last remaining companion, moving closer and sliding his half-filled wine glass across the table. 'Got anything to tell?'

'About Kaupff?'

'Whatever you can give me. I'm all ears.'

Robert swallowed a mouthful of beer. 'The Franks really think the boy's death was an accident. You won't get any more from them.'

'Hmm.' Davis pondered the situation while the singer raised an arm in synchrony with her voice, though it was not the band to which both men gave their attention, but the door. 'I'm sure the Franks will have more to say once you get to know them better.'

Robert felt he knew them too well already. He could easily imagine the three of them sitting at a table here; Miriam scowling while Arthur downed litres of German beer; Dot clutching her handbag and saying she needed to Blue Cat off to the loo.

The door opened and it was Dora who reappeared.

'Our great writer must have found another friend,' Davis observed. 'Wanda isn't the best-looking tart here, I suppose.' He turned to Robert. 'You know you'll be rewarded, don't you? Give me a little and you get a little. Give me more and the prize gets better. Money, privileges, power, sex – every man wants something different, but we have everything here. You might even be allowed to leave.'

'You mean the others . . . ?'

Davis smiled. 'What do you think? Would we let an idiot like Forsyth or that pansy Harvey go back outside and spill the beans? Already they know far too much. But let's not darken the mood – don't you love the atmosphere here? A secret bar in a secret town – and on the other side of that door another secret. A world within a world. Who do you want to fuck, Coyle?'

'Wanda,' he said at once.

'Wanda?' Davis rubbed his chin. 'Following in the giant's wake, so to speak.'

'She's the one I want.'

Dora was at Vine's table, taking orders from the night school. Davis waved across to the professor to make her turn; and when she did, Davis pointed at Robert, at the door, and she understood at once. Someone else would have to serve the scientists.

'She's all yours,' Davis said as Robert got up to follow her, making his way past Vine's table while the band began the next love song in their list.

'Come and join us afterwards,' Vine called to him above

the music. Robert nodded, then went to the door being held open for him.

13

Dora silently beckoned him through, out of the noisy blue-lit bar and into a corridor, illuminated by red neon tubes, whose featureless walls, painted matt black, were interrupted at regular intervals on both sides by small windows at head height. Robert paused to look through one and saw a naked woman sitting on a chair. It was like a miniature bedroom sparsely furnished with the essentials of the trade, which included a sink and bidet, some items of lurid lingerie hanging on a rail, a table strewn with magazines and a whip. The girl was alone and appeared oblivious to her exposure, nonchalantly examining the big toe of her right foot, raised by the practical but ungainly crossing of one leg over the other. Her belly sagged above a dark bush of pubic hair.

'That's Shelly,' said Dora. 'Would you rather have her?' Perhaps Shelly heard, because she raised her face and stared at Robert through the window. Shelly looked blankly at him, uncrossed her legs and spread her heels on the floor, then began to stroke her bush in what seemed like a standard and formalized invitation. Robert turned away, too embarrassed to look further. 'Come on,' said Dora, leading him along the corridor. Each window had a coarse pink curtain inside; some were open, revealing the room's solitary occupant, skimpily dressed or wholly naked, while other curtains were drawn closed to hide girls at work with their clients. In the space of only a few metres Robert saw as many as twenty prostitutes: women with the ample figures of tribal fertility icons; flat-chested girls so thin you could count their bones. Blondes, brunettes, redheads; breasts standing proud like small-nosed puppies, sagging like a basset hound's ears; buttocks smooth as butter or puckered like lemon peel. There were girls who looked as though they might still be at school, women old enough to be his mother. And as well as these, there were the equal number unseen behind closed curtains, reminding Robert of the corridor in the College where everyone was 'in' or 'out'.

Dora stopped at one of the curtained windows and fumbled with something brought from her pocket which proved to be a small key. Somewhere beneath the window there was a lock, too inconspicuous for Robert to have noticed in the dark, and with a quick twist and push she opened the handleless door in which the window was set; a door – like all the others on the corridor – rendered invisible through being perfectly flush with the matching black wall. 'Come,' she said. The light was already on, a white bulb that seemed unduly bright, more geared to efficiency than atmosphere. She closed the door behind him, sealing it with an iron security bar made to withstand the most determined of drunk intruders, and then with her back to him began to pull her white top up to her shoulders, exposing the black bra she wore beneath.

'Stop!' he said.

She turned, her clothing still raised in her hands. 'Sure, there's no hurry.' Covering herself again, she came towards him and reached a firm hand onto his crotch. This morning, in the crowded elevator, Rosalind had brushed her fingers, accidentally or otherwise, against his penis, and the transitory thrill had almost lifted him off his feet. Dora's hand was as lifeless and functional as the electric light that hurt his eyes.

'I don't want sex with you, Dora.'

'My name's Wanda.'

'That's not what you told me this morning.'

She moved away from him; her face looked worn. 'You've got a poor memory. I told you that when we're in the Blue Cat different rules apply. People have new identities here.'

'It's a charade.'

'Yes,' she said. 'It's the only way it can work. The men who fuck me here go home to their wives, then I see them next day in the College and offer them a cup of coffee and a biscuit, and everybody acts like nothing happened. That's how it is.' With a single swift action she pulled her top over her head and stood before him in her bra. 'Let's get on with it, soldier.'

'I told you, Dora, I don't want sex.'

'And I told you, my name's Wanda. How about some sucking?' Again she reached for his crotch, intending to unzip him. He backed away.

'What will you tell Davis?' he asked. She looked puzzled. 'He'll want to know if we did it.'

Dora gave a laugh. 'I'll say anything you want. I'll tell him you fucked my brains out.'

'But we don't have to do it, right?'

'I won't lie for you, soldier. If I lie, I do it for myself.' She kicked off her high-heeled shoes, slid her skirt to her knees and stepped out if it. 'Are you a top or a bottom man?' she asked coolly. 'Do you like to see tits first, or cunt?'

'I don't know why you're doing this.'

'I'm doing it because we both have to, so we might as well get on with it.' She pushed him gently back until he sat down on the bed, then she pulled off his boots and began to loosen his trousers. 'This is my job, it's how I survive. And you're a man. You've got a thing that has a mind and needs of its own.' She drew his cock out of his loosened trousers and began stroking it like a mouse. 'You come in here saying you don't want to do it, but I've heard that before. I've had men weep on me, spill their tears on me, tell me their problems, say they only want someone they can pour out their heart to. One man had just buried his wife the previous day. But they all end up fucking me, even the man who lost his wife. They've all got this thing that controls them.' He had gone hard in her hand but was still determined to resist.

'I only came here because I want to talk to you, Dora.' She put her moist lips over the swollen end of his penis, the most astonishing sensation he had ever known, and for a moment he was unable to do anything except marvel at the pleasure. Then he pushed her clear of his lap. 'You don't have to do this. Why can't we talk?'

She looked up at him with an expression of pity. 'You're wrong,' she said. 'We do have to do this. You're a man with a hard cock and I'm a slave. We don't have any choice.'

'I want to help you.'

'Help me?' She laughed mockingly and stood before him

with a challenging air. 'All right, I'll tell you what to do. Go out there and start a revolution, change the fucking world. You're a soldier, aren't you? Get hold of a machine gun and shoot every bastard sitting in that bar, every single one of them. That'd help. Otherwise let me do what I have to do with that stiff cock of yours, because as soon as it pumps its stuff into me you're not going to feel like talking to me anymore, are you?' She jabbed his chest to make him lie back on the bed, his legs still dangling on the floor, and pulled his trousers and pants off before removing her own remaining underwear. Then she straddled him, rubbing her crotch against his as she unbuttoned his shirt.

'I can give you money,' he said. 'Look in my pocket – they've given me lots.'

'Those stupid vouchers? They're worth nothing to me.' She was sliding herself over him and he was desperate to have her, just like Davis wanted. She moved away and got off the bed to stand on the floor beside him, looking down at his sweating, panting face. 'You don't understand anything at all about this place, do you?'

'What . . . what do you mean?'

'There's a very strict rationing system here.' She turned, and he watched her rump retreat the small distance to the other side of the room where her skirt lay on the floor. She lifted and folded it, bending over the small white cupboard on whose top she placed the garment neatly, displaying her buttocks like the meat the butcher had used this afternoon to tease and taunt a queue of women. She turned again. 'Your vouchers are no good to me – I can't buy anything useful with them. But if you aren't going to run out and start castrating every man in the Installation, there's one way you really can help me. The daddies who come here, they bring me things. Food mostly. That I can use. I don't want your talk, soldier, I don't want you telling me how sorry you feel about me, because I can't eat talk, I can't wear talk. Talk doesn't keep my toes from getting so cold that I cry with pain on my way to the College to hand out biscuits to the men who fuck me. Talk doesn't stop my belly rumbling. Your talk is as worthless as your book of vouchers. So fine, you don't want sex with me; in that case get dressed and get out, because I don't want talk with you. If you want to help me, come back tomorrow with something for my stomach – you're not rationed and your vouchers could feed me for a month. Then if you want to stick your thing in me it's up to you. Do it now if you want.'

He was still painfully aroused, but as he looked at her, propping himself on his elbow on the bed, he saw a human being in need. All the doubt that had been submerged beneath the effects of the drug or the machine in his pillow or whatever it was they had used to brainwash him became focused, like sunlight through a lens, into a small, brilliantly intense spot of burning anger; a white star of indignation. He didn't have to accept any of this. She must have seen the change in his face; she came back to the bed and knelt on the floor beside him. 'Life's not so bad,' she said. Then she took his rigid penis in her hand and with two or three swift flicks brought business to an end. She got up and fetched a roll of paper towel for him, carefully mopping droplets from the bed and floor while he attended to himself. 'Feeling better now?' she asked, going to throw the used towels in the swingbin beside the sink and then washing her hands. He nodded meekly, got up and dressed himself while she did the same. Soon they both looked as if nothing had happened.

He reached into his trouser pocket and brought out his voucher book. 'How much do you want?' he asked, an air of apology in his voice.

She gently pushed his hand away. 'Free introductory offer,' she said. 'When you come back, bring me a present. Some meat, say. Or chocolate; the real kind, not the horrible fake stuff they foist on the low-category workers. I need a new pair of gloves, too.' She held up her right hand and extended the fingers which not long before had brought him gratification; they were long, thin and elegant.

'You have beautiful hands,' he told her.

'They're the hands of a musician,' she explained. 'Nowadays they wash toilets and pull cocks.' She said it simply, without any hint of malice, and he took her outstretched fingers in his.

'Why are you here, Dora? What did you do?'

'Nothing,' she said. 'Absolutely nothing. Maybe I'll tell you my story when you come back with a present for me – but remember, I'm not a little girl who gets ecstatic over pink ribbons or the smell of roses. I can't eat ribbons and roses. This is how I survive, and if I live long enough without going mad, I might even make it out of this shithole one day.'

'I'll see you tomorrow,' he said. Then, before she could finish lifting clear the iron bar that blocked the door from intruders, he took her round the waist and kissed her on the lips. It was a long, loving kiss, and she tasted to him like the sweetest thing in the world. He no longer needed artificial courage; here was the sort of woman for whom he could happily risk his life.

She let go of the bar and pushed him back firmly, staring at him with anger. 'Never do that again, soldier, do you understand? You can touch me any place you like, stick your thing where you want, as long as you pay. But never kiss me. That's what people do when they're in love – and in this place there is no love.' She opened the door and waved him out of her room. 'You know the way.' Then she closed the door, and he heard the iron bar drop back in place. He stood waiting for a moment, but nothing happened; he wondered why she had become so hostile. Eventually the curtain swished open; he glimpsed her arm at it but not her face, and when she moved away from the window he saw that she was completely naked again, going to sit on the wooden chair near the bed, not meeting his gaze as she slumped languidly in anticipation of her next visitor, and looking just like all the other women trapped here.

14

When Robert stepped back into the bustling, blue-lit bar, he found it transformed by what he had witnessed. The same sequinned band was still going through its faded repertoire, and at every table, laughing customers continued to be served by the pretty and obliging hostesses. Yet it was all a pretence, like the toy money in his pocket. Across the room, Forsyth and Harvey had both returned to sit with Davis, but none of them noticed Robert. Vine waved to him.

'Join us now.' Vine's students were intently discussing some calculations scribbled on a napkin; Robert sat down beside the professor, and with a fatherly smile, Vine filled a spare wine glass then topped up his own. 'A lot better than the mulled stuff earlier.' He raised his glass to clink a toast. 'Here's to a successful mission.'

They sipped together, and Robert watched the physicists, who seemed very agitated over something called zero-point energy. 'Is it true Kaupff never comes here?'

Vine nodded. 'He's not gregarious. The life of the College suits him perfectly; he thrives on isolation.'

'Perhaps there are other reasons why he doesn't come. Maybe he disapproves.'

Vine looked at him with eyes skewed by alcohol. 'Disapproves? I'd hardly call Heinz a prude.'

'But the women in there are prisoners . . .'

'No, Robert, they all volunteer freely. Some are Category O, it's true, but working in the Blue Cat isn't part of their compulsory duty – they want to earn some extra money, and who are we to criticize? I tell you, the women like it, otherwise they wouldn't do it.' He grinned. 'Your objections seem a little belated, given that you've already spent what I can only assume were a very enjoyable twenty minutes in there.' Robert felt a flush of shame, which Vine noticed. 'Ah, *post coitum omne animal triste est*. Have your fun then punish yourself with regret later. Don't be a fool, Robert; the sexual instinct is the most natural thing in the world, and the Blue Cat exists precisely so that high-level workers at the Installation won't be bothered by frustration, and hence can be more productive. I'm a happily married man and I don't have any need of the girls here –

though strictly between you and me, I might occasionally make use of them – but for lads like you and your fellow recruits, it's a stark choice between prostitutes, masturbation, or propositioning women in the street, and as you realize, there aren't enough of them to go round. So, enough of this hypocrisy. Come here and discharge yourself whenever you feel the call of nature, and think no more of it. There are matters of far greater importance which need to be discussed.' He grew more serious. 'I heard about your score in the telepathy test today.'

Robert looked across the room and saw Davis staring steadily at him. 'I'd better go back . . .'

'No,' said Vine, calmly patting Robert's arm. 'When he wants you he'll let us know.' Davis's eyes were on someone else now; Willoughby was returning, and squeezed himself into the space the recruits made for him, looking flushed and overheated.

'Hope he doesn't have a heart attack while he's here,' Vine said sardonically. 'But tell me, how long have you been aware of your telepathic ability?'

Robert shrugged. 'I'd never noticed it before. I'm completely surprised.'

'From what I hear, that's quite normal. According to Rosalind, if we did regular tests and visualization exercises in schools, we'd probably find that as many as ten per cent of children have strategically useful skills. She's certainly come up with some remarkable data from her work so far – I'm truly amazed. You know, I'm a physicist of the old school, and I always thought of mind-reading as nothing more than a music-hall trick.' He leaned closer to Robert. 'Did you really play fair, or was there any cheating?'

'I give you my word, sir . . .'

'This mission is very important, you know that. Careers are the smallest thing at stake.' Vine nodded towards the distant figure of Davis, who was ordering more drink or sex from a waitress at their table. 'When they send a Party man to keep watch, you know they mean business. And it's always the same; they say there's a spy on the loose, so that we'll all suspect one another, and if the mission fails they haul away one of the team and put a bullet in his neck for espionage.'

'You've seen it happen?'

'Many times,' said Vine. 'When I was on the Pluto project, the head was accused of sabotage and relieved of his duties. Not long afterwards it was announced that he'd died of a heart attack.'

Robert looked across at Willoughby's rosy face; the writer was agreeing to some new proposal from Davis. 'Do you think the academician might be in line for one?'

Vine tutted at Robert's naivety. 'If he croaks it'll be because of some mistake made on the outside. No, if anyone should worry it's Kaupff, Simmons, Bradshaw, me. We know how it's done. The head of Pluto was given a hero's funeral, his widow got a huge pension. So you see, Robert, I'm not particularly concerned with niceties like the ethics of prostitution. I simply want to know if you're a psychic or a charlatan, because good men's lives depend on it.'

'I told you,' said Robert, 'I give you my word. Rosalind held up the cards and I wrote down what I thought – red or black.' He saw Forsyth getting up to follow another girl to the brothel; Forsyth saw Robert, too, and again gave his jubilant thumbs-up before disappearing. 'This whole mission is inside people's heads,' Robert said to Vine. 'The only way I'll ever see space is by telepathy – the capsule's a charade, isn't it?' The musicians on stage were accepting the feeble applause of the crowd as their shift came to a welcome end.

'You're wrong,' said Vine, putting his glass on the table and stroking its stem. 'The capsule's real – we don't think we can detect scalar waves adequately from the Earth's surface, though obviously we're trying. I'd happily show you how we're calculating the frozen star's radiation flux – an elegant idea initiated by one of Kaupff's former students, a fellow called Hawkins – but I see it's time for you to return to your table.'

Davis had given the signal. Robert rose, glanced at his watch and saw from the glint of its brass hands in the low light that the time was almost midnight. 'Do you always stay here so late?'

'The nights are our pleasure,' said Vine. 'We make them last as long as we can. Sleep is something most of us have learned to do without.' He looked over towards Davis's table. 'Now go and be nice to the commissioner. If he asks, tell him my heart is in good working order and I hope it has another ten or fifteen years of patriotic work left in it. My liver, of course, is another matter.' Vine drained his glass and beamed, but in his eyes there was sadness.

Robert found Davis, Willoughby and Harvey sitting quietly together, their conversation exhausted but their escape still not in sight. His return prompted Willoughby to break the silence. 'Behold the brave pioneer!' he said as Robert sat down beside Harvey. 'Do you know the poem?'

'It sounds familiar.'

'Familiar!' Willoughby rolled his eyes, then looked towards Davis, whose attention was elsewhere. 'I really must have a word with the Inspector of School Literature and Ideology.' Willoughby began reciting some lines that sounded to Robert as if they could have been sung by the mediocre band, though Willoughby declaimed them with a pedagogic lyricism which implied them to be high art.

Davis ignored the poetry, and when it was finished swung his gaze towards Robert. 'Was she good?'

'Yes.'

'Did you come inside her?'

Robert wondered whether to lie, but the sheer hatred he felt for Davis left him unable to invent. 'I got a bit too excited.'

Davis laughed. 'An eager young prick! I'll bet you shot far.'

The commissioner glanced at Willoughby as if for support, but the writer appeared to share Robert's distaste. He scratched his beard and declared, 'I've had a great time but now I need to sleep.'

Davis nodded brusquely and said he would order a car, then looked at the two volunteers. 'Your absent friend is doing all the fucking for you tonight – why not go and join him? Even if you've got no spunk left, you could watch and see what a real man does.'

Both recruits stared at the table, neither able to meet Davis's eyes. Robert said, 'I also need some sleep.'

'Me too,' Harvey added immediately.

'I see,' said Davis, as a girl arrived at their table. Robert recognized her – a plump brunette whom he had seen naked in a cubicle not long before.

'Is there anything I can do for you gentlemen?' she asked brightly.

'Go and speak to George,' Davis instructed her. 'We need two cars.'

'I don't mind walking,' Robert interrupted. 'I'm sure it won't take more than twenty minutes, even if I get lost a few times.'

Davis stared at him suspiciously while the girl stood waiting. 'Why do you want to walk?'

'I need the air, that's all. But I don't want to break any rules.'

Davis maintained his penetrating study of Robert's demeanour, as if performing a mental feat more intricate and challenging than anything being undertaken by the night school of physicists at the other side of the room. 'Your request surprises me. But you're perfectly free to walk if that's what you wish. The Town has no curfew, and as long as you can show your papers if you're stopped by security, you'll be home soon enough. Turn right when you go out of here and you'll soon find the main street.'

'I'll walk with you,' Harvey told Robert.

'You make a lovely couple,' Davis said with effortless malice, then told the girl, 'Only one car, going to the Lodge.' She left to do his bidding, her hips swaying as she went to speak with the doorman. Davis stood up. 'Now, if you three gentlemen will excuse me, I shall go and see the entertainment next door. I wish you all a good night.'

They watched Davis proceed stiffly and without any sign of intoxication across the room, pausing only to exchange a few words with Vine. 'Let's go,' Robert told Harvey. 'Goodnight, Mr Willoughby.'

'See you tomorrow,' the writer replied with a sleepy nod, and Robert wondered if Rosalind was still in his bed at the Lodge, awaiting the great man's alcohol-scented return. The two volunteers lifted their coats and made their way to the exit, where the doorman stood at the foot of the stairs blocking their way.

'Your car isn't here yet, sirs.'

'We're walking,' said Robert.

The doorman, who had the fist-sculpted face of a prize-fighter, looked puzzled. 'Why walk?'

'We want to,' Harvey insisted, buttoning his coat.

'I hope you know the house rules.' The doorman managed to sound both benevolent and threatening.

'There's no rule against walking home.'

'I mean about the girls,' said the doorman. 'Are you meeting any? They're only allowed to do business here, not outside. If they want to give you a free fuck it's up to them, but it has to be in your own bed – no knee tremblers against a wall.' Even the simple act of walking, Robert reflected, was tainted in these people's minds. The Blue Cat was supposed to be a way of freeing men from sexual need but had exactly the opposite effect. 'I wouldn't want you lads getting into any trouble,' the doorman continued. 'It'd give me a lot of bother, you understand.' Then he turned to lead them up the steps to the locked door. 'So you promise me you're not doing business?' With a jangle of keys he let in a welcome waft of cold night air. The recruits stepped outside, and the doorman's craggy features hardened. ''Cause if you do, it's the girls that come off worse. Don't make problems for them. There's always as much snatch here as you could want – you can even spend the night if you need to. And if you want it outdoors, let me know and I'll see what I can do.'

They wanted only to get out, and after giving their assurances once more, the door closed behind them and they made their way in grateful silence, walking beside the featureless brick wall of the large warehouse from whose crowded basement no sound or glimmer was permitted to leak. White floodlights at the top of the warehouse lit their way, but the opposite side of the street was dark and appeared to be waste ground where buildings had once stood, a few pale slabs of concrete bearing testimony to their demolition. Robert followed Davis's instructions to turn right, but there was no sign of the main street; only a further succession of warehouses, leftovers from an earlier Installation project, empty and derelict in appearance. It was an eerie place, and although neither man wished to talk, both felt compelled to. 'Did you really do it?' Harvey asked.

Robert knew what he meant. 'She tossed me off.' Harvey took in the information but said nothing. 'How about you?' Their footsteps were echoing in the quiet street and they spoke in what was almost a whisper.

'I couldn't do it,' said Harvey. 'I told you what happened today with Rosalind, when she stood outside the toilet. She made a switch come on inside my head and I was like an animal. But then she must have switched it off. I couldn't do anything with Beth. She'll tell Davis.'

'Don't worry,' said Robert, but he knew how feeble his assurance must sound. When Davis had left them it was to receive a full report from the girls.

'Do you think it's true, what Davis said about my mum? How could he know? Do you think Mr Wilson was really spying on us when he used to come and give me extra reading lessons?'

They rounded a corner and Robert recognized the bowling alley. They were in a familiar part of Town now. Soon they came to the park; both knew their way from here, though they had to go in separate directions. 'I'll see you tomorrow, John,' said Robert, then watched his friend walk off into the darkness. The sky was still as cloudless as when they had looked through Kaupff's telescope. Robert savoured the stars as he walked with his hands pushed deep inside his coat pockets.

After a while he heard a noise; he turned but saw no one. He walked on, still thinking of the night's strange catalogue that had included the rings of Saturn and a woman's lips. Tomorrow he would buy her a pair of fur-lined gloves, some meat . . .

When he heard the noise again it was already too late: he was being grabbed from behind. Something hit him hard between the shoulders; he staggered and swayed then fell to the ground as a kick impacted on his side. It was only when a hood was put over his head that he began to think clearly: they're going to kill me.

15

There must have been something inside that hood; Robert could still feel its sickening aftertaste when he regained his senses and found himself unable to open his eyes, a blindfold having been secured tightly round his head. His hands were bound on his lap and he was sitting on what seemed to be a rickety wooden chair. His immediate thought was that he had been brought back to Davis's interrogation room, but the chemical in the hood had failed to knock him out completely, and he was sure it could only have taken his attackers a minute or two to bring him here.

'Can you hear me, Robert?' a man was saying to him through the darkness. 'We're your friends, we don't want to hurt you. We only need information.' Robert felt a hand on his shoulder; startling at first, but its pressure was light and somehow reassuring. The fingers moved towards his face and gently lifted his chin. 'Can you breathe freely? Do you need water?'

'What do you want?'

Another man spoke more harshly. 'Did you have a good time in the brothel? Which girl did you rape?'

'Quiet, brother,' his softer-voiced companion interrupted. 'Robert, we know why you've come to the Installation. We know about the mission.'

'The Red Star?'

'That's right, Robert, we know about the Red Star. And the radio signals. We know the Red Star is beaming messages to Earth.'

'Is it?' said Robert.

His interrogator paused.

'He's lying,' the other man said.

'Maybe not,' countered the first. 'Robert, what frequency are they searching?'

These were the spies Davis was pursuing. 'Who are you?' he asked. Then suddenly his head was spinning and it was as if he had been hit by a rock. The blow to his left cheek sent him flying towards the floor; his fall was broken by the arms of one of his captors.

'Brother!' the first man hissed, cradling Robert from further injury. 'We are on the Lord's side and ours is the way of peace!'

'The Lord is a man of war,' the second replied, and Robert felt himself being hauled by him back onto the chair. 'You're going to tell us everything we need to know, Coyle, otherwise I'm going to kill you. I set before you life and death: choose life.' The man's grip loosened and he stepped away on the creaking floor, leaving the other to resume his questioning.

'What's the frequency? Please don't fear us, Robert, we're good people.'

Robert's military training had included a session on just this sort of eventuality: the enemy capture you know will never happen. The simulation, he now realized, had been about as realistic as a plastic dummy in a resuscitation class.

'This is a waste of time,' the second man snarled. 'We'll get nowhere without some persuasion.' Robert felt something push against the side of his head. 'Want me to put a bullet in you?'

He was sure he was about to die, but it wasn't his life that now rushed before his bound eyes. Instead all he saw was a woman's delicate hand, her nimble fingers, a jet of fluid and the Milky Way spreading across the sky. He chose what he intended to be the last word he would ever say. 'Dora.'

'Who?'

He had managed to live another second. 'I wanted to help her. I hate everything there.'

'That's right!' It was the first man who spoke again; the gun moved away from Robert's head. 'We have to put an end to evil, and closing down a brothel is only the tiniest part.' A door opened; Robert heard footsteps coming into the room, light but firm as they approached, filling him with even greater fear. 'We live in dark times, Robert,' his interrogator continued, 'but we can overcome evil with good. You want that, don't you? How are we going to help Dora and the others?'

Robert remembered what she said: get a machine gun and kill everyone. 'Are you trying to start a revolution?'

'We've already begun. But you need to tell us the frequency.'

'Please, I don't know anything about it.' Another blow, a slap this time, still painful but less surprising than before. And in response to it, a new voice.

'Don't leave marks on him.'

It was a woman, and he recognized her at once. 'Miriam!'

There was silence, then a low curse. 'Get her out of here.'

'Help me, Miriam,' Robert gasped, strangely elated at having found something in this hell he could identify. The enmity between them was trivial now; she was his saviour, his comrade, his sister. He imbued her with all the hope he had of escaping this place alive. 'I warned you about the radio, didn't I? I took risks for you.' Hands fell again upon his head; he flinched and braced himself for more pain. Instead he felt the blindfold loosening; he blinked his irritated eyes as the small, slightly cluttered and perfectly ordinary living room of a house came into view, a setting altogether more mundane than the bare cell he had imagined. There was Miriam, arms folded, her face stern. There too was the retreating man who had chosen to let Robert see; the mild interrogator whom he now recognized as Miriam's boyfriend, Tim. And there was the third man, looking downcast, seated on the arm of a red settee, loosely holding an empty beer bottle in his hand, its neck the gun that had touched Robert's forehead. These three were only playing at being revolutionaries; they appeared incapable of doing much harm. Robert saw that his hands were bound with nothing more than sticky tape; the rest of him was unconstrained. He could easily make a run for the door.

'Now you know who we are,' said Tim. 'If you like you can have us all shot, and our parents too.'

'I don't want that.'

Miriam stepped forward. 'You were right, I was using the radio, and thank you for warning me. We were trying to find the frequency.'

'Of the Red Star?'

She nodded, and Robert felt more confused than ever.

'A better world is about to emerge,' said Tim. 'A new age is dawning. The star is the sign and we are the magi.'

'What are you talking about?'

The other man explained. 'Miriam works inside the College, she hears things, sees documents she shouldn't. Kaupff thinks the star is alive, conscious, sending signals to Earth.'

'You've got it all wrong,' said Robert.

'But Kaupff is an atheist, a materialist. He can't appreciate the spiritual side of life. He hasn't been praying. He hasn't received the word of God.'

'And you have?'

Anger flashed on the man's face; Tim saw it and calmed him. 'Peace, brother.' He turned to Robert again. 'We aren't afraid to become martyrs. Whatever happens, very soon our souls will ascend to heaven, because the whole world is about to witness the second coming of our Lord Jesus Christ.'

Robert was dumbfounded; these people were harmless but mad. It was best to appear cooperative. 'What do you want me to do?'

'Keep us informed. Tell Miriam whatever you find out about the star.'

He wondered if they knew of the capsule; they'd probably see it as a plan to shoot down Jesus with a missile. Tim went out of the room, and while he rummaged noisily in what was probably an adjoining kitchen, Robert looked steadily at the other two fanatics, his diminishing fear being replaced by a sense of power. 'All right,' he began saying to them, 'you can trust me . . .' He stopped when he saw what Tim, coming back into the room, held in his hand. It was a long carving knife, glinting as he approached. Panic flooded back and without any further hesitation Robert jumped from his chair and ran for the door, his bound hands held in front of him like a battering ram. Tim moved to block his way; the other man grabbed Robert's waist and Miriam screamed.

'Don't cut him!'

They held him down on the floor; Robert gave a shout for help while Tim, throwing the knife to one side, desperately tried to cover his mouth. 'You fool – I only want to free you! Let me get the tape off, then you can go home.' Robert stopped struggling, Tim retrieved the blade and carefully sliced through the binding while the other man maintained a cautious grip on Robert's shoulders. When it was finished they helped him to his feet and led him out of the room to the front door, which Tim opened, revealing the dark and empty main street of the Town. 'Peace be with you,' he said, gently pushing the dazed soldier outside and immediately closing the door on him.

Robert instinctively broke into a run that carried him all the way back to the Franks' house, where as soon as he reached his room he collapsed fully clothed on his bed, not stirring until a heavy knock startled him awake in the darkness.

'Seven o'clock,' Dorothy called through the door.

He switched on the bedside light and looked disbelievingly at his wristwatch.

'Sausage and egg?'

Robert called back a yes, finding his throat hoarse from cigarette smoke or the chemical he had inhaled, and when he came out of his room he noticed that Miriam's door lay open, and her room was dark. He washed, then went downstairs to the kitchen, where Mrs Frank was frying his breakfast and Mr Frank sat reading the *Daily Worker*, a picture of normality. Beside him, neat and unperturbed in her grey suit, munching a slice of toast as if this were a morning no different from any other, sat Miriam.

'Well, if it isn't the partygoer himself!' Arthur ebulliently declared, folding his newspaper and gesturing with outstretched palm towards the empty chair whose back Robert clutched in need of support. 'How are you feeling?' Robert's hesitancy was caused by sheer bewilderment both at Miriam's presence and at her nonchalance, but Mr Frank interpreted it otherwise. Hoping for a manly exchange, Arthur's smile exuded so much bonhomie that he resembled a panting dog waiting for a stick to be thrown. 'Headache?' he asked jovially.

'A bit,' Robert replied, sitting down and glaring at Miriam, who ignored him. She must have slipped out after her parents went to bed and returned before they woke. 'And how are you today?' he asked her lowered head while she buttered another slice of toast.

She looked up. 'Me? I'm fine. Mum, did I tell you I might be late tonight? We're doing a stock check.'

Robert boiled with inner rage. As casually as he could manage, he asked, 'Did you do anything special last night?'

'No,' she said, holding the knife firmly in her hand. Mr Frank, whose ability to read human emotions was only a notch or two above total illiteracy, nevertheless sensed some chemical reaction at work in the air between them, and with his unerring talent for misinterpretation took it to be a nascent flirtatiousness.

'Miriam never goes out,' Arthur said apologetically. 'Or hardly ever. I'm always telling her she should be going to the dancing, then she could meet a nice boy.'

'At the Blue Cat, perhaps?' Robert asked pointedly. Mr Frank looked down at his empty plate and folded newspaper and gave a cough of embarrassment; Miriam stared fixedly across the table at Robert while her mother put his food before him and sat down on the remaining chair.

'Nice girls don't go there,' Miriam said icily.

'I see,' said Robert. 'And I take it you're nice.'

Mrs Frank had no difficulty perceiving the flying bullets. 'We'd all better eat up and get ourselves ready,' she said encouragingly.

Robert took a few mouthfuls and tasted nothing. 'I fell and hurt my head last night,' he told Arthur, who looked at him with concern but decided it must be a laddish boast rather than a request for medical assistance.

'Too much Victory?'

'Somebody punched me.'

Now the Franks were both alarmed. 'That's terrible,' said Dorothy. 'Did you report it to security?'

'You've got to be careful, Robbie,' Arthur added warily. 'Some of the boys here are apt to be hot-headed – they get jealous of these glamorous servicemen who come in and take the best girls. And there are some places in Town that are best avoided.'

'Well, Robert?' Miriam interrupted. 'Are you going to report it?'

He looked straight into her brazen eyes. 'No,' he said. 'I won't.'

'I think you should,' Mrs Frank insisted.

Robert wiped his mouth with a paper napkin. 'It was three stupid kids who should have known better. They're too pathetic to be worth reporting. But, Miriam,' he added, speaking earnestly to her, 'if you should happen to go out, I really think you should take care about who you see and where you go.'

'I'll second that,' Mr Frank said heartily. Dorothy was less sanguine.

'What do you mean?' she asked with a worried tone.

'Robert, is there something happening at the Installation that we should know about?'

'Lots of things,' he said, 'though not the sort I can talk about.'

Once again Mr Frank made the coughing sound that signalled closure. He refolded his already neat newspaper, stood up from the table and announced that he was departing. Miriam rose too, and Mrs Frank asked Robert if he'd like any more food before his car arrived.

'I would, thanks,' he said, his appetite restored now that he had been able to vent a little of his anger. 'And I plan on walking to the College.'

Arthur's eyebrow cocked. 'Are you allowed?'

'I sometimes do,' Miriam said confidently. 'As long as your papers are in order there's no problem. Perhaps I'll see you there later, Robert.'

'I'll look forward to it,' he told her as she breezed out to the hallway to put on her coat. Then she and Mr Frank left together to catch their bus to work.

Dorothy returned to the stove with Robert's plate, reheated the frying pan and cracked an egg into it, leaving it sizzling while she plucked two leftover sausages from under the grill. Robert watched her with the same detachment he had felt while trying to fathom her daughter. 'Has she got a boyfriend?' he asked.

'Who, Miriam?' There was a smile in Dorothy's voice, but when she looked round and saw Robert's seriousness, her expression changed to suspicion. 'No.' She turned off the gas and scooped the cooked egg onto Robert's plate, brought it to the table and sat down, pouring herself a cup of tea from the pot. She was wary of Robert's purpose but spoke with forced lightness. 'Miriam's a lovely girl, don't you think?'

He pushed some food into his mouth and mumbled polite agreement while Dorothy watched him over her steaming teacup, waiting for him to add more. Then she said flatly, 'Where did you two go last night?'

'I went alone.'

'She left after Arthur and I went to bed.'

'Not with me.'

'But you know where she went, don't you?'

He laid down his knife and fork, held the pink-edged paper napkin to his lips once more and stared at Mrs Frank, trying to decide how much to tell her.

'Say it wasn't the Blue Cat, that's all.'

He shook his head. 'No, not there.' He dropped the crumpled napkin beside his plate and dissected a blackened sausage. 'I only went there because I had to. I saw Miriam afterwards.'

Mrs Frank sighed. 'I hope you're telling the truth. The girls there are desperate and think they'll get privileges but Miriam doesn't need that, she has prospects. I don't want her making the same mistakes . . .' She trailed off, touched her grey hair, took a sip of tea, and it sounded as if she knew all about those curtained cubicles.

'We didn't do anything. We're not . . .'

'You could help her.'

There was a hardness in her face that Robert had not seen before. 'How?'

She put down her cup. 'Miriam wants to get away from here and I don't blame her, even if it means we never see her again. The only way is for her to marry a leaver.'

The proposal was more blatant than anything Robert had heard from Mr Frank, and nearly made him bolt on his food. 'We're not a couple. And even if I thought I could love your daughter, I'm certain she'd never love me.'

'I'm not talking about love. Arthur and I have got savings.'

He couldn't believe what he was hearing. 'Are you trying to sell me your daughter?'

'Our money's no use to us here,' she continued, seemingly intent on striking a good deal. 'I've always known there was only one thing it could buy, and that would be Miriam's freedom. All you have to do is marry her, set up home together outside the Installation for the statutory year and a day, then divorce her.'

'I can't do that.'

'Why not?' She appeared genuinely perplexed. 'You'd pay for a woman, wouldn't you? Why not get paid to have one? Or are you too proud for that?'

'There are things about Miriam you don't know.'

'Such as?' Dorothy raised her chin defiantly, as if waiting for the punch that Robert had been preparing for someone else since the moment he woke up.

'She has a lover – she was with him last night.'

'You're lying.'

'They meet here, or at his place.'

Mrs Frank spoke with a mother's fierce pride. 'Miriam wouldn't do that behind my back. She has principles, beliefs . . .'

'You mean she's a Christian?'

'Yes,' Dorothy declared. 'Just like I am, and there's no law against it.'

'He's called Tim.'

She was momentarily silenced, then laughed. 'Tim? Is he the big secret you want to floor me with? They've been friends for years – they study scripture together.'

'They were the ones who attacked me.' He told her everything, and her eyes widened as she listened.

'This can't be true,' she gasped. 'She could have us all . . .'

'Don't let her out at night, keep her under lock and key and never tell her what I've said – otherwise I might be the one who's shot.'

Mrs Frank nodded meekly. Now it was Robert who was in charge of the household – though Arthur need never know of the quiet handover of domestic control.

'I have to go,' he said. 'There's only one more thing I want to say before we go back to pretending nothing happened. I like you very much, Dorothy – you've shown me nothing but kindness. But I don't like your daughter at all, and if I help her it's only for your sake.'

Mrs Frank nodded again, still more humbly. 'Miriam isn't the easiest of people . . .'

He left her sitting at the table, looking dazed by what she had learned, and went out to the hallway. He was at the foot of the stairs when he called back, 'I need a bag, a rucksack perhaps. Do you have one?'

There was a moment's silence from the kitchen while Mrs Frank collected her thoughts. 'A bag? Yes, I can give you one.' She came out a moment later with an old canvas knapsack.

'That'll do,' he said, taking it to his room where he collected his coat and dropped *Rocket to the Stars* inside, fastening the leather-strapped buckles as he came back downstairs and wished Mrs Frank goodbye.

'Thank you,' she said when he stepped outside.

'It's too soon for that.' He slung the bag on his shoulder, dug his hands into his coat pockets and walked down the path.

16

Dawn was breaking, and already the people of the Installation were going about their business. Some shops were opening, and buses sped past every now and then along the otherwise empty roads, carrying workers to the Plant. A few folk, like Robert, preferred to walk, so he didn't feel out of place in the quiet trickle of pedestrians until an engine rumbled behind him; not a bus this time but the familiar white car that rolled alongside, its driver nodding towards the empty front seat. Robert stopped and so did the car. He approached and opened the passenger door.

'Good morning, sir,' the driver said, leaning across and exuding both subservience and superiority; the pride of a man required to wait on others, and therefore more than happy to carry out any command that might involve ordering someone else.

'I'd rather walk,' Robert said curtly, still holding open the door.

'My instructions are to bring you to the College.'

'I know how to get there.'

The driver's smile hovered between laughter and a sneer. 'Sir,' he said, 'I have clear instructions.'

'Does that mean I have to follow them?'

Now he sneered. 'Get inside, please. Otherwise there will be consequences.'

Passers-by ignored the scene as Robert climbed into the front passenger seat; all were familiar with the moment when a person is picked up off the street, and the correct response is to look elsewhere. But Robert was not being arrested; he had merely lost a small battle with the man whose job it had been for the last couple of days to ferry him around the Installation.

'I wanted to buy some things on the way,' Robert explained.

'We can stop for them if you like.' The driver seemed completely unruffled now that he had bent the volunteer to his will. His eyes never left the empty road while he followed its straight course with the care of a test candidate. 'What do you need to buy?'

'Some meat.' Robert saw a change in the driver's impassive profile; a raising of his eyebrows and the puzzled crinkling of his weathered forehead.

'Meat to cook? Or do you want to feed a dog?' A sardonic pout came to his lips. 'Have you found yourself a pet?'

'It's for my landlady. She's been very kind to me.' The driver nodded sagely in response, evidently not believing a word of it. 'I think I might also buy her a pair of gloves . . . and some chocolate.'

'Santa Claus has come a few weeks early,' the driver mused complacently. 'Your landlady's a lucky woman. She must treat you well. Very well indeed.' Soon afterwards he said, 'Here's your meat.' They were on the main street, passing the pub in which the recruits had drunk yesterday, and the car came to a halt a few metres further on, outside the butcher's, where already there was a queue of women waving ration books. Robert was about to climb out but the driver stopped him. 'I'll go,' he said. 'It's better. Got your vouchers?' Robert handed over the booklet and the driver went to see what was on offer, walking briskly inside the shop to the front of the queue, where the women stood aside to let him haggle with the butcher in his bloody apron, thick bare arms crossed over his chest.

Robert fidgeted in the car's small seat; his knees were pressed against the grubby glove compartment, and when he tried to adopt a more comfortable position the flap dropped open. Papers were crammed inside, but also something else. Letting the flap fall fully, Robert saw a small black automatic pistol. He glanced once more towards the shop, satisfied himself that the driver would not return swiftly, then reached inside the glove compartment to touch the gun's dull metal, sliding his fingers beneath the handle and finding the weapon far lighter than anything he had used in his military service; more like the kind that a D5 man might conceal inside his jacket. Taking it out of the glove compartment but keeping it low in his lap, Robert found it was fully loaded. And as negotiations reached a conclusion inside the butcher's shop with the exchange of several vouchers for a small brown-paper bag passed across the counter, Robert decided he would give Dora a more useful gift. He hurriedly opened the rucksack at his feet, hid the gun there, then closed the glove compartment and restored as much of his composure as he could before the returning driver had even reached the shop's open doorway. What he was doing was potentially a capital offence but he had no fear of consequences, only a sublime indifference when the driver climbed back in and passed the package to him along with the depleted voucher book. Robert could feel the meat's soft, moist bulk inside its wrapper. 'What is it?' he asked.

'A kilo,' said the driver, 'so you can think yourself lucky.'

'But what kind?'

The driver laughed hoarsely. 'It's a kilo, I told you. Don't ask me what the animal's name was – we weren't that intimately acquainted.' He started the car with two or three turns of the ignition key, and Robert slipped the package into his bag on the floor, being careful not to open it too widely.

'Where now?' the driver asked, startling Robert, who thought their destination was to be the College. 'You said chocolate, didn't you?'

Robert wanted only to escape before his theft was discovered, but he knew the most dangerous mistake he could make would be a sudden change of plan. 'That's right, chocolate. And a pair of warm gloves.'

'I know just the place,' the driver said, turning into a small side street lacking shops which Robert took to be a short cut, though they soon pulled up at a terraced house through whose small lace-curtained window could dimly be seen the limbless mannequin of a dressmaker. 'You'd better go and choose. What sort of hands has she got?'

Robert was absent-mindedly gazing at the dummy's narrow waist and smoothly swelling breasts. 'Who?'

'Your landlady – you want to buy her gloves, don't you?' The driver must have seen the dreamy look on Robert's face, because he added, 'You do mean your landlady, don't you? Or might there be some other young woman you want to buy a present for – a friend you met in the Blue Cat, perhaps?'

'That's right,' Robert conceded, lacking the power or will to deny it.

'I thought as much,' the driver said with a satisfied air. 'Go in there and get what you want.'

Robert realized what a perilous situation he was in. Left alone, the driver might decide to look inside the glove compartment. 'Come and help me.'

'I'm no expert.'

'But you must know a lot more than I do about what women like.'

This scrap of flattery brought the sardonic smile back to the driver's lips. 'I know what the girls in the Blue Cat like, if that's what you mean.' He opened his door, Robert did likewise, and the driver led the way to the dressmaker's door, ringing the bell and waiting until a small, elegant middle-aged lady appeared.

'Good morning, Mrs Baxter, I have a gentleman here who's looking for ladies' gloves.'

'You'd better come in, then,' she said, showing them to the front room where the mannequin stood proudly on a tall metal pole. Here was both sitting room and shop; behind an armchair, dresses were ranged on a rack; a glass cabinet displayed female underwear whose frilled edges had the untouchable beauty of submerged anemones. The whole room smelled of women, Robert thought; the secret aroma of that other planet where one half of humanity so comfortably resides.

Spectacled Mrs Baxter, prim as a headmistress in her black cardigan and pearl necklace, went to a tall, highly polished wooden chest with many drawers, one of which she opened. 'Is it for a formal occasion?'

'More for warmth,' said Robert.

She turned, looking at him almost with disdain. 'I see. Everyday winter wear, then?' She reached into the drawer. 'How about these?' It was a fur-lined pair made of suede, and Mrs Baxter laid them across her wrist like strangled rabbits.

'They'll do.'

'Well, that was an easy choice,' the driver declared, wondering why his presence had been thought necessary.

Mrs Baxter shared his distaste at such hurry. 'Might I show you some others? They're not for every day, but they'd make a very fine gift.' While Robert held the thick suede gloves, Mrs Baxter brought out three more pairs, each a work of art. One was black and covered in tiny sequins, another was richly embroidered with a dense pattern of flowers while the third was so marvellously diaphanous, lilac coloured and made of what appeared to be silk, that the pair seemed almost too flimsy to wear. Yet when Robert stroked and held them he immediately sensed the sweet touch of Dora's fingers, as gentle and delicate as the interior of her mouth. He raised the gloves to his lips as if to kiss them; involuntarily he had been overcome by an urge to smell them.

'That's the sort of thing a young lady likes,' the driver confidently asserted. 'You can take it from me.'

Mrs Baxter looked modestly downwards while the two men silently assessed the proposed purchase. 'How much are they?' Robert asked.

She raised her eyes and pursed her lips. It was a matter for discussion. 'He's with the College,' the driver explained. 'He's on D book.'

'Then we could say fifty for both pairs.' Though she looked like a headmistress, Mrs Baxter had the shrewdness of a businesswoman.

'Fifty for two pairs of gloves!' the driver complained.

'That's no ordinary pair,' Mrs Baxter insisted, nodding towards the ones Robert still held lovingly. Even more than the full-bosomed mannequin in the window, these soft gloves were a tangible simulation of the object of his desire. He reached into his pocket and brought out his voucher book.

'You're either mad or in love,' the driver told him.

'What's the difference?' Robert said, tearing out sheets of coloured paper that Dora considered worthless.

Mrs Baxter took the gloves but not yet the payment. 'I'll wrap them for you.' From out of the drawer she lifted a small, flat box of white cardboard, filled with fine crêpe paper which provided a bed for the most extravagant purchase of his entire life. The suede rabbits were an unwrapped afterthought, tossed onto the closed box when Mrs Baxter sat at her desk to write out the receipt and complete the transaction. Then she handed the items to Robert.

'You've made a very good choice,' she said, showing the men out. 'If any young man had bought something like that for me when I was a girl, I'd have . . .' she paused, lost for words. 'I really don't know what I'd have done.' With this comment, spoken as Mrs Baxter opened the front door to release her customers from her feminine world, the meaning of Robert's gift assumed a startling clarity for him. Whether it was with vouchers or with gloves, or with meat or anything else, the only commodity he could buy was sex. It was rationed exactly like everything else.

'Chocolates next?' the driver asked when the door was closed behind them and they stood facing the parked car.

'Never mind about that,' said Robert. The only gift that mattered was the loaded one in his rucksack.

17

They now went straight to the College, where the driver halted at the checkpoint to be scrutinized by the armed guard. It was the usual routine procedure, but Robert clenched his knees nervously over the bag at his feet when the guard approached and the driver wound down his window to call a friendly greeting.

The guard grunted in response, steam curling from his lips into the cold air, then nodded towards the car's passenger. 'Authorization?'

Robert had only his military papers and identity card; he hadn't been issued with any special pass for the Installation and had never yet been asked for one. It was as if the rules had changed now that he had something to hide. He was about to speak, but it was the driver who saved him. 'He's with Professor Kaupff's group, surely you know that.'

'I need to see some authorization.'

The driver chuckled. 'You're new here, aren't you? I'll

show you the mandate, then we can get a move on before our balls freeze.' It seemed as if he was about to stretch across to the glove compartment to retrieve what he wanted, but the driver's grip rested instead on the gear stick as he put the car in neutral, then reached inside his leather jacket and brought out what looked like a photocopy of an official state document, stamped with the government seal. He passed it through the open window and the guard inspected it with great deliberation, though it was probably unintelligible to him.

'Very well,' the guard said at last, handing it back. 'Move on, please.'

They sped past the raised barrier, the car's acceleration indicating the driver's displeasure. 'Fucking new boy thinks he's going to be a general. He'll soon learn what's what around here.' They took the turn-off for the Lodge. 'Once you're posted here it's for life. No promotion, no change, no nothing. That's how the Installation works. Good pay, decent perks, no worries.' He glanced towards Robert. 'You've figured that out already, haven't you?'

Robert nodded.

'And if there's a nice young lady who likes fancy gloves, so much the better. I expect the two of you'll end up having ten kids and retiring to a flat in F District, if you don't get given rooms here instead.' They'd reached the forecourt, where the driver halted in front of the Lodge's main entrance and switched off the engine. 'I hear you had some kind of mishap last night.'

The comment came from nowhere and took Robert by surprise. 'What do you mean?'

'After you came out of the Blue Cat. This is a small

place, people see things. Got beaten up, didn't you? Jealous boyfriend, I expect. Never enough women to go round.' He leaned closer and lowered his voice; a gesture of comradeship rather than secrecy, since the nearest guard was standing at a far-off corner of the building. 'You take my advice – don't fall in love with her.'

'Who?' Robert feigned innocence.

'The one that's getting those gloves you paid a week's wages for, that's who. You're a newcomer, just like the lad down there thinks he's got to see authorization for every single person comes through his barrier. A few days of seeing the same faces again and again'll soon put him right. And you? I wonder how many times you'll need to get beaten up before you realize there's not a single woman here who isn't a whore.'

'What are you talking about?'

'I don't mean they all work at places like the Blue Cat, but they have to look after themselves one way or another. If they can get themselves a big man then maybe they can get out of here – but that's more than the lad down the hill will ever manage.' He had put on the handbrake and seemed set for a rest before the next journey in his schedule.

'You surely wouldn't call your own wife a whore.'

The driver was unperturbed. 'In this place we don't ask questions,' he said simply. 'When you're sitting up there in your room in the Lodge twenty years from now with your good lady wife, there's going to be half the men in Town have slept with her. They'll be passing her in the street, ignoring her, same as you'll be ignoring all the women you've known who've got married to your colleagues. That's how it works here. I don't say it's right or wrong, but when I see a young fellow in love then I can't help offering a word or two. But don't listen to me – you'll learn for yourself.'

'Thanks for the advice.' Robert got out, carefully carrying the rucksack, and walked to the Lodge's entrance lobby.

Jason was standing at the reception desk as usual, pointlessly inactive yet with the alertness of a basking chameleon waiting for an insect to come within range. 'Professor Kaupff is expecting you,' he said with a mildly impatient air, coming out from behind the desk. 'Allow me to take your belongings.'

Robert fumbled uneasily with the buttons of his overcoat, the incriminating rucksack hanging by one strap from his right shoulder. He had no choice but to pass it to Jason, then his coat, which the smooth-skinned butler took behind the desk and skewered deftly on a hook, while the bag, as if thought too coarse with its suggestion of rugged hill walks for such elegant surroundings, was secreted out of sight beneath. He then led Robert across the panelled lobby to the Maxwell Room, where they found Kaupff sitting with Professor Vine, the two of them drinking coffee from white china cups. A shiny steel coffee pot and a third, empty cup rested with the milk jug and sugar bowl on the small table between the scientists' leather armchairs. Kaupff stood up; Vine remained seated.

'Good morning, Coyle,' Kaupff said, approaching to shake the recruit by the hand while Jason quietly retreated. 'I trust you're not too hungover after your night on the tiles.'

Robert glanced across at Vine but saw on the seated

professor's smiling face no record of the Blue Cat, other than a general ruddiness of complexion brought on by many years of excessive drinking, to which last night's bottle or two of wine could hardly have added. 'I feel fine,' he said as he received the old man's grasp.

'I'm relieved to hear it.' Kaupff waved towards an empty armchair. 'Do sit down so that we can run through today's programme. Coffee?' Robert shook his head, sank into the chair, and realized how much more sleep he needed. Kaupff sat too, then Vine placed his coffee cup on the table with a clink of its saucer and began the meeting.

'Yesterday Professor Kaupff explained to you how to screen out electromagnetic radiation. Do you recall the method?' It was a kind of exam, and Robert didn't have a good track record with those. Even telepathy couldn't help him now. Vine saw his confusion. 'A metal box? Don't you remember that electromagnetic waves can't penetrate it?'

Robert said meekly, 'I don't have a good memory.'

Vine and Kaupff looked at each other knowingly. 'Alpha interference?' Vine said, and Kaupff nodded. Then he asked Robert, 'What about gravity? Is there any way of removing its effects?'

Robert could think only of the gun in the bag beneath Jason's desk.

'The lift,' Kaupff prompted. 'Think of the falling elevator compartment I drew yesterday on the blackboard. When you fall you are weightless and hence free of gravity.'

Robert's theft had made him free; falling was what he wanted.

'Here's something for you to think about,' said Vine.

'An airliner is flying through the sky and a man jumps out of his seat waving a gun.'

'What?'

'It's a thought experiment,' Vine explained. 'Let's try it.'

And all at once he was there, a passenger in seat 13C gazing out at white clouds rolling like cauliflower far beneath, about to bring the gun from his rucksack and point it at the crisp firm breast of air hostess Barbara Perkins, the same actress they saw in some other show. It was on a television screen a thousand million light years away. 'And there are cracks in our close too.'

'I beg your pardon?' said Vine.

'Slippage,' Kaupff murmured. 'Robert, how old are you?'

'Twelve.'

'And where are your parents?'

'The aliens took them and gave me new ones.' He came to. 'What did I just say?'

The two professors were staring at him; Vine glanced at Kaupff. 'Has she used the invasive transducer on him yet?'

'No, later,' said Kaupff. 'Robert, you understand that we want you to help us detect signals from the visiting object. We think it must be emitting scalar waves, but they're easily swamped by electromagnetic or gravitational fields.'

'Somebody fires a bullet,' Vine continued. 'The bullet falls.'

Barbara Perkins is moving in a parabolic arc towards an unconscious lady while a male passenger in seat 16D – married with two children, the director of a pet-food company – gets out of his seat some distance behind the hijacker, who hears what's coming, turns and faces his assailant with gun raised.

'*Mission: Impossible.*'

'Not at all, Robert,' Kaupff assured him. 'There's nothing impossible about the mission. Difficult, certainly. Dangerous. One could even say . . .'

'Potentially lethal,' Vine concluded. 'But never mind about our thought experiment, Coyle, I only wanted to explain to you the principle of equivalence, which says that all things fall equally.'

'A wonderfully socialistic principle, Robert.'

'So if we want to detect scalar waves with minimum interference, we need a metal capsule in free fall. A bullet with you inside it.'

An aeroplane that could fly as fast as a bullet. 'Concorde,' said Robert.

Again the professor's faces were blank but intrigued. 'A fine and noble sentiment,' Kaupff observed, taking a pencil and notebook from his jacket pocket and jotting something. 'Peace and harmony between nations – or even between worlds.'

'Why did I say concord?' Robert asked them, confused. 'What did it mean?'

Kaupff put away his notebook. 'You're already receiving faint signals from the visitor. They don't make any sense; they're random patterns but your brain interprets them as words. When you're flying in the capsule, connected to the right equipment, we'll be able to understand those signals.'

Vine explained, 'The non-invasive transducer has attuned you.'

'You mean the thing in my pillow that made me ill?'

'The new device is more refined,' Kaupff said in what was meant to be reassurance but instead sounded sinister. 'You'll be driven to the research centre in a while to try it out. You'll suffer only a little discomfort.'

'No worse than a trip to the dentist,' Vine added, then stood up. 'If you'll excuse me, I have to go now.' He walked briskly out of the room, leaving Kaupff and Robert sitting silently together.

For a few moments the old professor toyed with his cup before returning it to the table, then he stared at Robert with eyes well trained in concealing emotion. 'Have you looked at Goethe yet?' he asked, and Robert shook his head. Kaupff tutted disapprovingly. 'I expect you had a late night at the Blue Cat.'

'I read *Rocket to the Stars*, though. I brought it with me.'

'Did you learn anything?'

Only that the doomed monkey in a spacesuit was a pitiful sight; a helpless creature unaware it was being sent on a one-way mission. 'Free fall is what happens when a spaceship orbits the Earth, isn't it?'

'Yes,' Kaupff agreed, 'that's one way of achieving it.'

'So I'll be weightless?'

'Completely,' said Kaupff. 'We have to be sure you won't feel nauseous.' He didn't know that Robert was already gladly tumbling. 'But let me tell you what Goethe said about the universe. *Only through love do we come to her. She is all. She is whole and yet always unfinished*. Does that make sense to you?'

'Yes.' Robert could see Dora, and he could see the pistol in her hand.

'And Goethe said that when we observe nature we study ourselves. We want you to become one with the Red Star, organically connected to the life of the cosmos; the new transducer we're about to test on you will help make this possible, though it seems the process has begun already. Information is reaching you from a distant world – perhaps an entirely separate universe.'

It sounded as crazy as Tim and Miriam's apocalypse. 'Rosalind told me she could make people see God using magnets.'

'They only think they see God,' Kaupff corrected. 'There is no God.'

'How can you be so sure?'

Kaupff prickled. 'Because I am a scientist, a materialist and a Marxist.'

'But what if this other world I'm getting messages from is heaven?'

Kaupff laughed derisively. 'Well, just think how lovely it will be when you get there.' Then he added seriously, 'Indulge in childish superstition if you wish, but there is no room in this mission for thumb-sucking bedwetters who believe in angels and tooth-fairies.' There was a harshness in Kaupff's words, a cruel mockery almost like Davis's taunting last night. 'Was your mistake about your age a Freudian slip, Coyle, or the neural noise I took it to be? Are you a man or a boy?'

'Which would you prefer?' Robert said boldly.

'What do you mean by that?' Kaupff's eyes expressed indignation, but also, Robert thought, understanding.

'I need some air,' said Robert. 'Let's go outside.'

Now Kaupff's watery blue eyes narrowed with suspicion;

he spoke softly. 'Come not between the dragon and his wrath. You displease me, Coyle.'

'The breeze on the bowling green might help.'

The professor nodded curtly and stood up; Robert followed him out into the lobby and towards the reception desk where Jason greeted them with a deferential smirk. 'I shall be needing my outer coat,' Kaupff informed the butler. 'Do be so good as to fetch it for me.'

'Certainly, sir.' He came out from behind the desk and walked smartly away to Kaupff's rooms.

'He's able to let himself in?' Robert asked when he was gone. 'You trust him?'

Kaupff straightened. 'I have nothing to hide. I'm a patriot.'

The tension remained while the two men waited in silence. Robert could see his coat hanging, the rucksack was out of sight, and he wondered if he should retrieve the items himself, but didn't want to appear in too much hurry. It seemed far too long a delay, though only a couple of minutes passed before Jason returned carrying Kaupff's grey winter coat over his arm, as well as a green woollen scarf; a thoughtful addition showing unexpected familiarity with the professor's wardrobe.

'Thank you, Jason,' Kaupff said, taking the garments and wrapping himself warmly while the butler fetched Robert's belongings, passing him the rucksack only once the recruit had finished buttoning his coat with fingers made clumsy by unease. The bag, when he took it from Jason's slim hand, appeared to have lost none of its incriminating weight, and soon the men were outside in the cold sunshine, on their way across the courtyard.

Kaupff tried to lighten the mood. 'This is a beautiful place to live, don't you think?' The high walls and tall leaded windows of the Lodge instead struck Robert as resembling a prison. They reached the path through the trees and Kaupff walked with hands clasped behind his back, breath billowing as they crunched over dry twigs. 'I've paid a price, of course. On the outside I could have been famous – I might have won a Nobel Prize. But I love my country, Robert. Sometimes we have to make sacrifices for the greater good.'

The sacrifice uppermost in Robert's mind was the kind made by Dora. 'Who decides the greater good?'

Kaupff halted. 'Do you doubt the value of this mission, Robert?' They were at the spot where Davis had hidden while spying on them.

'Only as much as I doubt everything in the Installation. Do you know what goes on at the Blue Cat?'

'What does that have to do with anything?'

'Women are abused, violated. They're kept like animals. What sort of greater good is that?'

Kaupff resumed walking. 'There are many things in our society that are far from ideal. But we mustn't let that distract us from the basic principles of justice and equality on which our society is based. Patriotism means love, and love must be unqualified. It's our country, right or wrong. We have to do our duty.'

'Even if it means a woman spreading her legs for a brute?'

'Even if it means death.'

They had reached the disused bowling lawn with its view of the Town, wreathed in chimney smoke and looking small and dismal in the morning sunlight. 'You speak of love, Professor, but only of loving countries or stars or the universe. What about people? Don't they matter more?'

Kaupff stared down at the lawn, still damp with glistening dew, and said nothing.

'After I left you yesterday, Davis questioned me.'

Kaupff looked up, startled. 'Why?'

'He's searching for spies.'

'I know that,' said Kaupff, 'but what help could you give?'

'None,' Robert told him. 'But later, when I came out of the Blue Cat, I was attacked by a gang, beaten up.'

Kaupff's expression distorted first in surprise and then, as the implication of the news struck him, in near panic. 'Did they hit your head? Did you lose consciousness? Robert, if any cranial damage has been done, it could wreck our plans. What were you doing getting into drunken brawls?'

'They weren't hooligans,' said Robert. 'They're subversives. They interrogated me about the mission.'

Aghast, Kaupff shook his head in sorrow and fear. 'This is a disaster . . .'

'No, they're harmless fools – they think the Red Star has been sent by God.'

Kaupff held Robert by the shoulders. 'We have to tell Davis at once – they must be rounded up and shot.'

Robert stared incredulously at him. 'You want them murdered? What are you – a scientist or a thug?'

'They're terrorists, Coyle, and if you won't tell Davis then I will.'

'That wouldn't be wise.'

Kaupff released him. 'What are you talking about?'

'It's you he wants arrested.'

He blinked and jerked his head backwards in stunned disbelief, recoiling from the verbal blow. 'Me?'

'If believing in God makes you a terrorist then what about fondling a man?'

Disgust filled the professor's face. 'How dare you.'

'Davis saw you hugging me. And in your bedroom . . .'

'Nothing happened. Do you think the place isn't bugged? Would I be so stupid?' The professor was proud, defiant, but also faltering.

'Innocent actions can be misinterpreted, good intentions can have bad consequences. Should someone be shot for good intentions?'

Kaupff laughed feebly and evasively. 'If you're suggesting . . .' He trailed off.

'Davis claims that when you taught at a school here years ago you interfered with a boy.'

'That's a damnable lie.'

'I hope so.'

The change in Kaupff's bearing amounted almost to a physical collapse; he was as battered-looking as anyone can be while still standing. 'So you're protecting me as well as the Christians? And do you think I'm a harmless fool, too?'

Robert bit his lip, then said, 'Right now I don't know what you are.'

Kaupff slowly put his face in his hands and a moment later started to weep. Robert watched the old man's shoulders shake, a little at first, then more strongly as the sobs attained a forceful rhythm, but the volunteer offered no comforting hand. Instead he took the rucksack from his back, loosened its buckles and reached down inside, feeling the cold, soft package of meat, the box with its precious gloves, and the gun. What he brought out was Kaupff's book. 'I wanted to give this back to you,' he said, holding it up. Kaupff glimpsed it through the fingers on his face, then hid his reddened, puffy eyes without a word, so Robert placed the book on the damp grass at the professor's feet. Then he fastened the rucksack, slung it on his shoulder, turned and walked slowly back to the Lodge.

18

The car was still waiting for Robert in the courtyard, and soon he was being taken to the research complex as arranged. He saw the great hangar where the simulator stood; the car continued round it to smaller buildings adjoining the rear, an architecturally incoherent collection of low concrete structures with the functional drabness of a community hospital, some of whose offices and workshops Robert had seen yesterday.

They halted and Robert got out. 'Thanks,' he called to the driver, who simply nodded in the direction of the wide glass door behind which Rosalind could be seen waiting. The door slid open and Robert entered what was indeed very much like a hospital reception area, though without patients or milling staff, a care home for ghosts. It reminded him of the place they'd stretchered him to after he became ill – the place where everyone thought he would die.

Rosalind, in a woollen skirt and sweater, was the only person to be seen, and she was in a hurry. 'We must begin,' she said crisply, directing him to follow.

'Are the others here yet?'

'Which others?'

'Harvey and Forsyth.'

'I've no role for them in this morning's activities,' said Rosalind, leading Robert along an empty, windowless corridor that smelled of bleach. She walked quickly, so that he found himself trotting behind her clicking heels, watching the smooth, rhythmic flick of her rump.

'Did you have a pleasant time at the Blue Cat?' she asked over her shoulder with a coldly ironic air.

'Delightful,' Robert told her tartly. 'And did you have an enjoyable discussion with Brian Willoughby in his room?'

'The man's a genius.'

'He showed up later at the Blue Cat.'

'I know,' said Rosalind. 'I persuaded him to go.' They had reached her office which Rosalind unlocked, ushering Robert through and instructing him to deposit his bag on the floor, his coat on the peg inside the door she closed. 'Has Kaupff told you what we'll be doing?' He turned and saw her gaze move down his body as though he were a living specimen about to be vivisected.

'He mentioned a new machine.' Robert looked around the room and saw only the familiar furnishings, the rug with its scatter cushions. 'Where is it?'

'Let's start with meditation,' she said. 'Lie down and close your eyes.'

'You mean I don't have to break my legs attempting the lotus?'

'It isn't necessary. Relax and let your mind become empty.'

He did as she ordered, feeling immediately more peaceful once prostrate and in darkness. He could even see stars.

'What's alpha interference?' he asked, and her voice came to him through interstellar space.

'It's the effect we want to measure. Scalar waves could create electrical signals in your brain; thoughts or impressions.'

'You want to read my thoughts?'

'No, we want to understand their source. A piece of matter falling into the frozen star could make ripples that you see as a cloud or a flower.'

'Or God?'

'Anything. We don't care about the subjective response, only the physical stimulus.'

He was floating, though no longer in space. There was a river with some kind of monument beside it. 'What if I see something beautiful? Something amazing?'

'The particular illusions your brain creates aren't our concern. They're noise – we want signal.'

A boy and a girl were beside the sluggish river, which wasn't particularly beautiful as there was an old shopping trolley in it. Robert opened his eyes and saw Rosalind looking down at him. It was only then that he realized he had become erect. 'What's going on?'

'You tell me.'

'You're making this happen, aren't you? Beaming things into my head.'

'The only signals you're getting are from the frozen star,' she said. 'Everything else is noise.'

'What about flashing your legs at us yesterday? Humiliating Harvey?'

She folded her arms and considered the specimen lying before her. 'My studies suggest alpha interference should be strongest in sexually aroused subjects. This isn't about teasing or titillation, it's an attempt to detect scalar waves.'

'And this is the antenna?' Robert asked, waving indignantly at his bloated groin.

'It's a carefully controlled experiment.'

'I suppose every time you make love it's a kind of experiment?'

'Not at all,' she said calmly. 'There's a distinction between work and pleasure.'

He sat up. 'What kind did you do with Willoughby yesterday?'

'That's none of your business. You'd have no qualms about firing a missile at innocent people if someone ordered you to do it, but you seem to think there's something wrong with using sex as a way of expanding human knowledge.'

'Sometimes missiles are necessary.'

'Sometimes sex is.'

'So instead of blowing up people you blow up cocks? You know, Rosalind, I don't think you like men very much.'

She gave a dismissive toss of her head. 'I don't see how you can possibly have enough evidence to say anything at all about who or what I like.'

'You're wrong,' said Robert, rising to his feet. 'I can read you more clearly than your playing cards.'

She stared witheringly at him. 'You don't know as much about this as you think.'

'I know how you do tricks like this,' he said, pointing at the still stiffened member jutting awkwardly inside his trousers. 'This isn't science, it's a game – energy beams as a way of playing with men's minds.'

'I told you already, there's no beam here.' She stepped away from him and moved towards the desk, propping herself against its edge. 'Sexual arousal is a crucial part of the experimental conditions. Any feelings you have about that are your business, not mine. You're a piece in a machine, Coyle, and if the only way to make you function properly was to give you the Blue Cat treatment then I'd do it. In my career I've killed rats and monkeys by hitting them on the head with a hammer – holding some dirty little soldier's cock is a lot less unpleasant.'

'Then you're worse than a fucking whore.'

'Everything you say to me gets recorded in the official project records.'

'Good.' He paced towards her bearing a grim smile of satisfaction. 'Then the official record will say you're a stuck-up bitch who likes teasing men's cocks because that's the only part of them you can have any influence over.'

'You're so very, very wrong, you foolish and obnoxious little boy.'

'The record will also say you're a charlatan whose only qualification for the high-level support you've received is a nice pair of tits and a willingness to show off your legs.'

She gave a laugh. 'Go ahead, little soldier, get it all off your chest. If anyone's got problems dealing with the opposite sex then I think we can see which one of us it is. You simply can't believe that someone like me, one of those objects you fuck in the camp brothel or think about while wanking yourself to sleep, could actually make a contribution to human understanding. I'll happily put on record the uninformed criticism of a spotty nineteen-year-old who happens to be the right size and weight to fit in the space capsule and possibly has above-average psychic ability; but if we take away the playing-card trick, Coyle, you're nothing, and I want you to remember that.' She went towards the door. 'Come with me now. We're going to the laboratory.'

They walked in icy silence until she paused to indicate a toilet. 'Go and empty your bowels and bladder,' she instructed. 'Nothing else.'

'Aren't you going to come and keep watch like you did with Harvey?'

She ignored the comment and instead pointed to a closed door further along the corridor. 'Meet me there once you're ready. I need to prepare the apparatus.' She began to walk on, then after a few paces stopped and turned. 'Remember,' she said. 'Only bowels and bladder.'

He went inside and did his best to comply, but was tightened by anxiety at the thought of what Rosalind might have in store. He finished and went to the door she had indicated, opening it to see her standing in readiness in the starkly lit laboratory.

It was a plain, white-walled room, eight or ten metres across, not particularly clean in appearance, with a cluttered workbench running all along one side, on which electronic equipment was littered in varying stages of assembly or repair. Of more immediate concern to Robert when he entered, however, was the wheeled, steel-framed hospital stretcher in the centre of the room that stood bathed in the astringent glare of an adjustable overhead lamp. Rosalind was beside it, snapping on a pair of latex surgical gloves. 'Close the door and take off your clothes.'

'All of them?'

'At least the lower half, though it's better to do a full strip in case of soiling.' She went to the workbench and attended to a multi-switched device whose tuning dial she twirled with her gloved hand, the protective covering on her fingers clearly being for her own hygienic benefit rather than his. He undressed and hung his clothes on a steel peg near the door, finishing with his underpants, which served as a last, mildly ridiculous garland. She turned and looked at him. 'When did you last ejaculate?'

He was standing with his hand over his crotch. 'Why do you need to know?'

'You don't need to know why I need to know anything at all, Coyle.' She was holding an electrical cable in each hand, one red, the other black, both connected to the device on the workbench and terminating in a pair of black rubber suckers. 'Have you had sexual intercourse in the last twenty-four hours?'

'No.'

'Have you masturbated?'

'No.'

She nodded at the stretcher, which was covered with an absorbent paper sheet. 'Come and lie down, please.' He did as she ordered; the harsh brilliance of the lamp hurt his eyes until she redirected the angle of its beam to highlight the film of nervous sweat on his abdomen. 'I don't want you to be afraid, Volunteer Coyle. It might disrupt the experiment. I also want you to be completely honest with me. Have you ejaculated in the last twenty-four hours?'

'Yes.'

'By means of what stimulation?'

'A woman.'

'How?'

'Her mouth. Hand.'

'Did you ejaculate inside her?'

'No.'

Rosalind rubbed a cold gel on Robert's forehead and told him to lie still while she attached the rubber suckers of the electrodes, then turned again towards the workbench, fiddling intently beyond his view. He thought he heard the strident leap of an electric spark, but felt nothing. 'Did you enjoy it?' she asked without looking at him.

'Probably not as much as you're enjoying this.'

When she approached again he saw there was something new in her hand. Made of gleaming metal that looked like polished steel, it resembled in size and shape the end of a broom handle, and was attached by a long spiral cable to a controller on the bench. 'Believe me, Volunteer Coyle, this is no time for impertinence. The quantity of ejaculate is related to the manner of stimulation and is of great relevance to my research. Was it the first time you had been with this woman?'

'Yes.'

'In the Blue Cat, I expect.'

'Of course.'

She tapped the steel rod in her hand like a policeman's baton. 'The girls there are experts. We can only guess, but let's suppose you lost four cc's.'

'Does it matter?'

Rosalind resumed her preparations at the workbench. 'What was her name?' she said over her shoulder.

Robert at first resisted making any reply, then realized how much he wanted and needed her here. 'Dora.'

'Oh, her,' Rosalind said casually. 'The tea lady. I've heard she's good. Couldn't you afford more than a hand job?'

Why didn't he fly off the trolley and beat her? Was it because of the pacifying effect of the electrodes stuck to his head, or because he'd been brought up to disapprove of violence against women? No, the truth was that he lay still because he knew he had agreed to all of this in advance. 'Do you ever go there?' he asked.

'The Blue Cat? Sometimes.'

'I mean, do you work there?'

She laughed. 'What do you think I am? I don't need to sell my body.'

'But if you did?'

'Then I would.' She came back from the bench, not carrying the shining poker this time, but instead what looked like a helmet of metal wires. 'Raise your head a little while I put this on you,' she ordered.

'What is it?'

'The focusing device.' She held it in his view while she examined its connections, lavishing on the contraption all the care and tenderness her experimental subject was denied. It was an elaborate filigreed crown whose jewel was a small glass sphere, oddly crude in appearance, like a child's marble.

'The lens doesn't look very clear,' said Robert.

'It's not for focusing light,' Rosalind told him brusquely, then held the crown close above his face while she gave the electrodes on his forehead a further check. 'This is our latest version of the non-invasive transducer.'

'The thing that was under my pillow?'

'That was a prototype.'

'And did it have a marble in it too?' Robert was staring at the rough greenish globe, seeing in its fragmented reflections a distorted geometry of his surroundings.

'A large proportion of the Plant's current activity is devoted to the production of this glass,' she said with a casualness born of pride. 'It has to be incredibly pure.'

There aren't many things in the Installation of which that can be said, thought Robert, and he felt the marble press against his head when the crown was fitted firmly on to his scalp. Rosalind instructed him to move his head so she could make sure the fit was neat, and he was reminded that his chief qualification for being on the mission was that he was the right size.

She went back to the bench, then returned with the poker whose spiral cable dangled from her hand. 'This is the invasive transducer. Now turn yourself onto your left side, facing the far wall.'

'Why?'

'You'll find out soon enough.' As he rolled she pushed his shoulder to encourage him to take the required position. 'Bend your leg, that's it.' She adjusted the crown on his head, then a moment later he felt something cold and wet on his anus, and a finger burrowing inside.

'What are you doing?'

'Sterilizing you. Why are little boys always so bad at wiping themselves?'

He heard her walk to the bench where she flipped a switch with a loud clack, followed by an electric hum. 'Relax,' she said, coming back, then without any further warning he felt the metal rod being shoved into his rectum.

'Aargh!'

'Don't move; it needs to reach the right spot. Think of anything you like, but don't twitch the probe out of position.'

It was nearly clawing at his stomach. She must have found the place she was looking for, because the hum changed in pitch and at exactly the same instant his penis spontaneously inflated like a party balloon. Rosalind glanced over his shoulder and murmured with satisfaction at what she saw.

'Right on target – my aim's getting good. Enjoy this, Robert; some people pay good money for it.'

She left the probe parked deep inside him and walked around the trolley, stopping in front of his aching groin. With gloved fingers slightly blackened from workbench grease, she lifted the end of his penis and prodded its firmness like a fussy customer in a fruit shop. Then she looked at his perspiring face and stared into his wide, helpless eyes. 'I bet even that whore of yours couldn't make you this hard.' She returned to the workbench, her every retreating footstep echoing in Robert's ears, and as he gazed at the far wall, its posters and notices above the white enamel sink unintelligible at the ninety-degree angle from which he had to view them, he wondered how much longer this would go on. When she came back in sight she was carrying a tube-shaped flask which she slid over his member. 'Get ready for the finale,' she announced, stepping back to the controls.

He could hear another sound as well as the hum; it was a rhythmic beep, which he thought at first might be his heartbeat. It set a different pace, though, slower and more steady, and in the long moments while he waited, he began to sense some profound connection between this steady chirp and the workings of his own mind. The wires on his scalp were transmitting something to the pinging box on the bench; they were draining thoughts, fears or other sensations and turning them into a simple mathematical wave that Rosalind could record in her notes: the material basis of human consciousness. As he lay in dread of what might be about to happen, he found a single supportive companion in that recurring beep, the scientific correlative of his soul. Every part of his body was tense and painful, including his head, where the glass marble rested like an insistent thought, and into which a dull, nauseous ache had been introduced by Rosalind's insults, and perhaps too by some return path of those electrical wires she had stuck on his scalp, stirring up an unnatural circulation of his mind and making it turbid. Yet out of that sickening confusion of impressions something clearer was beginning to emerge; something was dawning inside him in those infinitely compressed moments which seemed to him so interminable. It was a simultaneous craving and loathing; an urge to confront the invisible monster hurtling across space to meet him, yet also to fly from it. Yes, here it was, seen through melting glass: the Red Star, accelerating in its plummet towards the stretcher where he lay, opening itself like a carnivorous blossom, about to swallow him whole.

His body exploded. There was a blue flash, he would recall later, and the room went a searing white, then black. He had been on the verge of entering the Red Star, and it had been the most terrifyingly beautiful moment of his existence. It was over in less than a second.

'Let's see if you filled it,' said Rosalind, coming back round. She lifted the flask, held it close to his face and showed him the thick grey contents, swirling them like a satisfied alchemist. 'I think we tipped six mils.'

He was drenched in sweat, every part of him tingling, and the beep he heard again was a rushed staccato only gradually returning to its former state. He watched Rosalind take the flask to the sink and pour away the semen, then she filled the vessel with a burst of water, leaving it at the side for more thorough cleaning later, and came back towards him carrying a stiff wad of paper towels, her eyes never leaving his barely diminished erection. 'Time to switch off,' she said, walking past and going to the workbench. The control clacked, the hum stopped and Robert softened.

'Are we finished?' he asked weakly.

'I only need to get a little more of your baseline brain function . . . There, that should do it.' She came and pushed the paper towels into his hand and carefully disconnected him. 'Give yourself a quick clean – I'll take you to the shower in a moment. Was it good?'

He rolled onto his back, wiping his groin and clammy abdomen. 'I think I saw the Red Star.'

She nodded approvingly. 'What did it look like?'

'Not like anything. It had no shape or colour or texture. It was invisible but I could somehow see it.' He sat up, turned to dangle his legs over the side of the stretcher though still feeling too feeble and unsteady to stand, and saw Rosalind unwrapping what proved to be a coarse paper gown which she handed to him.

'I'll need to study your brain pattern in detail, but at a first glance there appear to be spikes I haven't encountered in other subjects. I'm very hopeful it could be the scalar-wave influence we're looking for.'

Robert looked closely for the first time at the instruments on the bench. 'How many men have you done this to?'

'A few,' said Rosalind. 'But as the technique improves I'm able to get more reliable results.'

'You mean your aim gets better with that cattle prod?'

She snorted. 'That part's straightforward; it's getting the right brain signal that's tricky. Ejaculation just happens to be a good way of raising activity in the appropriate cortical area.' She watched as he wrapped the gown around his shoulders. 'Making a man hard is the easiest thing in the world.'

'You have such a black-and-white view of the human male.'

'Based on ample empirical data,' she said. 'I know you all have your personalities and your hobbies, but let's face it, you're all the same. All the art, all the wars, all the civilizations and their discontents, they're all about a bag of flesh that gets pumped full of blood.'

'I'd better take that shower,' said Robert, standing up

from the stretcher. 'But tell me, is there any man in the world you can respect?'

'Professor Kaupff,' Rosalind said at once.

'And what's so special about him?'

'It's simple,' she said. 'He's the only man here who's never wanted to fuck me. He's never tried it on, never made a pass, never looked at me like I'm meat.'

'That's only because he's queer.'

'And you only say that because you're jealous of him. Now take your clothes and go to the shower block just beyond the toilet – you'll find everything you need there. Wash the filth off, then go and get yourself some lunch.'

19

Cleaned, dressed and with no trace of his ordeal left lingering in his body, Robert made his way to the dining area. The place had not yet begun to fill, and he quickly collected the meal of the day, a gravy with some macerated flesh in it billed as Irish stew. At the till sat the same plump and blowsy girl he had seen yesterday, who took his voucher book and tore out what he owed. 'Made a friend here yet?'

'What do you mean?'

'You know, somebody to walk out with.'

It was an expression he'd only ever heard used by people of his parents' generation, but the checkout girl was no older than himself. 'You offering?' he asked playfully.

'Depends if you're asking.'

He realized she was serious. 'Sorry, I've got someone.'

Her face changed. 'Well, you're a fast worker, then.'

She put his voucher book back on his tray and he went to choose a seat, opting for one that was well away from her. Soon afterwards he felt a hand on his shoulder; it was Colin Forsyth, smiling broadly and carrying a full plate of stew in his other hand.

'Hey, college boy, guess where I've been.'

The cheerfulness seemed forced. He deposited his food on the table and sat down beside Robert, who could think of only one place that might make Forsyth so excited. 'Blue Cat?'

'Fuck no,' he said, starting to eat ravenously and speaking with his mouth full. 'Simulator.'

Robert felt strangely envious. 'What's it like?'

'You'll see. Been up to anything?'

Robert had no wish to recount his torture. 'Lectures, boring stuff. Tell me about the simulator.'

After being so keen to mention it, Forsyth was oddly reluctant to elaborate. 'Fucking tiny,' he said with a laugh.

'We could see that from the outside.'

'Aye, well be sure to scratch your arse before you have a go because there's no chance of moving once you're strapped in. No light either – pitch-black in there. Who'd you shag last night?'

'No one.'

'Ought to do it when you've got the chance.'

'Why?'

Forsyth paused. 'Because every fuck could be your last.' The mask of jollity was falling.

'What happened in the simulator?'

'Nothing.'

He carried on shovelling food into his mouth, but Robert could tell he'd been through an experience as bad as his own. 'Did it shake you up?'

Forsyth ignored him. 'I'm trying that redhead next time if I get the chance.'

'And is that how you deal with it?'

'Deal with what?'

'You know what I mean.'

Forsyth put his fork on his plate. 'No, I don't know what you mean.'

'Deal with the fear,' said Robert.

'Like you never feel any?'

'That's not what I'm saying.'

Forsyth looked as though any further provocation might set him fighting. 'What exactly are you saying?'

Robert raised his palms in a placatory gesture. 'I'm on your side, remember?'

'Sure, us against them.' There was sarcasm in Forsyth's voice as he picked up his fork to finish his meal. 'What about Harvey?'

'Haven't seen him today.'

'I expect he's been thrown off the mission after the way he behaved last night. Talking back to a Party man like that, when all he had to do was go with a whore.'

'Harvey's got problems,' Robert said, immediately feeling as if he was betraying a secret. 'Family problems, I mean. Sick mother.'

Forsyth's sarcasm thickened. 'Oh, that explains everything, then. Better not shout too loud at the poor thing.' He stared at his empty plate as though he had no memory of eating what had been on it.

'What happened in the simulator?' Robert asked again.

'Nothing,' Forsyth insisted. 'Absolutely nothing.' He looked up. 'But you're right, I was scared in there. Shit scared.'

'Was it the darkness, the spinning?'

He shook his head and gave a contemptuous laugh, but the contempt was directed at himself. 'I thought I was going to die in there. I'm a soldier, it's supposed to be what I'm trained to deal with. Not like that, though. This was just blind terror.' He swallowed hard. 'You know, only one time in my life I've been as scared as that, when I was a wean. My dad locked me in a cupboard for dogging off school, said he was going to leave me there till I starved.'

'How old were you?'

'I don't know, six or seven. And seeing as I'm not very bright I believed him. The simulator brought it all back – for a moment I was that wee boy again, trapped, screaming for my maw. I shat myself.' His head sank in shame. 'Reckon I'll be going the same way as Harvey.'

'Not necessarily.'

'Didn't think it'd have that effect on me – I've been in armoured cars, locked cellars, all sorts.'

'They're playing tricks with our minds.'

'Some trick. But it's down to you now, college boy.' He looked towards the door. 'Here she comes.'

Rosalind had appeared at the entrance, and approached them with a stern expression. 'Can either of you two shed light on Volunteer Harvey's whereabouts? He's gone missing.'

The men were aghast. 'I walked home with him last night,' said Robert.

'I was only informed a few moments ago – security are on full alert.'

'Have you spoken to Commissioner Davis?'

'No, but I assume he's in charge of the search.'

'It's his fault Harvey's done a runner,' said Forsyth.

Rosalind's eyebrows rose. 'That's a grave and reckless allegation. It'll be officially noted.'

'Won't make much difference,' said Robert. 'This mission's record is bad enough already.'

She stared at both men, suddenly aware she was dealing with a minor mutiny. 'Well, Rosalind?' Forsyth taunted. 'Is it my turn to be ejected?'

She glanced round the dining room; no one was within earshot but she looked ruffled. 'This is not the place . . .'

'Go on, baby, sling me off the mission.'

'We can't discuss it here.'

'You've got college boy all to yourself now.'

'Don't get any romantic ideas,' Robert interjected. 'She's not the type.'

'Be quiet, both of you.'

'So tell me, Rosalind,' Forsyth demanded, 'am I in or out?'

'Your heart-rate and blood-pressure readings were a little high . . .'

'He was terrified!' Robert burst in. Forsyth flinched but said nothing; Rosalind looked round the room again with mounting confusion. 'All these readings of yours aren't just pen-tracks on a roll of paper, they're people's feelings.'

'You don't know what you're saying.'

'You're playing games with our lives.'

Her composure returned. 'I assure you both that this is

no game. Forsyth, you'll be assigned other duties – you won't be flying but you're still part of the mission. And, Coyle, as soon as you finish eating we need to go to Professor Kaupff's seminar in the education centre.'

Robert pushed his half-empty plate away. 'I've had enough.' He stood to follow her out and gave Forsyth a parting nod. 'I'm sorry for what I said. No one doubts your bravery.'

Forsyth looked broken. 'Good luck, college boy.'

They walked in silence back to Rosalind's office; it was not until they were nearly at her door that she said under her breath, 'What an odious man.'

'Who? Forsyth?' Robert watched her bring out her key. 'You're surely not claiming moral superiority, after what you did to me in the laboratory?'

She unlocked the door and stood waiting while he went in to retrieve his coat and bag. 'At least I didn't rape you.'

'That's a matter of opinion. And are you telling me Forsyth's a rapist?'

She nodded. 'He was due to stand trial before he came here. He volunteered so he could escape a court appearance.'

Robert buttoned his coat, unable to decide who were the Installation's monsters and who were its heroes. 'So do you think we're all like him?'

'I've got more important things to think about.' She watched him pull the rucksack over his shoulder. 'What have you got in there?'

'Nothing much.' He made to leave but Rosalind blocked his way.

'What kind of nothing?'

He shrugged. 'A few things I bought this morning.'

She folded her arms, still barring his exit. 'So when you say nothing you mean something. Show me.'

Fear seized him. 'Why?'

'I want to see.'

He tried to be light about it. 'You think you can simply order me around?'

'Yes, I do.'

'What if I don't want to open it?'

'Then I'll do it for you.'

She reached out and Robert wondered what he was going to do when she saw the gun. He could say that it was his weapon and he was authorized to carry it; that he was given it by Harvey; that he didn't know how it got there; it was all a mistake. He could pull it out in an instant, point it at her forehead, punch a neat crimson hole in her smooth brow and watch her tilt backwards into the empty corridor like a felled tree.

He took the bag from his shoulder and put it behind his back with a teasing smile. 'It's a secret.'

'I already told you, I don't play games.'

'But you like mysteries, don't you?'

'I like solving them.'

'And once you've solved them, what then, when everybody's thoughts have been turned into waves and numbers in your machine? Is that your idea of happiness?'

'Are you trying to insult me or flirt with me?'

'Why not flirt? You said it yourself, every man in this place who isn't a queer makes a pass at you. When's my turn?'

'Don't flatter yourself.'

'And what about in the lift, when you touched me?' He brought the bag from behind his back and let it dangle from his hand; he had distracted her sufficiently. 'What sort of game was that?'

'I don't know what you mean.'

'Oh, you do, Rosalind. You may be cold and clinical in your work, acting like an insensitive robot because that's the only way you can get ahead, but you're still a woman. And women are all the same.'

She smiled thinly. 'Tell me about it, since you're such an expert.'

'You want a dashing knight who'll sweep you off your feet, care for you, give you babies and a nice home.'

'Not all of us are quite so unrealistic. And in case you've forgotten, we had a revolution in 1946 so that we could get rid of bourgeois fantasies. I'm a worker and a patriot, Robert, just like you. Yes I have feelings, we all do, but in a place like the Installation, feelings only get in the way.'

'Have you never been in love?'

'I'm in love with my work and my country. They've never let me down.'

'You sound like a disappointed woman.'

'Don't go thinking you can cure me.' She stepped closer and lowered her voice. 'You think you understand so much – but you know nothing. You talk about trivialities and you miss everything that's significant. Do you think you were brought here for a romantic adventure? Stop and consider for a moment where you are, why it was created.'

'To make the Bomb.'

'Yes, and all the other projects: the missiles, fighter aircraft, spy satellites. What do they have in common?'

'This is a military research base . . .'

'Death, that's what this place is about. That's its purpose. We've all got a gun at our head and the only question is how long we can keep the trigger from being pulled, yet you don't see it. You're too busy trying to fall in love, too upset I'm not some silly girl in a pretty dress who'll hold hands with you.' She reached down towards the bag in his hand. 'Show me your secret.'

There could be no escape; he awkwardly loosened the buckles, his fingers mutinous with anxiety. She peered down into the aperture he created.

'What's in the box?' she asked, seeing the uppermost item.

'A present.'

'So that's it; a gift for your lady friend. Underwear, I expect.'

'Never mind what it is.'

'Surely I can take a peek?' She began to reach inside the rucksack and Robert rehearsed the surprise and shock he'd show when the gun was found; but first she prodded the brown-paper bag that covered it. 'What on earth's this?'

'Meat.'

She drew out her arm in disgust and looked at him with a puzzled expression, then broke into a laugh. 'You really do know the way to a woman's heart.'

'And you don't know the way to anyone's.'

Her face froze. 'Close it up before the stink escapes, and make sure you don't leak blood on the floor. There's a car waiting outside for us.'

20

Kaupff was standing at the blackboard ready to begin when Robert and Rosalind arrived for the seminar. Davis was in the same back-row seat he had occupied the previous day; Willoughby sat beside him. Vine and the other physicists were there too; the only absentees were the four recruits who had all been eliminated.

Kaupff showed none of the grief Robert had seen a few hours earlier. 'Close the door and let's begin,' he ordered, sounding mildly impatient at the enforced delay. Robert did as he was instructed, then went to join Rosalind in the front row, placing his rucksack beneath the table.

Then Kaupff began. 'Last night some of you looked through my telescope. I told you about Kant's theory that the universe undergoes perpetual evolution through a balance of opposing forces. Goethe sought to understand life in similar terms; yet Marxism teaches us that the balance cannot be static: every part of nature contains its own antithesis, its own negation.' He looked solemnly at Robert. 'The more fully we live, the more certainly we die.'

There was a cough from the back row as Willoughby prepared to interrupt. 'This is all very fascinating, Professor Kaupff; but is it really relevant to modern physics?'

'Absolutely,' said Kaupff, his enthusiasm undiminished. 'Kant understood that gravity dictates cosmic evolution; we now know the natural endpoint of this process is gravitational collapse, the formation of frozen stars, black holes, whatever we care to call them.' His voice quickened as he elucidated. 'The visitor to our solar system represents the highest form of evolutionary progress. The approaching Red Star is living proof of the Marxist theory of universal history.'

A murmur ran round the room.

'Physics went somewhat astray in the nineteenth century,' Kaupff resumed. 'Kant's insight was forgotten; there arose a bourgeois misconception that the universe moves constantly from order to chaos. But as we know from theoretical studies of collapsed stars, entropy is a measure of information, not disorder. What capitalism sees as a dungeon of disarray is instead a region of maximal content, ultimate order, purest simplicity. We should regard the Red Star not as destroyer of information, but as processor.'

Again Willoughby interrupted. 'Please, Professor Kaupff, I am not an expert in this field and I confess I am struggling to connect the eclectic flow of your ideas into a coherent whole. Can you tell me who was responsible for this work you cite on the entropy of collapsed stars?'

'Various physicists contributed,' Kaupff told him, 'but some very crucial and remarkable work was done by a former student of mine named Hawkins.'

'Ah, yes,' said Willoughby, nodding with what appeared to be sudden recognition. 'His story made waves beyond the rarefied world of theoretical physics; and I know that it was also this Hawkins who proposed that collapsed stars must emit radiation.'

'Exactly,' Kaupff agreed. 'Their entropy corresponds to a temperature, leading to the so-called Hawkins radiation whose scalar component, in our model, should be detectable through its effect on living tissue.'

'But it's not officially called Hawkins radiation anymore,

is it?' said Willoughby, revealing rather more expert knowledge than he had previously admitted. Robert looked round and saw that he had a small pile of books and papers on the table before him. 'And poor Hawkins is no longer alive. A pity that his short career should have been marred by public utterances on subjects he was not qualified to speak about.'

Kaupff gave an impatient shrug. 'Such misdemeanours are irrelevant to the present discussion.'

'In an article published in a foreign magazine he described himself as a positivist, meaning he thinks physics can only explain experimental outcomes, never the underlying truths. Yet Lenin explicitly denounced such views in *Materialism and Empirio-Criticism*. We see the misfortune that can arise when a specialist strays beyond his field of competence.'

'Of course I am familiar with all this,' Kaupff said wearily. 'But you puzzle me, Academician Willoughby. You are a writer I respect and admire, and I invited you here to the Installation because I thought you would be enthusiastic about the exchange of ideas between artists and scientists which I believe essential for the progress of our socialist society. Yet you belittle my efforts; you think Kant belongs only to philosophers, or Goethe to poets. That certainly wasn't the approach Engels took in *Dialectics of Nature*.'

Kaupff appeared indignant rather than anxious; Robert had warned him of the danger he faced but the professor had ignored him; too old, too proud, too stubborn to listen. Or perhaps he genuinely believed in the power of genius to triumph over mediocrity.

'Continue your talk, Professor,' Davis ordered. 'You were talking about information processing.'

Kaupff nodded, unshaken by the intervention. 'The scientifically qualified among us know we can think of any natural process as a form of computation; but what sort of computer is the Red Star? Where does the information come from, that it sends to us as scalar waves? If the highest form of biological evolution is consciousness, might not gravitational evolution reach the same apex? I believe the Red Star is a naturally evolved extraterrestrial intelligence with which we can hope to communicate.'

Now there were gasps; yet Kaupff was still oblivious to the ambush everyone else could see him walking into. He was a man made reckless by the speed of his own thoughts, by the purity of his convictions, by the intellectual shallowness he perceived in those around him. 'The cosmos is evolving towards universal consciousness. The old theories of Kant, Fichte or Schelling must be recast in a wholly Marxist unification of general relativity, quantum mechanics and information theory: a transcendental materialism.'

Throughout the audience there was stunned silence until, from the back of the room, Willoughby began clapping his hands. 'Bravo! Well done!' Like any Party dogmatist he was not a man to whom irony came easily; his tone was instead sourly sarcastic. 'To have unified Schelling with Marx – that is really quite an achievement! Schelling, whose ramblings Coleridge so ably plagiarized. And I know you're something of an expert on Coleridge, Professor.' Willoughby began studying one of the pages of notes on the table before him, then recited what he saw. '*The high spiritual instinct of the human being impelling us to seek unity by harmoni-*

ous adjustment, and thus establishing the principle that all the parts of an organised whole must be assimilated to the more important and essential parts . . . Do you recognize that, Professor Kaupff?'

'Of course I do; it's from *Biographia Literaria.*'

'Indeed,' Willoughby agreed, 'and immediately afterwards you quote Marx: *The worker produces capital and capital produces him.*'

Kaupff froze, realizing where the page, and all the others in front of Willoughby, must have come from. 'Those are my private notes,' he said quietly.

'No,' Commissioner Davis interjected. 'In the Installation there is no private property. These notes – which we found secreted in a box carefully hidden in your bedroom – are the property of the state, and you have no right to withhold them. Such subterfuge is serious enough in itself; but then we have to consider the content of the notes, which it has been Academician Willoughby's onerous task to assess.'

Willoughby sighed. 'It has been wearisome work; worse than any of the undergraduate essay marking I used to have to do, because although young people often write rubbish, it is at least the innocent rubbish of childhood, and can be corrected. This, though, is incorrigible.'

Kaupff was finally beginning to understand that the circle was closing. He rubbed perspiration from his forehead. 'What do you mean? My notes consist of quotations, nothing more.'

'Ah, but it's how those quotations are arranged,' Willoughby insisted. 'You cannot pretend that your work – your monumental labour and futile drudgery – is meant to be without meaning. No, the meaning lies in the choice and the positioning, over which you appear to have taken much care. Thus we find Marx made a footnote to Coleridge; Engels an afterthought to Goethe; Lenin an appendix to Confucius or Giordano Bruno or Raymond Lull or anybody else it pleases you to stir into this vertiginous melange, this iridescent potpourri of half-truths robbed of context and given new, false ones; this intellectual abortion of which it can truly be said that it is an eclectic pauper's broth of the most despicable kind.'

'It is nothing . . .'

'Professor Kaupff,' Davis had risen to his feet. 'You are hereby relieved of your duties as head of the mission.'

'What!'

'You will be escorted to the Lodge and will remain there until we receive further instructions.'

'This can't be happening,' Kaupff weakly pleaded. 'Under what authority . . .?'

Davis had come out from behind the table where the damning documents lay piled and now walked to the front of the room. 'Sit down,' he told Kaupff, who slid onto a chair at the side of the blackboard. The commissioner then addressed the assembled company, nearly all of whom shared Kaupff's sense of shock. 'As of this moment, Professor Vine is acting head of the mission. On behalf of the Science and Defence Council of the Central Committee, I wish to thank Professor Vine for bringing his concerns about Professor Kaupff's recent behaviour so swiftly and promptly to official attention.'

Robert looked round at Vine and saw a man whose head was bowed in shame.

'We all admire the great patriotic work which Professor Kaupff has done in the past,' Davis continued. 'We shall never forget how his inventions helped repel our foreign enemies. But now the enemy walks among us. The Installation has been infiltrated by spies, saboteurs who pose as loyal workers then seek to undermine our freedom and way of life. In these dangerous times we must look closely at every man and we must ask: is he one of us, or is he one of them?' Davis swung round to face the accused who sat slumped beside him. 'Which are you, Professor Kaupff?' The physicist remained silent, and Davis turned to his audience again. 'He promised to tell us the full nature of the mission today, and I will not disappoint you. Here, in simple outline, is the scheme which Professor Kaupff seriously asks the Central Committee to regard as a viable means of investigating the frozen star.' He brought a piece of paper from his jacket pocket, unfolded it and began to read.

'*A capsule is launched containing an adult male human whose neural tissue serves as a detector of scalar radiation. The tissue is suitably prepared using electromagnetic fields, and the extraneous influence of gravity is removed by making the capsule follow a free-fall trajectory.*'

He turned to Kaupff once more. 'This is all about trying to communicate telepathically with the star's mind, isn't it?'

Kaupff nodded. 'We have found a suitable subject in Robert Coyle.'

'Is that so?' Davis said rhetorically. 'And have you told Coyle exactly how his flight is meant to proceed? What about that preparation using electromagnetic fields?'

'He knows,' said Kaupff.

Davis fixed Robert with his stare. 'Oh, he knows. Then I pity him; but let me enlighten everyone else.' He continued to read. '*The carrier field is applied cranially, but endogenous excitation is also produced through automated induction of penile orgasm.* In other words, during the whole of the flight, Coyle has an electrified rod in his rectum, making him ejaculate at precisely the right moment. Is this not the most obscenely ridiculous idea that has ever been proposed? Ah, but there's more. Not content with anally violating our fine young serviceman, Kaupff proposes an even greater atrocity, and the hideous truth lies in that innocent-looking requirement of free fall. Has he explained that one to you yet, Coyle?'

Robert looked at Kaupff and saw once more the pitiful expression the old man bore this morning when he had stood sobbing on the bowling green. 'No, Commissioner Davis, he hasn't explained.'

'Then I shall. It is an awkward but inescapable consequence of physics and economics that a rocket cannot be launched into Earth orbit from Britain. Instead, to send the capsule aloft, it must be slung beneath the fuselage of a specially modified SN53 jet bomber. Taken to an altitude of forty-six thousand feet, the capsule is then released, sending its grotesquely impaled occupant tumbling weightlessly inside it. Only in this way, Kaupff claims, can the effects of gravity be sufficiently eliminated so that the star's waves can make some impression on the subject's brain. But how much time will be needed for pen recorders on the ground to be able to chart a useful amount of mental data? About ninety seconds, Kaupff estimates. And how much time would that leave for the capsule's parachute to open? Not long enough.'

'You mean . . .'

'That's right, Coyle. There's no parachute. As Kaupff puts it in his memorandum, *Preservation of some electronic instruments will be possible if thickly encased in blast-proof containers, but all living tissue in the capsule will be destroyed on impact. It is not expected that post-mortem analysis will yield useful data.*'

'I was going to tell you everything, Robert,' said Kaupff, 'but not like this.'

Davis resumed his denunciation. 'What kind of man could devise such a plan? The Central Committee were puzzled but felt obliged to give Kaupff the resources he required, knowing what he had achieved in the past. Even so, it was decided that special monitoring was required, and now we know the sad truth. Immersed in his secret researches, bewitched by the ramblings of alchemists and poets, ignoring the advice of those who could so easily have rectified his errors, Professor Kaupff has strayed completely off the path of socialist science and into the ideological wilderness. He is not a saboteur, but a fool. Well, let him savour the romantic literature he enjoys in the long and healthy retirement we hope will keep him from causing further damage . . .'

'It could really work!' Kaupff insisted. 'The method is extraordinary, but so is the phenomenon we are trying to investigate.' Finding no response from Davis, Kaupff instead appealed to his colleagues. 'You heard me explain the science in many lectures before now – you listened and you agreed it was worth attempting. You could have said no, but you didn't. Were you too cowardly then to disagree, or are you too craven now to say otherwise?' His eyes were moist and pleading, like a beaten animal's, and Robert thought of bringing the gun out of his bag so as to end this misery. First Kaupff, then Davis, Willoughby, Rosalind . . . as many of them as there were bullets in the pistol. Instead he spoke, and though Robert's gaze was on the professor, what he said was aimed at all of them. 'I hate you.'

Davis came and stood before him, leaning over the desk which separated them to place a benevolent and fatherly hand on the shoulder of the young recruit. 'You speak like a patriot, Volunteer Coyle, but there is no need for hate, only pity, and gratitude for the achievements of the past, which Professor Kaupff's present mental disturbance need not eclipse. We know you would gladly give your life; but the motherland detests unnecessary sacrifice. Professor Vine will redesign the mission, and we trust him to find the best solution.' He turned to Kaupff. 'We also trust that you, sir, will accept with due dignity the irrevocable decision of the Science and Defence Council of the Central Committee. You are free to return to the Lodge.'

Kaupff looked startled, then strangely grateful. Davis was not going to arrest him after all; he was not to be shot. Kaupff got to his feet, shakily at first, straightened as best he could, and looked at his colleagues. He spoke softly but clearly. 'I thank you all for your friendship. I have complete confidence in Professor Vine who will, I am sure, continue to build on what we have achieved—'

'Please, Professor,' Davis interrupted. 'This is not the time for a retirement speech. Go now.'

Kaupff stared down at his feet, a final hesitation, then raised his face and walked firmly towards the door, never looking at Robert or any of his colleagues, all of whom slowly turned their heads to follow the lonely course of his retreat. When he opened the door, two armed guards were waiting there, and it was with this escort that Kaupff departed, their footsteps echoing along the corridor as they receded into the distance, getting steadily fainter while everyone listened as though to the beating of Kaupff's own heart, terminating eventually with the heavy banging of a far-off door.

'Professor Vine, I now hand over to you,' Davis said. Vine came to replace him at the front of the room.

Vine struggled to speak, though there was little for him to say except that the meeting was adjourned. It took a moment for those present to make sense of all they had heard, then there was a scraping of chairs and a sullen procession to the door. Of the stunned witnesses to Kaupff's downfall, most began returning to their offices in silence, while Robert walked alone along the corridor to the lift. He heard Willoughby's voice some distance behind, turned, and saw that the corpulent academician was coming in the same direction with Rosalind. The couple met Robert's gaze but on their faces there was no trace of sympathy or any human warmth, and rather than share the lift compartment with them, Robert decided to take the stairs he reached beforehand. He pushed open the swing doors on the stair-well, and Rosalind caught up with him. 'Wait – I want to talk to you.' It sounded more like a command than a request. Willoughby excused himself with a nod and walked on without a word to the lift. 'This is a disaster I never expected,' she said quietly.

'You mean you weren't part of it?'

She looked disgusted by the suggestion. 'How can you say such a thing?' They began descending the stairs together; it was a bare, inhospitable and echoing place in which to discuss Kaupff's fate, and they spoke in anxious whispers.

'Whose side are you on, Rosalind?'

'Nobody's. When one man goes down we can't let him take the rest of us with him.'

'So much for all your loyalty and admiration: you didn't say a word in Kaupff's defence, and all you want now is to save your own skin.'

She stopped. 'That's right, I do.' When he looked at her face he was surprised to see a tear on her cheek, fear in her eyes.

'You were prepared to let me die.'

'Everything was going to be explained properly so you could decide.'

'I don't believe you.' He carried on indignantly down the steps; Rosalind's pace behind him was more hesitant. 'You're a liar and a coward,' he said over his shoulder.

'I'm a human being and there are times when I regret it.' He turned and saw more tears. 'You asked me if I was ever in love: the answer's yes. With Heinz.'

'Kaupff? But he's . . .'

She shook her head, choking back a sob. 'Oh, shut up, Coyle, you understand nothing. Yes, I'm a coward and a liar. I'm a woman and I'm scared. But however much you hate me, don't blame Heinz. If it could have been him in the capsule instead of you, do you think he would have said no?'

Robert ignored her and went down into the foyer where researchers were milling around; he looked among the crowd for Dora but saw another woman at the trolley. When Rosalind reappeared beside him she had dried her eyes and restored as much of her usual aloofness as she could manage. 'Your friend must have got the day off. Better find her before that meat in your bag goes rotten.'

'I will.'

'You think I'm no better than a whore, don't you?'

'The ones at the Blue Cat are infinitely better than you.'

'No,' said Rosalind. 'We survive: they've got their way, I've got mine.' She stood before him and stared into his eyes. 'You think we planned to kill you – you're wrong. You're dead already. As soon as you passed the perimeter fence, as soon as you entered the Installation, that's when your life ended. Because this place is hell, and you're never getting out of it.'

He brushed past her with mute contempt and walked across the foyer to the stout, middle-aged woman at the trolley. 'Where's Dora?'

'Off sick,' was the complacent reply.

'Where does she live?'

The woman raised her snub nose in a gesture conveying it was none of his business but she'd tell him if he could make it worth her while. He brought out his voucher book and she cast a precautionary glance over her shoulder before tearing out a slip and stuffing it in her overall pocket.

'Just off the main street, first right after the housing office, one with the blue door – she's upstairs.'

He was still memorizing these directions like a schoolroom verse when Rosalind came and took him by the arm, leading him back to the side of the room. 'Wait here for me while I find out what happens next.'

'No,' he said bluntly. 'I'm going for a walk. Might even do a runner like Harvey.'

'Don't be a fool, you could be next on Davis's list.'

He was unruffled. 'If he's got me marked then nothing's going to save me. But if you can't look after your volunteers then soon there'll be no reason why anyone should want to save you either, so perhaps you'd better start treating me a little more pleasantly. You need me, Rosalind. I'm the only one who passed your playing-card test – I'm the most important piece of your apparatus.'

She leaned close to his ear. 'Don't be so sure of that, Coyle. I faked the test results.'

'I don't believe you.'

'Heinz wanted a telepath and I gave him one.'

'You're lying.'

'It's every man for himself now, and I can easily find another like you. So off you go.'

21

Rosalind's taunts didn't scare him, and though he wondered if he might be stopped by the guard outside, he was free to proceed as soon as his identity had been checked. It was all a most uplifting illustration of how the Installation preserved the freedoms its citizens enjoyed: Robert was at liberty to go almost anywhere he wished, precisely because everywhere was so identical.

Walking into Town in the fading afternoon light, he saw a familiar figure on the opposite side of the street, wearing a suit and proceeding purposefully past a row of offices. It was Lachlan Macleod, one of the first of the recruits to have been eliminated. Robert hurried across the road to greet him. 'Lachlan!'

Macleod stopped but had a puzzled, embarrassed air. 'Look at you,' Robert said teasingly. 'Suit and tie, eh? Have they given you a desk job?'

He was still staring blankly. 'Do I know you?'

'What are you talking about!'

'I think you must be mistaking me for someone else . . .'

Macleod began to move on; Robert blocked his way. 'Don't play tricks, Lachlan, I know it's you. I can go along with all the secrecy shit but don't pretend you've never seen me. We were all supposed to be in this together, weren't we?'

The man's face remained unaltered. 'If you'll excuse me, I have to get on with my work.' Robert stood aside and watched him go past, disappearing soon afterwards into one of the offices. No, he wasn't mistaken – Macleod looked different in a suit but not that different. They'd done something to his brain.

Robert was sickened but not surprised: this place was hell, forgetfulness its only possible comfort. He went on until he reached the darkening main street, following the directions he had been given until he came to Dora's blue door. It was a terraced house like most others in the Town, with the ubiquitous white pebble-dash, stained by years of harsh weather, giving it the dismal air of a seaside cottage washed far inland. There were two doorbells; Robert pushed the upper one, waited, and when no response came he stepped back, looked at the upstairs window whose curtains were closed, then tried the bell again. This time, after another wait, he saw the curtains twitch, and a few moments later heard feet coming down the stairs inside. The door opened only wide enough for Dora to check who was there, and for Robert to see that she was wrapped in a long, drab dressing gown. She looked tired, unwell, and not pleased to see him.

'Go away.'

'No,' said Robert.

'I'm not working today.'

'I brought you a present.'

'I told you, I'm not working.' She tried to shut the door but Robert kept it open with his shoulder and foot. She was too weak to push him out, and soon relented. 'Why are you doing this?' she said, stepping back to let him in, then closing the door behind him before any more of the freezing winter air could enter.

'I wanted to give you some things,' he repeated.

'Come and let's get this over with,' she said, leading him past the chipped door of the lower flat and up a narrow carpeted staircase that creaked beneath their feet. Her door at the top stood open, and when Dora showed him in and closed it, Robert found himself in a place reminiscent of Kaupff's bachelor apartment in the Lodge, with a similar tiny kitchenette adjoining the small living room, and doorways leading off to the bedroom and bathroom. Here, though, there were no books and few possessions of any kind, the only glimmer of humanity that seized his gaze being some artificial flowers crowding from the neck of a glass sauce bottle on the windowsill. Robert took the rucksack from his back and opened it. The meat had lain there for several hours now and had leaked blood through its brown-paper wrapper onto the box containing both pairs of gloves. The gun, too, was slicked, but undamaged. Robert brought everything out except the pistol, apologizing for the mess.

'It doesn't matter,' said Dora, taking the paper package first. 'That's what meat does.' She pulled away some of the wrapper and inspected a corner of red marbled flesh, finding it to her satisfaction. 'It looks good,' she declared with the authoritativeness of a connoisseur, raised it to her nose and sniffed, then took it to the kitchenette and put it safely in the small fridge. Next she came back to examine the white box, smeared pink along one of its narrow sides. She opened it and took out the thick winter gloves that lay on top of the folded crêpe paper. 'These will do,' she said simply as she put them on and flexed her fingers, turning her hands and enjoying the warmth she felt, seeming almost unwilling to take them off. Robert, who had remained standing all this time, was beginning to appreciate how cold it was inside the flat.

'Look what else is in the box,' he urged. 'Inside the paper.'

Giving him a suspicious look, Dora removed the thick gloves and returned to the open box she had lain on the simple dining table. Robert watched her peel back the paper, but when she saw his most precious gift she looked less delighted by it. She lifted the fine gloves and held them hanging limply in her fingers like withered stems.

'Do you like them?'

'They're beautiful,' she said politely. 'They're very, very beautiful.' All at once Robert realized that beauty was not what Dora wanted or needed. Without trying them on, she put the gloves back in their container, folded the paper across them, and tried to wipe away the blood from the box with a fingertip dampened by saliva. She wanted to keep them in good condition so that she could exchange them for more meat, more warm clothing. Their only value to her, Robert knew, was whatever material necessity they could be traded for. 'Thank you,' she said, then she opened her coarse robe and let it fall to the floor, standing before him in a flimsy nylon shift that made her look more emaciated than he remembered.

'Put it back on, don't get cold . . .'

She pulled the shift over her head, leaving herself completely naked. Then she went to the bedroom door and pushed it open. 'It's best if we do it here . . .'

'No!' Robert remained where he stood, angered by the callous equation she made between his gifts and the sex she thought he now expected.

'All right, if you prefer.' She came back, kneeled on the floor at his feet, and reached for his belt. 'Shall we start with some sucking?'

He took hold of her face and raised it so that he could see the hopelessness in her eyes. 'I didn't bring you presents for this.'

'Then why did you bring them?' She was unbuckling his belt.

'I came because I love you.'

A smile haunted the corner of her lip, as if she'd heard an old joke from childhood that still retained something of its risible innocence. 'Then let's make love, baby.' The belt was undone; she lowered his zip, his trousers began to slide down his hips. He pulled them up and moved away from her.

'Don't do this to me,' he pleaded. 'You're sick and I came and brought you something to make you happy.'

'I'm sick from being punched in the stomach by a punter last night,' she said. 'But don't feel sorry for me. We all must do our patriotic work.'

He sat down on one of the threadbare armchairs; and seeing that he was not to be removed so easily, Dora took the other, pulling her dressing gown over her body to stop herself shivering.

'Let's talk,' he said.

'Sure, we can talk. Some guys only want that, though you can watch me doing things if you like.'

'Stop it! I'm not a punter and you're not a whore. We're human beings, and I came because I wanted to see you and be with you. Is that so hard to understand?'

'No, it's perfectly easy,' she said. 'But although it's what you want, it's not what I want. We can talk, fuck, anything you like, but not for free. And I don't take presents for nothing. Whatever I get in life, I pay for it. The meat's worth a fuck, so are the thick gloves.'

'And the beautiful ones? The ones I imagined seeing on your hands that'd make you look like the woman you deserve to be?'

'They're worth lots of fucks,' she said. 'A whole week's

worth. Or lots of talk if that's what you prefer, and if you want me to say I love you I'll do it as much as you like. I'll be any girlfriend you want me to be.'

'I really love you, Dora. The truth of it came to me like a blinding light.'

She smiled again at the old joke. 'I must be at least ten years older than you. Not old enough to be your mother, but old enough to know that at your age, love is something you carry round inside yourself, ready made, until you find someone who'll let you shower them with it. OK, so you showered me last night. It could have been anyone. What about the scientist I saw you with yesterday at the education centre?'

'Rosalind?'

'I think that's her name. Takes milk and no sugar. She's younger and prettier than me, and she's got a better body – so why aren't you in love with her? Or did you go off her and then start on me instead?'

Robert sat in the uncomfortable armchair feeling unable to offer any counter-argument. He hardly knew Dora; the fantasy in his mind had little to do with the underfed woman sitting opposite him. He didn't feel ready to give her the most important gift in his bag. 'Go back to bed,' he told her. 'Get some rest.'

She stood up, wrapped the dressing gown round her shoulders, and went towards the bedroom, stopping to pick up her nylon slip from the floor. 'Come with me,' she said in a voice that was suddenly both kind and needy, so Robert followed. The bedroom looked squalid and untidy; a red plastic bucket stood on the floor at the head of the bed. 'I've thrown up a few times,' she explained, and Robert thought he glimpsed a trace of vomit clinging stubbornly to the inner wall of the rinsed container.

'Why did he punch you?'

'It's what some of them are like. One of your crowd, I think; horsey face.'

'Colin Forsyth?'

'I don't know. It doesn't really matter.' She dropped the robe again so that she could put on her slip, and her nakedness was somehow less wonderful to Robert than the sight of her once she was lying covered with the blankets pulled up to her chin. He sat beside her on the edge of the bed, looking down at her face, which was more childlike now, enabling him to imagine what she must have looked like in better times.

'Why did you get sent here?' he asked.

'Someone had a grudge against my husband.'

'You're married?'

'Are you surprised? I had a life on the outside. My husband had a good position in a steelworks, I was a music teacher in a school. We lived well. Then another man in the factory wanted Adam's job – you know how it is. He dug up evidence of corruption – Adam said it was mostly lies, he'd done no worse than anyone else. But he was convicted of fraud and we both lost our jobs. Then the slide began – one thing after another until we had nothing left, no marriage, no hope. I ended up here; I don't know where Adam is now.'

'And children?'

He saw her eyes well up. 'I can't talk about that.' Any she had, Robert knew, would have been given to a more law-abiding family for adoption; that was how things worked, and he had never until now questioned the justice of it. Dora's punishment, he realized, was not to be allowed to forget the life she had left behind.

He lowered his face onto hers and felt her tears against his cheek; her skin was unexpectedly soft. He kissed her hair. Soon it was their lips that met; hers were chapped and gnawed but yielded to his completely. She freed herself only to tell him to get into bed; there was no more hostility now. He quickly undressed and slid beneath the blankets.

'You're so warm,' she said, snuggling against him, even wanting to wrap her toes in the cosy embrace of his feet. She buried her face against his neck and he drank the scent of her hair.

'I really love you,' he said.

'Then make love to me.'

With an initial fumbling that made them both laugh, he did as she asked. There was no thumbs-up to the crowd, no ceremony; instead he got inside the capsule, exploring its dark confines; an unexpected ridge, a slight bend. He was safe and comfortable here, feeling on his ear her rhythmic breathing that aligned itself like an oscilloscope with his own internal frequency. They were floating together on scalar waves, rising, and he began to see the Installation far below as a diminishing map. There was the Town, all of it, like a smoky fuzz; and there the Plant, the College, the outer perimeter with its rows of wire, its watchtowers and minefields, and then the surrounding hectares of forest, crowding with the perspective of altitude until the Installation was a tiny bald speck among the trees. They were high enough to call it space, this throbbing ether they shared, in which she gave voice to what he was thinking.

'I love you.'

They were there: the event horizon was opening and the singularity stood naked before him, an infinite pearl. This was how space and time began and this was where it ended: the limit and purpose of everything. Whatever had gone before was only a crude simulacrum of what he now experienced; for this was heaven, and he was like a wheel being turned by the force that moves stars.

Exhausted and at peace, he slumped with satisfaction. He never wanted to stir again; he wanted to die like this. Dora eventually gave him a push so that he rolled beside her. He cuddled her again, but she was warm enough by now; there was a resistance in her body. She hadn't flown to the same place after all.

'You'd better go,' she said.

'Why?'

'I'm not supposed to have visitors. And I need to sleep. I'm working at the Blue Cat again tonight.'

'Do you have to?'

'Yes.'

He got out of bed and walked naked to the bathroom where he hurriedly cleaned himself at the cracked sink. In a blue and white cup stood two toothbrushes. Visitors, he realized, were a transgression she allowed herself as long as the terms were right.

He went back to the living room and lifted his rucksack from the floor, took it to the bedroom and stood before her where she lay covered, too weak even to get up and wash. 'I brought you one more thing,' he said.

'You've already given me enough.'

'It's the most important gift.'

She looked at him with what Robert at first took to be coldness, then realized it was pity. 'Stop now,' she said. 'Get dressed and go.'

'Did our lovemaking mean anything at all to you?'

She paused, then slowly shook her head. 'When you see a beautiful thing in hell it only makes the suffering harder. Don't you understand? I can't let it mean anything. You'll be gone from this place soon enough but I won't. This is my world – I have to survive here.'

He reached inside the bag and brought out the weapon. 'This is what I wanted to give you.'

She stared at it in bewilderment. 'Why?'

'You told me last night you'd like to shoot everyone in the Blue Cat, start a revolution.'

She looked at him warily. 'I never said anything of the sort. Take your gun and get out of here.'

'Don't be afraid of me,' he pleaded, waving the pistol despairingly as he stood naked in the room. 'All I want is to help you. This is a way.'

'Who do you want me to shoot for you? The one who punched me?'

'I don't want anything except to help you. I took so many risks bringing this.' He placed the gun on the bedside table. 'There are people here who want to change things. They're organizing themselves; I could put you in touch with them.'

'Get out of here.'

'Why must you be like this?'

'I can look after myself and I don't need your help. Never mind about the gun, leave it here. I know how to get rid of unwanted things.'

It was a strange end to a love affair that never happened. Stealing the gun was an imaginative act; the use it might serve was imaginary too, and so was the love that motivated the theft. They were voltages in his head. Robert dressed himself, aware of what a fool he had been.

'You know how you could really help?' Dora said when he was almost ready to go. 'Take the gun and use it yourself. That's what I told you last night. Kill the bastards.'

He'd had so many opportunities. Davis, Willoughby, Rosalind, Kaupff – all of them in the seminar room. But he knew the truth. 'I can't.'

'No, I can't either,' said Dora. 'We're good people. We let the bad ones take all the power.'

He pulled on his coat, lifted the empty rucksack, then leaned over the bed to kiss her. She offered him her cheek.

'Goodbye, Dora.'

'Goodbye, soldier.'

He turned and went out, closing the bedroom door to try and seal in whatever warmth the two of them had generated, then left the flat and went down the creaking staircase and into the dark street where he immediately saw the familiar white car parked on the opposite side of the road, its headlights and engine switched off. The rear door opened and a voice called across. It was Davis. 'Come and join me, Coyle.'

22

Robert crossed the road and climbed into the car's back seat beside the commissioner. The driver was different this time; a fair-haired, younger man, but he stared ahead in the customary way and said nothing. Davis leaned towards Robert and gave him a pat on the arm. 'Was she good?' He laughed at Robert's silence. 'Don't be shy – we're all men here. It's the one you were with last night, isn't it? Wanda, Dora, Zelda – a name for every occasion.'

'I won't be seeing her again.'

'Good idea,' Davis agreed. 'O's have their uses but fraternizing with them can only lead to trouble.' Then he instructed the driver to set off; there was no indication where their destination might be, but the car went as slowly as usual. This was not like a normal arrest.

'Now, then,' said Davis, getting to business as the car moved through the dark, deserted town. 'What more can you tell me about Kaupff? Have the Franks given you any useful information?' Robert could see no point in Davis's questioning except as a way of exercising control. Kaupff was ruined, wasn't that enough? But Davis had other ideas. 'This investigation has taken an intriguing new turn,' he said while they proceeded along a quiet road Robert had not seen previously, the floodlit buildings on either side soon giving way to dimly visible uncultivated moorland. 'Harvey turned up.'

'Where?'

'In the river, dead.'

Robert was stunned; contending possibilities quickly

flashed through his thoughts of accident or suicide, the latter seeming likeliest.

'It was Kaupff,' Davis declared. 'He hasn't confessed yet but the evidence is clear; it's a repetition of what he did years ago to the Frank child. Sexual assault, then drowning the victim. The doctor who examined Harvey's body said there was clear evidence of anal penetration.'

'Rosalind must have done the experiment on him too.'

'I expect so,' the commissioner chuckled. 'But the experiment is secret – a bruised arse isn't. We've got him nailed.' Davis turned and peered through the window into the night. Every so often they would pass the broken shadow of an old, disused concrete bunker beside the road. 'This is where they tested some of Kaupff's earliest bomb designs, before the Town was created. I expect we could get cancer just by setting foot outside the car.'

'What will happen to him?'

Davis shrugged. 'He'll retire honourably, and with any luck he'll have a heart attack not long afterwards. But for now, keep watch on Vine, Rosalind and the others.'

'I'm still part of the mission?'

'Of course!' cried Davis. 'You've passed every test so far – and I don't mean medical checks or mind-reading tricks, which are the least important element as far as the Central Committee are concerned. No, what they want is their own man inside that capsule, maintaining a close check on things. Someone who can be trusted absolutely, whose only loyalty is to the State. You rejected Kaupff in exactly the right way, same as you've dropped that tart you were with. This is what we need, Coyle – men of integrity and unshakeable principles.' He lowered his voice. 'You realize, don't you, that even a redesigned mission could still prove fatal?'

Robert said nothing. He was a coward who had renounced the only people he cared about; he was doomed and he deserved to die.

'We'll have to see what sort of new design they come up with, but whatever the outcome, you can expect the highest rewards. If your duty is to live, you'll be well looked after until the end of your days. And if things have to go otherwise, your family will receive those benefits on your behalf.'

Looking out, Robert saw in the distance the twinkling lights of the Town; and from the other side of the car he noticed tall security fencing beside the road, with impenetrable pine forest beyond. They were wheeling round the Installation's outer perimeter, performing the highest and most lonely orbit its topography allowed. They could go on like this forever, circling the closed universe where Robert's only task was to fall according to the dictates of gravity.

'Does anyone ever leave the Installation?' he asked.

'Certainly,' said Davis. 'Willoughby's going back to his wife and kids and his endless meetings and cocktail parties, and I expect he'll write a few more of those dreadful books of his.'

'But will he really go? Or will he simply disappear from here?'

In the gloom of the car, Davis's teeth could be glimpsed shining between parted lips. 'Some questions cannot be answered, Coyle, so don't ask them. Rosalind was assigned to monitor Willoughby and she did a fine job. Now you must monitor Rosalind. I've told her to watch you, so you can expect to find yourself in her bed soon enough. Give her a good hard fucking and submit a full report afterwards.' They drove on in silence for a while until Davis said suddenly, 'You know you had a very lucky escape? Those infiltrators could easily have killed you.'

Robert's heart sank even further: Davis knew about Miriam.

'This morning we caught the one with the radio,' the commissioner explained. 'He was trying to send coded messages to his American paymasters – had a transmitter hidden inside an electric heater.'

No, that didn't sound like Tim or his Christian comrades.

'We don't think he leaked anything useful to the Yankees but he squawked soon enough when we collared him. And do you know who his accomplice here was? A trusted citizen who'd been giving apparently loyal service for years, when all along he was a saboteur waiting to be activated.'

'Who?' Robert asked nervously.

'Your driver. He was coming to pick you up at the College when my men arrested him; as soon as he realized what was happening he grabbed for his glove compartment and tried to get hold of something, the officers thought it must be a gun or a bomb and took cover but all the poor sod could come up with was his papers and a photo of his wife that he showed them while they put the cuffs on him, crying like a baby.'

So Robert had stolen the pistol from the one man who might have made good use of it. He had foiled the rebellion he'd half-heartedly yearned for.

'You were being driven round this place by a spy, Coyle.

But we know you didn't tell him anything; we'd have beaten it out of him by now if you had.'

Robert could see the driver in his mind, wearing his crumpled coat with dandruff on its collar, haggling in the butcher's shop, or passing comment on a pair of gloves. He could see him being kicked in the face, his mouth bursting in a bloody spray of loosened teeth. Robert had disarmed a spy. He was a hero.

'Mr Kelly came to get you instead,' said Davis, nodding towards the driver, 'but you'd already buggered off on foot. So now let's take you home.' He gave instructions to the silent chauffeur and soon they were re-entering the Town, following the familiar streets until the car halted outside the Franks' house.

Robert saw no lights inside. 'I don't think they're back from work.'

'If you've no key I'll have the door opened for you.'

'Do you need more information on them?'

Davis shook his head. 'We've got Kaupff; the baby can rest in peace. Don't go out tonight, have a relaxing evening with the Franks. Tomorrow we begin in earnest.'

Robert got out, and as soon as he stepped away from the vehicle it moved off. He let himself into the house, switched on the hall light, hung up his coat and the empty rucksack that was stained with a small patch of dried blood, and went upstairs to the darkened landing. When he pushed his bedroom door open he was so startled by what he found that he gave a cry.

Miriam was there, kneeling on the floor, her ghostly face illuminated only by the glow from the old radio hissing quietly in front of her. She turned and looked up at him with an air of displeasure at having been interrupted in her prayers.

'I didn't expect you to be here, Miriam. You frightened me.'

'I always get home early on Tuesdays. You ought to know that.'

'Should I?' He came in and closed the door, leaving the light off, not wishing to disturb her any more than he had to. He sat down on the bed and stared at the radio to which she had quickly returned her attention. 'Still trying to contact the Red Star?'

She nodded. 'It's so near now.'

'I've seen it already.'

Miriam swung round in the eerie gloom. 'What do you mean?'

'I've been there in my mind, it's beautiful. It really is heaven. But everyone has a different idea of what heaven is.'

'If you've seen it then you should kneel here with me and pray.'

'What for? Salvation? Freedom?'

'Try and you'll find out.'

He came and knelt beside her on the floor. It was ridiculous, being on their knees in front of an ancient Bakelite radio; they were like primitive tribal villagers worshipping a technological icon dropped from an aeroplane. The radio hummed and crackled, and from time to time Robert thought he heard the faint intimation of a far-off dance band. It was stupid – but when he closed his eyes and let himself relax he felt a welcome peace; the same relinquishment of effort he had experienced in hospital, critically ill, while the loudspeaker at his ear relayed the voice of the Red Star. Yes, that was when his spirit had died, and since then his soul had been in limbo. The sound was a liquid background, a gentle surf reminding him of Dora; and she was right, the woman breathing beside him now could be anyone, the love within him was a beam he could project on any surface.

An hour later, Mrs Frank came in noisily carrying the shopping bag she had filled as best she could on her way back from work. She knew her daughter would be in, but the sight of Robert sitting with Miriam in the kitchen gave her a pleasant surprise.

'I'm not going out tonight,' he said. 'I hope that's all right.'

'You're eating with us? That's lovely! And what have you two been up to?' she asked innocently. The look that passed between Robert and Miriam made her pause, but she didn't follow it up. 'I'm doing curried mutton – how does that sound?'

'Perfect,' said Robert.

'Well, I'd better mutton myself out of here and into the living room to get the table ready. Let's eat in there, shall we? We can make a wee night of it. Arthur will be so pleased.'

She bustled out, and Robert looked again at Miriam, who, like her mother, could wear entirely different faces depending on the circumstances. 'Shall we tell her yet?' he asked.

'Not yet.'

Mrs Frank came back. 'Miriam, why don't you get off

your bahookie and give me a hand carrying these glasses through?'

'Why don't you ask the lodger, Mum?'

Mrs Frank stopped in her tracks and looked at both of them. They were all three playing a kind of charade, and they were at the point where any of the players might decide to abandon the script and the whole pretence it represented.

'Here, I'll do it,' said Robert, getting up. 'You and Miriam can take care of the cooking.'

When Mr Frank returned later, the house was filled with the appetizing smell of the meal that would soon be ready. He came striding to the kitchen, addressing his good lady wife before he had even entered from the hall. 'And what culinary delight is my darling angel preparing for us tonight . . .? Why hello, Robbie, are you getting ready for another night with the lads?'

'He's staying here,' Mrs Frank announced. 'We've all decided to have a wee night together.'

'Go and look in the living room,' Miriam told him, and when Arthur went there he saw the table elaborately decked with all their best plates and cutlery, paper napkins at the ready and even three candles glowing at the centre beside an open bottle of wine.

For a moment he was speechless, beaming with a child's delight at the rare spectacle his family had prepared for him. 'What a lovely idea,' he said at last. 'What a really lovely thing for us all to do.' Robert had joined him from the kitchen; Mr Frank turned and looked at him. 'It's an honour and a pleasure having you with us. I hope you're in no hurry to leave.'

Mrs Frank decided to change out of her everyday work clothes into something more suitable for the evening. She disappeared upstairs, taking Miriam with her. 'Fancy a beer?' Mr Frank asked his guest, his smile broadening when Robert said yes. 'Lads' night in, eh?' he said with a wink, going to the kitchen and coming back with a litre bottle of Victory and two glasses. 'Sit yourself down, Robbie. How's your day been?'

'Don't ask.'

'Aye, they work you hard here. But there's nane like Installation folk!' He passed one foaming glass to Robert and took the other to his armchair. 'And you're an Installation man now, Robbie. You're one of the best. Cheers!'

The beer quickly made Robert's head feel light, and it was pleasant for him to be able to sit back and be treated with such warmth. He was ready to be pampered and cosseted, and the Franks were determined to oblige.

'But tell me,' Mr Frank said in a low voice, while the women were still absent. 'Have you . . .' he glanced round to check that the living-room door was closed. 'Have you found yourself a lassie here yet? I don't mean those girls you-know-where. The regular sort.'

'As a matter of fact I have.'

Arthur's face fell. 'I see. Well, if you need to bring her back here, that's OK. But, you know . . .'

'I'll be discreet,' Robert promised.

'Because it's not a big house and the walls are a bit thin. Might be frightening to anyone who doesn't understand how it is that a man and a woman . . .'

'I know, you told me before.'

'Frank by name, frank by nature – that's me. But what's she like, this lassie? Might be someone I know.'

'Might be,' Robert agreed, then fell silent as footsteps came down the stairs. Mrs Frank entered wearing a dress with a bold geometric pattern, a string of large artificial pearls at her neck, and matching earrings.

'Doesn't she look great!' said Arthur, getting to his feet and putting down his almost empty beer glass on the coffee table before going to her. 'You look just like the girl I married.' He swung round to Robert. 'And I'm needing my eyes tested!'

'Och, Arthur,' said his wife.

'No, seriously, Dot, you look fantastic. And here's my wee daughter looking magic too.' Miriam came in wearing a dark blue dress that was plainer and more old fashioned than her mother's; but she'd put on make-up, too, and her red lips and full bosom reminded Robert that when they had knelt together in front of the crackling radio she could have been any woman in the world.

They sat down to dinner, which Mrs Frank served single-andedly by means of many journeys to and from the kitchen. A small hatch cut in the wall would have made it all so much easier, Mr Frank observed, but such modifications contravened regulations, and this led him into a lengthy speech about the structural details of the house, its wiring and plumbing, and the various problems encountered in other dwellings of the scheme, none of which Dorothy could solve by trying to change the subject when she sat down to eat with them. In fact it was only Miriam who was eventually able to silence her father by tapping her knife against her wine glass and saying, 'We have an announcement.'

Mr Frank's mouth stood open in mid-vowel, the uncompleted word being 'generator'. His wife took over. 'What do you want to announce?' An optimistic smile was rising on her face which had nothing to do with the wine she had drunk. 'And who's "we"?' For Mr Frank, his beer-warmed mind still swirling in a circuit diagram of its own making, the penny had yet to drop.

Robert spoke. 'We want . . . I mean, Mr Frank, I'd like to ask if . . .'

'We're getting married,' said Miriam.

Arthur's mouth showed no sign of closing; his wife was already crying. 'Oh, Miriam, I'm so happy!' She got up and went to hug her daughter while the news reached Arthur's brain and set about creating a further flood of tears.

'Thank you, Robbie!' he gasped, choking back his emotion. 'Thank you, son!'

No one really noticed the curried mutton after that, but Mrs Frank didn't mind. The wee night was declared one that would go down in Frank history. The clearing of the table gave Dorothy another chance to pull her daughter away, leaving Mr Frank to reiterate his joy through successive stages of inebriation.

'You said you'd found a lassie . . .' Arthur said with some concern.

'I meant Miriam.'

'Oh, that's all right.' Then another thought struggled across his mind. 'She's never, you know, been with anyone. You'll have to . . .'

'Don't worry, I'll look after her.'

Fresh tears welled in Arthur's eyes. 'My wee daughter! Only seems yesterday when she was on my knee with a dummy in her mouth. Used to want to play horsey all the time, and now she's a woman. I'm getting old. I hope you'll give us lots of grandchildren, mind!' Robert smiled, and Mr Frank let his thoughts dwell on lost times. 'We've had our share of misfortune, you know that. Losing wee Jamie could have destroyed us and it nearly did, but I was never going to let one tragedy cause another. There's always a ray of hope even when you feel you're in a living hell, same as there's always that speck of sadness though you're the happiest man on earth, like I am now, because whatever happens has to for a reason, that's what I think. Let me tell you an old story, Robbie – a bit of Installation history, from the time long before they made the Town that's here now. I'm talking eighteen hundreds, when this was a pit village called Kenzie and the weans used to get taken to the baptismal font and sold to the mine owner before they even had their first teeth. And two wee weans, maybe seven or eight year old, they fell in that river, same as my Jamie did. I read about it all once. And a fellow, name of Deuchar, student at university, he was going past, jumped in and tried to save them. He could have drowned himself. But he didn't – it was the weans that died, same as my Jamie did. So even if there'd been somebody who saw my boy when he fell in, there was no saving him. The water's too fast when it's in spate – you'd need to be an Olympic swimmer. It's not easy for me to talk about it, Robbie, but me and Dot never discuss this and I'm only glad I'm going to have a new son now that I can share these things with, but I tell you, when I remember what the wee lad looked like with his eyes still open . . .'

'Please,' said Robert, 'we don't have to do it all at once. There'll be time.'

'No,' Arthur insisted, 'I want to tell you this now, on the happiest day of my life. I really mean that, because being happy doesn't mean forgetting what's happened. We're all going to be happy remembering Jamie, and maybe you'll even want to call your bairn after him, I don't mind what you do about that. I only wanted to say that the fellow Deuchar, you might have heard of him from your history lessons. He was the James Deuchar that formed the Scottish Socialists. And when I read that he'd once tried to rescue two weans from that river that took Jamie, I thought to myself, what if Deuchar hadnae made it? What if he'd drowned like the weans? Don't you see, Robbie, for all we know, the whole of history might have been different. But it couldn't be different, because everything happens for a reason, and if James Deuchar had thrown his life away then maybe we wouldn't be here, there'd be no Installation, I'd never have met Dot, there'd have been no Jamie, even though we had to lose him so soon. And if somebody had been there beside the river and saw him bobbing past and jumped in, he could have died as well as Jamie, and what then? There's maybe someone alive right now, here in the Installation, who'd be dead for no reason, and they'd have missed all these years we've seen. I'm sorry, I'm rambling, but do you see what I'm saying?'

'Yes, I see,' said Robert. 'Sometimes we make sacrifices

for the greater good. I suppose that's what James Deuchar believed.'

'Of course he did,' said Arthur. 'That's the meaning of socialism. I'm not an educated man and I haven't read all these clever books by wise people, I'm just an ordinary working bloke who does the best job he can and likes a wee beer when he comes home at night, that's all I am, a common working man who's never raised his hand to his wife in anger and only to his offspring when he had to. But the way I look at it now, if somebody had gone and killed himself saving Jamie then there'd be one person more and one person less, and instead of us grieving it'd be another family. What happened to Jamie was an accident and nobody's fault, it was plain bad luck, but if it hadnae happened then we'd have had two children growing up in this house and they'd both be here still. You'd never have been billeted here and you wouldn't be engaged to my daughter now, and the weans you'll have one day would never get the chance of living. So I look at the future, Robbie, and I think of they kiddies yet to be born and I tell you from the bottom of my heart, thank you for letting me die a happy man. Thank you for giving Dot a chance to find peace in her heart. Thank you for making Miriam happy. Love her and be good to her because she deserves it.'

Robert listened in pained silence. In the kitchen, Miriam was describing to her mother the deal that had been struck. Yes, they would marry, but they would never sleep together as man and wife. If Robert survived the forthcoming mission, he would take Miriam and her parents out of the

Installation and she would be free to divorce him after the statutory period. If he died, all would receive the same benefits, the only difference being that Mr Frank need never know the marriage was a sham. So Robert had made his sacrifice. Looking at Arthur's reddened eyes he wondered if, by saving the landlord's only surviving child, he was making a gesture equivalent to Deuchar's so long ago. He was saving a woman he didn't even like, while those he loved and respected were left to fall alone. Did it make him the noblest of men or the most pitiful? Robert didn't know. The ladies came back and saw Arthur's face; theirs too were marked by a heaviness and shame that Arthur was thankfully unable to notice. Then they went back to pretending, and of those present, it was only Arthur, his cheeks traced with two thick lines of tears, who could honestly claim to be the happiest alive.

23

Try to see him now, though in the capsule the only light is the glimmer of a control panel flicking into activity to signal that the descent is about to begin. It's exactly like the simulator, so cramped that any movement is impossible, and Robert could almost be fooled into thinking this was only another rehearsal and not the real thing, but for the steady roar of the mother jet preparing to abandon him, and the gentle rise and fall of the bonded vessels' mutual passage through periodic pockets of mild turbulence.

Forty-six thousand feet below, Kaupff is about to be buried with full honours and Vine is under arrest. Rosalind is in the control room, watching the twitch of pen recorders monitoring Robert's thoughts. On the scrolling paper, six jagged lines unfold in partial synchrony portraying mental divisions of which Robert himself is unaware, considering himself of one mind, determined in what he does.

'*Can you hear me?*'

There is no radio in the capsule; nothing that the ground crew and the helpless passenger could possibly say to each other. But Robert hears.

'*I am the voice of the Red Star.*'

Only the sudden flicker of the feeble lights, strangely bright to his starved eyes, tells Robert that the drop is about to happen; but those lights were put in place for the sake of the maintenance technicians working on the apparatus before it was launched, not for him, and soon they switch off again, recreating the perfect darkness deemed essential to the operation and made legible on the ground in another alteration of pen tracks.

'*I am the one who brought you here, made every shape you saw, every phantom. Now we must go to another place.*'

Then it happens.

There is no tumbling of the capsule; the aerodynamic predictions are of an accuracy that gives cheer to the anxious physicists. Yet for Robert it is not the instantaneous sensation of perfect weightlessness he had been led to expect. Instead it is as if he is rising. He sees Dora, as pure and naked as he is, in that other capsule in the Blue Cat with its curtained window where she too is alone, opening a drawer in her sparsely furnished cell and lifting out the gun he gave her. He tries to call out but the barrel is already hard against her skull like the glass marble focusing everything on his; the shot is fired and she is falling while a dark red spray ribbons from her head across the room. The redness Robert flies towards is darker still; invisible and benevolent in its infinite orbit, its endless cosmic loop.

'*Your life is over, Robert – but not your story.*'

PART THREE

1

Standing at the kitchen window, looking over the sink into the back garden he had tended for nearly fifty years, Joe Coyle was displeased. 'It's that damn cat again.'

'Maureen's?' said his wife, slowly entering the kitchen with the cool teapot she'd brought from the living room, leaning on her metal walking stick. The transistor radio, ignored on the shelf, was tinnily talking about another suicide bomb in Iraq.

'I'll get it this time,' Joe vowed, reaching for the pink plastic water pistol he'd parked in readiness beside the draining board.

'Better be quick,' Anne warned while he filled it. 'I just hope she doesn't see you.'

'Who, the cat? That's the whole idea.' He slowly opened the window.

'No, you daftie, Maureen. I don't want her getting upset.'

Their neighbour had bought the animal to ease her widowhood but Joe was unmoved. 'I keep telling her not to let that damn moggie come in.'

Sam Dunbar was only sixty-two when he had the heart

attack, lean and suntanned, not long back from Tenerife. Right after his best round of golf in years, the way he'd have wanted to go, everyone kept saying at the funeral. Maureen so brave about it. But Joe and Anne knew more about loss than she ever would, and they'd no need to go spoiling other people's gardens over it.

'I'll get you this time, you wee devil!' A thick bright stream arced from the pistol Joe shoved through the open window, and the cat dodged and leapt, unimpressed, to the foot of the privet hedge, where it lingered insolently, eyeing him from a safe distance before turning to slide beneath the foliage with a final triumphant flash of its anus. 'And don't come back!'

'It's only a cat, Joe.'

Happened in the clubhouse toilet, Joe heard from the friend Sam was playing with that day. Wondered what was taking him so long, went to check, had to climb over the locked cubicle and there he was, face down on the floor in his own urine, trousers in a knot round his ankles. Poor Maureen. To lose a spouse is a terrible thing at any age – but your own son? No, you'd need to bury a thousand husbands and a million bloody cats before you knew that burden.

'Better close the window before we get cold.' With a twinge of pain, Anne propped herself on one of the high wooden kitchen stools and leaned her stick against the neighbouring table. She'd been on the waiting list for a hip replacement for the last four months. 'This leg's giving me H-E-double-L today.'

Joe turned. 'Did you remember your blue pills?'

Anne nodded. She and Joe were in life's extra time,

medical science's gift to humanity, when every day becomes a row of slots in a plastic drug dispenser.

'Those blue pills are no better for you than the old ones,' Joe grumbled.

'Doctor thinks they're worth a try,' said Anne, turning off the radio.

'Doctors? Don't trust any of them. They get fat off kickbacks from the pharmaceuticals and that's the only reason you got prescribed they blue pills.'

'Dr Roe's not like that,' Anne said patiently. 'She thinks I need my calcium building up.'

'Then why don't you drink more milk? Or eat chalk, that's what pregnant women used to do. You know, a lot of the time the doctors aren't giving you real medicine anyway. The drug companies need guinea pigs, so the doctors give half their patients the real thing and the other half a placido.'

'Placebo.'

'You think it's going to cure you, so you feel better.'

'And what's wrong with that?'

'It's not real, that's what's wrong. It's fake.'

'If it makes you feel better then I don't care how it works. And Dr Roe says these blue ones are helping my calcium.'

Joe tutted and looked out the window in further search of the cat, almost disappointed it was gone. 'Take some bicarb, that'd do you as much good.'

'It'd only make me burp.'

'If you're needing calcium, that's where you'll find it. Better still, dissolve it in milk.'

'With a piece of chalk?'

Joe went to the cupboard and opened it. 'Should have some here. Baking powder would do . . .' He rummaged intently.

'Are you sure there's calcium in bicarb?'

'Of course I'm sure.' He was reaching through an archive of spices amassed over many years and never used.

'But it's bicarbonate of soda,' said Anne. 'I'm sure soda isn't the same as calcium.'

Joe stopped, extracted his arm from the cupboard and looked at his wife with a puzzled expression. 'Aye,' he said after a pause. 'You're right about that.' Undeterred, he resumed his probing. 'The calcium's in the bicarbonate bit.'

'I thought that was carbon.'

'Well, you would do,' Joe muttered, 'seeing as you never learned any science. But it's not just carbon, is it? It's bicarbonate, and that means carbon with some calcium in it. We'll soon have your bones sorted, pet. Look at me . . .'

'Aye, just look at you.'

'Hardly a day's illness in my life, and you know what that comes down to.'

'Luck?' Anne suggested.

'No,' said Joe. 'It's because I stay away from doctors, they're the ones that kill you. My wee cup of parsley in the morning keeps me right.' For years it had been his habit to drink an infusion of the herb in warm water with his breakfast each day; he'd read somewhere that it was good for you and he'd been confirming its benefits ever since. 'I keep telling you to try it, Anne.' He'd been telling her this for a decade and a half, and Anne had long ago decided that the drink was disgusting as well as useless, but as long as it kept Joe happy she had no reason to complain. 'I'll bet there's calcium in parsley, that's why I've never needed my joints fixing.'

'No,' said Anne, 'there's other bits of you suffered instead.'

Not only was there no bicarb; Joe saw that his parsley supply was running low. 'I'll take a wee walk into town,' he decided, closing the cupboard door.

'You do that,' his wife agreed. 'Calcium off down the road and I'll wait here till it's time for my next blue pill. And if I see the cat again I'll give it your apologies.'

2

The kid was in WH Smith in Kenzie town centre looking at the PC games and like hanging around but not too much because rule number one is not to be conspicuous and the only way to knock something like a PC game is pretend you're going to buy one as in you'd like your dad or your grannie to buy you one but they don't know anything about PC games so they've asked you to choose and then you're looking at them, flipping them forwards one by one on the display rack, sometimes lifting one out to look at the cover, like you're meant to be there and everything's fine.

That's the First Law of Life, kid reckons, twelve years old so he's been around, seen a few things though not enough, never enough. Whatever you're doing, act like it's what you're meant to do. Maybe it isn't, maybe you should still be with one or other of the dinosaurs, your dad Stegosaurus who's meant to be looking after you this weekend but doesn't give a shit, or Maiasaura who's gone on a two-day shopping trip with those old hags she refers to as 'the girls' and expects you to be dropped off by Steg tomorrow night so you'll be, as Maia puts it, 'fresh for school' the following day, like you're a pack of strawberries in ASDA.

But the kid is not with Maia, he's not with Steg, and he's not a soft fruit reduced for quick sale. He's got a life to lead and he's made his decision. Time to move on from the Cretaceous era, leave the reptiles to cope with the meteorite that's about to hit them. At least it'll make them talk to each other for once. Missing child: who's to blame?

You do it all in strict accordance with the First Law. Tell Steg you're going shopping, then he swings his head from the football game on television, open can of Heineken cocked in his hand, says, 'Eh?' Might as well have told him you're leaving on the next space shuttle. Going shopping, you repeat, as in going out, duh. 'Who with?' asks Steg, the way he knows he has to, being the responsible adult in charge and so forth, and you tell the spiny lizard that you're meeting up with Spud and Marko at the Springdale Centre like you always do. He thinks about it. Commentary from the television, camera pans, tiny ball you can't even see, cheering. Can of Heineken stays completely immobile in his hand, way things look when a giant rock enters the solar system a billion miles away. Don't worry, Dad, it's cool. You and me and Glasgow Rangers will all still be here a thousand years from now, like don't worry yourself about it.

'All right,' says Stegosaurus. 'Be careful. And don't be too late.'

What the fuck, thinks the kid, is that supposed to mean?

Here he's now in WH Smith, looking through the PC games deciding which to knock, and Steg's telling him to be careful. Damn right he's careful, he could get lifted for this. Society's to blame, that's the trouble. Through a process of evolution it's come up with stuff like football and beer and the men such as his dad who consume them all brainlessly, swinging their tails through the primeval forest.

You're going to knock a game, you've got to do it right. He's got the two wee magnets in his pocket, trick he learned off the Internet, fools the inductance loop they've got in the security machine at the exit if you know the move, and he knows it. He'll walk clean past the barrier, did it last week with *Gore War II: Vengeance Day*. Security guard'll be standing there in his stupid uniform looking like he's the presidential escort from Uzmania and the kid'll go by with a great big grin on his face and a new game inside his jacket. It'll work because he knows the magnet trick and more importantly he knows the First Law. Act like it's meant to happen.

But which game? It's the usual problem: too much fucking choice. Does his head in. Even in school dinner, it's like computational nightmare, combinatorial hell. Thing is, the kid wants to try everything. As in, you've got three things on the menu, ABC, and can only take two, so kid likes to sample all possible combinations, namely AB, AC, BC, on successive occasions. What you might call an urge for completeness, though Maia reckons it's a form of obsessive-compulsive autistic-spectrum hyperactive Asperger's blah blah blah inherited from Steg, while Steg couldn't give a shit. Other example: clothes. As in, five pairs of socks, one for each school day, each pair different, Maia's decision, reasons of hygiene. Cleaned each weekend by Maia while the kid is with Steg who hasn't evolved the capacity to work a washing machine and even if he had, couldn't be arsed to open the fucking door and push the button.

The problem. Five pairs, P_1 through P_5, and five days, D_1 through D_5, commonly known as Monday to Friday. One solution: P_n on D_n, where n runs 1 through 5. That's how dumb morons with no imagination would do it. But how many other ways? As in, one week you do pairs 1,2,3,4,5 in standard order but then next week you do 5,4,3,2,1. They're all clean, aren't they? There's no Law of Life says you've always got to wear the Pringles on Wednesday.

Solution. By choosing a different ordering each week, the kid can get through the whole cycle in 120 weeks. Which means he'll be fourteen by the time he finishes and he'll have new socks by then so it's basically shit, but he still has to try a new permutation every week, he really has to. Because that's The Way He Is.

You watch a DVD, *Taste of Blood*, say, he liked that film. Maia was pissed off when she found out Steg had let him see it but it wasn't so scary, they only made it an 18 because it's got the word fuck in it and who the fuck says that a twelve-year-old can't be allowed to hear the word fuck? It's not like grown-ups don't say it all the time in front of their fucking offspring when they're fucking well coming to collect them and wanting to know what the fuck the kid has been eating all weekend, like has it been sweets and fish and chips as usual you fucking moron? And so on. Well, then, let's say for the sake of argument (some argument) that it's *Taste of Blood*, certificate 18, on sale in the

DVD section of WH Smith but not worth knocking since the kid's seen it already.

Here's how it works. You get the basic movie: watch that first. But then there's Commentary, and it's cool to watch the whole film again with Commentary. And there's Special Features. Deleted Scenes. And of course Subtitles, the kid being particularly fond of watching films with English For The Hearing Impaired. Makes him aware of stuff he hadn't noticed. Such as his sense of hearing. Though what he'd really like is a Special Feature which is Commentary For The Hearing Impaired, like all these people off-screen would be shouting really loud, it'd be excellent.

The trouble with these Features is that a ninety-minute film turns into a six-hour marathon. At first the kid went for a totalizing approach but it was too much hard work and nowadays he has to be more selective though he still tries to see all the trailers, out-takes and deleted scenes because if he can't get to watch them he feels edgy and wishes he'd like never started you know.

So he's standing in WH Smith in his light blue jacket that he's unzipped and he's deciding which game to knock and it's like the whole choice thing again, the agony of having too much. When you're a dinosaur everything's easy. You've got the kind of teeth that grind plants or the kind that tear meat, simple. But then evolution happens, diversification, the kid's seen it all on Discovery Channel, he's an infomnivore. Evolution creates variety aka consumer choice, which is good. That's progress. It's PlayStation, Xbox or PC. And the kid has opted today for PC, something of a miracle, really, that he's managed to settle on one out of three, though anyone taking the longer view of this, as in the kid himself, knows that the present scenario is only stage two of a grand trilogy, so to speak, because he knocked a PS2 last week and he'll be back with his little magnets for the Xbox version to complete the set.

That's what it's all about: completing the set. Like you're a boy and you need to find a girl otherwise you don't have the full series, you're sort of a pilot episode with no conclusion. You've got to find a girl and go through all the permutations with her but the kid doesn't think he'll ever find a girl who can recite the complete episode list of *Doctor Who* series one to three in the correct order, which would be his kind of girl. Someone like Rose, the Doctor's assistant in series one and two, a perfect ultimate time-traveller's fantasy babe.

The kid's best friend Marko told him that Sarah Walker wanted to go out with him and the kid went and asked Sarah about it and she laughed. So now the kid has put Marko on the Death List, which is the names of all the people who'll be incinerated when the meteorite hits Earth. There'll be this huge explosion spreading like a tsunami of liquid fire, shattering every window pane in his school and demolishing it, circling out to consume the Springdale Centre and all its shops, even WH Smith where he's standing now, everything turned to lava and ashes, rolling across the town and hitting the flat where his dad the Stegosaurus has been living since he moved out, a bright flash drowning the television screen and the walls imploding, the Heineken can melting as its contents vaporize. It'll all happen, it really will.

The kid's going to survive, though. His mum and dad,

his friends, his enemies, his teachers, they're all doomed because they don't know the Way It Is. They don't know that cosmic disasters are the norm, they've been happening for billions of years, again and again, like changing your socks. It's a great big spin cycle and planet Earth's number is going to come up soon, has to. And the kid's making damn sure he'll live through it.

That's why he's run away. Steg and Maia are no use to him: they're extinct already. Marko and Sarah Walker can burn too. The kid knows he'll need food and shelter and a change of clothes after a day or two but he couldn't exactly walk out of his dad's flat with a Samsonite full of worldly possessions, could he, duh? The First Law says you always act like it's meant to be this way, and he's meant to be running away with nothing except a couple of magnets, but those magnets are gold dust, he's tried them and he knows. Any shop he pleases, he can walk past the security barrier, so who needs money when you've got a pair of neodyms? It's almost as good as Doctor Who's psychic paper.

All right, here's the plan. Knock a game and go round to Spud's house, offer him it for a fiver. Tell Spud there's more if he wants, tell him there's a trick to it but don't give too much away. Thick Spud supplies petty cash, maybe a place to sleep tonight, bedding. Spud is temporarily useful but not to be retained for too long since he's on the Death List, he's one of the drowned, not the saved. Spud is a dinosaur of the small kind, sort of a raptor. He's extinct.

Could be any game as long as it's one that Spud hasn't got already, but the kid wants this to be part two of his grand game-theft trilogy so he goes for the PC version of the PS2 game he knocked last time. Spud hasn't got it, the kid's pretty sure about that. Life is so darned sweet, he thinks. Stealing is the sweetest feeling in the world.

For a long time the kid has been stealing from Stegosaurus on a regular basis and his dad is so fucking brainless he hasn't even noticed. The kid thought to get some cash before leaving Steg's flat but the only liftable stash he found was a couple of pound coins, sort of loose change you'd throw in a charity tin, and how much do you have to steal from a Stegosaurus before he gets the message that you exist? More than a couple of pounds, that's for sure. Kid should have lifted the flatscreen out the living room, that would've left an impression.

Stealing is basically so simple, as in you lift something, like a PC game on a rack in WH Smith, and you act like you're reading the stuff on the cover, in accordance with the First Law, while holding the neodyms, one in each hand, being careful not to let them click strongly together which is not only noisy but also damn painful if you get your skin caught between the powerful magnetic pair. And you do the move, the one you've practised and done before so you know it works. You lean towards the sloping rack like you want something from the top row which is furthest from you, you lean into it and over, and your jacket is sort of like a tent of theft, a robber's hideaway, a crook's curtain that covers the left hand's deed while the right is used for misdirection. The game's inside your jacket in less than a second, safely tucked in the pocket they always put there so you can steal things, because why else would you want a pocket in such a stupid place?

It feels so good, the weight of that game in the kid's pocket. So hard and heavy and it's cost him nothing. It's his way of saying: you're all on the List. This shop is going to burn and I've saved one little plastic box with a shiny disc inside it. You're all going to die and this shiny piece of plastic is going to survive. Or something. To be honest, the kid doesn't really know why stealing feels so good, he guesses it has to be some kind of Darwinian adaptation, as in there used to be people that were honest but the environment has changed, their strategy doesn't work any more. His dad the Stegosaurus says if you want to get anywhere in life you've got to work hard, like at school and stuff, and look where he is now, sitting in front of the television with a can of Heineken in his hand, waiting to be annihilated. It's well sad, so it is. The kid's dad works in logistics whatever that means and apparently spends most of his day dealing with emails. That is so fucking dull. That is like the biggest and dullest thing you could ever imagine. That is like walking really slowly across the primeval swamp swinging your big spiky tail and all you do is eat leaves all day long. Eat leaves and look for another dinosaur to do sex with. And hope nothing interesting ever happens, you've got big bony plates on your back to make sure of it. Something interesting comes along, those bony plates will bounce it away and protect you. Don't even need to turn your head to look at it. That's what his dad's like.

He said be careful and the kid is being careful. He's knocked the game, he's walking to the door. Steg said don't be late and the kid is going to be late, very late indeed. So late he's never coming back and it feels terrific.

Thing is, there's stuff in the world the kid needs to see. As in really go there, not just watch it on cable. India, say, or the Antarctic. Hospital operating theatres. The tunnelled maze of a sewerage system. The kid needs to see these things, just like he needs to go through every possible ordering of his socks or the features on his DVD, because otherwise he feels edgy, and the kid feels edgy all the time at the thought of that great big world escaping him, all its channels going on without his presence. Boardrooms, locker rooms, motorways, tree houses, abandoned cottages, frozen lakes; all the things he's seen in pictures, on a screen or in his head. The bit where some railings are bent and a small kid can pass through; the spot on the planet where a lion is eating a springbok right now; mountains, mountaineers, mountaineers right at the top of mountains and others at the bottom; the people in the mountain shops who sold the mountaineers their gear; it's all happening, it's all there in the Special Features menu of life on Earth, makes five pairs of socks look so damn easy to get through, and the kid is missing it all but he needs to consume as much as he can before the meteorite hits because That's The Way It Is, makes him so edgy to think about it, walking towards the exit, seeing the presidential guard of Uzmania, actually an old guy who's looking the other way, staring out into the street, and the kid thinks I bet he's as sad as the rest of them because he knows inside his heart, in that place where we know things but don't know that we know them, he knows we're all going to die, the power switch is going to be flicked, the screen's going to go dead and we'll hardly have begun to go through those Special Features. He knows it and I know it, thinks the kid, but I know more than him because I've seen the Death List and his name is on it. And the kid walks right past him, straight in front of the presidential guard whose line of sight encourages the kid to gaze momentarily skywards: an aeroplane, a little dot in the sky full of people who are going to die too when the meteorite comes and the power switch gets flipped. It's all reality, hyper-reality, ultra-reality, the infinite matrix of nows and happenings and the kid has made his choice, he's outside in the street, the neodyms worked and the inductance loop was foiled. He's free. He knocked the game and he's a winner.

3

Joe Coyle was studying the herb section in ASDA. 'Take a look at this,' he said to a passing assistant, a girl of eighteen or nineteen who stopped to see what he wanted. Mr Coyle was holding a small cardboard box of dried parsley. 'Fifty-seven pence,' he said.

'That's right.'

'For twenty grams.'

'Yes,' said the girl.

'And do you know how many grams there are in a kilogram?'

'Eh?'

'One thousand. That means you're charging £28.50 for a kilo of parsley.'

The girl looked puzzled. 'You want a kilo of parsley?'

'Not at that price!' Mr Coyle laughed. 'I could grow a kilo of parsley in my garden for nothing.'

'Then why don't you?'

Joe smiled and took a breath. He couldn't see why this assistant was being quite so dim, though they always were, whenever he challenged any of them about the price of dried herbs. 'It's not even parsley you're paying for, is it? It's mostly cardboard. And the glass jars are worse.'

'Packaging costs money,' the girl conceded, willing to give up half a minute of box-stacking to hear him out.

'So really when I come here I'm buying a lot of cardboard and plastic with a bit of food thrown in for free?'

'I suppose so,' she said. 'You could always go to the fresh fruit and veg section.'

'But you don't have parsley there.'

'Don't we? We should. Come and let's have a look.'

She led him along the aisles to a part of the store he knew perfectly well – he came here every day. Like a hunter anticipating the smooth operation of a well-laid trap, Joe watched the girl pick through coriander, basil and thyme, all sprouting delicately from plastic pots in cellophane wrappers.

'No parsley there,' Mr Coyle declared triumphantly.

'It's better value than the boxes.'

'Not if it isn't there, though. You can't call empty space good value. Zero pence for zero grams.'

She turned and looked at him. 'You could always do your shopping somewhere else.'

An older female staff member approached and intervened. 'Morning, Joe, how's Anne?'

'Not too bad, Agnes.' The young assistant slipped quietly away, leaving her superior to deal with the customer's complaints, which suddenly had nothing to do with parsley any more. 'Have you seen what's going on in your wine display?'

'What's that then, Joe?'

'Come on and I'll show you.' Mr Coyle snaked back through the aisles with his new companion, walking briskly with the air of an expert, until they reached a dense array of dark bottles. 'Says here it's three for the price of two.'

'So?'

'But that's for the Cabernet Sauvignon – all these bottles are Merlot. Are they in the same offer?'

Agnes looked ruffled. 'Maybe there's been a mistake . . .'

'Great way to sell wine, isn't it – pretend it's reduced when it isn't?'

'That's not how it works, Joe.'

'Not that I'm accusing you personally, mind. I know your hands are tied by the people at headquarters. Same in all the shops these days, the staff have got no control over what they sell, it's all decided by the ones at the top who only look at balance sheets and never spend a day on the shop floor seeing what people actually want . . .'

'I'll get it sorted, Joe. Mind how you go, and give my love to Anne.'

Then Mr Coyle was alone with the Merlot, still not sure if three bottles would cost him £8.58 or £12.87. It was the Australian kind he liked, always thought it funny that you could get wine from Australia, place full of kangaroos and boomerangs, Robbie had one of those but could never make it come back. No, we can't make anything come back. Chile, too, he didn't mind drinking Chilean wine now Pinochet was gone, damned CIA with their coup against Allende, long time ago, of course, but you need people with long memories to bring the likes of General Pinochet to account – and who was the biggest friend of that murdering bastard?

'Maggie Thatcher,' he said to the person who happened to be passing. It was the girl again.

'Eh?'

'That's who looked after him when he came here.'

Her face screwed up in the sort of puzzlement she'd felt when failing maths at school. 'Are you still looking for parsley?'

'Oh, never mind,' Joe said with the resigned impatience his years entitled him to. Young people these days only want to listen to music squawking out their damned earphones, interested in nothing but internets and eye-pods and God knows what else. All it'd take would be another Pinochet or Thatcher to show up on *Big Brother*, as long as they were good-looking and ran around showing off their bare arse, and everybody'd love them. Death camps and slavery – these kids'd vote for it on their mobiles.

He went to the checkout empty-handed. No wine or parsley today. 'Cheerio, Agnes,' he called as he walked past the fag desk but she didn't hear him.

It was sunny outside and the *Big Issue* seller was up for a wee bit banter as usual. 'How's business?' Joe asked him.

'Not sae bad.'

'You do realize you're being exploited, don't you?'

'How's that, then?'

'Look at the price on the cover – how much does it really cost to staple some pages together? Where's all the extra money going to, that's what I want to know.'

'I don't think it works like that.'

'CDs are the worse thing,' Joe opined. 'I mean, what are they? Bit of plastic, no moving parts, £15.99. Saw one the other day, they wanted more than twenty pounds.'

'Outrageous.'

'Where does it go, this money we throw away? Do you know how much they charge for parsley in there? A weed, for God's sake.'

The magazine seller shook his tanned and leathery head in sorrowful agreement. 'There's nae justice in the world, that's for sure.'

'And did you notice when everything started to change?'

'When was that, then?'

'1979. Year Maggie Thatcher got in. That's when it all started.'

'Aye, she was a bitch for sure.' The magazine seller looked old enough to remember her but could have been aged anywhere between twenty-five and sixty.

'Plant I used to work in,' said Joe, 'out at Clydebank, thriving business. Kind of heavy industry that made this country great. What happened to it?'

'I can guess.'

'The asset-strippers moved in and sent us all right down the Swanee, four hundred men. We'd had problems there all through the seventies, of course.'

'Three-day week, winter o' discontent . . .'

'Aye, all that. I was union treasurer.'

'It was a different world then.'

'Certainly was,' said Joe. 'And when they launched the coup they knew who they were after.'

The *Big Issue* seller's eyes shrank even smaller in his sunburned face. 'What coup was that, then?'

'The one that put Maggie in. It was the CIA did it, same as Chile, only this time they managed without the aeroplanes and missiles. Blowing up an elected president wasn't good for their image, even if he was a Marxist.'

The magazine seller was struggling to keep up. 'Marxist? Who was that – Jim Callaghan?'

Joe shook his head. 'No, you've got to go back to Wilson. I never liked the man much and I'd hardly call him a socialist but he was still too left-wing for the Americans, too dangerous. That's why they made him resign and then they put Callaghan in his place.'

'I don't quite remember that . . .'

'Oh, it was a surprising thing. One minute Wilson's riding high in power, the next he's resigning for no reason. They say now it was because he thought he was getting that . . . what do you call it? Thing where you lose your memory.'

'Alzheimer's?'

'Aye, that one. But it was a plot. The CIA bought Wilson off and put in Callaghan, then he turned out to be a dud so they picked Maggie.'

'Bingo.'

'Too right,' said Joe. 'Look what she did for America.'

'And look what she done for us.'

'Exactly. Wrecked all our heavy industry, sabotaged the unions and the labour movement with moles and infiltrators, put millions of people out of work. It's obvious, isn't it? She was a CIA stooge, and every prime minister since then's been one too.'

The *Big Issue* seller nodded. 'You've got a point there.'

'And that's where all our money's going,' said Joe.

'Siphoned off to America. The stooges get a kickback and wind up millionaires while we go to the wall. Everyone that buys a copy of your magazine, most of it goes to Uncle Sam, and where does that leave you?'

The seller shook his head. 'Stood here like a lemon.'

'And it's just as bad in there,' said Joe, pointing to the ASDA entrance behind him. 'All these supermarkets are owned by Americans now, same as everything else, and do you know how much they charge for parsley? £28.50 a kilo.'

'That's a lot of cash.'

'A big con, if you ask me,' Joe said. 'Biggest con in history.'

The magazine seller looked doubtful. 'You think so? What about Jesus getting married and having a wean?'

Joe nodded. 'All right, maybe that was equally big. But you know what else they do? They put the wrong labels on things.'

'Who? The Americans?'

'The people in ASDA – it amounts to the same thing. They put a wee label saying three for two, but they deliberately stick it in the wrong place, so there's us filling our baskets thinking we're getting a bargain . . .'

'When all along we're spending more money.'

'That's right,' said Joe. 'And a nice big cut goes straight to the Yanks so they can keep fighting their wars and telling us all how free we are. You know, I wouldn't mind them so much if they could only talk better. Why do they have to drawl all the time like they own the place?'

'But they do,' the *Big Issue* seller said with a shrug, and Joe left him to his task, crossing the street and walking past the parade of small shops whose names changed, it seemed, almost every week, as one after another tried to compete with the big supermarket nearby. The Common Market had a lot to do with it, of course. A car beeped when Joe crossed another street, impatient young type in a suit, fancy Mercedes, thinks he's something special but ought to know you should give way to pedestrians when going round a bend – don't they do the Highway Code any more? Not that Mr Coyle ever took lessons but there was no need when he was young, public transport being what it was. Common Market was Ted Heath's big idea – Joe remembered giving Robbie stickers to take to school and give to his pals, 'Say No to Europe', and then Robbie coming home saying Mr Tulloch thought integration was a good thing, well he would say that, wouldn't he, damn fool Liberal voter with all his German writers he made Robbie read, filling his head with foreign nonsense. What's wrong with Scottish writers? Aren't there enough of them to keep anybody busy for a lifetime?

The things being said about Mr Tulloch now – that article in the local paper claiming he interfered with a boy, total slander but when a man's dead and gone you can say what you like about him, that's the problem. If Tulloch was alive they could ask him. And if Robbie was still with them they could have asked him too. But there was never anything like that, Robbie would have told them if there had been, they were always frank about everything.

Joe stopped in his tracks, a wee thought had flown inside his head like a bumblebee. Something else he was meant to be getting. Retraced his steps mentally, backwards across two streets, *Big Issue* seller, ASDA. Was he meant to buy wine? No, it was a con in there. But he'd walked into town looking for something apart from the parsley he never bought. Something Anne wanted. It was tapping and nagging, the bumblebee against the window pane, up and down and never finding an exit.

Joe walked on. If a bumbee stung a bumbee's bumbee, what colour would the bumbee's bum be? Like it was yesterday, explaining it to Robbie, the wee soul, five or six year old. Bumbee tartan, he told him. What's that, dad? A kind of tartan. What kind, says Robbie. Kind that's fake.

Not that Mr Tulloch was ever a practising, no evidence of that despite whatever they people he used to teach are saying now, thirty or forty year after the event. Of course he was a nancy but things were different in they days, effeminate wasn't the same as being a bum-bandit. Didn't even occur to Joe and Anne to worry. World was simpler then. Now it's full of paedophiles who've learned how to do it from web rings, probably would never have hurt a fly if they hadn't found a name to give themselves, make them into a community. European Economic Community, that was the next stage of German grooming after they stopped calling it Common Market. Joe told his children at the time, they were eating their tea in the living room and Ted Heath showed up grinning on the evening news, saying how it was an end to conflict, and Joe said to Robbie and Janet, the Germans tried beating us on the battlefield and they couldn't do it, now they're going to take over another way instead. There they were, the Krauts, lost the war, whole country in ruins, and America bought them wholesale with the Marshall Plan. They own the place, Mr Coyle said, both his children looked round and for the first time it was like they didn't believe him, not only Janet but Robbie too. That was Tulloch's doing.

European Union they call it nowadays but how long before it's United States of Europe, Joe wondered. They've even got all the wee stars on their flag, just like the Americans, next they'll put stripes on it, tiny at first so people won't notice – they'll be too busy watching Yank rubbish on the telly – but the stripes'll get bigger until one day it's the American flag flying all over the continent, everybody spending dollars and cents instead of euros and cents. But he was no fool, not Joe Coyle, he was as smart as the next fellow, and he'd go on speaking his mind till the day they came and shot him.

Now where was it he was meant to be going?

4

The kid's away, the magnets worked, he's round the corner and legging it. But don't forget the First Law: act like this is meant to be happening and people will believe it. As in slow down, take your time. Kid gets to the big swing park and reckons he'll take five on the empty bench in the corner. Sits and pulls the game from his inside pocket and it's like totally crap but Spud'll give him a fiver for it, as in instant money, and he can do this anywhere he wants, go in and swipe as long as it's got the right kind of security tag, they nearly all have because it's one company does ninety per cent of in-store security systems and if their system's got a loophole the size of Gibraltar it's not his problem.

Only himself on the bench and a woman with two little girls at the other end of the park, he watches them on the swings, matching skirts and bare legs waving. Kid was their age once, a long time ago. He was a child then he stopped, gave it up as a bad habit. He must be twice as old as those girls. They've got like their entire life to lead all over again before they even catch up with where he is now, and by then he'll be gone. Correction, they'll be gone, because they're probably on the Death List.

If the kid could live his life again he'd make sure he did everything differently. Same as he does with socks. First you do the life where your parents don't get on and you get sick to death of both of them and you run away. Then you do the life where everything's cool – but maybe you run away for the hell of it. Then something else. And so on, never repeating, because only losers do the same thing twice.

A programme he saw on TV: one hundred things to do before you die. Only a hundred? Like, not a zillion? And anyway, most people manage maybe ten. They never get to be millionaires, never form a rock band, never write a novel, never appear on television. Instead they go through the jungle swinging their spiny tails and they don't see the meteorite above their head.

A man loitering at the edge of the park, old man in a long dark coat, forty something, same kind of age as the Stegosaurus. Is he with the woman and the little girls? No, more likely a flasher or a paedo, either it's the woman he wants or it's the girls or it's the kid himself. One hundred things to do before you die: run away from home and get sexually assaulted in a swing park, no that was never on the list. But then, why not? I mean, thinks the kid, if you're going to do everything, like absolutely everything in every menu and submenu that life can throw at you. Well, it makes you think.

Here's what the kid thinks. The universe is infinite, right? He knows it's infinite because he saw a *Horizon* programme that said the Hubble Space Telescope took a photograph of the cosmic microwave background radiation. Was it Hubble or was it WMAP? Never mind – and now the woman's telling her daughters it's time to leave, like maybe she saw the old man and her pervert alarm went off.

Let's say it was WMAP, purely for the sake of argument. Took a photograph of the cosmic microwave background, which is so to speak the afterglow of the Big Bang that happened 13.8 billion years ago – the kid knows this stuff by heart. And they took the photograph to this big room where a whole load of scientists looked at it with a magnifying glass, because the thing about the picture is that it's got lots of spots, it's kind of grainy like when you look at a screen too closely. And the size of the graininess tells them the shape of the universe, because if space is curved then the pattern gets distorted. This is what the kid knows, and he sees the old man coming into the park at the same time as the lady and the little girls go out. As in, I've only just run away and here comes a pervert to get me, exactly like they say always happens.

All of this started with a particle or a singularity or something that exploded 13.8 billion years ago and nobody, absolutely nobody on this planet we call Earth, knows why it happened. Thing to do before we all die: figure that one out. But it happened, and it made this spotty picture of microwaves that the scientists looked at under a magnifying glass, and they said: this proves space is flat. And that means space is infinite. So by looking at this little photograph through a magnifying glass they proved that space goes on for ever and ever and ever and ever and ever and ever and ever . . .

'Hello, kid.'

The guy has walked right across the empty swing park from the gate at the far end to the bench where the kid sits, all in the time it takes to think about a little photograph of an infinite universe.

'Hello.'

'Mind if I sit down?'

'No.'

And suddenly it's like the kid is a kid. His magnets can't deal with this one.

'You're all alone here.'

'Yes.'

'That's odd.'

'I don't think so.'

'Don't you have any friends?'

'Sure I've got friends. Lots of them.'

'You're very lucky. Friends are important. You know, there'll come a time in your life when you realize that friends are the only important thing, nothing else matters. And the only way to have friends is to be a good person. Are you a good person?'

'Yes.'

'Always?'

'No, not always.'

The man smiles and nods. 'I like that. I can tell you're an honest person, and being honest is good. Have you any idea who I am?'

The kid's throat is so dry. 'No.'

'I come from very far away. You might not think it from my accent but it's true. I'm on a mission.'

'What sort of mission?'

'Never mind. But I saw what you did, stealing the computer game. It's in your pocket, isn't it?'

'No, and if you're a store detective you've got no right to search me . . .' The kid gets up but the stranger stays calm, waving his hand as if none of it matters.

'I saw you stealing, so I know you're not always honest.'

'But I had to do it. I can't explain why, I needed to, that's all.'

'Don't worry about it,' says the stranger. 'You're a kid and it's what kids do sometimes. There are worse mistakes a person can make, and I should know. Are you going to go home now?'

The kid hesitates. 'Maybe.' He sits down again. 'What did you mean about being on a mission?'

The man takes a deep breath, more of a sigh really, like this is something difficult for him to talk about. He's got like a lined old face but sort of distinguished. 'I've been travelling for a long time and now I'd like to find my way home.' In other words the complete opposite of what the kid plans on doing. The kid wants to travel. He wants to see the world.

'Have you seen the world?' the kid asks.

'I've seen many worlds.'

Kind of thing the Doctor might say. Guy's nothing like

David Tennant or Christopher Ecclestone, or even Tom Baker or Peter Davison in the old *Doctor Who* episodes the kid's seen on DVD, lousy stories with cheap special effects that Steg likes because he grew up with them and can't appreciate how generations move on, can't understand that being 'classic', i.e. old, isn't necessarily the same as being good. This guy's sort of classic-looking, though. Dark hair with only a little grey at the temples, big long coat; he could be a regenerated Doctor in a new series. He'd need an assistant. Kid asks, 'What's your name?'

'Can't tell.'

'Can't or won't?'

'Both,' says the stranger. 'Can't implies won't.'

An adult who understands logic: kid likes that. Definitely an extraterrestrial feature. 'How many hearts have you got?'

'None – I left it in San Francisco.'

'Not two?'

Guy looks at him, puzzled. 'Why should I have two?'

'Nothing,' says the kid. 'I was thinking of Doctor Who, that's all.'

'You think I'm an alien in human form? A spaceman?'

Kid laughs. 'Of course not, duh. I'm not an infant or a retard.'

'Because in a sense you're right.'

Kid stops laughing. 'What do you mean?' he asks quietly.

The stranger is perfectly matter-of-fact about it. 'You could say I'm a spaceman.'

'What, you've been up in the International Space Station or something?' Loads of people have done it, even like schoolteachers and tourists; it's cool but not impossible. Probably on that list of one hundred things.

'It's not all about going up, you know. Sometimes spacemen have to fall.'

'And you fell in Kenzie?'

Guy nods. 'Yup.'

The kid's fuck-around detector is on full power but it's like the guy's got some magnetic bypass because the kid's almost believing him. 'You mean you're not a paedophile?'

The stranger smiles and shakes his head. 'Not a paedophile, not a store detective. A spaceman.'

Here's how it works. Some scientists get a photograph of the microwave background radiation and use it to prove the universe is infinite. Which means there's more than enough room for all the infinite atoms to be in every possible arrangement, just like the kid's socks, and it doesn't matter how much time you've got, like whether it's a year or a billion years, because all of that space makes up for it. In an infinite universe anything is possible and everything is certain. You go far enough, there's a bunch of atoms arranged to make a world just like this one, with a WH Smith in it and a kid who decided to steal a game, or maybe a different game, and you go farther still, there are worlds where the kid stole every possible game, one world beyond another for ever. A googolplex things to do before you die, all happening at once right now in an infinite universe. That's the Way It Is.

'I don't think you're really a spaceman.'

'Why not?'

'Because . . .' Kid can't think of a good reason except

that if the stranger were a spaceman then it would be an Interesting Thing and the human species, as in his father, has evolved to repel Interesting Things with thick bony plates. Kid says, 'Prove it.'

'I don't have to.'

'Tell me what space is like.'

'You can see it over your head every night. It's no secret.'

'Where's your spaceship?'

'I don't need one.'

'You mean you teleport, flap your arms, what?' He sees the stranger get to his feet. 'Sorry,' he says, 'I didn't mean to insult you or anything.' Only he thinks the guy is ninety-nine point nine recurring per cent certain to be a lunatic.

'You need to go,' says the stranger, looking down at him.

'Where?'

'Anywhere.'

It's a cusp kind of a moment. Like the kid knows, suddenly he knows in that blinding all-illuminating way, that this is for real, if he wants it to be. He's got the Special Features page up and there's a link saying Normal Life (Like Dinosaurs Lead) and there's another underneath it says Crazy Life (Like You Want) and the remote's in his hand and it's his call. He says, 'Can I go with you? On the mission?'

'It's not a good idea.'

'Only for a little while. Maybe I can help you go home. You know, like ET.'

He mulls it over then says, 'How did you do it?'

'What?'

'Take the game out of the store without setting off the alarm?'

The kid smiles. 'I have access to superior technology. I can walk into any shop and take whatever I want. Cool, huh?'

'Does it work on cash machines?' the guy asks immediately, making the kid give a start.

'No . . . I don't do cash machines. Not yet.'

The stranger looks disappointed. 'Still,' he says to himself, 'it could be useful.' Then he says to the kid, 'I need a place to stay tonight. I'm going to reconnoitre the area, see what I can find.'

'I need a place too.'

'You do? Then why not search as well? Let's meet here at seven o'clock and we'll see how we're both getting on. Now go and do your duty.'

The kid gets up, pauses, waits for something else, another word of explanation, or thanks, or anything, but the stranger isn't going to give it. There has to be something, though, a sign, a sonic screwdriver, a Tardis in the bushes. Kid says, 'Why won't you tell me your name?'

'I can't, it might compromise the mission.'

'Not even like your initials?'

Now the guy sits down, kid's still standing. Role reversal. 'All right,' he says. 'RC.'

'RC?'

'That's my initials.'

Richard Carter, Robin Cuthbertson, Rohinder Chowdury . . . a thousand million trillion possible combinations in an infinite universe, and the remote's still in the kid's hand and he doesn't know which special feature is Spaceman (Interesting) and which is Sicko Dick Swinger (Run Like Fuck) but he's not running because in his own weird way this guy's kind of a classic as in he doesn't even have a name and that's cool. So the kid turns and walks while the stranger stays on the bench. Sort of a start your life all over again kind of a moment as in everything's been switched around in his head, black to white and left to right and time rewound, the kid walking out instead of the stranger striding in. That's what it's like in an infinite universe where anything is possible and everything is certain. That's the Way It Is.

5

'More than twenty,' Joe was saying to his wife as he came into the living room. He was just back from ASDA and on the way had been picking up discarded rubber bands from the pavement. He held the day's takings in his outstretched hand like an accusation. 'Two dozen in one stretch of road.'

'Such a waste,' Anne agreed from the settee where she sat with a book at her side, enjoying a temporary respite from pain.

'What I want to know is why the postmen can't put them in their pockets and reuse them.'

'It wouldn't be hard.'

'But no, they've got to take the elastic off every bundle of letters and drop them in the street. Dogs could choke on them.'

'You can't stand dogs.'

'Or children maybe.'

Anne frowned. 'Would a wee child swallow a rubber band off the road?'

'It could easily happen,' Joe insisted. 'Don't you remember how Janet used to be always picking things up from the ground.'

'She didn't eat them, though.'

'Aye, but she might have. Anyway, don't get me off the point, Anne, we've got to look at this logically. Twenty-four rubber bands in one wee stretch in one day. If you multiply that up to the whole country in a year you'd get . . .'

There was a long pause.

'A lot of rubber bands,' Anne suggested eventually. 'Something for you to think about in the toilet.'

'How do you know I'm headed there?' Joe asked, puzzled.

'Because we've been married nigh on fifty years, Joe, so you elasticate off upstairs.'

He nodded and left the room; Anne heard the heavy creak of his footsteps as he rose, then lifted the book to carry on reading. It was what she mostly did nowadays; sometimes she'd look at the television but she preferred reading because with a book you never feel lonely and if you wake up in the middle of the night it's better than listening to rubbish on the radio with a wee earphone like Joe, you might as well switch on the light and open your book and in a moment you're away with the story, you forget all your aches and pains and your troubles. Telly's for youngsters but it was old people must have invented books because they're the ones that get the benefit of them.

There were plenty around the house, books that Robbie left behind, many of them with his name pencilled inside, sometimes a date too, fixing them in time like butterflies on a pin. Everything's in the past eventually, that's the plain truth of it, and fretting over it's like worrying yourself about a few wee rubber bands. Anne opened her book at the page she'd marked; it was a very old book with a tattered red cover, the gold lettering on the spine faded and almost illegible, but the pages were still crisp and clean looking. Some of those paperbacks of his were falling apart already, gone yellow and foul and not worth opening but kept in a box because they could never throw anything out that was his, twenty-five years next week, she'd sent the In Memoriam to the local paper. But this book Anne was reading now was at least as old as she was, no, more, and here it was in her hands, a wee bit musty and ragged but perfectly useable. That's how they made things back then, built to last. And now? If it's last year's thing it's out of date. Chuck it away and buy another.

The name inside the cover isn't Robbie's. The handwriting is the kind of copperplate she was taught at school and the signature is G. B. Tulloch; she knew his first name was Gordon but never learned what the B stood for. Brian or Bernard, perhaps, or his mother's maiden name. Brown, Baillie, didn't matter, really. Poor old fellow died alone in that house of his and got found by a neighbour; bit like Sam Dunbar, only they found Sam a lot quicker.

The book is called *Wilhelm Meister's Apprenticeship*. Been sitting on a shelf for years; it never got put away in a box because the hardbacks looked nicer and this one was an antique, Joe thought it might be worth a bob or two seeing as it was so old, though one time Anne looked in a second-hand bookshop she saw hundreds as ancient and in as good condition and some of them were going for 50p. Place was like a cross between a graveyard and a jumble sale and she walked out wishing she hadn't looked. No, she'd never go on one of those antique programmes and hand her book over to some expert in a linen suit who'd open it and push his glasses up his forehead and hand it back and say it was worthless. All they want is money, those people on the telly, all they see is the monetary value in everything.

For a long time she thought the book was in German because the only words on the spine were *Wilhelm Meister* and underneath it the name Goethe. Robbie had some other old books that were completely in German from when he learned the language, it was Tulloch advised him to do it, and she'd glanced in one or two and seen that horrid way they used to print, reminded her of old Adolf and made her feel sick. Joe said they shouldn't even have such stuff in the house, said Goethe was a Nazi and for all Anne knew maybe he was, but you've got to live and let live.

What surprised her about *Wilhelm Meister*, though, when she eventually decided a week or two ago to start reading it, was how easy it was to follow. She could never be doing with those books she had to read at school, long-winded and full of descriptions – there was one by Walter Scott, *Waverley*, sent her completely to sleep. And then that time she took Robbie to the doc for his bed-wetting and the old fool suggested *Ivanhoe* – and Anne going to the library to look for it! In those days she thought doctors knew everything and you just had to do what they told you, but poor Robbie was as bored as Anne had been and it didn't do his vivid imagination any good.

It was old Mr Tulloch found the answer. He'd read a lot of books even though he was a science teacher and he knew the good ones, the ones that don't fade. *Wilhelm Meister* gets going right away, Anne found, there's no messing about, no fancy writing in it, just a straightforward story about a boy who's got a dream. He's seen a puppet show and all he wants is to be in the theatre, it seems like the most exciting thing there could be. Reminded Anne of the way Robbie used to be about space. So this lad Wilhelm falls in with a load of actors and he's in and out of love, some of the women are good and some of them mess him around – well, who knows how Robbie got on with that part of life, he mentioned one or two girls he knew at the uni and some came and visited him near the end but she and Joe were never the sort to pry. Anyway, this Wilhelm fellow theatres off on all sorts of adventures and spends a lot of time rehearsing *Hamlet*, that was a bit Anne wasn't so keen on. Awful lot of talk about *Hamlet*, she could have done without that, couldn't see the point at all. Maybe Goethe ran out of ideas and decided to talk about somebody else's book instead of his own. But then Wilhelm makes his big discovery – he's never going to make it as an actor. And that's so true to life, because we all start out with dreams in our head and then they fade, one by one, and we learn to adjust. Anne wanted to be Judy Garland once. Now all she wants is for her turn to come in the hip-replacement queue. She heard the toilet flushing upstairs.

Poor Wilhelm, finding out he can't act. Except that the story still isn't finished, because then he meets up with a doctor who knows how to treat depression, and gives Wilhelm a book about religion, and Anne had about as much time for that as she did for *Hamlet*, but once Wilhelm has finished reading the book he winds up in this nice big country estate and that's where she'd got to now, the third part of the novel. And this is where it all fits together at last – the actors, the book about religion, a young boy Wilhelm adopts – they're all part of this bigger story, because we realize the whole thing has been organized by a secret group called the Society of the Tower, sort of like the Freemasons or the Rotary Club. All the way through, Wilhelm has been bumping into various people, and now they turn out to have been members of the Society in disguise. Maybe that's not so realistic, but it's still like life because when you look back on it, thought Anne, you see how things have happened that didn't mean anything at the time, but afterwards they do. Lots of wee incidents with Janet, for example, all showing how she'd grow up and leave Kenzie and change her name and identity and want nothing more to do with her parents as if they never existed. There's a pattern. Call it destiny or fate or whatever you choose, there's a path you follow – even if all you wind up with is a dodgy hip that gives you H-E-double-L. We get older and we get wiser and it's no use trying to persuade the young about it because if they've got any luck they'll have their chance too and one day they'll know. Not that Robbie had the chance.

'About a million,' Joe said, coming back in and twitching the curtain to see what was happening across the road.

'A million what?'

'Rubber bands,' he told her. 'Or something like that,

thrown away every day, and we pay for it in stamps. Just think what you could do with them.'

'Hold letters together?'

'Aye, you could do that.'

'But that's what they do already.'

Joe laughed, threw up his hands in despair at the sort of intellect he had to deal with, then went to the kitchen to put on the kettle while Anne tried to carry on reading, though she couldn't decide if she liked Goethe's Society of the Tower with all its secrets and rituals. One of the leaders is a shifty character who's already set up a branch in America and wants to have it running in every country in the world – a bit like the CIA if Joe was to be believed. A year or two ago Anne read another book of Robbie's, *The Castle* by Franz Kafka, and that was all about a fellow like Wilhelm Meister, coming to a place and finding the people there were in on a big secret that he knew nothing about, or maybe there was no secret but he only thought there was. So you've got one book says wouldn't life be lovely if there were people pulling all the strings for us and controlling what happens, like they're gods, and you've got another book saying it would be hell. And there was Joe, bringing back two mugs of tea, who'd spent all his life saying we should be socialists and now he wanted to start a campaign to save rubber bands. Well, thought Anne, if I could have another life I'd go to university and study all sorts and then maybe I'd know what to make of it.

'Do you not remember what it was like in the war?' said Joe, handing one cup to Anne, who nursed its warmth in compensation for the forsaken book. 'We couldn't go throwing away rubber bands then, could we? They needed rubber for the guns and planes and ships.'

Really it was iron they collected, all those railings from every part of the country, given up gratefully by cheering patriotic folk who never minded if the iron was the wrong kind and ended up being dumped at the bottom of the sea, but the detail mattered little to Joe, who had a faraway look in his eyes, a ragged-shorts and shrapnel-collecting look as if in his boy's mind he was following the swift whip of a Spitfire worked by a twisted rubber band, zooming over a grey Gorbals skyline.

Anne asked him, 'Where exactly did they use the rubber?'

'On the tyres. Round cockpits, doors, nose cones, anywhere they needed a flexible seal.'

Balancing a rubber ball on the end of a nose – you'd need a flexible seal for that. 'What about guns?' Anne quizzed. 'Where do they put rubber in a gun?'

Joe shook his head. 'I don't know, it's not the point. But think of what gets wasted every day.'

Anne thought about it.

'Can't go on, can it?' said Joe. 'We're going to run out eventually, but do the Post Office care? Not a bit, because it all fits in with their privatization plans, big con they've been plotting for years, even when they first put up the Post Office Tower, and that was a story too. How many times have I said to the postman when he comes to the door, here would you like these, and given him a handful of rubber bands? And he always looks at me like I'm an idiot.'

Anne thought about that too.

'But they're the idiots,' said Joe, 'if they think they can

go on throwing away rubber bands, and you know who's behind it all?'

'Who's that, Joe?' Anne asked dutifully.

'It's the people running this country, that's who. They don't want to save and recycle and make life better for ordinary folk like us, they only want to strip this country of every asset it's got.'

'Like rubber trees?'

'Don't be facetious, Anne, these days it's a synthetic composite they make from oil and the Americans have been in a panic about it ever since the first North Sea rig went up. They want to see this country run out of everything so we'll buy from them instead. They're halfway there already, all they need do is make sure we keep throwing away enough stuff that's perfectly useful.' Joe drew breath then swigged his tea, still standing at the window surveying a world he held in a contempt so profound he almost didn't notice it anymore, like the weight of a limb.

'It's not worth getting het up about.' Anne looked at the wall clock. 'I'm needing to take my next pill – I left them in the kitchen.'

'Those pills are hopeless,' said Joe, about to go and get them for her when he stopped. 'I meant to get you bicarb. Totally slipped my mind.'

'I know.'

'Why didn't you say?'

'It didn't matter.'

'But you need it for your indigestion, don't you?'

'Oh, never mind about that, Joe. Just fetch me my pills.'

He brought what she wanted then said, 'I'll go back into town.'

'You stay here, you daftie.'

'But I went all the way there and walked out of that shop with nothing. Too busy thinking about the wine – you know what they're doing?'

Anne nodded patiently. 'I know.'

'Won't take me long to go back. Could do with another walk.'

She knew why he was so restless; this was always a difficult time for them, every year when it came again. And a round one, twenty-five. Silver, like they ought to celebrate. He could have his walk and she could finish her book. 'Get some eggs when you're out.'

'Eggs?'

'We're needing some.'

'Could have told me that earlier.'

'I didn't think of it,' said Anne. 'Write it down so you won't forget. Don't want another wasted journey.'

'Aye,' Joe muttered, 'so much waste. And we know who's at the back of it all.'

6

This is so the most exciting thing the kid's ever done it's like unbelievable he's a real-life spy a real-life assistant to a spaceman and he's going round Kenzie with a game he's knocked inside his jacket. If his Stegosaurus dad could see him right now he'd be. Actually he probably couldn't give a shit.

Plan A was go to Spud's and sell him the game but now the kid's thinking he should ditch Spud who's on the Death

List anyway. The kid's more interested in the Stranger aka RC who still might turn out to be a paedophile or a murderer you never know but the kid can look after himself and won't take any unnecessary chances because the Stranger might also be the Doctor or the equivalent as in real life well you never know that either, the kid thinks, I mean how would you know it if you met a genuine Time Lord? When Rose Tyler went to school they must have kept telling her Never Go With Strangers, I bet they had those lessons even way back then, the kid thinks, but she went with the Doctor and became his assistant and all sorts of cool things happened like when she got her DNA inside a Dalek and gave it emotions. You've got to keep an open mind.

He's decided to take the path that goes beside the river, place where you only go if you're on a date or pushing a buggy or you're a smelly old fisherman or else, as in this case, you're a runaway carrying stolen goods. It's very much a life-on-the-edge sort of place. River's so sluggish it looks like it needs a kick up the arse, shopping trolley stuck in the middle of it all tangled with weeds and rubbish. Things to do number zero: push a shopping trolley in a river. Like so totally pointless. Though he'll probably try it one day, maybe tonight if he feels like it since he won't be home.

He's got that one covered already. A quick call on his mobile and Stegosaurus is now convinced the kid's sleeping over at Spud's. The most rudimentary bit of fact-checking would have blown that lie out of the water like a duck on the end of a shotgun pellet but Steg's not up for that kind of labour-intensive childcare strategy as in call Spud's parents and confirm. Couldn't give a shit as long as he's got the flat to himself so he can watch his pay-per-view porn channel tonight without embarrassing-offspring interference. As in, can I watch too? And Steg like no you can't and I wasn't watching it anyway. It's on his credit-card bill for Christ's sake!

Two girls up ahead, under the concrete bridge where the road crosses the river, walking slowly and chatting the way girls do, like they're all the time flirting with someone invisible. Mature girls, maybe fourteen or fifteen, not from his school he thinks, in any case no reason why they should recognize him which is cool because staying incognito is important while he's on the run, except that one of them is looking at him, blonde girl, nice eyes, makes him feel wobbly. It's sort of a riverside-path opposite-direction opposite-gender confrontation kind of event where the two girls are coming his way and taking up quite a lot of girl-shaped space with their arms and hair and so forth and he's coming towards them and his eyes connecting with the blonde girl's and somebody's going to have to make way as in step aside but that's kind of an acknowledgement of the other's existence which is so to speak a delicate issue.

'What you got in there? A gun?'

It's the other girl speaking to him, the brown-haired one, and it's only now that the kid realizes he's walking with his hand inside his jacket, holding the stolen game. Girl's looking at him with a come-on-then smirk like she's already halfway through the Bonus Features menu vis-à-vis the opposite sex as in she's done it and put the phone shots on the web to prove it and can say what she likes. 'Well? Gonnie shoot me?'

The kid wants to pull out a sonic screwdriver and stun her. The Stranger would know how to sort it out but the other girl, the blonde one, she joins in like it's a double act. 'What're you hiding?' she says, only sweeter, like she thinks it might be a bunch of flowers for her or a box of chocolates.

'A game,' he says and brings it out and before he even knows what he's saying or why he's saying it he goes, 'Do you want it?' and hands it towards her.

She's looking at it like it's some incredible thing materialized out of thin air as in Tardis or other transdimensional object and the other one's got like 'this boy's mental' written all over her face but not the blonde girl who's acting like it really is a box of chocolates. The kid repeats the offer but not by saying anything because right now he can't. He stretches his arm a bit, waves the game towards her like he's tempting a pony with a piece of hay, wants to stroke her nose sort of thing.

'Did you steal it?' says boss girl, ever wise to the ways of the world, and the kid wonders which answer scores more points.

'It's mine,' says the kid.

'I can see that,' she goes, 'but I'm asking if you stole it. Still got the wrapper and everything. Bet you've been in WH Smith and knocked it.'

'What if I have?' says the kid, and the blonde girl's looking at him in silence. Like he's the Stranger and she knows he's a thief, murderer, pervert et cetera but so what?

'Maybe we'll shop you,' says the brown-haired girl, still smirking.

'Why would you do that?' says the kid.

'Cos,' she says, and the kid sees she's rolling gum in her mouth, first time he's noticed, blends so well with the way she talks.

The blonde says, 'It's wrong to steal.'

'What's wrong with it?' says her friend. 'As long as you can get away with it.'

'It's wrong, that's all,' she goes, and says to the kid, 'You should take it back to the shop.'

Boss girl says, 'You're mental,' then her mobile rings, she's got Black Eyed Peas on it, and she gives her head a toss when she puts the phone to her ear. As in contemptuous, thinks the kid. And now she's talking to some boy at the other end like there's nobody else in the world, as you do, like her friend and the kid and the river have all been sucked into the Vortex and there's just her and the phone and the crackly voice on it and the kid thinks you're on the List, you and your boyfriend, you're right at the top of it.

Kid says to the pretty girl, 'Take it,' like he's still holding it out but she doesn't want it.

'I can't. It's wrong.'

And he chucks it in the water, just like that. Disappears in the brown flow and sinks from view in a circle of spreading waves and the boss interrupts her conversation as in pulls the phone a wee bit from her ear as she turns to look and says, 'Fuck!' and then at the kid and goes 'Fuckin dickhead!' and at her friend and goes, 'Did you see what that mental cunt done?' and then she laughs and says into the phone, 'You should see this fuckin lunatic we met, lobbed a brand-new game in the river,' and then a moment later to the other girl she goes, 'We're seeing Kyle, OK?

C'moan,' and makes to leave but the blonde says no, tells her flat, doesn't want to come.

Second moment of disbelief for the boss. 'What, you want to stay with this prick?' Then second moment of bursting out laughing. 'You two are as bad as each other!' But there's no more to be said – the boss stares at the pair of them and finally gets the message. 'All right, fuck off,' and she turns and away she goes, fat arse swinging in her short skirt, never looking over her shoulder but texting on her phone instead.

Blonde girl says to the kid, 'Why did you do it? First steal it, then throw it away?'

Kid shrugs. 'Cos.'

'Cos what?'

'Dunno. Felt like it, I suppose.'

She says, 'My name's Jodie.'

'Cool.'

'Like the actress, you know?' But the kid doesn't. 'Jodie Foster. My mum wanted to call me after her. And my mum's called Dorothy because of *The Wizard of Oz*, can you believe that?' The kid believes but doesn't see the relevance, as in it's only a name so what difference does it make? But doesn't say anything. She goes, 'What's your name?'

'Doesn't matter.'

She smiles. 'Mystery man, eh? Go on, tell me.'

'I can't.'

'Why?'

Pair of them standing beside the river, nobody else about. Sort of romantic. Never mind the shopping trolley and the smell and stuff. 'Thing is, you're right about the game. I knocked it. I've done stuff that's wrong.'

'It's not so bad . . .'

'Not just that. Other stuff.'

She's looking at him in this penetrating way like she's trying to read his mind. The kid likes it. Only people ever try to read his mind are teachers reckoning he hasn't done his homework, but this Jodie, it's as if she cares about him.

'Go on,' she says, 'what's your name?'

'I'm not telling. It's best if you don't know. I'm . . . I'm on a mission.'

Slight raising of her eyebrows. As in, I don't really believe you but if you want me to then I'll believe because I care about you. 'A mission?'

He goes, 'There's this man I met in the park,' and he tells her. Not everything, he knows he can only go so far. And her eyebrows come down again and make a frown.

'Be careful! He's probably a paedo.'

'No, he's not one of those, I know what they're like. My guess is he's escaped from prison.'

'No!'

'And I want to help him. Cos I've run away too. We're like these two people who don't fit in anywhere and nobody wants us.'

She reaches out her hand to him. 'Don't think that way.' And she puts her hand on his arm. It's like there's electricity flowing through her fingertips into his body, pumping energy inside him. It's like she's got this magic power of caring what happens to him. Right now his mum's away shopping with the Hags and his dad's picking his nose in front of the television and here's this girl called Jodie that he didn't even know ten minutes ago and she's like the most wonderful thing in his life. That one touch of her fingers on his arm and it's like he's seeing a thousand million zillion futures that could lead from this moment and he's only allowed to choose one of them because God is such a boring bastard.

'I'm seeing him later,' he says. 'I'm meant to meet him in the park.'

'Don't go.'

'I want to.'

'Then I'll come with you.'

'What, so he can murder you too?'

She says, 'I want to know who he is and what this is about.'

And they start walking. It just happens, neither of them say, 'Let's walk,' or propose they take a vote or anything, but there they are, walking along the path beside the river. And next thing they're holding hands, both a bit embarrassed at first, but they soon get used to it once they work out where their fingers ought to go. Funny, they used to hold people's hands all the time – their parents, or their partner's in school whenever they had to go on trips in pairs. But that was years and years ago and they've forgotten what it's like. You probably start out knowing everything when you're a baby but it gets wiped and you spend the rest of your life having to relearn it, or so the kid thinks.

They get to an old monument with a bench in front of it. There's been someone lit a fire at one end of the bench and left it black and charred so the two of them have to sit close together at the other end, and after a while the kid puts his arm round her. River's full of rats and shit but right now it's the most beautiful spot in the universe. And the kid's got his arm round her thinking this is what I ran away to find, this is the answer, the missing piece, the full set.

She goes, 'You can kiss me,' so he does. First time he's ever properly kissed a girl and he feels like the game must have done when it fell in the water and disappeared. He's at the centre of a whole lot of spreading rings, vibrating waves putting him in touch with the furthest end of the galaxy. Her lips are so soft and warm, full of a life that's not his but she's letting him share a little piece of it. He wonders if he's meant to put his tongue in but she solves the dilemma by gently pushing him away. 'Enough for now,' she says with a smile, like she only dares allow herself a bit at a time, frightened of enjoying it too much.

He looks round at the monument behind and finds himself reading the inscription on it.

ON 31ST DECEMBER 1860, DURING SEVERE FLOODING, JAMES DEUCHAR, 20, A DIVINITY STUDENT AT GLASGOW UNIVERSITY, LEAPT INTO THE RIVER NEAR THIS SPOT INAN ATTEMPT TO RESCUE GEORGE LAIDLAW, 5, AND MARY LAIDLAW, 7, WHO HAD FALLEN IN. HAVING SAVED THE YOUNGER CHILD, MR. DEUCHAR RETURNED TO SEARCH FOR THE GIRL, WHO WAS WASHED UP ALIVE FURTHER DOWNSTREAM. MR. DEUCHAR, HOWEVER, PERISHED IN HIS NOBLE ENDEAVOUR. THIS MONUMENT TO HIS HEROISM WAS ERECTED BY PUBLIC SUBSCRIPTION, 3RD JANUARY 1863.

'Look at that,' he says.

Jodie reads too. 'That's terrible.'

'Happened so long ago.'

'It's still terrible.'

They both turn from it and look at the river in silence. Too shallow to be a threat to anyone unless they drank it. What if James Deuchar had lived and the children had died? Menus and submenus of human existence, hundreds of people alive today because of what that crazy superhero guy did in 1860, perhaps even Jodie or the kid, which is so cool, like everything's connected and means something. He says to her, 'If you fly far enough in space there's another planet just like this one. Only that guy Deuchar didn't get drowned.'

She's looking like this is rubbish but I'll believe you if you want me to and she goes, 'Is there another you and another me on that planet?' and he goes, 'Sure.' Why not? It's what they saw with their magnifying glass, said so on the Discovery Channel. She tells him Jodie Foster was in this film called *Contact* about an astronomer who gets sent instructions from aliens to make a spaceship and she builds it and goes to see them. And he decides to tell her everything.

'The stranger I met in the park – he says he's a spaceman.'

She laughs then sees he's serious. 'You don't believe him, do you?'

The kid shrugs. If we live in an infinite universe et cetera. Which we do.

7

Joe Coyle liked something to listen to while he was walking, and it was always his transistor radio with an earphone. You get these young ones with an enormous thing on their shoulder, ghetto blaster, music pounding out. Do they think they're clever? Is their musical taste so superior to everybody else's that they've got to inflict it on the entire population? One time, Joe had a quiet word with a group of them, kiddies probably no more than eleven or twelve year old. What did one of them say to him? 'Fuck off, you old git.' And the rest of them laughed. Circle of smirking weans, deserved a good cuff round the ear, and Joe Coyle realized he was scared of them. Scared because if he lifted a finger they'd have the law on him. Or one of the brats might pull a knife. Or his heart might give out like that fellow's over by Gippen, took on a crowd of yobs who were vandalizing his neighbour's car, wound up dead. World's gone mad.

Joe Coyle was walking back into town, back to ASDA, fact of the matter's that he was finding a way to pass a Saturday afternoon needed passing. Being a non-driving moderate-drinking football-hating pensioner with a semi-invalid for a wife, well, there wasn't a lot else for him to do, was there? Take up fishing, maybe, though he'd seen the price of rods in the Argos catalogue and it was outrageous really. No, a man's legs are his best entertainment. When the kids were still with them, every weekend, the family walk. You lose the family but you don't need to give up the walk.

He gave his earphone a twist so he could hear better, turned up the volume, and listened to *Any Questions*. Panel of experts, so called, commenting on current affairs. Always guaranteed to set Joe's blood boiling. One talking now, it was that fellow, what's-his-name, wanted to be party leader and it came out he was sleeping with his secretary. Current affairs indeed. Then a woman, Joe knows her voice, can picture her face, a Blairite clone. Thirty years a Labour Party member, so he was, then they made it New Labour. And you know whose idea that was. Even the union went down the pan. Used to be called the ATWU, been that since it was founded, then they got in some marketing agency, load of kids with suits and expense accounts, and forty thousand quid's worth of subs went on coming up with a wee picture of a daisy for a logo and a new name, Together. Meant to be a trade union, not a pop group!

This daft woman talking in Joe's ear, she was driving him nuts. Thirty year ago he was working forty hours a week at the plant, plus overtime, plus he was coming home and dealing with union business until midnight, plus there was branch meetings, plus he was out there at every election canvassing for the Labour Party, plus he was bringing up two weans to know the difference between right and wrong. And this stupid wee lassie on the radio? Thirty year ago she probably wasn't even a sperm and an egg though already by then she'd got her career mapped out as New Labour spokesperson on community relations.

Now it was the presenter talking, they wanted another question from the audience. Joe could think of a few he'd like to ask, but the one they got came from Susan Wells who's thirteen years old and comes from Little Norton. Joe turned up his radio another notch to hear what the girl would say, and it was almost like struggling to catch birdsong, this flutey child's voice reading the question she'd brought. Joe had to wait for the presenter to repeat it.

'*What is truth?*'

That was it: three words so short and simple that for a moment neither the audience nor the panel knew how to respond. '*There we have it*,' said the presenter with an ironic smile in his voice. '*Who'd like to kick off with that one?*'

Some posh bloke pitched in; MP, millionaire, archbishop, whatever. '*Truth means different things to different people and in an integrated, multicultural society we need to respect that. Of course there are certain core values we all share and uphold: the sanctity of life, for instance, and respect for individual freedoms. But it would be quite wrong to believe in some kind of one-size-fits-all approach.*'

Next it was the fellow who'd been screwing his secretary, and of course he agreed entirely. '*We really need to look at it in terms of individual rather than collective truths, all of us moving forward together while retaining our rich diversity of traditions and beliefs.*'

Then the clone, firm but conciliatory, way they're trained to talk. She'll be Prime Minister one day, thought Joe. '*In a healthy democracy, instead of there being one monolithic truth, there are lots and lots of them, all having an equal say and contributing to the debate. To give an analogy, when I was growing up there were four television channels – now there are hundreds, and we've got the Internet too, all feeding us so much information that we can't possibly keep track of everything. So we're a society of surfers and choosers, cherry-picking whatever suits us, whether it's our religion, our politics, our taste in fashion and so on. Some people might find that disorientating but really it's the triumph of choice, and that has been the greatest achievement of global civilization in the last half century. Now there are no ideologies, no rule books we all have to follow.'*

'*So truth is whatever we want it to be?*' the presenter intervened.

'*I suppose you could say that,*' the clone agreed. '*Within reason, of course.*'

Joe stopped to take a breath, leaning against a railing. Had he ever heard a group of sane adults talk such utter gibberish? Disorientating? Too right it was, to have this sort of nonsense piped in your ear. And what was all that marching about, that he and Anne and millions more had done? Were there weapons of mass destruction in Iraq or weren't there? Not a difficult question, yes or no would do. But all you could get from these political jobsworths was evasive guff about everybody being right in their own way.

Joe pulled out the earphone. I'll tell you what's truth, he thought to himself. Truth is that I'm standing here, the sky's blue, two and two make four. Truth is all the things that happen, all the experiences, the good times and the bad, things you wish weren't true but they are. He felt a pain in his chest, took another breath, calmed down. He damn well wasn't going to be finished off by the idiot southerners on *Any Questions*.

He took the small black radio out the breast pocket on his T-shirt and swivelled the tuner. The dial was marked only with numbers, that's what they're all like nowadays.

Used to be you had a list of cities, permanent as the exchange rate, a gold standard of world frequencies: Vienna, Madrid, Paris. Robbie loved playing with the radiogram, thrown out long ago when nobody wanted it, not even the charity shops, though it still worked. Joe was for keeping it but not Anne. Can't keep everything, she said. Got to let go. Joe's dial was marked, however, by fine lines of Tipp-Ex indicating his favourite stations, and on abandoning *Any Questions* he moved up the scale in search of better wavelengths. Pushing the earphone back in place, he heard a medical programme in which a doctor was offering advice on healthy eating.

'Plenty of fresh fruit and vegetables, of course. And don't forget the herbs and spices, because recent research shows these can contain high concentrations of useful antioxidants. But don't overdo it, because some of our tastiest herbs owe their flavour to natural toxins designed to deter insects, and although not harmful in the amounts we use in cooking, you wouldn't want to be brewing them up to make your morning cuppa.'

Joe's blood ran cold. All that stuff he'd heard was a lie. Fifteen year ago the doctors were saying you should drink parsley and he'd been doing it ever since. Now he knew the truth: he'd been a guinea pig in an experiment. Those bastards were out to kill him.

He thought about it all the way to ASDA, got there and knew Anne had wanted him to buy something, told him to write it down. He hadn't, never needed to, always carried the list in his head, but this parsley shocker had fair floored him – a junkie at his age! And a herbal one at that. Anne would no doubt tell him he was being a big daftie but he'd heard it with his own ear (the left one, his best). Not like he was starting to hear things, the way Robbie did, first sign he was getting ill. No, old Joe never had a day off sick in his life, only way they could get him out the plant was redundancy, but he'd been noticing right enough that if he ran out of parsley and skipped a day or two he sometimes got the shakes.

Freezer cabinet – is that what Anne was wanting? Load of processed burgers full of dead pets that ran away and got caught – Maureen Dunbar's cat'd make a good sleeve for a fur coat and a packet of mini-Kievs. No, try the next section, frozen desserts. Anne must have said ice cream, Joe thought, here we go, American type she likes, always coming up with new flavours. Picture of the pair of them on the back, jolly men with beards, wonder if they're real? All gets made in a factory somewhere, they con you into thinking it's home-made. Sliding open the freezer, reaching inside to retrieve a tub so cold it stuck momentarily to his fingers, pulling it from the frigid steam and closing the door, then reading the description on the side. '*There's nothing we like better than rowing on the beautiful rivers and lakes of Vermont, and that's how we came up with this great new addition to our range. Rich vanilla ice cream, luscious Vermont maple syrup and miniature chocolate rowing boats in a mouth-watering tide of gorgeous caramel. We love it!*'

Joe tipped the tub to see the name on the lid. 'Caramel Oargasm'. And wee kiddies could see it there in the freezer, it wasn't like it was on the top shelf or anything. Fine if they want to have X-rated desserts and put them out of reach but this was where anybody could get it. 'Mummy, can I have a caramel orgasm?' Used to be you couldn't even say 'pregnant' in public, and then they wonder why there's all these perverts and weirdos?

He tried to think what he needed and soon was in the herb section. 'Take a look at this,' he said to a passing assistant, a teenage girl. 'Fifty-seven pence.'

She looked displeased. 'We've been through this. Try fresh herbs another day.'

'What?'

She walked on, ignored him. He was a customer and she'd treated him as if he didn't even exist. Who the hell did she think she was? Young kid with purple hair and a head full of pop music, thinks she's too good to worry herself with an old man like Joe Coyle, is that it? And what did she do about Iraq?

Hang on, rewind. Strange sense of déjà vu like he'd seen it in another life but no they really had been through all of this already and he'd momentarily forgot like it was blanked out, bit of the tape that didn't record properly. It was all that parsley. Fellow on the radio, professor somebody or other, bloke who knows about these things, said there's something psychoactive in the plant and that's why people have been using it for generations not realizing every time they put a wee sprinkle on their steamed cod or roast lamb they're getting high on it. OK in moderation, professor somebody or other says, but two cups a day? We're talking brain, liver and lung damage, doc says, legs crossed behind his big desk and sitting back with a sorrowful shake of his head. Do you not mind that man lived on carrot juice and when they found him dead on his bed he looked like a carrot?

Joe felt suddenly breathless, all that green juice poisoning his system – and there was him thinking it was doing him good! He was turning into a walking wreck so he was, and all because of those damned Americans. Stay calm, big fellow. You were on the cigs for long enough until you gave them up and that was no problem. You decide something and then you do it. No need to be emotional about it like a blubbering wean or a woman. Twenty-five year next week and you've survived that one, haven't you? Two wee cups of parsley every day, what's that? Maybe shortened your life by a year or two, call it ten if you like. In which case you died last week . . . no don't think that way.

He walked to the end of the aisle and saw the cash desks with queues at each, people stuffing groceries in bags, but it was the sunshine beyond that drew him, sucking his gaze like a buzzing fly's, his feet knowing where to go even if his mind was somewhere else, and soon he was at the entrance, the *Big Issue* seller with his stray-dog look standing only a few yards ahead, but before Joe could cross the threshold he heard a deep male voice.

'Excuse me, sir.'

Startled, Joe turned to see a uniformed security guard at his side.

'You didn't pay for that.' The guard was pointing at the ice cream Joe raised into full view, feeling guilty and confused.

'Sorry . . . I totally forgot.'

'Come on, Joe.' It was his friend Agnes, appearing from nowhere and rescuing him. 'Here, I'll do it for you at the cigarette counter.'

Joe meekly followed. 'I'm getting awfie forgetful.'

'Comes to us all, Joe,' Agnes said before stepping behind the counter and instructing the assistant at the till to deal with his purchase. Agnes took the tub from him and squinted at the lid, then laughed. 'You saucy old devil. It's good, mind you.' Then she saw Joe's face and the look of humiliation it bore. 'Hey, don't you go losing your marbles too soon, Joe,' she said. 'Anne needs you more than ever.'

'I know,' Joe said softly, and the assistant handed him his ice cream in a carrier bag.

'We've all got our crosses to bear,' said Agnes. 'Mind yourself.'

Joe left the supermarket and when he saw the *Big Issue* seller again it all came to him, he'd been here already today. He'd long been forgetful but that was age, it was normal. This was worse. This was CIA-sponsored parsley poisoning. But it wasn't too late to cure himself; if he could beat the cigs he could kick the weed, and he wasn't feart of a wee touch of the shakes. Breaking into a brisk walk he soon felt more positive, buoyed by a convert's faith as he reflected on what a fool he'd been, surprised he never peed green with all that toxic juice in him, might do yet, but why don't they bring back the wee Edgar Allan under the bed? Would save all that traipsing round the landing from bedroom to bog every night and good for the environment too – one flush in the morning and it's gone. He'd suggest it to Anne, though he couldn't imagine her squatting for a jimmy riddle in the small hours. How did our grandparents manage, Joe wondered; they had arthritis in those days too, and a trip outside to the cludgie come daybreak. The smell of wood and poo, the smooth worn seat beneath your wee bum and the sunshine leaking through the cracks in the planks. How fondly he remembered it all.

A walk along the river, that'd be nice. Joe made his way through the town centre until he came to the bridge, then took the steps down to the waterside path where a man of similar age held a rod over the idle flow. 'Only thing you'll catch in there's Wheel's disease.'

'Whissat?'

'You know, thing you get off rats.'

'Ah'm no fishing for rats.'

'I know you're not. But there's a disease you get off them.'

'You mean rabies?'

'No, Wheel's disease.'

'Same thing as rabies, isn't it?'

The conversation went on for some time and gave Joe considerable satisfaction, particularly when a brown rat was sighted near the opposite bank, but then it was time for him to say cheerio and move on, and when Joe reached for the transistor radio in his pocket, intending to switch it on and retrieve his earphone, he was reminded of the contents of the carrier bag still dangling from his right hand which bumped against his chest as he raised it. Looking into the bag he saw a fawn-coloured trail of melted ice cream oozing from the softened cardboard tub.

'All because of that damned drug,' he muttered, looking ahead along the path and seeing a litter bin he could make use of. As soon as he reached it he put Caramel Oargasm and its grinning transatlantic creators where they belonged, and in a further public-spirited gesture decided to pick up one or two crisp packets that lay beneath the bin, either fallen out or more probably tossed there by kids who found it too much effort to dispose of their waste properly. It gave him renewed strength, a sense of righteousness, and he strode vigorously along the canal to the accompaniment of the afternoon jazz programme on Radio 3.

More than half an hour he walked, a good couple of mile, until he was beyond the town and surrounded by fields, the water looking cleaner here though he still wouldn't trust it. And over there in the distance, the place he suddenly realized he'd been unconsciously drawn to as if by a malignant magnet. Site where the military installation used to be.

The base was gone, thank God, but the land round about looked little different from when it was taken off the farmers. Compulsory purchase order, they called it, part of the Cold War effort, officially it was described as a testing range and signs went up on the perimeter fence warning of live explosives beyond. All Joe's protests had done nothing, the leaflets and the meetings and the marching with Anne in those days when their joints were still capable of political action. Half the town were up in arms about it but to no avail, the fence was up, and far behind it, out of sight and mostly hidden by trees, a complex of low-rise prefabs grew, housing whatever it was they did in there.

For the most part nobody noticed, except when the big guns were fired. Every weekday afternoon they'd go off, the exact time never fixed so the booms came without warning, singly or in groups. Joe never heard them because he was at work but it was worse than ruddy Concorde, Anne said, she was hopping mad about it, could still hop then. Houses shook, windows cracked, tenants' associations held more meetings and nothing got done. Installation wasn't even marked on the new Ordnance Survey map came out, only the re-routing of the roads round an empty grey patch, and how do you get rid of something that doesn't exist? Joe never believed it was guns in there, more likely some new bomb or secret fabrication process; but everybody got used to it, even the cows in the surrounding fields that would graze on through the banging, it was said, without so much as batting an eyelid.

Robbie used to go playing in those fields at weekends with Scott Campbell. Two of them would ride there on their bikes, couple of mile from home, but you never worried in those days, looking for frogs, flying their kite. And wandering round the installation where they weren't meant to go. That's how it started.

Joe hadn't seen another soul for the last quarter of an hour but now he caught sight of a young man ahead, chap in his forties maybe, coming into view round the bend of the river and walking towards him. Looked familiar; Joe thought he knew him but the other man showed no sign of recognition as he approached. Not an angler or a bird-watcher, just a walker like Joe himself, yet with a sense of purpose in his gait.

'Aye there,' said Joe, trying to remember where he'd seen the man before. Was it the fellow moved in at the end of the street? Couple with two wee kiddies, whole scheme was getting taken over by a new generation now the first wave was dead or going into retirement homes.

'Hello,' he said. Even sounded familiar. The two men eyed each other.

'How's it going?' Joe asked open-endedly, hoping a bit of banter would help the penny drop. Music was still playing in his earphone.

'Fine,' said the stranger, neither elaborating nor moving on.

It was starting to give Joe the creeps, knowing this bloke but not knowing how he knew him, or why, or where. He pulled out his earphone and then, with some embarrassment, said, 'You look like you don't remember me.'

'I don't.'

'Joe Coyle.' Saying his own name, hearing how defensive the words sounded, made him feel almost a stranger to himself.

The man showed a flicker of understanding, a movement of his eyebrows, but it was not a gesture of warm acquaintance. 'I don't live in these parts.'

In Joe's hand, the earphone continued to emit its tinny rhythm like a trapped insect. 'You're not from here? That's funny, because you're awfie familiar. Did you live here before and then move away? Maybe you went to school with Janet or Robert, you look the right sort of age—'

'Are they your children?' the stranger interrupted.

'Yes,' said Joe, feeling as if he was being interrogated.

'And did they leave?'

Joe took a breath. There was something uncomfortable about this conversation, as if it had a deeper meaning he was incapable of fathoming, though he knew it was only small talk with somebody he must have met before, maybe when the fellow was still a boy which was why it was so hard to recognize him. 'They're both gone,' he said.

'A lot of people move away from here.' There was a new note of sympathy in the stranger's voice.

'My daughter's living God knows where,' said Joe. 'My son died when he was nineteen.'

'I'm sorry to hear it.' He sounded as if he meant it.

'He's been gone longer than he was alive,' Joe said softly. 'Doesn't feel it, mind. But what about you? Are you visiting family?'

'You could say I'm here on a mission.'

Joe's heart sank – now he understood why the fellow had come over so concerned and understanding all of a sudden. Hadn't struck Joe as an evangelist but you never know where these people'll show up next – the door-to-door business must have gone slack and now they were trying a riverside approach, John the Baptist sort of thing, though this missionary had a rough look about him, more Livingstone in the jungle than the clean-cut style you usually see hawking salvation. 'Good luck to you,' Joe said, cutting short the conversation before he could get handed a leaflet. He was about to move on.

'I'm looking for somewhere to stay.'

'I can't help you there,' Joe said at once, feeling instantly threatened.

'I heard there was a hotel near here.'

'Now I'm with you,' said Joe. 'You mean the Lodge.'

'That's the one. Some people in town gave me directions but they weren't very accurate.'

Joe pointed away from the riverbank across the fields to some thick woods. 'It's right in the middle of they trees, that's why you couldn't find it. But I wouldn't go near it if

I were you. Used to be a military base there, they closed it after the Cold War ended, cleared the land and redeveloped it. They say it's safe and there's no contamination but they would, wouldn't they? Chance for somebody to make a quick buck. And the sell-off was a dodgy affair, it went to some consortium runs conference centres all over the place, but why here? Who'd want to come here for a conference? I reckon the answer's in the name.'

'What do you mean?'

'Place used to be a private estate, belonged to the Logie family, then it got sold to the military; and next thing you know, the army's selling it back again, to this chain the Logies have got shares in. A nice wee deal between the Grand Master and his fellow members in the top brass with their funny handshakes and rolled-up trouser legs. It's Freemasons run that place. Why do you think they call it the Lodge?'

The stranger took it all in like there was nothing in the world could surprise him. Maybe he's one of them too, thought Joe, then watched the fellow walk by after they'd exchanged a cursory farewell. 'I hope your mission's a success,' he called after him, but the stranger didn't turn, either failing to hear or else ignoring him. Opus Dei, they were probably at the back of it, running the Lodge as a training camp. When Janet disappeared his first thought was she'd joined that shower, because he knew she'd converted to Catholicism after her time as a Buddhist, but no, it was a New Age commune they eventually got a postcard from, said she was happy and they were never to try and contact her again or come looking for her, well it's all brainwashing whatever name you want to give it and no worse than being a parsley addict when you come down to it but Joe was on to that one, he'd got it sorted. He wasn't going to end up like the daughter he'd lost, high on dope and God knows what else and living on lentils because it's bad karma to kill a fly never mind a cow.

And the son he'd lost. Joe looked again towards the far trees and thought of Robbie and Scott playing round there, two helpless wee specks on the map, straying towards the grey. Joe never quite got the truth of it, but Robbie claimed he and Scott managed to get through a hole in the fence and inside the installation. Two boys playing soldiers in a top-secret base. Anne never believed it, nobody did, called it another of Joe's conspiracy theories; but they could call it what they liked, Joe didn't care. It was still the truth by any name.

He left the riverside and walked up to the quiet country road that would take him home, retuning his radio to listen to the news and who was this coming on, my God he might have known. David Luss MSP, education spokesman. Fellow who sat in Joe Coyle's living room thirty-odd year ago with fumes belching out his pipe, head of science at Kenzie High, Robbie knew him for the fool he was though Janet took a shine to him, maybe because he spent his lessons talking about John Lennon or Chairman Mao instead of teaching anything. Didn't hurt his career, though. Joe had monitored his progress over the years; a steady move up and to the right as the arse-licking toady free-lunched his way from Trotskyite shop steward to respectable school inspector to elected politician in a nice suit and tie with a fair bit more weight on him than he'd had that time Anne cooked for him.

'We have to remember that education is our top priority because this nation's children are our future.'

Aye, you tell them, thought Joe. Tell them how you never really gave a damn about the workers but socialism happened to be the fashion at the time, like flared trousers and sideburns, and soon as it went out of style you changed your stripe. Yes, you were the one ended up chief commissioner for schools, calling on teachers to break the strike they'd voted for.

World's full of shits like him, thought Joe, the item on the news washing over him like foul rain. Finger in every pie that could fatten his reputation, like that nonsense about poor Mr Tulloch in the local paper last few weeks, grown men saying he'd made a pass at them when they were teenagers, all lies. And who's come out of the woodwork to take the glory? David Luss, of course; said he was the one reported Tulloch at the time, no evidence mind, but as a conscientious colleague who put the interests of children first, etc., etc. Forced a good teacher into early retirement, more like dismissal, and what did Tulloch do? Topped himself with a bottle of paracetamol. Well done David Luss, spokesman for education.

A car beeped and swished past Joe, too fast for the small road and probably on its way to the Lodge. Sam Dunbar was a Freemason too, Joe remembered; half the GPO were in it, exchanging code words on the fairways. Maybe the Angry Brigade had a point, trying to blow up that control tower of theirs; but what did Robbie find in the installation? No microwave dishes or armed guards; didn't even see any buildings. What Robbie said he found was marbles, great big piles of them heaped like waste, mountains of dense green glass. What they were for, nobody knows; even after it was all over and the base got closed, still there was never any explanation of those marbles or even an admission they existed, as if everyone had only dreamed about them. But they were real.

Two lads who wandered up the wrong path and next minute they're jumping on these heaps of magic glass, imagining they're on another planet or whatever; the marbles, millions of them, crunching and rolling beneath their sinking feet, the boys laughing and shouting and never for one moment thinking there could be any harm in it because that's kids, you can't blame them, it's the ones who are older who should know better. Like an enormous playground they've stumbled into, not a soul about, nobody to tell them off or object when they start picking the marbles up and lobbing them at each other, dodging round the mounds trying to take cover, could easily hurt yourself with one of they marbles, not as big as golf balls but a fair bit of weight in them. And something strange about their surface, not perfectly smooth like an ordinary marble but grooved and wavy, like they'd come out an irregular mould. Nuclear waste, that's what it was.

Middle of the Scottish countryside, aye, put it there in case something goes wrong. Don't want an accident anywhere near London, do we? Oh no, that'd be terrible, that'd get on the news. But if a few more Scots die of cancer nobody's going to notice, are they? And put a fence round it all to be on the safe side, but these fencing contractors, Joe had seen how they operate. Got a wee stretch nobody notices – save yourself some wire. Cut corners, reduce your overheads, increase your profits, take the rest of the afternoon off and play a round of golf, whatever. Anything the hell you like as long as it means you don't have to shift your weight more than the bare minimum, it'll all get hushed up anyway if something goes wrong, so there's two wee kiddies walking in like it's a swing park and they're playing on irradiated waste from those shells the army's testing there. Or if it's not radiation it's chemicals, who knows what it was, when all you get is denials and even your own wife doesn't believe you.

As far as the boys were concerned it was something to play with, pile of marbles, take some home as souvenirs. Joe never knew anything about it until long after when Robbie started getting the headaches, hardly a wink of sleep some nights and the doctor was no help, prescribing analgesics for the symptoms and never troubling about the cause. Joe found it under Robbie's pillow: a marble. Anne already knew because she was the one made Robbie's bed every day and said a bit of glass couldn't be the trouble, hardly pressed his skull, but it wasn't the pressure troubled Joe when Robbie said where it came from. Joe held the sphere aloft and in its watery refractions saw the connection.

He threw it out, evil relic of his son's trespass. But that was a mistake, because whenever in later years Joe aired his theory about his son's disease and death, his words were received in contemptuous silence, the evidence being missing and presumed buried beyond the tender reach of any Geiger counter or more probably non-existent. Nor would Scott Campbell verify Robbie's story, sensitive more to his own self-preservation than to historic record: said they'd played in the estate before it was redeveloped but never again once the military moved in. All lies. They were in there, again and again, nobody knew but Robbie saw the secret complex. Yes his mind was confused, it started then with the headaches when he was twelve year old and only got worse, but that was a symptom of the poisoning.

Now Scott's got two grown-up kids of his own, Joe reminded himself, they're all healthy and happy. And Robbie's dead. One wrong path, a big heap of marbles, a boy's life, for what? All so the government could test their weapons at the installation, never admitting the cost of it. All because America needed to hold on to its colony in the North Sea. For their damned greed Joe's son had to die.

8

So it's seven o'clock in the evening and this guy's waiting in the park like he said he would, not in the fenced-off play area where the swings are, but on a bench on the grassy part outside, and the kid's with Jodie, watching from behind a row of bushes that must have got planted by the council to make the park more like a countryside sort of effect though the twigs are full of drink cans that people shove in like it's a bin and on the dry earth at the kid's feet he sees a condom as in probably used but he's not exactly going to check, is he? Well, duh.

Jodie reckons it's ninety-nine point nine per cent certain the guy's a paedo. She's fourteen years old and she knows a paedo when she sees one, they've all got this slimy Mr Ordinary look about them and RC fits the bill perfectly. She whispers in the kid's ear, if you go with him he'll rape and murder you. Or maybe just show you his dick or something, and they both try not to laugh while they hide behind the bushes.

Kid thinks, somebody must have had sex here, which is so pathetic. Or did they leave the condom on the ground as kind of a showing-off sort of thing as in pretending they'd had sex? Or maybe it's a balloon, the kid's not entirely sure. And he isn't sure about the stranger either, because there's a zero point one per cent chance the guy's all right. He says to her, don't worry, I can handle this, and she says, I'm coming too. No you're not he says, oh yes I am, and it sort of goes on like this, quite romantic and impressive really, as in heroic, like in a film. Except it's all happening in this crummy park. And the kid says, I'll go on ahead and you cover me.

'Cover you?' She doesn't watch the same kind of films.

He says, you keep watch and if the guy starts strangling me or pulls his dick out or whatever then you scream your head off. You do know how to scream, don't you? She nods and the kid gets out from behind the bush – she watches him walk across to the bench where the guy's sitting, facing a different direction so he doesn't see at first, and right now it's like the kid's this tiny dot in an awesome universe, as in here he is, he's run away from home, been on the loose all afternoon and now it's nearly dark, he's stolen a game from WH Smith and found a girlfriend well not officially as in they've not formally decided to go out with each other but they held hands and kissed and so forth and that was all quite impressive, and here he is, then, this little dot walking across the grass thinking, I wish you could see me right now, as in his father the Stegosaurus who couldn't give a shit, and his mother the Maiasaura who's with the Hags on their shopping weekend and so basically couldn't give one either. And Spud and Marko and all his friends, well, sort of friends, as in scholastic acquaintances so to speak, meaning they're the kind of people he sits next to in lessons or the dining hall but when it comes down to it they're in the non-shit-giving league too. The whole world and the whole universe couldn't give one except of course for Jodie who's watching him walk across the grass and is ready to scream at a moment's notice, like she's got it lodged in her throat same as the stranger's got something he's hiding and about to pull out as in a knife or his dick or whatever it doesn't really matter, thinks the kid, because the thing is, when all this is finished at least I'll have done something, as in not sitting in front of television with a tin of beer in my hand waiting to die.

And the stranger turns and sees him. 'Hello,' he says.

'Hello.'

'I didn't think you'd come. I'm glad you did.' The stranger reaches for something and it's like the kid is watching all of this from a million miles away, like he's in a little spaceship flying above the Earth, and the stranger's searching inside his coat, in that pocket they give you so you can steal from shops, and it's not a knife or gun he brings out but a little wallet kind of thing, as in for keeping credit cards, kid's seen them before and when he grows up he wants one, it'll be absolutely filled with cards, all gold. Stranger opens the card wallet and there's only like two or three in it, he takes out a card and puts the wallet back where he got it, and he holds up the card for the kid to see as if it's impressive but it isn't gold or platinum or whatever other kind there is, like Spud says there's an iridium card now because people have got so rich the platinum one isn't good enough anymore, but this one the guy's holding looks more like the swipe card the kid uses to pay for his school meals.

The guy says, 'I have a job for you,' and he hands the card to the kid. 'You've got a trick with magnets, I've got one with cards.'

Kid takes the card and looks at it and he's thinking, please don't scream now Jodie because everything's under control and I want to know what all this is about. Card's totally blank except for the magnetic strip on one side.

Guy says, 'I want you to take this to a cash machine and put it in. The PIN is 1729. Get five hundred pounds.'

Kid stares at the card. At the guy. At the card again. 'Why can't you do it?'

Guy smiles. 'It's a test. I want to see if you'll come back.'

'And if I don't?'

He laughs. 'Then you'll have got yourself a lot of money. And nothing else.'

Kid thinks about it. 'And if I come back?'

Guy leans towards him. 'Then we can discuss the mission.' Says it in sort of a kind but serious way. In a totally *Doctor Who* way.

'I'm going,' says the kid, and walks back towards the bushes with the card in his hand. He looks towards the place where Jodie is hiding and tries to signal to her with his face that everything's fine, smiling and mouthing like a complete idiot, but he knows the guy must be watching him and Jodie must be watching the guy, so when he passes the bush he says quietly to her out of the corner of his mouth that she'd better follow him when she can but not to let herself be seen and then he keeps going, he knows where to head with the card, a five-minute walk to a line of shops nearly all closed now and not too many people about and he doesn't even look round until he's almost at the ATM and when he does he sees that Jodie must have been ten paces behind him all the way as in so embarrassingly uncool of him not to have noticed even though they're on an illegal top-secret mission.

'He gave you his card?' whispers Jodie, catching up, and the kid decides she should be the one puts it in the cash dispenser because he's a kid and it looks suspicious but she's fourteen as in basically a woman like she's got breasts and make-up and so forth and nobody's going to hassle her so he tells her the deal and passes the card to her, they're both looking straight ahead and walking and the card's going from his hand into hers, sort of romantic really, he feels for a moment the touch of her fingers, then she's like examining the card she's got in her hand saying oh my God, very quietly, and they're at the ATM, all lit up like it's an ice-cream parlour in the wall or something, place where grown-ups get their treats, and she's saying this is so wrong and the kid says what do you mean?

They're standing at the machine and she says I'm only doing this for you, not because of whatever the weirdo says. She's like half looking over her shoulder all the time and it's making the kid nervous, then she puts the card into the slot and the machine sucks it in and for a moment nothing happens like this is all going to go horribly wrong, kid thinks, as in cage descends from the sky and traps us or great big plastic bubble comes out of the machine or a robot arm with a claw on the end of it grabs me by the throat and sirens wail and there's this voice saying intruder alert intruder alert and so forth.

Then he remembers the First Law. Act like all of this is meant to be happening. And it works, because the screen is asking Jodie to enter the PIN so he tells her and she taps the keys. Then it's asking which service she requires like this is all so absolutely normal and she selects cash withdrawal and the next moment she's like keying five hundred pounds which is so totally unreasonable because the kid's sure there's meant to be a limit or something but the machine doesn't blink, she asks for five hundred pounds and its little computer circuit says sure, five hundred pounds, be my guest, but first take back your perfectly legitimate blank card with a strip of videotape stuck on it, and the machine rolls it out slowly like a piece of gum for Jodie to take. Please wait for your cash, it says, and if there's going to be a cage falling from the sky then this is the moment, police cars screeching round the corner, as in the stranger in the park is a plainclothes detective from the child-catcher unit.

Clunk. That's what five hundred pounds look like.

'Shit!'

'This is so wrong,' says Jodie, as in repeats, but she takes the wad and folds it so quickly and naturally it's like she wrote the First Law herself and the kid didn't even get a chance to see what sort of denomination the machine chose though he thinks it's twenties which means there's twenty-five of them in the wad she's pushed inside her bra. As in those twenty-five pieces of paper are touching her actual breast. Or one of them is, the lucky twenty-fifth on the outside of the wad, and the kid thinks about this while they walk silently back, as in the Queen has got her nose on Jodie's nipple which makes it all so much more real somehow. He doesn't know if he'll ever get to see Jodie's breast and in fact he doubts it quite a lot and in a way he's glad because although he's plenty old enough to run away from home, steal from shops and banks and get involved with dangerous criminals, he doesn't quite feel ready yet for a full physical relationship with a female.

'What do we do now?' he asks her, neither looking round, both expecting the flashing blue light of a police car to start following them.

'You give the paedo the money and the card,' says Jodie. 'Then we run like hell and forget about this.'

He admires Jodie, as in he can see why people might confuse her with some film star she's named after and he's never heard of but knows is this really kind of strong character. Feisty, that's the word he always hears. It's what woman are meant to be, and Jodie's feisty. The kid wonders if boys can get to be feisty too but he's not really ready yet for a fully feisty lifestyle, and in any case maybe it's strictly a female thing, like you'd never call a girl handsome it would be meaningless.

He knows that basically Jodie feels sorry for him because he's a young kid who's run away from home and when they held hands and kissed and so forth it was kind of a sympathetic gesture as in offering somebody a cup of tea and a biscuit sort of thing because a woman like Jodie is really more interested in somebody who's maybe like sixteen or seventeen or even drives a car. She's not going to hang out with a young kid except out of kindness or curiosity or because her friend happened to get called away. All of which sort of makes the kid really hate being who he is and the age he is so to speak which when you think about it is only a matter of when he was born as in the year and there are all these other twelve-year-olds like him in other time zones for example the Victorians and the Saxons and the Romans that he learned about at school so boring and they all grew up and died, even the little children who got saved from the river, and when you think about it that way, the kid thinks, it's like we're all dead already as in we're somebody's past. So stealing really isn't such a big deal. Kids stole in Victorian times and nowadays everybody feels sorry for them.

'Here's the money,' says Jodie, stopping and reaching inside her top. They're nearly back at the park but not yet in view of it and even if they were the kid wouldn't be looking at it because the only thing he can see right now is Jodie's hand reaching feistily inside her underwear and pulling out a warm wad of twenties that she presses into his fingers. As in this paper has touched her breast and now he's holding it, really and truly, and all he wants to do is put it up to his nose and smell it. He wants to be that money.

She gives him the card too. 'Go and see the weirdo, then split, got it?'

She's definitely the one in charge, or thinks she is. And something inside the kid tells him: Jodie, you sound just like my mother. He has a right to decide, doesn't he? The stranger gave him the card and trusted him to go to a cashpoint and pull five hundred pounds. Or rather didn't trust him – he did it as a test and doesn't care if the kid comes back or not. Guy's probably got ten cards like this one and could find ten more kids, sort of a Fagin kind of character only this guy doesn't even steal because the money came out of a machine and not somebody's pocket. And the kid has passed the test, or will pass once he hands over the goods. But Jodie's setting a different kind of test, as in he's got to do what she orders and the kid's not entirely happy with this because it's not like they're actually going out together or anything. She's basically this bossy girl who feels sorry for him because he's run away and so forth but he didn't run away so he could get bossed around. He says, I'm going there alone.

'I'll keep watch again from behind the bushes. I'll scream if there's trouble.'

'No need,' says the kid. He's got it all under control. 'You'd better leave.'

She stands there looking at him like she's thinking, is that it? Sort of a romantic moment. Because the kid has realized two things. One: he's got a card that gives him access to unlimited cash. Two: he doesn't need to take orders from anyone. And thanks to both of these things, he's risen in her estimation.

She says, 'Will I see you again?'

He laughs. 'Nothing's going to happen to me . . .'

'I don't mean like that. Do you want to see me again?'

'Yes,' he says. Then adds, 'Once all of this is finished.' It's sort of heroic, they're both like these tiny dots. Only he's a bigger one.

'Bye, then,' she says.

'Bye.'

He watches her turn and walk away and the roll of

money is curled in his hand which is safely inside his pocket, where the card is too, and he can feel how much power it gives him. Like every game or DVD in the whole entire world that he could possibly want. They're his, and all the extras. It's like the menu of his life has expanded. He walks to the park alone.

Kid sees the stranger sitting there, bit of a smile on the guy's face but not much, like he's pleased but not too surprised. Nobody else in the park, usually get older kids this time of the evening but it's like maybe the sight of the stranger scared them off, thought he might be police or community worker which is even worse in a way, but the kid's pleased he's got the stranger all to himself, not even Jodie watching, because this is his adventure and he has to deal with it alone. So he hands over the wad, guy reaches from where he's sitting on the bench like he hasn't moved all this time the kid was away, takes the money and folds it into his pocket, might as well be toilet paper, takes the card too. Says nothing.

'Did I pass the test?'

Guy nods. Stands up. Looks taller than the kid remembered, almost like a god. 'Let's go.'

'Where?'

'You'll see.'

They walk. No conversation, no discussion, they just walk, and soon wind up back at the riverside path, kid says to the stranger I was here before but the stranger isn't interested. They walk.

He thinks, maybe he's going to try to kill me. Maybe he'll pull me behind some bushes and slit my throat. Or he'll rape me and slit my throat. But the kid isn't scared. If it comes to it, he can handle himself. He can fight, run, scream. And anyway, the stranger isn't going to hurt him, he isn't a paedo, kid can tell. He's a spaceman. They're on a mission and that's all that matters. They keep walking.

'It's over there,' the stranger says suddenly. They're like basically nowhere.

'What is?'

'Place where we're staying tonight.'

Pretty obvious when you think about it, which is what the kid does now, as in they've been going all this way because it's getting dark and they need somewhere to stay. They've walked right out of town to a bit where the kid never goes and there's fields and stuff around them, sort of generic boring countryside kind of scenario and already too dim to see much anyway except a glow of light beyond some trees.

Stranger says, 'There's a hotel over there. I went earlier and booked us a room.'

It's kind of exciting and scary. Like they're doing a sleepover together. And he's like this forty-five-year-old axe-murderer or whatever.

'Cool,' says the kid.

'We're going to head over there now,' guy tells him. 'I've already checked in so all you need do is let me pick up the key, then we go to the room. You don't have to say anything, got that?'

Kid nods. Suddenly it's all so real. As in instructions and so forth.

Stranger says, 'Don't talk to anybody and it'll all be fine. But as a backup, you need to know the names we're using. The story is that you're my son, understand?'

Kid nods again. Head feels loose at the neck joint.

'Good,' says the stranger. 'Your name is Felix.'

'Felix?' the kid echoes.

'Yes, Felix,' the guy echoes back. Two of them standing there in the twilight beside the river, midges swirling, kind of a tense sort of moment.

Kid says, 'Why Felix?'

'It doesn't matter.'

'Is it like a code?'

'Never mind. You're Felix and that's that. Try it. What's your name, kid?'

Comes out soft and hesitant. 'Felix?'

'Say it with more confidence. What's your name?'

'Felix.'

'Again.'

'My name is Felix,' says Felix.

'There you go,' says the stranger, 'you've grown into it.'

'And what's your name?' Felix asks him.

The guy looks down at Felix, stooping so as to bring his face closer. 'My name is Robert Coyle.'

Kid rolls it in his head like a gobstopper. Robert Coyle. And the more he rolls it, the more all the colour comes out of it. As in he knows it's a made-up name and doesn't really mean anything, because names are just like this combination of letters out of zillions of equal possibilities. But names are what you grow into, and already he's liking being called Felix, a cool name, sounds right for a runaway carrying out a dangerous mission with an alien. Robert Coyle is more like a camouflage sort of thing, kind of name you could give to anyone.

'Hello, Robert,' says Felix.

'Wrong,' Coyle says at once.

'What do you mean?'

'You never call me Robert,' says Coyle. 'You call me Dad.'

It all feels pretty natural really. As in he's got himself a new dad, and even if this guy is an axe-murderer he couldn't be much worse than Stegosaurus, who right now is holding a tin of beer in his hand and wishing he could win the lottery some day. But there's only one way you can be sure of winning the lottery and that's to cover every possible combination. Like socks – or names. For this mission, the kid is Felix Coyle and his dad is Robert. Next time they'll be different people. One life, one ticket – that's for sad losers.

'It's called the Lodge,' Coyle explains, leading his son up from the riverbank to the dark and empty road. 'Walk behind me, keep close to the hedgerow, and we'll be there in less than ten minutes.'

Kid obeys, figuring after a moment that the Lodge must be the name of the hotel, but is it real or do they put up a new sign every day? Better if they did, thinks Felix, keeping pace with the adult in front. Every day a reinvented world – he'd complete the mission and go back to find that Jodie was called, whatever, Nathalie or something. Like everybody keeps being this new person, the same but different, maybe you'd recognize them in the street but maybe not, and in an infinite universe that's the way it's got to be, the scientists proved it. There was that film, *Wizard of Oz*, Jodie said her mum was called Dorothy after it. And she gets blown away and everything goes in colour and all these really really like boring hick dead-end useless people get a life at last, even the schoolteacher that turns into a witch because she's basically quite an interesting character when you think about it. And the thing about those guys with the magnifying glass is that they showed it has to be real – the witch, the yellow-brick road, the whole damn package. They're all arrangements of atoms and letters and numbers on a lottery ticket and every story you can possibly think of is true. Felix can see the hotel now, they're walking up the driveway and it's got sort of a magic-castle look to it, he thinks, though basically that's an effect of the lighting which makes it seem mysterious and dramatic and so forth, in daylight it's probably nothing, like just somebody's big house or whatever. But right now it could be Oz, it could be the planet Gallifrey, it could be like any menu in the whole of creation.

Kid heard once that the Wizard of Oz is basically God, it was on some TV documentary he skipped through, archive footage, interview with Liza Minnelli and so forth. Only the Wizard's not God because he turns out to be this crummy shyster, guy who's the fairground magician in the other world, it's all a trick with mirrors and stuff to make him seem so powerful when actually he's nothing. Somebody on the documentary, professor with funny glasses, saying it's like Hitler or Stalin or whatever, as in this little guy with a megaphone, all these leaders are wizards or something like that, kid changed channels and watched a thing on MTV instead. So maybe the spaceman Robert Coyle's like this kind of a fake wizard, telling Felix to walk beside him and slow down, take it easy, now they're stepping into the entrance lobby of the Lodge, wood-panelled sort of a place with antlers on the wall and a guy behind the desk looks like he's a reptile. Maybe Robert Coyle's a fake and a rapist and a murderer but the reptile couldn't give a shit, he's handing over the key and Felix is being gently urged by his father towards the lift at the far end of the lobby next to the entrance to some kind of posh lounge. Maybe it's all fake – the lift doors opening, the mirrored compartment unoccupied and inviting the two of them to immerse themselves in its gleaming interior during their short ascent. Sure, it's fake and make believe and the whole of it could burst like a bubble and blow away like spit but the point is that nobody cares and that's the First Law of Life. Act like all of this is meant to be happening.

9

Joe's slippered feet were propped like clock hands on his favourite footstool while he watched the evening news over the rim of his whisky glass. 'He's looking old these days.'

'Who?' said Anne, glancing up from her book.

'That newsreader. Gone awfie grey.'

The presenter was describing the worsening situation in some place no one had ever heard of. Fraudulent elections, ethnic tensions, resurgent fundamentalism. '*Now there's concern about what the Pentagon thinks could be a nuclear-weapons programme.*'

'Here we go again,' Joe moaned.

'What's that?'

'Next in line for Uncle Sam's shooting gallery. Hope they know how to build decent air-raid shelters.'

He'd been in a foul mood since coming back empty-handed from his second pointless trip to ASDA. Anne knew he just needed to get out the house, September was always the hardest month for them both. She looked at the screen and saw a shabby street lined with flat-roofed concrete buildings; a crowded open shopfront where a swarthy-faced man, backed by shelves of glass jars, was leaning on the counter trying to hear the portable radio perched beside him. Others listening too, all male, from small boys to a toothless satchel-faced greybeard in dark robes, huddled intently.

'See his T-shirt?' said Joe, pointing at one of the younger men. 'Hard Rock Café. And a Coke bottle in his hand.' Already the shop had disappeared forever, but not the image in Joe's mind. 'That's how the Yanks do it – sell it to them first, and if that doesn't work then blow them up. They'll be doing it to us one day.'

'Bombing us?'

'Aye, the moment we stop paying the protection money. Nearly happened under Wilson and they soon sorted that, didn't they?'

'Best not get worked up about it,' Anne said gently. 'And you don't normally start on the whisky so early in the evening. What's happened to your parsley? Did you run out?'

Joe scowled at her. 'I'm reckoning I need to cut back on that. Maybe not so healthy as I thought.'

'Better than whisky, though.'

He raised and admired the well-filled glinting crystal tumbler in his hand. 'At least it's Scottish so it can't do me too much harm. If it was good enough for my faither then it's good enough for me.'

Joe's faither had died of a heart attack at the age of sixty-seven and as Joe always said, there are three reasons why Scotland has the highest heart-disease rate in the developed world: too much booze, too much work, and too much stress off the English. Anne watched him swirl and swallow the golden liquid, pitying the defiant belligerence in his voice but feeling powerless to ease it. 'Your parsley's Scottish, isn't it?' she said.

'Produce of more than one country,' Joe said darkly.

'But one of them might be Scotland,' she suggested somewhat desperately, aware that a leaf-sorting process with the aid of a magnifying glass stood about as much chance of success as the Pentagon's proposed search for uranium in this new country they were talking about on the news, thought she'd seen it mentioned once in a cookery book. Probably more of a cumin and cardamom kind of place.

'It's all genetically modified crap nowadays,' Joe said. 'It was on the radio, how parsley's got a kind of drug in it.'

'Never.'

'So that's me finished.'

'It surely won't kill you.'

'No, I mean finished with the parsley. From today I'm a rehabilitated junkie.'

'But what about your whisky? Has that not got a drug in it?'

'Aye,' Joe conceded. 'But I know where it comes from and what it's doing to my system. You go in the supermarket and buy all your food that's full of additives and God knows what, you could be putting anything in your body. You look at the kids today and think what it was like when we were young. It's the food and drink that does it, the tap water too, for all we know. Turning everyone into yobs and zombies. Them with their ASBOs or whatever they call it.'

'I think the telly's got something to do with it,' Anne said, then tried to return to *Wilhelm Meister*, which she hoped to finish before bedtime, though in this final section she'd found herself getting a bit lost. So many of the characters were turning out to be miraculously connected to ones she'd seen before, like the poor wee kiddie who'd been abused and was getting looked after by a man with no name, and now it was sounding like this man was really the father and it was his own sister who was the mother, well, it was like something off *Jerry Springer*, but old Goethe must have known what he was doing and planned it all beforehand because that was surely how any book got written. Or did he make the whole thing up as he went along? It had never really occurred to Anne before – perhaps some writers put down a sentence and then another and another and they keep going just to see where it all ends. So there's no plan. Things happen, same way they do in real life. The book was saying nothing's an accident, everything's connected, call it conspiracy or politics or the mind of God – but the book itself was an accident. There were countless others Mr Tulloch might have given Robbie to read but this was the one that came off his shelf. It had an introduction at the front, Anne hadn't thought to look at it before now but was in need of guidance.

'To the great mass of readers, who read to drive away the tedium of mental vacancy, employing the crude phantasmagoria of a modern novel, as their grandfathers employed

tobacco and diluted brandy, Wilhelm Meister *will appear beyond endurance weary, flat, stale and unprofitable.'* Not much explanation there, and hardly a good advert by the book's own translator, Thomas Carlyle, who you'd think would have been a fan. '*Few among us will disturb themselves about the allegories and typical allusions of the work; will stop to inquire whether it includes a remote emblem of human culture, or includes no such matter; whether this is a light airy sketch of the development of man in all his endowments and faculties – or is nothing more than a bungled piece of patch-work, presenting in the shape of a novel much that should have been suppressed entirely, or at least given out by way of lecture. Yet every man's judgment is, in this free country, a lamp to himself; whoever is displeased will censure; and many, it is to be feared, will insist on judging by the common rule.*' It really wasn't so bad; she'd been enjoying most of it, apart from all the stuff about *Hamlet.*

'Our generation knew hardship and suffering,' Joe said to his wife, or the screen, or himself. 'That's why we wanted to do something about it. Now it's a wee bit entertainment on a news channel, firework display in some country nobody cares about. We knew what it was to be in an air raid but it's a dying memory, that's the problem. Going to school next day,' he bleakly reminisced, 'seeing an empty desk for a kid that was killed.'

'Mmm,' Anne said from her book.

'If ever we get a socialist back in Number 10 we'll have B52s coming over the scheme faster than you can blink.'

Anne looked up. 'Do they still have B52s?'

'Of course they do.'

'I thought it was cruise missiles and stealth bombers now.'

'Comes to the same thing. They've got the whole place mapped out, Anne. GPS and all that, it's a con. Make everyone desperate to drive around with a wee bugging device the army can home in on. Did you not hear how they killed that fellow in Iraq?'

'Who was that?'

'One of the leaders. Made a call on his mobile phone and they had a missile ready and waiting to fire. Bang.'

'Sounds a better way of fighting a war than blowing up civilians.'

'Would be if they could fire their missiles straight.' He flicked through the channels and paused at an arts-review programme, a sculpture exhibition in a white-walled Glasgow gallery. 'Look at that, load of RSJs in a warehouse.'

Anne glanced at the brightly painted lumps of metal and agreed they looked like items in a children's play park. But that's art: make things up without a plan and let people figure it out for themselves. When old Goethe was Wilhelm Meistering away he didn't know how the story was going to end; it was a game, and maybe that was why Robbie liked it so much at fourteen or fifteen years of age. He was making up stories himself by then, like that nonsense about going inside the installation, his headaches getting worse though the doctors were still saying it was migraine and he'd grow out of it. And the voices: Robbie was afraid to tell his father about them, as if they were evidence of mental weakness, but Anne understood because sometimes she heard things too, ghosts or spirits or more probably the workings of imagination, though with Robbie it must have been different, a symptom of something organic. The cancer was alive in his brain sooner than anyone realized.

She stared at the arts programme, which left the playground gallery for a group of studio pundits. '*Now theatre*,' said the presenter, a woman with a posh Edinburgh accent, '*and a new production of the hit Broadway musical whose name we've got to be careful about saying correctly*.' The poster flashed on the screen showing the title in big letters: *F*U*C*K*.

'That's the absolute limit,' Joe blurted. The whisky glass was tilted before his lips and he looked unable to decide whether to tip and spill another warming sip into his mouth or send it flying in the direction of the screen.

The presenter spelled it out. '*F.U.C.K. stars Kieran Holloway and Stacey Rowlands in the story of a group of women call-centre workers who lose their jobs and decide to start a nude housework agency, making a strict rule that anyone offering clients more than dusting and ironing will be instantly sacked, as the title says, "for unlicensed carnal knowledge"* . . .'

'Can you believe that?' said Joe. 'A musical called fuck.'

'I've heard of it,' said Anne.

'Heard of it?' Joe boomed with volcanic indignation. 'Of course you've heard of it, you hear it every time you walk past any kid in the street.'

'No,' said Anne, closing the book she would have to finish later. 'I mean the musical.'

'It's disgusting, calling it a name like that.'

'Only a word,' said Anne. 'They had *The Vagina Monologues*.'

'Bloody nonsense.'

'And there's FCUK.'

'Another disgrace.'

Anne smiled. 'We've been eating coq au vin for years and it hasn't killed us.'

Joe couldn't see the funny side of it. He turned up the volume to hear what the panel thought of it, the first speaker being a dour man with thick-framed glasses and no hair who said he thought the anodyne songs in *F*U*C*K* were exactly the kind of thing American special forces could use as a torture method on detainees.

'There, you see,' said Joe. 'Says it's like Anaddin.'

Beside him sat a middle-aged woman with a ring through her nose. '*I loved it!*'

'Might have guessed,' Joe moaned.

'*It's Aristophanes meets* The Full Monty *with a score worthy of Sondheim.*'

'God help us.'

'I'd like to see it,' said Anne.

Joe's eyebrows nearly shot off the top of his overheated head. 'What! How can you be interested in that trash?'

'But it's a comedy,' said Anne. 'And the title's not a swear word, it's initials.'

'So that's all right, is it?' Joe took a hefty swig to calm himself.

'It's like *M*A*S*H.*'

'Mash is something you have for your dinner, not an obscenity.'

The reviewer on television was still enthusing, and just getting into her stride. '*It's a genuinely subversive vision of female empowerment.*'

'Let's see what else is on,' said Joe, aiming the remote.

'No, wait,' said Anne. 'Why don't we try and get tickets?'

'Are you kidding? I'm not going to see that rubbish.' He finished his whisky and stood up, swaying momentarily.

Anne watched the familiar pantomime of indecision. 'Are you F.U.C.K-ing off up to the loo, then?'

'Eh?' He hadn't quite heard her.

'Nothing.'

Joe stretched and flexed. 'I'll maybe go out for some air.'

She looked at him sympathetically. 'Try and relax. Fifty trips to ASDA aren't going to help anything, especially when you come back empty-handed every time.'

'I'm not going there, Anne . . .' He looked like he didn't know where he was going. He needed some kind of escape, that was all.

'Sit down, Joe. It's always like this every year and we get through, don't we? It's another day, that's all.'

'What, like it's only a word? Only initials?'

'That's right. One more year and we're still here, you and me.'

'And Robbie isn't.'

'I know that,' Anne said quietly. 'But Wednesday'll pass and that'll be another anniversary over with. Why don't we go and see a musical for a change?'

'No way,' said Joe. 'I'm not wasting money on American drivel like that.' He was still standing with his empty glass in one hand and the remote control in the other. He tossed the remote on the chair where he'd been sitting and went to the kitchen to put the glass beside the sink while Anne gazed at the closed book on her lap and thought of all the years that had come and gone like this. A moment later she heard the clunk of the front door as he went out.

10

They've reached their room for the night, Felix and his dad who unlocks the door and switches on the light, ordinary-looking hotel room, Felix follows him inside and sees two single beds, one of them crumpled like it's been laid on earlier, guy's trolley case at the foot of it, small black one standing upright with the handle extended. Guy must like to travel light. He closes the door.

'That's your bed,' he tells the kid, pointing to the one still untouched.

'But it's not time to sleep yet.'

'I know,' he says. 'I'm only explaining.'

'You don't have to.'

Tense sort of a moment, like you get in small spaces, especially when involving adult–kid interaction. They're meant to be father and son so might as well act like it. Kid sits on the end of his appointed bed and surveys the room, mid-price, kind this guy can easily afford with his magic card that buys anything. Remote control stuck on the side of the big black television set, sort of a plastic slot it fits into, remote holder, stops you losing it though not as practical as it looks because the whole point about a remote is that it isn't on the set. As in, it's remote, duh. Kid goes over and takes it from the holster while the guy kicks off his shoes and lies down. Kid returns to where he was sitting on the bed, presses the button and the television comes on, blue information screen about the channels available to guests as in which ones are the sex movies you need to pay for, Stegosaurus would like that, the kid's real dad, or is he? Says he's real but you never know, anything's possible. Top of the screen says *Welcome, Robert Coyle*. Like that's the name he used when he checked in and it's on the hotel computer, it's in their files, it's coming through wires from the front desk where the reptile sits and it's there on the television like it's actually true now. You see it on television, it's real. Kid stares for a moment at the information screen and there's like this really really poor music playing like in a lift or something only they didn't even have it in the lift. Violins and stuff. Kid starts going through the channels, guy lies with his eyes closed and doesn't care.

'I'm hungry,' says Felix, flicking the select button repeatedly. Old films, drama series, kind of crap his parents watch.

'I'll phone down and order us something,' guy says from his horizontal eyes-closed as in not asleep but sort of pretending to be kind of position.

'Isn't there a restaurant here or something?' Some art-review show on the screen, man with stupid glasses, people in a gallery.

'I don't want to go to the restaurant,' the guy says. 'It might compromise the mission. We need to stay here until morning.'

Kid thinks, I ran away for this and it's worse than an evening with Stegosaurus. Says, 'If I have to watch this crap all night I'll go mad.'

'Then don't watch it.'

'What else is there to do?'

Guy sits up. For a moment it's like the dreaded why don't we play Monopoly situation as in sort of thing Stegosaurus says whenever he remembers he's supposed to be somebody's father which is like when he runs out of beer or the adverts come on, but the crisis passes. 'What do you want to eat?'

'What is there?'

This kills some time. As in they look through sort of a big book full of leaflets and information and stuff that tells you what to do if you need a shirt ironing or a taxi or you're sick. There's a room-service menu and the kid opts for the double cheeseburger with fries but minus the salad because he doesn't like anything green that looks too much as if it was once alive. Guy phones down and orders, including a club sandwich for himself. Kid doesn't exactly know what a club sandwich is, but it doesn't sound like food for a spaceman on a mission. Not a real mission, anyway. More like a James Bond nineteen-seventies re-run kind of mission. There's kind of this post putting down the phone silence sort of moment and then the kid says to the guy, 'Are you really a spaceman?'

Guy looks at him. 'Yes.'

Straight question, straight answer. Like his name's on the information screen on the television so that's fine. Except it's not his name.

Kid says, 'Are you going to tell me about the mission now?'

'No.'

'But I thought . . .'

'Then don't think,' says the guy, lying down again to rest. 'You've passed every test so far, you're doing well.'

Kid wonders how many tests there's been. The card, coming here – what else? Is everything a test?

'There's a lot that's wrong with this world,' guy says. Well, duh. He raises his head, props himself by his elbow as he lies on his side and goes, 'The thing you have to understand, Felix, is that everything is connected. All the little pieces, all the things that on their own don't make any sense. When you put them together you see the whole picture.'

'Then why not give me the whole picture?'

'I can't.'

'Why?'

'Because if I did then the plan wouldn't work.'

As in, the only point of the kid being involved is that he doesn't get it. Well thank you, Mr Spaceman. Kid says, 'I could walk out of here.'

'Of course you could.'

'I could go to the police.'

'I know,' the guy says calmly. 'And you'd have nothing to tell them except that you stole something from a shop.'

'I could say you're a paedophile and you abducted me.'

'But that wouldn't be true.'

'Then what is?' says the kid. 'What exactly is true?'

Guy shrugs like he doesn't know. Or like he doesn't want the kid to know. 'The truth is that everything is connected.'

The kid's annoyed. Only reason he's here is because of that thing with the cashpoint card. Wants to know how it works and if he can have one too. Get one of those cards, you're set up for life. Never have to work, never have to worry.

Guy says, 'You've handled yourself perfectly. When we came here, in the lobby, that was most impressive.'

The kid feels proud. It's not often that people say he's done well. 'I've got a rule,' he explains. 'It helps me get through situations. I call it the First Law of Life.'

Guy raises an eyebrow. 'Tell me.'

So the kid does. 'Whatever happens, always act like it's meant to.'

Guy smiles. 'I like that. But you know, there's a Zeroth Law of Life.'

'Which is?'

'Whatever happens, it's meant to.' Then the guy lies down again and closes his eyes. So it's all a test and it's all meant to be a test and everything is connected. That's just about the sum total of what the kid has learned since running away and teaming up with this con man and it's worth damn all if you don't count the £500 wad which is the only good part. So why can't they move on to the Second Law of Life? Why go back to zero? Next lesson he gets, it'll be the Minus First Law and there's no knowing where it'll stop.

Kid stares at the suitcase at the foot of the guy's bed and eventually says to him, 'Have you got a gun in there?'

Guy opens his eyes. 'No.'

'Lots of spare socks?'

'None of your business.'

Kid keeps staring at the suitcase. As in, what's the point of it? Guy's got a card buys him anything he wants. Change of clothes – get yourself another £500 and buy it. Things get dirty, throw them away. What a perfect way to live, every day you buy a new life with your magic card. Kid thinks: that's my idea of heaven.

Guy says, 'Why not read something?', and now it really is like being with Stegosaurus who's got this thing that kids watch too much television nowadays and they should be reading books or going out on their bike though when did Steg ever do either of those?

'There's nothing to read.'

'Newspaper?'

Guy's pointing at something on the desk-type table thing over at the wall, a folded newspaper, and if it was Steg asking then the kid would tell him where to go but this has to be another test and if a man's got a card that works in any cashpoint in the universe then he's a man worth sticking with. The only kind of money that means anything is infinite money. So the kid mutes the TV and goes over to the table thing, maybe you'd call it a writing desk, headed notepaper neatly placed on it. *The Lodge*. And a white ballpoint pen with blue letters printed on the side, same fancy font. *The Lodge*. Like it's this really amazing brand. But only kind of hotel that means anything is an infinite hotel, and this hotel sure as hell isn't infinite. As in it's only got about twenty rooms or something. Kid saw a thing on BBC Four (don't ask why) about this infinite hotel invented by a man called Hilbert. You show up and they say sorry we're full. And you say no problem, why don't you ask all the guests to change room, then I'll be able to fit in. There's some way it works, kid can't remember now, but those scientists proved it's real. Kid lifts the ballpoint, clicks it a couple of times, figures it's crap and puts it in his pocket. Lifts the newspaper too, it's the local rag he never reads, his mum gets it, pictures of school football teams and sad losers doing sponsored walks. Left here so that guests can read the listings as in there aren't any, it's like here you are, suckers, you chose to stay in this crummy place, now see for yourself that there isn't a cinema or a restaurant or a club worth going to. This town is so full of nothing. This is like a totally finite town.

Kid opens the paper, looks at the pictures, doesn't see anyone he recognizes. As in this is his tiny little finite town and he doesn't know anybody in it and they don't know him. Which is good because it means he can walk up to any cashpoint and draw an infinite amount of money. Photograph of an old lady standing outside the town library, kid never goes there, it's for old people and random wasters who can't afford a computer. Old lady's been working there for a hundred and fifty years or something and now she's retiring well big deal. And on the opposite page, bald man in a suit, David Luss, education spokesman, visiting schools in the area, used to teach in one, like so what? Does he want a medal or something?

Kid turns the page and sees the notices. Births, deaths, marriages. Which is basically it, as in life. Three things, and they can't even put them in the right order. Though once you're over twenty-one you might as well be dead, kid thinks, as in everybody who ever did anything interesting did it when they were young. Maybe call it thirty at the outside, got to allow for late developers.

There's a section called In Memoriam and the kid knows what that means. As in somebody still remembers you.

He'll be there one day and it'll be the whole infinite universe that remembers him, they'll all have been to his funeral, music's going to be something by Nelly Furtado but he can't decide which. Nelly will be there in person, crying her eyes out, and it'll be most impressive.

Robert Coyle: forever in our hearts.

Kid reads it and freezes.

11

Joe didn't know where he wanted to walk but he needed to feel one foot going in front of the other, that was all. Easier for Anne since she was a woman, used to being in the house, but Joe was born to work, even if he'd been on the scrapheap since he was forty-five year of age. His son and then his job, both gone within the space of a year, and no hope of seeing either of them again.

Young kids loafing outside the chippie Joe passed, found himself momentarily bathed in light and warmth and the rich reek of vinegar and thought about getting himself a poke of chips and a pickled onion but kept walking, and behind his back, he could see it out the corner of his eye, they kids were staring at him like he was a joke.

Maybe it's a war they're needing, thought Joe. Not the computer-game kind they show on the news but the real sort, falls on your head and deafens you. Glasgow got hammert by the Jerries, so it did, though people only ever go on about the London Blitz, cheerful cockneys, pearly kings playing spoons. Anybody says Gorbals, it's all flick-knives and razor gangs and you'd think it was the ordinary folk there who were the enemy, which in a manner of speaking they were, mind, because before Churchill was ever fighting Nazis he was putting tanks in Glasgow to stop a revolution. Working class in those days meant nearly everybody, thought Joe, now all the work goes on in sweatshops some place other side of the world, might as well call it Gorbalistan, making the trainers and stereos for these kids hanging round the chippie in their FCUKs.

Taking his customary route through the town, he was soon looking down from the bridge to the river, eerie in the nocturnal lamplight but safe enough this end, stretch where people walk their dogs and the main risk is getting shit on your shoe. Joe descended the steps and surveyed the empty bank; a bat zipped and twirled like an overgrown moth. Kenzie never felt the Hun's wrath, wee mining town like hundreds of others throughout Scotland, but Glasgow and the Clyde, they suffered. And now we're all meant to shake hands and be pals in the United States of Europe.

Going to school, seeing another vacant desk; somebody's child, gone just like that, killed by German millionaire arms manufacturers, same as Robbie was killed by Uncle Sam, never mind what all they experts maintained with their fancy names for bad luck. Cancer happens, they said, but nothing happens without a reason. A bomb goes off, there's somebody made and planted it, even the kind explodes in a person's mind. No, Joe survived one war only for his son to die in another, and he could remember what it felt like, looking up and seeing that Jerry plane with big black crosses on its wings, six year old, peeing himself with fear, thought his mum must be inside the shelter after they got split in the rush. She'd left him behind and the Jerry was going to drop a bomb on him and he was going to die.

He felt a spatter of rain from the overcast sky but it quickly passed and the path remained dry beneath his feet. Before long he was at the old memorial with its bench half burned by vandals, the standard obscenity spray-painted on the side of the sandstone pillar like a casual afterthought. Evil wee bastards, thought Joe, but what else can you expect when they're getting bombarded day and night by the same foul message? His maw almost mental when she found him and got him inside, tears on both their faces. She simmered down and wiped her eyes and felt his pants that were all wet, nothing they could do about it in an air-raid shelter full of people, all as feart as he was, Joe knew now. That smell of piss you got in the shelters, he never understood as a child what it really meant.

First thing Joe thought when they planes hit the Twin Towers: now they know what it's like. Awfie sad, of course, terrible tragedy for all they innocent people, lives destroyed. But now they know. Six year old, looking up in the smoke-filled sky over Glasgow, seeing black crosses on a Heinkel's wing and thinking where's my maw? Now they know. Because when did America ever suffer an air raid? Only once if you count Pearl Harbor but by God did they make a fuss about it! The day that changed the world, a turning point in history, on and on and on and on about it, weeping and wailing like they were the only people on Earth ever got bombed. Of course it's sad but do they think it's so unusual? Just because it's right there on their doorstep, live on their television stations that are normally full of pop music and adverts and crap, a bit of reality for a change.

Second thing Joe thought: serves them damn well right. They treat the world like it's their bloody aircraft carrier, coming and putting their nuclear poison here, and the least slap they get they're greetin like there's no tomorrow. All they marbles Robbie waded in, Joe would have liked to drop them out an aeroplane on New York. Here you go, Yanks, have them back, we don't want them in our neck of the woods anymore. A hundred thousand wee glass globes falling out the sky like nuclear rain, every one of them a dead child. One dead child, Joe's own. One extra cancer victim, a statistic nobody wanted to count.

And how they damn well bleat about it. There was this fat American woman they interviewed on the telly, ordinary housewife in sunglasses loading her car at the supermarket and she was saying to the reporter, why do they hate us so much? Why are they jealous of what we've got? It was like she just couldn't figure it out, couldn't add two and two the gither in her fat skull and Joe damn near choked on his single malt as he shouted at the screen, remember Marie Antoinette you daft cow, let them eat cake.

He could still smell that shelter him and his maw were in while the sirens wailed. Sweat, piss and fear. And the dull thuds of bombs exploding, each a shudder that ran through the grown-ups wondering if it was their tenement had got hit. An old woman who kept saying the bombs were getting further away, said it every time one went off though they weren't. And his mother holding him in her arms, singing softly. She loved music, had a big harmonium in the house, used to fascinate him, though how did she ever acquire such a thing or learn to play it? All sorts of tunes; music-hall songs, folk ballads. Joe could hear one in his head right now, like a sea shanty whose reedy chords put the rhythm back in his step as he reached the end of the lamplit section of the riverside path and walked into the darkness, following exactly the same route he'd taken in daylight and had trodden a thousand times before that, a score he couldn't get out of his system. A sad song, it was, because anything you play on a harmonium sounds sad but also holy and uplifting, if only he could remember the words. His mother was sitting at the big black thing, pumping the bellows with her feet, the room dark with only a single lamp glowing beside her, throwing long shadows, and her hair tied up in a bun.

It was a sound in his head, but why should it have come back to him now? Joe didn't know and didn't need to think too much about it; instead he savoured the memory of his mother at the harmonium, such a sombre great thing like you'd find in a funeral parlour, but a lively tune she played for all its sadness, strange how you can have both at once. Not like your pop songs nowadays with their boom-boom-boom and only one topic, no, Joe couldn't imagine people of eighty year old, one day humming to their selves in a care home about get on down shake your ass baby. But your folk songs, they're the music of the ordinary working people, which is why nobody's interested anymore. Be a pop star, then you need never work again. A verse came to him:

> 'I wish the wind may never cease
> Nor fashes in the flood,
> Till my ane son comes hame to me
> In earthly flesh and blood.'

He remembered it now, song about a woman who's lost her son. Yes, that was why it had come back without him even noticing. Must have been swirling in his head while he watched the telly with Anne, swirling like the whisky in his glass; and like the alcohol, it had tilted his mind, stirring memories of his mother, the air raid, all the junk of his old and tired imagination, but at the centre of it was the frozen void where his child had been. It jolted him, this simple realization of the meaning of his own automatic actions, just as he was jolted but not surprised to find he'd already reached the stretch of bank running near the site of the old installation, where he'd met the missionary earlier. Another half-mile and he'd cross the bridge and take the circular route home, same as he'd been doing for years, even when the weans were wee and Janet would be complaining about the distance. Should've brought a torch with him, not the safest place for a night-time stroll, but it was the song in his head led him on.

It fell about the Martinmas
  When nights are lang and mirk
The wife's ane son cam hame to her,
  His hat was o' the birk.

'Cold blows the wind, my mother dear,
  O let me bide this night,
For I hae been beneath the ground
  Where shines no living light.'

'Are you an angel, son?' she said,
  'All clothed in birk sae dark?
Take off your mantle of cold clay
  And helmet o' the bark.'

'So let me be,' he said to her,
'Take not my garment firm.
My house lies neath the muckle wood
Where chides the chann'rin worm.

'A twelvemonth lang it gnawed my banes,
A twelvemonth and a day,
Now he is fat and I maun mak
The last step o' my way.'

The wheezy harmonium in the corner like the sound of angels and his mother working it with the same steady patience that made her push the steam iron over piles of white linen or turn the handle of the sewing machine. Life is work and when the work runs out you're finished so the fact of the matter was that Joe Coyle died long ago, he knew it. All those years he served as apprentice, journeyman, master of his tools, father of two children, gone and counted for nothing. Janet in a commune or a squat or God knows where, even changed her name, and Robbie gone to ashes and dust, his last months a torture as his mind went, talking to himself as if it was people in the room there with him. He'd always been one to make up stories in his head, thinking he was an astronaut or whatever, Anne reckoned those tales of his about going inside the installation were the same kind of harmless make-believe, but Robbie's illness, that cancer that got put in his skull, it was a black hole that sucked him right inside. It fed off his healthy young brain, ate it up, swelled to engulf him. In the end he couldn't hold a spoon or keep his head up to drink a bit of soup, howling with terror at nothing, fallen over the edge and there was no bringing him back. Joe holding his son's hand, seeing his boy's face like yellow wax and telling anybody that'd listen it was the installation was the cause, but nobody listened. His son's last word, a girl they never traced, a name that meant nothing. Dora.

Where we finally belong is the place a flame goes to when it's snuffed, a song when it's finished; the immaterial past. And if he could wind everything backwards, Joe thought, then he would, growing younger in his grief and stronger in his anger, to the day they turned Robbie into smoke and nothing, and further still, through the years till their son was a wee boy again, hiding his self in the cupboard under the sink, saying it was his spaceship. Back until he was conceived one night the pair of them never noticed, dissolved into a parting egg and sperm, unmade by life as surely as by death since both's the same in opposite order. Unliving but unmourned, and Joe pushing further through the years like a falling stone becoming swifter and more vigorous with each retreating second. Yes, he'd do it if he could. Robbie, Janet, Anne, his years at the plant, his whole life – take it and leave me only the sweet innocent start.

Still he could hear the harmonium as he walked, its music the anthem of that great leveller, the democratic socialist republic of death. Faither didn't like music, didn't like noise, so whatever memories Joe had of his mother's playing came from those moments when it was only the two of them; abundant moments. Then one day faither found a tiny hole in the instrument's side and declared it to be infested with woodworm. A single puncture, no more; Joe saw it at the end of his sorrowful mother's fingernail, the tiny black hole that threatened to spread and dissolve their entire house. So faither heaved the harmonium downstairs and through the close to the back midden where the dustbins stood and he took an axe and chopped it all to pieces with his strong bare arms, smashed and crunched that old harmonium whose split wood was pale and innocent beneath the dark paint, the dying instrument giving out a last plaintive chord, Joe remembered, before its keyboard scattered like loosened teeth beneath the fatal blow. It must have broken his mother's heart but she said nothing at all about it, and soon it was as if there'd never been a harmonium in the house. That's how we live with loss.

Something over there, other side of the river. A figure moving, Joe reckoned. Couldn't see the form, only changing shapes of darkness against the trees. Druggie hunting for a place to shoot up, couple fancying a spot of bum-freezing open-air sex. Mugger. The possibilities clicked in Joe's head like the chambers of a revolver and he felt fear, the thing he'd spent a lifetime trying not to show and most times managed. He stopped and stared across the river and thought of turning and going back because if there were hoodlums on that side they could have friends on this. But there was no movement now, and Joe satisfied his self with the tune in his head.

She's made to him a feather bed,
 She's made it large and wide,
Then laid her grey cape over him
 And sat down by his side.

Till up there crew the blood-red cock,
 And up and crew the white,

The sun crept o'er the hill o' stanes
And banished all the night.

'When sall I see you son again,
In pleasure or in toil?'
'When grow again the fallen leaves
That lie upon the soil.'

'Then fare ye well my bairn sae mild,
Fare well my ane pure heart,
Till we bide at the far green place
Where nane sall mak us part.'

He saw it now, a figure on the opposite bank, pale and motionless, almost as if hovering. He saw and understood.

'Robbie!'

The sound came out of him like air from a submerged jar, a name he called again.

'Robbie!'

For it was his son standing on the other side of the river, Joe was blindingly certain of it, and the fear drained from him, replaced by a giddy lightness. His own son, though why did he not wave back or call in response? Joe felt a tightness in his chest, he was almost panting with joy and astonishment, half expecting the apparition at any moment to resolve itself in his adjusting gaze to a misinterpreted fence-post or concrete slab. But no, it was a waiting human figure, and it was Robbie.

'I'm coming, son!'

Only one way to reach and save him, the water low enough even for an old man to walk across. Never mind the madness of it, Joe was seized by the power of love and hope, acting on instinct, following his feet into the cold flow that rose to soak his shins, his knees, the hidden stones making him stumble several times, but on each occasion when he looked up he saw his son still standing there, growing larger and more certain, his own son come back to him, as impossible as it was true.

12

Kid's like staring at the local newspaper and says to the guy still lying with his eyes closed on the bed, 'You're in here, Dad.' But before he can answer there's a knock on the door and it's their food brought on a tray by someone dressed as a waiter. As in, he's a waiter. Way the kid looks at it, if you're dressed as a waiter and you're carrying a cheeseburger with no salad and a club sandwich on a tray and you're saying 'room service' like it's a lovely sunny morning and you just woke up and feel glad to be alive when really it's late and you're beat and want to go home, well, in that case you're a one hundred per cent genuine waiter. Expecting a tip.

'Thanks,' says Robert Coyle, as in the one sitting up on the bed reaching into his pocket for change, not the one whose death notice is in the newspaper the kid folds and returns to the desk-table thing where it lives. Robert Coyle stretches a coin-loaded fist that the waiter's drawn to like a fish to a worm, taking the money with exaggerated gratitude then retreating through the door so the guests can eat the meal he's delivered. Kid thinks it looks like shit. Wishes they'd gone to Burger King.

'Get yourself a drink from the minibar,' guy says to him, nodding towards the cupboard under the television where the kid finds a fridge and gets himself a Coke. 'And bring me some mineral water.'

Then the two of them sit on their respective beds basically eating. Almost a family-type moment, as in neither of them saying much, until the kid decides he'd better mention the newspaper again because it's like the guy doesn't care that his name's in it. 'Robert Coyle, died aged nineteen,' he reads.

'It's not me.'

'But it's the same name. And look, it's next week.'

'No, it's not,' says the guy. 'It's the same date, but twenty-five years ago.'

'You know what I mean,' the kid protests, stuffing in another mouthful of unexpectedly satisfying carbohydrate. 'It's like totally freaky. Are you a ghost?'

Guy pauses momentarily over his club sandwich. 'What do you think?'

Kid doesn't know what he thinks. You dress and act like a waiter, that makes you a waiter, especially if you get tipped for it, but the kid doesn't know what a ghost ought to dress like or how it behaves. Not floating around with a white sheet over its head, that's for sure. 'You told me you were a spaceman.'

'So to speak.'

'And you've got like this magic card. Even if you aren't a pervert you're pretty damn weird.'

Guy munches and swallows and looks totally real, as in not a ghost, because ghosts you can see through, they're like this ectoplasmic thing. Says, 'What's the worst thing a person can do?'

Comes out of nowhere but the kid's used to weirdness from this guy. 'I don't know, kill somebody I suppose.'

'What if you're a soldier?'

'Then it's different.'

'And what makes you a soldier?'

It's got damn all to do with the newspaper and being a ghost and so forth and the kid realizes it's misdirection, like the way he stretched an empty hand in WH Smith to hide his stealing. 'If you're a soldier you've got like a uniform and an army.'

'What if there's no uniform?'

'There's still an army. That makes you a soldier.'

'And what if you're the last man left?'

Now he gets it. This guy, as in the Doctor, is the last of the Time Lords because the rest of his race were wiped out in the Time War and he's like this sole survivor. But that's shit because it still doesn't explain how he died twenty-five years ago but is able to eat a club sandwich. And when would Doctor Who ever eat a fucking club sandwich? Kid says, 'Even if you're the last man left and you've got no uniform you could still be a soldier.'

'So it would be all right to kill?'

'Depends who.'

'The enemy.'

'Sure, that's OK.' It's like, either Robert Coyle is the dumbest shit-brain in the galaxy or else he's playing some kind of game. And anyway, he isn't the same Robert Coyle, it's only a name. Like, if the kid called himself Jesus Christ it wouldn't mean he was the one in the Bible. Kid says, 'You stole the name, didn't you? You read it in the paper when you were here earlier.'

Guy nods pensively, like it's basically plausible, but then says, 'You're forgetting something.'

'What?'

'I used the name when I first checked in, before I got the room and had any chance of seeing the paper.' OK, so he's not quite the dumbest shit-brain. Guy says, 'Ever heard of identity theft?'

'Sure.'

'Well, it works best if you steal from someone who isn't in a position to complain.'

Now the kid gets it. Except that he doesn't. 'Dead people don't have bank accounts.'

'I'm not interested in anybody's bank account,' the guy says. 'I've got a card that gives me all the money I want. Only thing I needed was a name.'

Again the kid gets it. And again he doesn't. It's sort of like eating a cheeseburger and fries without the salad. Chew, swallow, digest, then wonder why. 'You could have made up any name,' he says. 'You didn't need to steal one.'

'But then I couldn't have gone to the registrar for a copy of my birth certificate,' the guy explains. 'Couldn't have got myself a national insurance number. And a passport.'

Kid gives a burp. 'I thought they've got like computer checks and stuff.'

'They have. They want to stop illegal immigrants. But I'm an ordinary British white man who's in a hurry and tells the nice young girl at the desk that he needs a copy of his birth certificate for a job application. And she believes me.'

Kid's eyes wander to the foot of the guy's bed and the dark trolley case standing there with its handle erect. 'Is that the honest truth?'

'Maybe.'

It's like the kid can believe whatever he wants to believe: this guy is a ghost or he's a fraudster. And it's like basically the kid doesn't care, as in it doesn't matter to him one way or the other because there are two options in the menu and the kid's got the remote. It's like what difference does it make? Truth is whatever we choose. Kid says, 'What's with the question about killing people? Was that a test?'

'Everything is a test, Felix.'

'And are you some kind of soldier? Is that it?' It'd be another option in the menu, and three's cooler than two.

Guy says, 'You think killing someone is the worst thing a person can do?'

'Sure, if it's not like a war situation, self-defence and so forth.'

Guy nods like he agrees. Says, 'Suppose you were in a world full of evil people. Or rather, a world where the system has made people evil. You get hold of a weapon, purely by chance. You could use it to kill evil people and start a revolution.'

'Go ahead, do it.'

'But then you're a terrorist.'

'No, you're a soldier.'

'All right,' says Robert Coyle. 'Let's say we go in my

time machine and we find Hitler when he was a baby. Would you pull the trigger on him?'

It's like one of those brainteasers they get in PSHE but the guy looks serious, like he's really got a time machine. Options: ghost, fraudster, soldier, Time Lord. 'Sure,' says the kid.

'You'd murder a baby?'

'It'd be for the best.'

Guy says, 'What if we go back further to make sure? Would you shoot Hitler's parents when they were babies?'

This is like so not relevant. 'Sure I'd shoot them, they're dead now anyway and it's not like it would make any difference.'

'And if I told you there's a child who has to die tomorrow to save the future of this planet, would you kill that child?'

The kid feels a shiver again, as in this is starting to feel uncomfortable. Change the channel. Kid asks quietly, 'What's the next step of the mission?'

Guy chews a moment, draws a swig of mineral water from the bottle, swallows and arrives at some kind of decision. 'We're going to the airport tomorrow morning. Plane to catch.'

Kid's stomach tightens. As in this is serious. Ghost, fraudster or whatever the heck he is, going on a plane with him is like running away big time, and it's like all at once the kid's looking for an excuse. 'I haven't got a passport.'

'You don't need one.'

'It's a domestic flight?'

'You won't be getting on the plane.'

'But where are you going?'

'Home,' says the guy. 'When the plane reaches the right altitude, I'm going home.'

It sounds weird. Kid stares at the black trolley case and all he can think is that this is even freakier than if the guy was a paedo. Guy starts waving his dick around, he could understand that, but all this altitude crap, he's lost. 'Why do I need to come with you to the airport?'

'When we get there you only have to do what I tell you. It won't be difficult.'

'You mean this is another test?'

Guy nods. 'This is the biggest test of all, Felix. A test of faith.'

'And if I pass?'

Guy thinks about it, shrugs. 'Then we'll see.' He can see the dissatisfaction on the kid's face. 'I'm not being secretive for the sake of it. These are complicated issues.'

'Oh, sure, too complicated for a kid.'

'No, Felix. Too complicated for an adult. Even I don't really understand it. But we live in a sick world . . .'

'Too right.'

'And the world needs to heal itself.'

Kid doesn't feel like listening to some grown-up sermon-type crap like he hears every week in school assembly when the head goes on and on about how we're all one big family, got to work together, blah blah blah. Instead, while Robert Coyle keeps talking to him, the kid tunes out and thinks about the other Robert Coyle, the real one who died at nineteen, which is sort of old but not old from a dying point of view, in fact it's impressively young. Probably crashed or OD-ed but maybe he got sick, it happens, kind of sad and embarrassing, those people you see in the news with their wheelchairs and bald heads and tubes up their noses, brave kid and so forth, not a rock-star way to go but just as likely when you think about it. And if the world's sick then maybe it's sad and embarrassing too, like all the other planets would prefer it if ours just got out of the way and died instead of looking ill and bringing everybody down. Brave little Earth, battling against the odds. Earth takes part in charity half-marathon. Earth gets award for courage. Earth loses fight. Rest in peace.

'So you see, Felix, everything is connected.'

Kid has no idea what Robert Coyle has been talking about but thinks he gets the drift. The right altitude is when the spaceman goes back to his galaxy far, far away. That's his mission.

'But now we need to get some sleep, Felix, we've got an early start tomorrow. Taxi's picking us up at five.' The guy stands up from the bed, puts his empty plate and water bottle on the coffee table, starts undressing. Like, this is it. Kid thinks, any moment now he'll be waving his dick at me.

Kid sweeps his last chip through a smear of ketchup, finishes his Coke and goes to the bathroom. Light makes a horrible humming noise or perhaps it's the extractor, sound matches the harsh white glare of the room. Maybe the kid should sleep here with the door locked. Maybe he should run away. As in, run away from running away, which would make him sort of a runaway squared. Has his real father even noticed? Has Stegosaurus phoned Spud's parents to check his son is sleeping over? Probability zero.

Kid takes a long leak, washes his hands and face, finds a tiny tube of complimentary toothpaste in a basket but no brush, so fingers his gums clean, stares at himself in the mirror. Everything you can possibly imagine is real somewhere. Like Stegosaurus phoning to check, it really happens. Probability non-zero, though pretty damn small. Wearing every sequence of sock. Kid hasn't got a change of anything – he'll be wearing the same clothes tomorrow with a probability of one, if the guy doesn't kill him tonight. And no pyjamas, like it's part of the plan. Naked boy found dead in hotel room with con man. That is so totally sad and embarrassing. That is so not going to happen in this universe.

Kid switches off the light and comes out of the bathroom and the guy's lying on his bed but under the cover now, on his back like a corpse, eyes closed. Looks like he's asleep. Left the kid's bedside lamp on out of consideration but switched off the rest, kind of a fatherly touch, so the room looks cosier now, softly illuminated by the single shaded bulb. And the guy's naked, at least his arms and shoulders are, so he didn't even take a set of pyjamas or a washbag out of his black trolley case that stands guard at the foot of his bed. Guy hasn't touched it. Padlock's still fastened, kid can see it from where he stands. As in he'll never know, and that's just how it has to be. You stay here, he's a fraudster. You leave now, he's a ghost. Let the ghost go home.

So the kid quietly, very quietly, lifts his light-blue jacket from the bed where he tossed it when he arrived. The neodymium magnets rattle in the inside pocket; kid thinks for a moment he's going to be rumbled. But the guy only gives a heavy breath that's almost a snore, he's truly asleep. Then the kid carefully folds his jacket over his arm, walks to the door, and a moment later he's free.

He's in the empty corridor, walks swiftly to the staircase

and goes down to the lobby but the reptile's at the desk and the kid hesitates, doesn't want to attract attention, what if reptile stops the kid and phones upstairs to check? Only a moment's hesitation but it's long enough to make the kid turn on his heels in strict accordance with the First Law of Life, like he's meant to be here in the lobby, on his way to that room he noticed earlier, posh place with its name in gold letters on a wooden plate on the open door, Maxwell Room, lots of people there, mostly women chatting among themselves, nobody turns a head when he slips inside and stations himself in a corner where he stands carefully examining a painting on the wall. Everyone thinks he's somebody else's kid. All of this is meant to happen.

'Ah, here they come.' Heads turn towards the doorway where a couple are entering, a bald old man with piggy eyes in a dark blue suit and a woman on his arm, she's like in her forties but he could almost be her father, smiling at everyone with the look of a politician. Kid twigs, it's the one he saw in the newspaper, David Luss with his wife or assistant or mistress or whatever, and the door being closed behind them, kid's got himself trapped in some kind of meeting and nobody notices or cares. The pair settle on a sofa and the woman does the introductions. 'David, as you know, has long links with this town, because he used to teach here. In fact he even used to teach me.' Blush of pride and chuckle of embarrassment, kid sees Luss's eyebrows rise on his empty forehead, a different kind of embarrassment. 'David plays a key role in shaping education policy, and that's what this informal get-together is about.' Kid wants to make a run for it, but now she's inviting someone else to speak, another middle-aged woman like one of the hags his mother goes shopping with, they all look the same with their lines and baggy faces and hairdos. This one's called Rosalind and might have been good-looking once.

'Thank you all,' says Rosalind, with a voice that's almost a purr. 'And thank you, Miriam, for inviting me here. Since many of you don't know me, I should explain that I first got to know Miriam at a holistic community where I ran a healing centre. I'm interested in meditation as a means of therapy and personal development, and I want to explain why I think meditation should be taught in schools.'

Then she goes into this long speech like you get at assembly, kind that sends the kid straight to sleep but he knows how to look awake and in any case everyone thinks he's only here because his mother couldn't get a babysitter. So the First Law is working really well and this Rosalind woman is going on about body and spirit and the word she keeps coming back to, holistic, like it's all to do with holes. Then she stops and somebody asks whether meditation should be taught in physical education or religious instruction. And Rosalind's like, do it everywhere. English lessons, maths. Get them all meditating for one minute at the start. Kid thinks this is way cool, like it's what he's been doing in lessons all his life as in falling asleep, only this time it'd be official and you could get a qualification in it.

David Luss speaks. He says he hears what they're saying about joined-up education and he's already argued for its implementation blah blah blah. Big long speech about how he's fifty-eight years old and can remember blah blah. How his professional relationship with Miriam has helped him blah blah. How he's devoted his entire educational and political career to furthering blah blah. It's all about dialogue and synergy as in everything's connected and the kid thinks that's what the guy upstairs was saying, only he sure as heck wasn't saying it like this. David Luss says he used to be a chemistry teacher blah blah, and Miriam's got like this twinkle in her eye, like she knew him then, like she worshipped him even then, like there's this story that only the two of them are ever going to know, like she's not really called Miriam.

Then it's Rosalind again. 'Everything has two kinds of explanation: a rational and an irrational. Science concerns itself only with the rational, so it leaves out half of human existence. We need to give equal weight to the irrational.'

Sounds reasonable, but when's the kid going to be able to make a dash for the door?

She says, 'All of us here have a professional interest in alternative knowledge systems: astrology, feng shui, crystal therapy. The education system betrays its students if it fails to give them sufficient grounding in these disciplines. It's all very well teaching children about the planets of the solar system, but are those planets merely lumps of rock, or are they spiritual presences in our lives? Shouldn't we spend an equal amount of time finding out how to do a basic birth chart?'

They're all kind of like muttering and agreeing with each other but not enough for him to slip away.

'Let's do a little experiment,' Rosalind says. Then she brings out this pack of playing cards and starts handing paper and pencils round the room and the kid's like holy shit it's an exam. 'I don't expect to get positive results from those of you already aware of your own psychic ability. I find, though, that this test can be a good way of uncovering hidden talent – it's one that every school should conduct.'

He's got to get out of here, they're all rustling pages and putting on spectacles like they're limbering up for a game of Pictionary and this is his moment, kid goes to the door and he's out without looking back, reptile's not even there now, it's like so totally easy, kid slipping on his jacket as he passes the empty desk without any slackening of pace because fact is, nobody gives a shit what he does, going through the revolving door and into the darkness of the night. He's walking away from the hotel, down the long driveway through the trees to the main road, and it's like so what? No searchlights or barking dogs or thunderous overhead helicopter mussing up his hair while a guy with a megaphone tells him to put his hands up. It's basically bye-bye and good riddance kid. Which is so not what this is meant to be about, as in who's going to show up for his funeral and the Nelly Furtado gig?

If he'd stayed with the guy he could have been famous. As in *Terrorist # 2: The Accomplice*. Boy in light-blue jacket seen near the check-in counter, wanted for questioning. His blurry CCTV image on *Crimewatch*. Stegosaurus seeing it and dropping his tin of beer. Maiasaura getting straight on the phone to the Hags. Barking dogs, helicopters et cetera. But he's walked out and it isn't going to happen, he's trying to retrace the route to town and soon realizes that's not going to happen either. As in he's so to speak lost. Generic unlit country road sort of scenario.

Kid saw something on UKTV History once, as in he watched three or four minutes of it, a record for anything on that channel. All about these terrorist groups in the sixties and seventies who had great names like the Weathermen or the Angry Brigade or Baader-Meinhof or the Red Army Faction, like they were basically pop groups, and they all had like long hair and beards and sweaters and did drugs and the girls all had this rock-chick look, getting led away in handcuffs like they were being busted for playing their music too loud. Nowadays if you want to be a terrorist you've got to be a dark-skinned Muslim, which is so basically unfair. Maybe Robert Coyle is like this white wannabe, kind of an Eminem deal, his fake passport photo will be in the newspaper: the lone bomber. Only the kid and Jodie will know, and it'll be so totally cool.

Kid hears a river as in it's under him and the road here is like this small bridge wide enough for one car, doesn't remember walking over it earlier but the river's how he got here so he tries to find a way down, settles for scrambling through bushes and feels a tear in his jacket, ends up on the bank. He can follow it all the way back to Kenzie or he can basically camp out as in lie down on the ground, it's not too cold, and if only Jodie was with him it'd be so romantic. Plan is to find her after the plane explodes and tell her the two of them have to go on the run, because even though all those people died the guy had to do it, as in he knew there was this child on the plane who was going to grow up into like the next Hitler, so he's basically a hero even though on the front page of the *Record* he's *Face of Hate* and in the *Sun* it's *Bastard* and the *Independent*'s got like something totally irrelevant. Only Jodie and the kid know the secret and they're going to share it forever in their little cabin where they'll have babies and buy everything mail-order off the Internet.

He walks fast while he thinks about it, everything's slotting into place like this is how it's got to be because he's learned that you can still be a hero as long as at least one person knows about it. Like you don't need to be on TV, there just has to be the one who believes, the one who cares, the one who makes your life mean something instead of being this unwatched programme. He's almost running and then he stops. Over on the other side of the river it's like there's this random old guy staring at him. Hard to see in the darkness but the kid can tell he's old because of the way he walks, can't be police but maybe he's like this plain-clothes anti-terrorist guest marshal they keep on standby in the hotel in case anybody suspicious checks in, and the old guy has come to a halt too. Maybe he's got like body armour under his zip-up coat. A walkie-talkie, a gun. Helicopter's going to fly over any moment.

The old guy's shouting something, kid can't hear but he can guess. Kid's thinking, better run, but his feet aren't moving, it's like he's busted big time. He's scared. And holy shit, the old guy's marching down to the waterside and now he's coming straight at him, wading through the river, like they gave him a wetsuit as well, in case of aquatic-chase scenarios. Only the guy's not so fast, he's knee-deep in cold black water, slipping and stumbling and looks like he might fall on his arse, kind of amusing. He's stopping for breath, it's taking him like ages to get across a few yards of river, and the kid's not so scared now because this is like not threatening it's just plain weird, he could run away if he wanted but he doesn't need to. He wants to know what this crazy old man really wants.

'Robbie! I'm coming!'

Kid can hear him now, like this sad old man making a total dick of himself, nearly across, looking up so the kid can see his face better now, covered in sweat and basically exhausted. The old man's panting hard, slowly coming to the edge, grabbing at reeds to steady himself and maybe the kid should help him up but he doesn't as in it's not like a crossing the road standard situation he's dealing with here.

'Robbie, it's me.'

The old guy's made it up the bank to the kid and he's standing there in front of him with water dripping off his trousers and his coat where it splashed.

'It's me, Robbie. I'm old now but you haven't changed at all.'

He's got like this look on his face which is sort of between hypnotized and delirious and basically out of his head, like whatever he's seeing isn't what's in front of him because the kid isn't Robbie but he isn't Felix either and if you're going to get through every submenu of life then what the heck?

'Hello,' says the kid.

'Oh, Robbie! Son!' He basically hugs him. Embarrassing sort of moment. 'I don't know how it can be possible . . .'

Kid's got an answer to that. 'Anything's possible. Everything's connected.'

Kid backs off a little and see there's stuff all over the old man's face like sweat or tears or river water, he's basically a mess, and his expression is sort of changing, he kind of nods like he gets it but his breathing doesn't sound right and his grip on the kid's arms has loosened, the old man's arms have fallen, his legs are buckling and he's going down on his knees as in praying and then he makes like this really disgusting grunting noise, the whole of his insides are rattling and his eyes are widening, staring, pleading, it looks totally scary. He's trying to say something, clutching at his chest. He basically dies.

It's like the kid's staring down at this dead old man who must have been on drugs or something, well, you hear about pensioners taking Ecstasy and so forth, their hearts can't take it. And now the kid's got like this situation to deal with as well as the other one, it's so totally interesting. But first thing he's got to do is get away from here and find somewhere to sleep.

13

Dawn breaks over Kenzie and Anne Coyle lies awake in bed, still waiting to hear if the police have found him yet. Across the whole of the dormant town, night's shadows slide and shrink; St Mary's church, the municipal library, the empty Springdale Centre, all welcome the new day, and on the riverside memorial, the painted 'fuck' becomes more clearly visible to an indifferent fauna. Anne finished her book hours ago, not long after Joe went out. A death and a wedding: the traditional endings in the story-book version of life. Happy ever after, on Earth or in heaven.

In the bushes beside the river where he slept, the kid wakes to hear birdsong and the flowing of the water. He looks along the path and in the distance can see the old man still lying where he fell; it seemed such a long way last night when the kid stopped running and lay down exhausted, but in the daylight it doesn't take him long to walk back to the spot, as if to make sure the old man really is dead, lying peacefully on his back but with his legs in a strange position. When he gets near, the kid sees the old man properly for the first time, his eyes wide open and staring straight up into the sky, his mouth open too, caught in the process of trying to frame whatever it was he wanted to say when he collapsed at the kid's feet. Long strands of grass fringe the old man's grey head, and on his coat some shiny dark insects patrol with forensic determination.

There was nothing the kid could have done, or can do now. It's time to move on. But first he stoops beside the body, half expecting it at any moment to leap back into life like the zombie in *Taste of Blood*. In games and movies nobody's ever truly dead, that's what makes the real thing so cold and final. What the kid wants to avoid more than anything is touching the old man's skin, but if he has a wallet somewhere, cash, the kid could use it. A pity the kid didn't take the magic card before escaping from the hotel, but he didn't dare risk it. A corpse is easier to steal from than a ghost.

The old man's back pocket is the place to try, but he's lying face-up and it's out of reach. The kid gives the body a slight push to one side, hoping to get a hand underneath, yet when the dead weight shifts it releases something trapped inside, there's a gurgling sound and the kid thinks he might throw up, he lets go of the body and it slumps back into its former position. The kid stands up and feels himself gagging, manages to hold it down. He ought to go now. The old man's death was nothing to do with him and he should forget it ever happened.

He hears a sound and looks up; an airliner high above, Robert Coyle on his impossible mission, the kid feels sure of it. The plane so high he can hardly see it, but he knows this has to be the one, this tiny dot where Terrorist # 1 is sitting in seat 13C, gazing out at white clouds rolling like cauliflower beneath him while an air hostess walks by offering coffee. The kid can see it all so clearly, the terrorist standing up waving a non-metallic weapon, saying, 'Nobody move. Nobody panic.' And everybody panicking.

But the plane's still up there. The kid watches the dot grow smaller, swinging slowly across the brightening sky, until he loses track. The mission has failed: the world has not been saved. There is still work to be done. The kid takes a last look at the old man whose face retains the rigid dignity of his dying moment, then sets off for town to seek the girl he loves.